SEMBI

A realm ruled by wealth
always in search of g

THAMALON U

The embattled patriarch i
of the proud Uskevren family.

SHAMUR USKEVREN

A woman with a past as shadowed as it is long,
now one of the most influential of Selgaunt's ladies.

THAMALON USKEVREN II

He stands to inherit all, if he can keep
himself alive long enough.

THAZIENNE USKEVREN

The poor little rich girl who prowls the city streets
at night—like mother, like daughter.

TALBOT USKEVREN

The second son carries more than one
potentially deadly curse.

EREVIS CALE

Trusted servant, master thief—he serves two masters.

LARAJIN

An innocent maid with secrets of her own—
secrets that course through her very veins.

SEMBIA

THE HALLS OF STORMWEATHER

SHADOW'S WITNESS
Paul Kemp
NOVEMBER 2000

THE SHATTERED MASK
Richard Lee Byers
MAY 2001

BLACK WOLF
Dave Gross
NOVEMBER 2001

SEMBIA

THE HALLS OF STORMWEATHER

Richard Lee Byers

Clayton Emery

Ed Greenwood

Dave Gross

Paul Kemp

Lisa Smedman

Voronica Whitney-Robinson

THE HALLS OF STORMWEATHER
Sembia

Distributed in the United States by St. Martin's Press. Distributed in Canada by Fenn, Ltd.

Distributed to the hobby, toy, and comic trade in the United States and Canada by regional distributors.

Distributed worldwide by Wizards of the Coast, Inc. and regional distributors.

Cover and interior art by Terese Nielsen
First Printing: July 2000
Library of Congress Catalog Card Number: 99-69356

9 8 7 6 5 4 3 2 1

ISBN: 0-7869-1560-9
620-T21560

U.S., CANADA,
ASIA, PACIFIC, & LATIN AMERICA
Wizards of the Coast, Inc.
P.O. Box 707
Renton, WA 98057-0707
+1-800-324-6496

EUROPEAN HEADQUARTERS
Wizards of the Coast, Belgium
P.B. 2031
2600 Berchem
Belgium
+32-70-23-32-77

Visit our web site at **www.wizards.com**

A tale in seven parts set within the walls of the mighty city of Selgaunt, which sits perched on the northern coast of the Sea of Fallen Stars in the realm of Sembia.

It is winter in the Year of the Unstrung Harp, 1371 by Dalereckoning. Sembia, guided by the many hands of her prosperous merchant princes, thrives.

Here we meet one of Sembia's powerful merchant lords and his family, the Uskevren.

THE PATRIARCH

The Burning Chalice

Ed Greenwood

"Any more business?" the head of House Uskevren asked calmly over the rim of his raised glass.

The lamplight flickered on the last sweetened ices and the wines served with them. The slight ripple of his set jaw behind it was the only hint of the disgust Thamalon Uskevren felt at dining in his own feast hall with his two most hated rivals—and creditors.

"Oh, yes, Uskevren," the man with silver-shot hair and emerald eyes so sharp they glittered said in an idle manner that fooled no one, "there *is* one thing more." Presker Talendar's smile was silken. "I've brought along someone who very much wants to meet you."

One of the four hitherto silent men who sat between Talendar and Saclath Soargyl—the fat, sneering son of a man who'd tried to kill Thamalon six times and hired someone else to bring down a sharp, cold end to Thamalon's days at least a dozen times more—leaned forward. Something that might have been the ghost of a smile adorned his face. It was the stranger in the doublet of green musterdelvys gilded with leaping lions, who resembled Thamalon's long-lost elder brother Perivel . . . as he'd been when young and vigorous, so long ago. Had Perivel found time back then to secretly sire a son?

Thamalon knew the other three silent diners at his table by sight. One was Iristar Velvaunt, a coldly professional mage-for-hire whose presence here this night must have cost the Talendars several thousand fivestars, at least. He was the whip to keep raised tempers from exploding into something more . . . or to blunt the many menaces a host might whelm against guests in his own house.

The man beside Velvaunt was Ansible Loakrin, Lawmaker of Selgaunt. Loakrin was the perfect witness and the owner of a face as carefully expressionless as Thamalon's own.

The third man, by far the shortest and fattest of those gathered at table, was a priest whose raiment marked him as a servant of Lathander, god of creation and renewal. The priest's name had escaped Thamalon, but several platters of nut-roasted goose had failed to escape the Lord Flame of Lathander—and three decanters of good wine were thus far very much failing to escape him as well.

They were witnesses, these three, here to watch the unfolding of whatever stratagem the man in green and Talendar had hatched together, and to keep swords from being drawn.

Thamalon inclined his eyebrows in an expression of casual interest that was very far from what he was really feeling. "And having met me . . . ?" he prompted gently.

". . . I found myself disappointed at the distantly formal nature of my reception," the man in green smoothly took over the sentence. "After all, Thamalon, I *am* your brother."

He paused to give Thamalon time to gasp and launch into loud and eager query, but the head of House Uskevren gave him only calm silence, one lifted eyebrow rising perhaps half an inch higher.

Before the stillness could stretch, the man in green drew himself up and said in ringing tones that could not help but reach the servants standing motionless along the walls, even to the maid busily dusting the farthest corner of the hall, "Let all here know the truth of my heritage. I am Perivel Uskevren, rightful heir of my sire Aldimar, and head of House Uskevren. This House is bound as I bind it, its coins flow as I bid, and as I speak, so shall Uskevren stand."

The words were the old formula, echoing Sembian law. The head of a house controlled its investments and business dealings utterly. If this truly was Perivel, Stormweather Towers—the Uskevren's fine city manor—had a new master. Thamalon would lose in an instant all authority over the wealth he'd so painstakingly rebuilt, and this stranger would rule here henceforth.

There was, however, a slight complication. Perivel Uskevren had been dead for more than forty years.

Thamalon's last memory of his brother came tumbling back into his mind, as bright and as terrible as ever. Stormweather Towers was in flames, and there was Perivel shouting defiance in the red, leaping heart of an inferno of toppling beams and roaring, racing fire, his sword flashing as he hacked and stabbed at three—three!—Talendars.

The horse under Thamalon reared in terror, its scorched mane and flanks stinking. It surged forward with a scream into darker, cooler streets, bearing Thamalon and his tears away from the crackling of the fire and the shouts of the slaughtered.

The house was but a blackened shell when he saw it again. Its ashes held the bones of many but yielded up no living man, nor corpse that anyone could put a name to. The priests questioned a few of the scorched skulls with eerie spells, then turned in weary satisfaction to name Thamalon Uskevren heir of the house and to present him with a bill for their holy labors. They, at least, had been certain that Perivel died in the fire. Of course, with the passing years their gods had gathered in every one of them, and there was none left to echo their testimony now but Thamalon.

So it was; so it had always been: Thamalon Uskevren standing alone against the foes of his family.

Alone again. He was growing very tired of this. Perhaps it was time to set aside politeness and go out like a lion. If he could just be sure of taking all the snakes who hissed and glided around House Uskevren with him, down into darkness.

And there lay the rub. The gods had never made it easy for Sembians to be sure of anything.

"I suppose, brother," Perivel was saying smoothly, "you wonder why I'm here this night in the company of men whose families have, in past years, been at odds with our own?"

He waited for Thamalon to bluster or protest, but the head of House Uskevren gave him no more than a silent, almost leisurely wave of a hand, bidding him continue.

The pretender's eyes flashed—had he deceived himself into seeing surrender in Thamalon's eyes?—and with a flourish he drew forth a sealed document from the breast of his doublet. Perivel held the parchment up to catch the lamplight, so everyone could see that the seal was unbroken. He looked at Presker Talendar, received a solemn nod of assent, and slowly broke the seal.

Iristar Velvaunt moved with the speed of a striking snake, long sleeves billowing as his arm darted out to lay one quelling, long-fingered hand on the false Perivel's arm.

When the pretender obediently halted, the mage murmured something and passed his other hand over the document. That hand left a slightly blue glow in its wake, which clung to and coiled around the parchment. All of the men at the table recognized it. It was a common shielding to protect the parchment from being torn, burned, or affected by other magics.

Velvaunt then gave an extravagant "proceed" gesture of his own, and the pretender triumphantly thrust the document under Thamalon's nose.

Thamalon read it calmly, not moving to touch it. It seemed that Perivel Uskevren owed House Talendar a lot of money, and had named as his collateral if the monies—seventy-nine thousand golden fivestars, no less—were not repaid.

The collateral was Stormweather Towers itself—the house Thamalon had rebuilt, every tinted glass pane and smooth-carved arch of it. The head of House Uskevren did not look at the huge marble-sheathed pillars that rose all around him. Nor did he spare a glance for the exquisite lamps of iridescent blown glass that hung above the table, whose cost outstripped that of even the ornately carved pillars . . . but his question seemed directed more at them than at anyone seated down the long, decanter-laden table as he gazed across the cavernous hall and asked gently, "And how is it that an Uskevren came to stand in debt to the Talendars, without any in this house knowing of it?"

"I am but recently returned to Selgaunt," the pretender said eagerly, "after years as a captive then a loyal servant of the Talendars, at their holdings in the distant land of Amn. I—I came to owe Presker Talendar the value of a ship that was wrecked on rocks near Westgate, as I was captaining it for the Talendars."

Clever. Thamalon took care that none of the dark anger gathering in him showed in his face. The downfall of the Uskevren in his father Aldimar's day had been trading with pirates—an offense then as now treated no differently under Sembian law than open piracy itself. Any payment Thamalon might make to this man who claimed to be his brother could be trumpeted by the Talendars as paying a pirate, proof that the Uskevren were again up to their old tricks. False claimant or not, the Uskevren would be ruined. For that matter, this claimant—Perivel or not—could be a pirate himself.

Persons convicted of piracy in Selgaunt were always shunned by citizens anxious to avoid sharing their fate: a month of hard and unpleasant labor (usually harbor-diving to plug leaks in ship hulls, or squaring and hefting quarried stones to repair the city wall), followed by the amputation of one of the convict's hands. The guilty were often sentenced to suffer the breaking of another limb as well by officers of the court, a wound that was left to heal by itself so that, as the saying went, "the pain will be their teacher."

At over sixty years of age, Thamalon would be worked hard for a month, while this pretender disowned him and plundered the family vaults—a family none would dare trade with thereafter, for fear of being thought pirates in their turn. The Uskevren would fall, and the Talendars would seize everything and no doubt make special visits to a whipped and groaning Thamalon Uskevren to torment him with the news of what they'd done with it.

He'd end his days mutilated and in pain, probably tormented by Talendar servants and hirelings sent to hunt and harry him in the streets to provide feast-table amusement with their reports. He'd heard of their doing so before with House Feltelent, breaking the fingers of a lone, blinded old man one by one as months passed, purely for cruel sport.

In Sembia, it was all too easy to ruin a man.

It hardly seemed more difficult to shatter an entire family, no matter how rich, proud, and historied it might be.

His father had died fighting against such a fate. Thamalon could do no less, whatever it might cost him, and no matter how sick he'd become of such skulking and strivings. Thamalon owed the ghosts of Stormweather Towers—and his children, their lives still bright with promise before them—no less.

He raised his eyes almost idly, face smoothly expressionless. Seventy-nine thousand golden fivestars was coin he did not have. Nor was it a treasure Thamalon would be willing to let any Talendar steal from Uskevren coffers, even if he'd had it to spare. Yet if he lost this his beloved home, the brightest and best of Selgaunt would shun him and his as paupers whose every coin might already be spoken for . . . and, again, the Uskevren would be ruined.

Ruin, ruin on all sides, and sinister smiles all down his feast table, from men waiting to see him fall into the doom they had prepared.

The Talendars were the oldest, proudest family in all Selgaunt. One did not lightly refuse the request of a visit from one of them. Foes and longtime rivals they might be—and they might well have earned their cruel badge of the Blood-beaked Raven many times over—but they could boast trading contacts, agents, and factors almost everywhere across the teeming continent of Faerûn. Only a fool snubbed the Talendars in Selgaunt.

"I anticipate you'll avoid any unpleasantness, brother," the false Perivel said heartily into the lengthening silence. "After all, you are the man they call the Old Owl . . . and all Selgaunt knows that Thamalon Uskevren is a man of his word—a man who takes care to keep *all* of his promises."

Thamalon almost laughed. So it had been said, repeated by Selgauntans over and over again as a business motto, ever since he'd once said such words in a speech. He'd known then, the moment they left his mouth years ago, that they'd someday be turned back at him.

The man who always kept his promises let his eyes wander down the table, allowing a smirk to crawl across his lips and cover the snarl he wanted to let slip. Let them wonder what mirthful secret he held; with a Talendar and a Soargyl at the table, they'd learn it was but a bluff.

They'd not, after all, come unprepared. Invisible daggerspurn fields sang around all of them, to turn aside any weapon an Uskevren might hurl, and hunger glowed in their eyes. They were ready and eager for Uskevren blood. Well, then . . .

Thamalon looked down at the promissory note again, and let them all wait for another tensely drawn breath before he raised green, glowing eyes from the parchment to regard the man who claimed to be his brother.

"I've never seen you or this document before," he said calmly to the pretender, "and this your signature fails to resemble any I've seen in our vaults. Prove to me that you are Perivel Uskevren."

This last, blunt sentence was dropped into the tense and waiting silence like a gauntlet hurled down in challenge. The men around the table seemed to lean forward slightly in excitement. The eyes of Presker Talendar and Saclath Soargyl gleamed with the anticipation of pleasure.

Thamalon never looked at them. His eyes were bright and very steady as they stared into the unfamiliar eyes of the man who called himself Perivel Uskevren. His gaze never strayed as he carefully handed the document not back to the pretender, but to the hired mage.

Velvaunt accepted the parchment with a smile that was almost a sneer. For all the attention the others at the table paid to him just then, he could well have saved himself the effort.

The little smile that curled the edges of Perivel's mouth never wavered as he stared back at Thamalon. His burly shoulders lifted in a slow shrug as he spread his hands and said mildly, "Bring me the chalice."

The smirk that rose into Perivel's eyes was a flame of pure triumph that told Thamalon two things: that this could not be his brother, whose quite different gloating smile Thamalon could remember very well, and that this impostor, whoever he was, thought he could prove himself to be Perivel Uskevren. Thamalon's older brother, the head of House Uskevren with the sole power to buy, sell, and forfeit its chattels, had been burned to ashes forty-odd summers ago.

Thamalon's hand never faltered as he set down his glass and rang the bell that brought his butler gliding to his side.

"Cale," the patriarch directed calmly, "fetch hence the chalice."

As the butler inclined his bald head and turned in smooth silence to obey, the triumph in Perivel's eyes became a blaze. Thamalon's fingertips found the familiar hilt of the knife strapped to his forearm, inside his sleeve. He stroked that hard, reassuring smoothness ever so slightly, out of long habit. Battle was joined.

That the man who called himself Perivel Uskevren knew about the chalice proved nothing. Half the elder houses of Selgaunt had heard of the Quaff of the Uskevren. It had been enspelled long ago by Phaldinor Uskevren's house mage, Helemgaularn of the Seven Lightnings, to keep revelers from stealing his mead. Its enchantments were later altered so that only one of the blood of the Uskevren could touch it bare-handed and not be instantly burned.

Burning was how Thamalon had first seen the large, plain metal goblet—or, withstanding snarling flames. It had been floating alone, dark and eerie in midair, among the roaring fires devouring Stormweather Towers. He'd stared at it in amazement ere his great-uncle Roel stormed out of the smoke to snatch him away from the fire and death and shattered dreams.

The chalice had been one of the few things to be salvaged from the ashes. It had been found standing serenely atop a charred mound that had once been the servants' quarters—and the servants—before they'd plunged helplessly into the inferno of the pantries beneath.

Stormweather Towers had fallen then. It must not fall again.

Somehow the sunlight streaming in the windows of the rebuilt high gallery never seemed as golden as the light that had fallen through the windows of the first high gallery. Back then the light fell onto maps and records, and Thamalon's own laborious copying as old Nelember had taught a quiet, chastened son of the Uskevren the history of his family.

A history that had begun somewhere else—his old tutor had never been very clear about just where—but sailed on ships to Selgaunt, there to rise in riches under Phaldinor Uskevren.

"Too bold to hide," the family name meant, in some forgotten tongue. Certainly Phaldinor had been by all accounts a gruff bear of a man, always lumbering into fray after fray and never backing down from a fight. He was a man as good as his word, as many folk learned to their delight—and some learned to their cost. Phaldinor the Bear used the coins spun into his hands by a fleet of merchant ships plying the Sea of Fallen Stars to sponsor armed expeditions into the peaks around the High Dale, to dig mines under the very jaws and talons of the beasts that made the Stormfangs—still dangerous today—so perilous then. Those mines brought back gold and silver enough to make the Uskevren the owners of much of Selgaunt, and enable Phaldinor to build himself a veritable palace. A straightforward man, he named it for its appearance: Blackturrets.

Thamalon had been born in that sprawling, indefensible mansion of orchards and gardens and watched Selgaunt gnaw away at field after copse after bower of its grounds, filling family coffers but searing away small corners of his heart with every felling and building. Wherefore his wildness had begun, a madness of youthful rebellion, which he'd fallen out of, shaken and sobered, bare months before the flames had claimed the grand new home of the Uskevren.

Prim, careful old Nelember had stepped into the chaos of Thamalon's heart and thoughts, and built a foundation of pride as carefully as any castle mason.

Pride in a family that was not without its faults. Phaldinor's first son, Thoebellon, was tall and strikingly handsome. In the words of Nelember, "he looked more like a king than kings ever do." He was also a hunter, wencher, and drunkard who squandered vast treasuries of family coins on dragon hunting, a sport at which the flower of the Uskevren was (luckily for him) an utter failure.

He hunted gentler prey with far more success, leaving a trail of outraged fathers and scandalized mothers clear across southern Sembia. That tactical error might well have hastened his doom.

Someone who was never found or even named stabbed Thoebellon in a forest one night whilst he was on a stag hunt, and his young son Aldimar became head of House Uskevren.

Aldimar was Thamalon's prim-lipped, disapproving father. His eyes were as hard and unyielding as two swordpoints, and his tongue never spoke to wayward sons save with cold, biting contempt.

Nelember had seen Thamalon's hard face as they talked of his father and had fetched forth the chalice from its locked cabinet at the end of the room.

"Think of your father, and touch it," the old man had commanded.

He'd never been allowed near the family heirloom that the servants called "the Burning Cup" before. More out of curiosity than anything else, Thamalon touched it. . . .

"Uncle," the young man stammered, blinking, "can you count coins at *all?*"

The great bear of a man belched, waved one blunt-fingered, hairy hand vaguely and rumbled, "By the handful . . . why?"

"Uncle Roel," Aldimar said in exasperation, "this chest was *full* a tenday ago! Brim-laden with Chassabra's housekeeping money; the servants' pay for a *year.* Where is it now?"

Roel belched again, thunderously. "Gone," he admitted sadly.

"Gone where?"

The bearlike man lifted the goblet that was never far from his hand, pointed into its depths, then upended it toward Aldimar. Nothing ran out. It was empty.

Thamalon found himself back in the high gallery, young again and drenched in cold sweat, blinking at the chalice on the table in front of him instead of the empty depths of Roel's unsteadily dangled cup.

Nelember wordlessly handed him a tankard of something

warm, wet, and steadying—pheasant broth—and offered the dry words, "Rich fathers always have such easy choices to make, hmm?"

Thamalon stared up at his teacher, then back at the chalice. After a long, silent time, he mumbled, "Just tell me; I'll hear and heed. I'd not touch that again."

The old tutor smiled grimly and said, "Think of it as truth, waiting at your elbow for whenever you disbelieve."

Thamalon listened and learned. Aldimar had been a quiet, studious youth who let his boisterous, hard-riding uncles Roel and Tivamon run the affairs of the Uskevren—until Tivamon was killed in a tavern duel fighting half-a-dozen fellow drunkards, all of different families, and none of them "noble." The day after the crypt had been sealed on his casket, the hitherto-quiet Aldimar firmly set his Uncle Roel aside and assumed control of the family.

Aldimar had by then grown into a man both young and inexperienced but lettered and shrewd enough to run a family. All he dreaded was Roel's revenge, but the old bear snarled once or thrice then took happily to spending all his waking hours (than just half of them or so) at wenching, drinking, and falling drunkenly out of saddles as he rode from one Uskevren hunting lodge to another.

In the fullness of time, Aldimar took a wife, Balantra Toemalar, a stunningly beautiful, soft-spoken lass from a Saerlunan family of old and respected lineage but declining wealth. They had two sons, Perivel and Thamalon, before a third birthing killed her and what would have been a daughter. Thamalon remembered best her crooning songs, dark starshot eyes, and the long tumbling wildness of her hair.

The elder son, Perivel, was his father's favorite. He was a handsome, strapping youth every bit the horseman his Great-uncle Roel was, but with wits as sharp as Aldimar's own. In his brother's shadow, Thamalon became the quiet, studious watcher . . . and, after Nelember's teaching on the heels of his wild days, the family coin-counter. He had a horror of empty chests.

Under Aldimar, the Uskevren clan soared to new prosperity, outstripping even its former greatness. Aldimar took a second wife, and grew steadily more gaunt and short-tempered even as his influence made him the uncrowned ruler of Selgaunt. Perivel seriously contemplated conquering Battledale. This contentious realm northeast of Sembia proper was to be Perivel's own province, what he hoped would be the "breadbasket to the realm," as well as his own source of endless riches.

Then it all came crashing down. A dying pirate revealed Aldimar's dark secret. Behind all the lawful land deals and loans to shopkeepers and cart-merchants, the Uskevren wealth was based on piracy. Through Aldimar and the family fleet, the Uskevren bought ships for pirates, fenced their stolen goods, and in return prospered from smuggling and from pirate gold.

Like a pack of wolves swarming a falling stag, rival families rushed in for the kill. Old business foes like the Soargyl and Talendars and grasping new-coin climbers such as the families of Baerodreemer and Ithivisk hired wizards to uncover the truth. When Aldimar ignored their visits and failed to appear before the probiters they complained to, they met to plan war, hammered out an agreement, and forthwith attacked Stormweather Towers seeking to seize—or butcher—Aldimar.

Being an Uskevren, of course, he defied them.

With a flash and a roar that split the night, the gate guard and his hut cartwheeled up into the sky amid rolling blue flames.

"*What* by all the bright gods—?" Perivel shouted, springing up from his game of chethlachance with a violent surge that scattered the pieces across the board and sent old Nelember ducking hastily away from the swing of the heir's scabbarded sword.

"Unless I'm mistaken," Perivel's father said quietly, standing like a dark statue by the windows, "that will be our friends of House Soargyl and House Talendar, come to call on me, and in a mood to demonstrate that they've forgotten how to open gates."

"Why, those *beggars!*" Perivel was almost speechless in fury, but not quite. A Sembian could give no higher insult than the word he'd chosen.

"Father," Thamalon asked urgently, his book flung down and forgotten, "what shall we do?"

Aldimar Uskevren shrugged, the weariness of the gesture leaving both his sons gaping at him in shock. "What else?" he replied. "Fight, and sell our lives dearly. If two of us fall, mind, the third must win free, to keep the Uskevren name alive for a day when revenge can be taken. I've no more the strength or the inclination for fleeing and dodging. Let it end for me here."

He drew a wand from one sleeve and a long knife from the other and strode forward, never seeing the stunned looks his sons traded with each other behind his back.

A moment ago the brothers had been idling away an evening waiting for their father to confide in them the details of his latest schemes. They waited for him to tell them just how startlingly steep the bribes he was going to have to pay to avoid being jailed over this piracy scandal would be. Now, it seemed, they were standing on their own battlements in a doomed siege, staring into their father's waiting grave . . . and perhaps their own.

Shouts and crashes rang faintly up the stairs from below, and the sounds of frantically running feet suddenly smote the ears of the three, as the House Guard whelmed in haste. Their sounds seemed to remind Aldimar of something.

"Nelember," the head of House Uskevren commanded

curtly, without turning his head or slowing, "get the Lady Ilrilteska and her maids away to safety as swiftly as you can. To Storl Oak by morning, if possible, but out of the city forthwith, regardless of what befalls hereafter. Hear you?"

The old tutor, as pale as the wax of the nearest candles, had to swallow twice before he managed to gasp, "Aye, Lord. Storl Oak it shall be."

Whatever Aldimar said next was lost in the splintering crash of the forehall ceiling coming down amid the shrieks of pantry maids below. Lightning flashed up the stairs, spitting sparks, and stabbed at the three Uskevren.

The Lord of Stormweather Towers sprang back and cast two swift, hawklike glances over his shoulders. His eyes flashed at what he saw and he snapped, "Stand away from me, both of you! What bright future will there be for House Uskevren if one bolt fells us all, eh?"

Perivel was shaking his head in disbelief as Aldimar's sons traded glances again and obediently drifted apart. Thamalon simply stared, open-mouthed and mute, at the horror so swiftly overwhelming his world.

There were heads bobbing amid the rolling clouds of dust below—helmed heads, advancing purposefully up the broad steps.

"Aldimar Uskevren!" a man shouted. "Miscreant and pirate! Yield to us!"

Aldimar flung up one hand in an imperious gesture commanding silence from his sons, and planted himself at the head of the stairs, thrusting his knife back in its sheath and shaking a second wand out of his sleeve.

Like the one ready in his other hand, it was a weapon neither of his sons had ever seen before, or known their father could use.

A lance of black magical fire leaped up the stairs. Where it struck, crackling, Nelember's head vanished from his shoulders. As the spasming body danced and reeled, another shout rolled up the stairs from below. It was a voice all three Uskevren knew.

"Aldimar," Rildinel Soargyl roared, his voice as deep as the snorts of the bull he resembled, "you are a dead man! Too craven to yield or stand forth and fight. I swear, we'll pull this place down until we find you or its falling crushes you. Where by all the coins Waukeen has ever forgotten are you?"

"Here, Rildinel," Aldimar called, in the mocking tones of a young lass teasing someone who searches for her. "Here."

As his old friend Nelember crashed to the floor beside him, both of the wands in Aldimar's hands burst into life, flooding the stairs with a sheet of white flame.

The men-at-arms rushing up the steps shrieked as they died, hurled off their feet and away by the power that seared them and melted their swords and armor alike. Below and behind the soldiers the three Uskevren saw a dark-robed figure reel and stagger amid the fading, darkening wandfire. An instant later, what was left of the forehall erupted upward through the solar, seeking the star-strewn sky. The explosion flung them all backward and smote their ears into ringing cacophony. It seemed that a mage had been unprepared for Aldimar's magic.

A shaggy head, dark and wet with blood, bounced on the steps beside Perivel's boots long moments later. All three men knew its staring face. It seemed Rildinel Soargyl, too, had been taken quite by surprise.

Well, nothing would ever surprise or disturb him again.

"I cannot but fail to observe, my sons, that House Soargyl has a new head," Aldimar murmured wryly. "Let us see if we can give them yet another before morning. Brutish ambition should be aptly rewarded."

As Perivel chuckled at this dark sally, his father's wands spat forth white fire again.

Only a few groans followed the second flood of flames.

From beyond the shattered solar came fresh blasts of fury, and the dainty Ladyspire Turret toppled slowly past their view, flames spewing from its tiny arched windows.

Thamalon saw Aldimar's face change, and swallowed hastily. "I-I'm sure she was elsewhere, Father," he managed to say. "The—"

Another explosion rocked the steps beneath their feet, an instant before the turret's landing made the floor heave, flinging them helplessly against the nearest walls. Dust puffed out of the joints between those massive stones as they staggered back and away from walls that were shuddering as if they were alive.

Perivel drew his sword with a snarl. "They're destroying the Towers around us!"

Aldimar nodded sadly as the thunderous grating of stone rose to a momentary scream, echoed around the three Uskevren as they found footing once more, then started to die away.

"The Talendars pay their mages well," the patriarch observed, when speech could be heard again. "They must often be consumed with a frustrated hunger to use all that hired sorcery—and lo! Here we are, villains and traitors whose presence can not be tolerated in Selgaunt a moment longer." The smile that crossed his face then was not a pretty thing.

"Find them, my sons," he commanded, "and slay me some mages. Let them rue the price of our passing."

Perivel strode to the head of the great stair, but the head of House Uskevren put out one hand to his elbow and plucked him back. The son was startled by the strength of his sire's grip.

"Not right down where they're waiting for you," Aldimar snapped. "Of what use to me is a dead heir?"

For a dark instant Perivel looked as if he was about to return his sire's snarl with interest, but that moment passed and he nodded slowly.

"The passage to the vaults?" Perivel asked, with a fierce grin. "Out to the stables and around to take them from behind?"

"Brother," Thamalon said urgently, pointing out one shattered window, "I think they're around by the stables already. The—"

A blue flare of magical light curled almost lazily up from the spread, upraised hands of a shadowy figure in the courtyard below. The light rolled forward through the dusty chaos of the Ladyspire's fall, to the gaping wound in the mansion walls where the turret had fallen away.

Through that opening eight armsmen of Aldimar's House Guard could be seen, swords and spears in their hands, cautiously probing every corner of the shattered chamber for intruders.

"No," Aldimar growled. "Fools—you'll all be slain! Get back! Get . . ."

His voice trailed away in futility. He had no spell to send his voice to them, and there was no way to save them. The deadly radiance was already rolling inexorably into the room. As the three Uskevren men watched grimly, the blue glow surged through the chamber like a storm-driven wave crashing through a flooded coastal forest. It swept away furniture and stiffly tumbling bodies, dashed lamps and mirrors into flying shards, and hurled statuettes to the floor.

"Tymora's . . . angry . . . talons," Perivel gasped slowly, as they watched the ravening magic roll on through the mansion, devouring stone walls as if they were made of butter, "how can we fight *that?*"

"Strike down its source," his father said crisply, and pointed one arm through the broken window. "Like this."

A ring on his pointing hand pulsed into sudden life, and the wizard who'd created the blue fire began howling and staggering in agony, his head blazing like a torch. Aldimar's sons looked at their father in fresh amazement.

What else had their have-nothing-to-do-with-such-nonsense-as-magic father happened to acquire in secret through the passing years?

"Father," Thamalon asked quietly, "isn't this your last chance to let us know secrets like these battle magics?"

Aldimar gave him a long look. "I expect to die before morning, but gods take me if I'll plan on it."

"We can't have more than a handful of guardsmen left," Thamalon said urgently. "The three of us may stand alone!"

His father shrugged. "What of it? While we stand, we'll fight—until there's but one of you left to flee. House Talendar has so many mages up its sleeves that I don't want one of you trying to get away a-clanking with magic . . . you'd be spell-traced and hunted down."

He turned back to the window again—just as it erupted inward in a storm of daggerlike glass shards and reaching tongues of purple and white flame.

Aldimar flung himself over onto his back and let the blast tumble him across the room, shouting, "Get *down!*"

Perivel hesitated for only a moment before following Thamalon in a dive to the floor. He was bare inches from landing when something dazzling surged over the balcony like a huge wave crashing over a beach and racing across the land beyond. The room exploded in light.

The floor rose to meet Perivel's chin, rattling his teeth as he fell, and air so hot that it blistered his cheek howled over him.

When he could see again, the air was full of a sharp scorched smell, and little fires were dancing in many places along the walls and ceiling. Somewhere in front of him his father made a horrible wet groaning sound.

"Father?" he called.

"I am that," came the reply, the voice so strained that Perivel scarcely recognized it.

Perivel found his feet, somehow, the room seeming to tilt and spin crazily around him, and tried to stride forward. It was like stumbling along the deck of a ship pitching in the worst swells of a storm. A red haze seemed to be creeping in around the edges of his vision, and behind him he could see Thamalon clawing his way feebly over the jagged remnants of what had been a gilded chair scant moments before. There was blood all over his brother's face.

"Perivel," the master of Stormweather Towers said calmly from somewhere amid the dust-choked chaos ahead, "stay back." His father's voice was raw with pain and still threaded with a wet bubbling, but at least it sounded like Aldimar Uskevren again.

"Father?" Perivel called, clambering on over shattered furniture, and fumbling vaguely for the sword that didn't seem to be in his hand any more.

"Perivel, keep *back.*"

The snap of command in his father's voice brought Perivel to a halt, blinking and peering. He was in time to see another turret, torn apart by spells, begin its deafening, ground-shaking fall to the earth below. He watched it through a larger opening than before. The row of windows was all gone, and the garden wall that had held them was also missing.

Perivel's thoughts ran on in dull confusion. At some time during his ruminations, as other spells rent the night outside, he fell back to the floor and rolled over to find Thamalon crawling up to him. The youngest Uskevren was blinking at his brother through a mask of blood. Clutched in one of his hands was Perivel's missing sword.

"Brother," he gasped, "I—"

Whatever he might have said next died, forever unspoken, as they heard their father murmur something that began too low to hear, and rose with terrible passion into words they could not understand. It was a surge of rising grief and fury that seemed to pull the floor under them into a matching rise and surge, like a wave racing toward shore.

The two brothers tumbled together in its wake, rolling

over and gasping in ragged unison at the fresh pains of being dragged over splintered furniture.

They fetched up against a toppled, now armless statue of a winged woman who'd always displayed more artful drapery than modesty, and found themselves facing the missing wall again—and their father.

Aldimar Uskevren was straddling a rising, rolling knoll of stone like a rider urging a galloping horse forward in a race. Bent low over floor tiles that were flowing as if they were made of sap or syrup and not rigid stone, he was moving away from them, surging forward on a magical wave.

He was heading for the huge opening where the solar windows had been, toward the courtyards below where the Talendar and Soargyl mages were standing. The stones moving with him were making horrible groaning, deep-voiced creaking sounds that almost overwhelmed the strange little voice coming from Aldimar.

The head of House Uskevren was humming contentedly to himself.

"Father?" Perivel called, "what're you *doing?*"

"Dying, son," Aldimar said deliberately, as the flood of stone took him out of the room and up into the sky. "I'm busy dying. Please don't bother me now."

The sons of the Uskevren found themselves clawing at pillars and the edges of rolling, broken rocks to keep from being carried out of the solar by the ongoing stream of stone. Aldimar was high above them now, the wave of stone blotting out the moonlight as it arched up and on.

There were shouts from the grounds below, and the flashes and crackles of several spells. One of them sent a web of crawling, clawing lightning across the huge tongue of moving stone. His sons saw Aldimar reel and writhe as its blue fingers washed over him.

"Father," Perivel cried, "why are you doing this?"

The head of House Uskevren twisted to look back at his

sons. "A man is but memories of deeds done, in the end," he bellowed. "Deeds measured by promises kept! Don't forget, both of you: Uskevren keep their promises!"

He gave them a wave that became a brutal, chopping signal to the magic he rode—and the wave of stone crashed down with sudden, terrible speed.

The shattered solar rocked as that fist of the stones hit the ground. Perivel and Thamalon clawed and sprinted and stumbled forward in desperate haste.

They were in time to see the terrible crash that transformed Marmaeron Talendar, head of the house of that name, and almost thirty armsmen and hired mages around him, into bloody pulp. They were in time to see their father's contorted body, reeling atop it all, consumed by the rushing, glowing energies of the magic he'd raised. They heard Aldimar's last, ringing cry, "Die, Soargyls! Die, Talendars! And know you full well at last: Uskevren *keep* their promises!"

The words were a roar above the rising dust, a call made loud by magic after the lips that had uttered it were burned to nothingness, and gone. Aldimar Uskevren was no more.

Perivel and Thamalon stared at the rubble-strewn courtyard through glimmering tears. Nothing moved in it now but the lazily curling dust—and one injured bird, who fluttered away from the cracked, crazily leaning fountain and flew drunkenly, in obvious distress, up into the ruined room where the guards had died, and out of view.

"F-father," Thamalon whispered. "You shall be avenged. This I swear."

"This *we* swear," Perivel echoed, in a voice like a gem-knife cutting glass. He raised his hand, and sketched a salute with the sword he held in it—not his own blade, lost again by Thamalon somewhere in all the tumbling, but the warsword that had hung in its case on the solar wall for as long as either Uskevren son could remember.

Blue fire ran along the blade, gathered in a cloud of spitting sparks at its tip, and spat a bolt of lightning across the courtyard. Perivel and Thamalon exchanged astonished glances.

"What other secrets does this house hold, I wonder?" the younger son breathed, watching the runes glowing along Perivel's sword.

His brother gave him a dark look. "Don't worry," Perivel muttered. "We're unlikely to stay alive long enough to find out."

He leveled the sword at the distant, leaning fountain, set his jaw, and watched the leaning stone topple slowly into complete collapse in the heart of leaping lightning.

On the other side of Stormweather Towers, another young, angry man with a sword in his hand glared at the lightning and snarled, "I thought you said there was no one left alive back there."

The panting, bleeding, bearded man crumpled against the gatepost shuddered as his shattered arm sent fresh agonies through him, bent his head for a moment to struggle against the pain, then sobbed as the man with the sword kicked him impatiently.

"C-crave pardon, Lord Talendar," the injured man gasped, "but I spoke truth. There was none but me and heaped stone there when I flew away."

"Then that must be Uskevren work," another of the men standing nearby growled, hefting his own sword in his hand. "So they do have a tame wizard."

"Aldimar Uskevren always claimed he wanted nothing to do with magic," a third young noble protested, waving a jeweled hand axe.

"Aldimar Uskevren made a lot of false claims, it seems," snapped Lord Rajeldus Talendar. He'd been head of his house for a bare handful of minutes, but already he was sounding more bitter, more serious. Ruling families did things to people, it seemed. They became far swifter at hurling orders about, for one thing. "We'd best be going. I'm not stumbling through a house roused against us, in the dark, if they've got mages awake and ready for us."

"It'll be worse on the morrow," rumbled the Lord Loargon Soargyl. He, too, had been lord of his clan for mere minutes, but it seemed to have sobered him as well. "They'll be ready for us. Just a pair of servants with crossbows could make scouring the house a *very* unpleasant experience." His brother Blester laid his jeweled axe back against his own shoulder, and nodded mute agreement.

"I've no intention of setting foot in this place," Rajeldus said grimly, staring up at the dark bulk of Stormweather Towers above them. "I intend to bring a ring of our own bowmen and stand well clear, behind it, as we burn it to the ground with all the Uskevren inside. We shoot down any who try to flee, and let the rest cook—at first light tomorrow."

He smiled bleakly at his own brothers, Marklon and Ereldel, received their nods of support, then turned again to face the two surviving Soargyl. "Are you with me?" he asked. "Or do our ways part here?"

Loargon Soargyl cast a longing glance at the mansion, seeming to realize that he'd never get an undisturbed chance to pillage the fabled wealth within. If the Soargyl were elsewhere, however, there'd be nothing to stop the Talendar from entering Stormweather in force, to plunder—and no argument he'd dare to raise later, to this cold-eyed young head of the Talendar, about their having done so.

The hand of a wealthy Sembian never hesitates to help itself to unguarded valuables.

"We'll be here," he grunted. "No fighting between us, and mind your bowmen know we're coming. First light in the morning it is. We burn Stormweather Towers and all the Uskevren together." He glanced again at the mansion. Smoke was still drifting from some of the holes in its shattered walls. "May the gods grant the Uskevren the fates they deserve."

"No need for that," Marklon Talendar growled. "We'll send them to their fates while the gods watch—and make sure of it all. This house must fall, both loudly and dramatically, so that none miss the lesson and dare to challenge our rightful supremacy in Selgaunt again."

Lord Soargyl gave him a long, dark, considering look, but made no reply.

The hard, familiar smoothness of the black, star-adorned hilt was growing warm under Thamalon's fingers. Those fingers that itched to pluck it and throw the dagger hard and straight into a few of those furious remembered faces.

Burn Stormweather and all the Uskevren together. They'd have succeeded, too, if it hadn't been for Roel's philandering. He'd evidently been seeing Aldimar's second wife, Teskra, for some time. . . .

Thamalon found himself shaking his head slightly in disbelief, as he always did when faced with this particular little truth. Ilrilteska, a delicate little beauty from House Baerent, was a subtle, superb actress and a practiced deceiver, though Thamalon had never seen so much as a hint of malice in her ways. He and Perivel had both been awed by her, and he could still scarcely believe that she'd found Roel's boisterous brutishness attractive. But, oh, thank the gods that she had.

"Thamalon—wake *up,* damn you!"

The voice was female, and as frantic as it was angry. Out of an endless inferno of dying Aldimars and burning

Stormweather Towers, in which he ran and ran through rooms of screaming, dying men, and could never find a way out, Thamalon came slowly, blinking, up to the light.

It came from a candle held in the bare and trembling hand of the Lady Teskra Uskevren, wax dripping down over her dainty fingers to spot his own bared shoulder. Someone—Teskra, no doubt—had bandaged the worst of his hurts, and put him to bed in one of the guest rooms, but his sword and armor lay ready on serving tables beside him.

Wordlessly Thamalon sat up and reached for the belt of the breeches he still wore, to have them off ere he donned his war harness.

"There's no time for that," Teskra snarled, eyes twin flames of fury. "They're here already, and I've used up all of my arrows. I haven't the strength to pull any of the war bows. Get your sword and come on! Perivel can't hold them off alone forever."

Thamalon discovered his boots were still on his feet. He scooped up his sword and a belt of daggers, and ran for the door, Teskra at his elbow. A slender sword bounced at her hip, and there were daggers strapped to her forearms. A House Guard's buckler bounced on the low-cut front of her silk blouse, serving as a crude breastplate, and another buckler was belted crazily to her right side. Thamalon recalled grimly that neither guardsman was likely to be alive enough to ever need either buckler again.

"How many?" he asked, letting his stepmother slip past him to lead the way.

"Sixty or so, at the start," Teskra called back, as she shouldered through a hanging and the usually closed panel beyond, into one of the secret passages. She had to slow down and cup the candle to keep it from going out, as they descended its steep, damp stone steps. "It was dark, then, before dawn, and hard to see. I think we've taken down more than half, though, and all of their bowmen. They're standing in a ring all around us, trying to work up dragonfire enough in their bellies to charge us. They wanted to burn us out from a long bow shot away but they'll have to carry their little fires right up to us now. Blester Soargyl tried a few fire arrows, but he can't use a bow. One of them came down almost in his own boot."

They shared a bark of hollow laughter at that, an instant before Teskra burst out into a ravaged room that had once been a linen cellar. She led the way, vaulting heaps of rubble, through a breach in the walls to where Perivel was crouching behind the spell-scorched remnant of a wall, grimly putting arrows in distant men.

He gave them a wild look, and snapped, " 'Ware either side, you two! They're creeping around along the walls where I can't see."

Thamalon looked obediently to the right, saw nothing, then looked to the left. Teskra was already crouching, slender and beautiful, and leaning out on one knee to peer around a corner.

Thamalon saw the blade flash down at her even before she screamed, and he got his own sword out in time to catch it and take it, ringing, into the wall scant inches from her hip. Teskra sprang up beneath the bound blades with her flickering candle still in her hand and thrust it into the face of the bearded swordsman.

His beard caught light with a vicious crackle. The armsman screamed hoarsely as he staggered back, waving his sword wildly to keep them at bay. Teskra flung herself around his ankles like a striking snake and heaved.

One of her daggers flashed out as the man fell—ready to stab as she climbed along his body—but the man's head struck the wall with a wet, heavy sound. His lolling neck as he plunged the rest of the way to the flagstones told her there'd be no need to slide steel into this foe.

Thamalon was already striding along the wall, anger

ising in him and with it a hunger—a need—to strike out at one of these men who'd slain his father and despoiled his home. He got his wish soon enough, striking aside a spear to take its wielder by the throat, spin him around into another armsman who'd been following him, then thrust his blade in, low and through, to pin him there. He took the man's own sword as the pinioned armsmen screamed and thrashed together. Thamalon used the sword to slash open the throat of the second man, then hurriedly retreated to where Perivel and Teskra were fencing with men who'd come at them from the other direction. Lightning leaped away from the tip of Perivel's blade as Thamalon arrived, and where it cracked, men danced and died.

"I've been trying to get Rajeldus or Loargon, but they keep well back and out of my view," Perivel gasped. "How fares it, brother?"

"Not well," Thamalon told him truthfully. "There's lots of smoke back there—and yonder, too. They must have set fires against the walls to burn down the house while we fought them here."

"I find myself unsurprised," Perivel told him grimly. "Recall you what father said about earning a stiff price for our deaths? Well, that's my work now. You're going to be the one to run—with Teskra—to carry on."

"Run, and leave you to die alone?" Teskra asked, color high in her cheeks. She flung a stone into the face of a Talendar man-at-arms and followed it with her dagger under his chin. His blood drenched her before she could spin away, but she never wavered. She used her knife as a handle to drag his sagging body sideways into the path of the next attacker. "Whose idea was that?"

"Lady, you do us honor," Perivel told her as he grunted and slung steel with all his might, fencing with a huge Soargyl warrior whose mustache and beak of a nose made him look like a walrus, "but we are bound to obey Father's last command to us. One of us is to bear you to safety, and stay alive this day to sire other Uskevren."

"To die in other battles, in years to come," his stepmother replied bitterly. "While I watch, without my Aldimar."

She spat in a warrior's face then drove her sword into the man, leaping high to put her shoulder against the wall and her boots into his chest. He reeled away with a raw cry of pain as her kick drove him off her blade. Teskra growled like any man, and bounded across the littered floor to drive her bloody sword into the neck of the man Perivel was fighting.

The smoke was growing thick around them, and from somewhere above and behind the three struggling Uskevren a roar was growing. It was the hungry roar of flames, sweeping through the rooms of Stormweather Towers . . . the roar of a family being swept away.

"You'd best be thinking about getting away," Perivel called to Thamalon, coughing as his cry took in some smoke. "I don't think they've got any mages or bowmen left here, but I can't see to shoot any more arrows."

Thamalon turned his head to shout an answer of defiance. Though fighting frankly scared and sickened him, it was not right to leave yet and abandon Perivel to the blades of a score of men on all sides, seeking his blood.

He never got that refusal out of his mouth. With a sudden boom, a beam gave way overhead and fell, trailing sparks. Blazing rubble cascaded down, forcing Teskra into a frantic leap for safety. Her knees took a startled Blester Soargyl in the throat, and he was still choking for breath when they hit the ground together. The Lady Uskevren's dagger busily rose and fell into his face and throat. . .

Thamalon made his own desperate, lurching run away from the blistering heat, shouldering aside a man who didn't even see him in the smoke, to drive aside the blade of a Soargyl armsman before he could run Teskra through.

As it was, his steel laid open her left side, leaving her sobbing and twisting in pain. Thamalon rained blows on the man's face until he fell, giving the youngest Uskevren room enough to stab the man.

Stormweather Towers was blazing away in earnest, heat shimmering everywhere the smoke didn't cloak all vision. Cinders were whirling in the heat, and somewhere nearby a warrior, caught under a fallen beam, was screaming as he burned to death.

"I should be thinking about getting away," Thamalon hissed aloud, as he floundered in smoking rubble, trying to fend off the blows of another Soargyl swordsman.

There was a sudden roar of flame and doubled brightness behind him. The heat suddenly intensified. Thamalon choked and staggered helplessly sideways before he dared to step away from his foe and look whence the fire flared.

Teskra was crawling toward him, gasping. Her long hair had come unbound, and was smoldering. Beyond her he saw a wall of flame, with two beams settling into it, like bright bars, as they burned through and sagged. Something dark was floating in midair in the heart of those flames.

A large, plain metal goblet, black but seemingly otherwise untouched by the fire. Could it be . . . the Quaff of the Uskevren? His father had talked about it, had mentioned something about it catching fire if someone not of the family blood touched it.

Thamalon set himself to meet a charge from the shouting Soargyl, intercepted both the man's sword and dagger with his own. Almost instantly he was forced to give ground, slipping and stumbling in the rubble underfoot as their bodies crashed together and the Soargyl's size and momentum drove Thamalon back.

A sudden burning to outstrip the pains of his real blisters made the youngest Uskevren grunt in pain and arch his bare bicep away from the swordsman's blade that had sliced it. Grinning fiercely, the Soargyl bore down, forcing the steel closer to Thamalon again . . . and closer. . . .

Teskra rose behind the man like a vengeful shadow and flung herself into the air to reach high and hard with her dagger. She cut his throat.

The Soargyl turned, gurgling, as his blood sprayed forth, and stared at her in disbelief as his eyes slowly went dark. He sank down and died. Teskra favored him with a mirthless smile, then looked up at Thamalon.

He was stealing another glance at the dark, eerie, floating chalice. She followed his gaze, drew in breath in a whistle of amazement, and said, "I'd forgotten it did that. Ald—your father showed me once, when we'd had too much to drink." Grief washed across her face for a moment. She swallowed, tossing her head as her lips trembled, then snapped, "Enough! It's high time you obeyed the orders of your father and your brother and took yourself away from here."

"With you, Lady," Thamalon reminded her.

Teskra nodded impatiently, peering through the billowing smoke, then her face tightened.

"Beware," she snapped. "You're but half-dressed, and there're a lot of men in armor coming this way. There!"

Thamalon followed her pointing hand, and the smoke obediently eddied away for a moment to reveal half a dozen men in full, gleaming plate armor moving cautiously forward, their faces hard and reflected firelight dancing down the blades of the long swords in their gauntleted hands.

"The three Talendar brothers," Thamalon said grimly, "and seven or so guards. We can't hope to stand against them and live."

Teskra shot him a glance, then unbuckled a leather thong along one forearm with deft, racing fingers.

She slapped one of her scabbarded daggers against his

own arm as soon as she had it free, tugged on the straps to lengthen them with cool skill, and met his astonished glance with the crisp words, "You're a dagger short, Tham. You never carry steel enough. Now wear this, and don't hesitate to use it."

Thamalon stared down at the knife long enough to see that it had a white star graven into its smooth black hilt, then lifted his gaze back to their foes.

The advancing warriors had seen and measured them, and cold smiles were beginning to slide onto their faces as they came closer, moving with unhurried care amid the sprawled bodies, falling embers, and rubble.

Teskra stared back at them, eyes narrow, seeing who moved with skill and speed and who seemed careless or slow or with a hint of clumsiness. Then she saw something else, behind them, and her face changed for an instant, before she looked quickly away.

There was a clatter of hooves on cobblestones amid the din of flames, falling beams, and men dying back where Perivel's blade flashed and darted. A horse reared up out of the smoke, its hooves lashing out, and one of the armored warriors fell. There was a rider on the horse, and he urged his mount on to strike down and trample another armsman, even as he leaned out of the saddle to hew a third Talendar.

"Roel!" Teskra cried joyfully, racing forward.

Thamalon stumbled after her, his own heart lifting. The bearlike man lost his balance, shouting in amusement as well as anger, and toppled out of his saddle to crash down atop a struggling armsman.

Roel Uskevren bounced. The armsman convulsed, then sagged and fell still. Thamalon's great-uncle never lost his one-handed grip on his reins. He was one of the few men in all Sembia with the strength to hold a snorting, frightened stallion from running away whilst wallowing on the ground. Roel found his feet with a bark of laughter, hauled hard on the reins to drag his horse back to him, and at the sounds made by a man charging up behind him, turned and struck the man's spear aside with a deftly timed slap of one great hand.

The bearlike Uskevren was swift enough to turn that slap into a punch—and the armsman ran right into his fist.

The armsman's helmed head snapped back, and his armored body ran on for a few loose-limbed paces, arched over backward, and collapsed. Roel saw one of the men he'd felled earlier scrambling to turn over and get up, so he hauled his horse back a few deliberate paces more until he could land a solid kick to the man's snarling face.

The man lost all interest in rising or battles or creeping fires for that matter, and Roel threw back his head and bellowed with laughter again. Teskra covered the last few running strides to him and bounded up to scissor her legs around his belly and cling to him, covering his face with eager kisses.

Thamalon stared at her open-mouthed for a moment, until Roel caught sight of him and let out a fresh roar of laughter. "Gods above, boy, have you never seen lovers together before? Your *face!*"

Teskra turned her head, not releasing herself from her perch, and called, "Thamalon, take Roel's reins and get gone!"

"No need, Tessie," Roel drawled. "There's horses for all back that way."

"The Soargyl and the Talendar—" she protested.

"All the ones who were guarding our horses are dead now. They emptied the stables before they attacked, I think, to stop you folks from departing in haste once the festivities began. I broke a sword doing it, but there's a dozen or so back there that won't be cooking any morning feast over *this* fire."

The bearlike eldest Uskevren jerked his head at

Stormweather Towers. The roaring was relentless now, and tongues of flame were leaping higher than some of the turrets.

"Thamalon, get a horse. We'll take Tessie here to visit her kin at Sundolphin House for the day. Don't know how those old leather-nosed Baerent witches'll take to her knives and the blood and all, but I don't much care, either. They'll want to gossip, you can be sure. Be nice to 'em, Tessie, will you? Not even the Talendars will dare to wade into *that* house with swords drawn. Run, now, lad—run! I see more Soargyl scum headed this way!"

"By all the gods," Thamalon muttered aloud. "He sounds almost happy at the prospect!"

As he trotted past, Teskra gave him a grin that told him she'd heard his words. She'd taken hold of the reins, so Roel could keep a blade ready in one hand, and apply the other to somewhere far more interesting. The Lady Ilrilteska threw back her head and gave the smoking sky a long, shuddering gasp as Thamalon ran on through thinning smoke. It was not a gasp of pain.

He found the horses snorting and stamping in fear at the fire and the human bodies sprawled in blood all around them. They were saddled and bridled, and their reins were all tied to the gate that led to the garden wall. He chose one he'd ridden before, grimly fought down its attempt to break free of him, and rode it back into the smoke. He had to whack its rump with the flat of his blade and saw at the reins to make it go into the smoke. Thamalon hardly blamed the beast for its reluctance, especially when he heard the clang of steel on steel from just ahead.

Smoke eddied once more, sliding away like a snatched cloak to reveal Roel and Teskra fencing with five—no, six Soargyl swordsmen. As Thamalon rode up, one of them screamed, threw up his arms, and fell over, his guts laid open.

That was enough for Thamalon's horse—even before

the blazing ember fell out of the smoke and landed on its withers.

The beast bugled and bucked wildly, stumbling to one side and nearly beheading a Soargyl with its hooves. Someone shouted and swung a sword at it, and it shied away so violently that it tripped on bodies and fell heavily. Thamalon kicked his legs clear just in time.

He clung to his saddle's high cantle as the scorched horse rolled, thrashing and shrieking in fear. By sheer strength he hauled himself into the saddle again as the horse found footing for a wild gallop.

From nowhere, a laughing Roel cut in front of Thamalon's horse, waving cheerfully with Teskra clinging to his back.

"Away!" he cried. "For other days, and glory then!"

He clapped his boots to his mount's flanks, and raced away into the smoke. Thamalon's terrified mount followed the stallion it knew, and they tore through smoke and toppling rubble together, plunging through streamers of flame to skirt the worst of the roaring pyre that had begun the day as the proud mansion of Stormweather Towers.

They came to a place where blazing beams were toppling and lightning was flashing forth. A sweat-soaked and bleeding Perivel was dodging and parrying with gasping speed and skill, in a room wreathed in flames. He held a dagger in one hand and a sword in the other, and needed both to hold Marklon, Ereldel, and Lord Rajeldus Talendar at bay.

Roel drew a sword from its scabbard and threw it, hard. End over end it flashed, to take Ereldel Talendar in the side of the head, biting deep.

Ereldel toppled slowly, like a reluctantly felled tree, as Roel bellowed, "I'll be back, Lord Uskevren! Save me some fun!"

Perivel managed a fierce grin in reply—an instant before Marklon Talendar delivered a two-handed cut that had all his strength behind it, and the aged sword in

Perivel's hand broke amid a flood of blue lightning that sent all of the combatants staggering back.

"I'll . . . be here!" Perivel cried, gasping for breath and snatching a sword up from a sprawled body. He waved it in the air and cried, "For Uskevren—*forever!*"

Rajeldus and Marklon Talendar recovered themselves, traded glances, and advanced in grim unison on the Lord of House Uskevren. Even as Thamalon leaned back dangerously in the saddle of his racing mount to shout a warning, the blazing beams above Perivel Uskevren groaned and began to fall. The subsequent crash, and the roar of bright flame that went up in its wake, was the last of Stormweather that Thamalon saw that day. His terrified mount carried him through a choking billow of smoke, and away.

The star-adorned hilt of the knife in his sleeve was as smooth as ever. Thamalon let them all wait and wonder what was behind the gentle, wry beginnings of a smile that he'd left on his face, and went striding down the shadowed halls of reverie once more.

His mount had thrown him in its frantic gallop across Selgaunt, dashing him senseless until the sun was well up the next day. Roel went back to the fire in a vain attempt to drag forth anyone still living, and emerged from its searing flames so badly burned that he looked more like a monster than a man.

The man the Uskevren servants called the Great Bear never regained his health and seldom left his bed as that terrible year dragged on. On more than one night Thamalon found proud Teskra weeping alone in one of the turret rooms, emptying a decanter without bothering with a goblet, and staring out over the lamplit streets of cruel Selgaunt.

He never spoke a word of reproof to her but instead sat with her. Usually she said nothing, but simply offered him the decanter—and usually he accepted it for a swig or two. He sat with her until morning, cradling her against his chest if sleep claimed her. For such a small, dainty thing—she always seemed more a little sister to him than a second mother—she snored like a horse.

After Roel went to his grave, she did not tarry long before following.

Thamalon tried not to look at the pity in the eyes of the few servants who stayed with him, as he grimly began the long task of picking up the pieces. He left Selgaunt for some years, leaving Stormweather in ashes, to trade in Sembia's humbler ports and even into the neighboring kingdom of Cormyr. Slowly he rebuilt the family fortune, but it was work he might have abandoned in despair had he not met and wed Shamur, and found her fierce temper, wiles, and battle-boldness awakening something warm in him again.

Uskevren shipping fleets meant piracy in the eyes of Selgauntans, so Thamalon avoided the traditional work of his family. Instead, he bought and sold land until he became shrewd at it, anticipating where cities would expand, and which trade routes would rise in favor. What coins he made, he spent sponsoring the crafters most Sembian merchant clans of note preferred to ignore and belittle: the common folk working as finesmiths, woodcarvers, jewelers, and the like.

He rode with them through lean times, dealing fairly, and to them the name Uskevren came to mean not "dark, lawless pirate" but "loyal friend." He sold their wares into the cities, made them wealthy, and in doing so refilled the Uskevren coffers. In Sembia, to rebuild wealth is to rebuild one's name . . . and so the spring came when the Uskevren began to restore Stormweather Towers, returning to Selgaunt as if they had never been away.

The whispers began, of course, and were fanned by houses—Soargyl and Talendar prominent among them—who were not pleased to see a vanquished rival return, but Thamalon Uskevren dealt fairly in the trading halls of Selgaunt. This was something other proud houses were seldom seen to do.

When troubles erupted, the family guard Shamur had founded, trained, and secretly tested to weed out the disloyal proved their worth. Several of the most troublesome Soargyl and Talendar "disappeared."

Mages were hired. Mornings found more sprawled bodies, and Soargyl and Talendar warehouses and ships burned—just as Stormweather Towers had burned.

When the cost grew too high, the only fires that remained were smoldering in Soargyl and Talendar eyes, but the two families no longer dared to openly attack Uskevren or family retainers in the streets.

Years passed, Stormweather Towers arose from its ashes in opulent glory, and most folk in Selgaunt came to respect Thamalon's honesty, fearless but polite dealings, and quick business wits. The Uskevren family was truly prosperous, highly regarded—and well-supplied with foes—once more.

Far too well supplied with foes, it seemed. . . .

"Butler!" the man who claimed to be Perivel Uskevren boomed suddenly, "I bid you bring hence all my beloved kin. I desire them to be present, to bear proper witness as I reclaim the wealth that is rightfully mine."

The butler, Erevis Cale, seemed to hesitate for the briefest of moments. He'd already passed through an archway into the gloom of a low-lit passage beyond, and it was hard to be sure if he'd properly heard the pretender's order at all.

Damn all the dancing gods, Thamalon thought, this man *might* be Perivel—or might be anyone who had access to a captive Perivel and a lot of time to question him about family matters.

Thamalon raised his eyes at the sound of faint rustling in the feast hall balconies, caught sight of a sleeve he knew to be his daughter Thazienne's, and dropped his gaze again to the foes at his table. His sons and daughter would have had to be creatures of leaping lightning to have responded so swiftly to any bidding from Erevis Cale. One of the other servants must already have warned them of what was brewing in the hall.

The head of House Uskevren drew in a deep breath and thought, Gods above, let my children keep silent until at least the testing is done.

With this hired mage swollen with deadly spells and the lawmaker in attendance, it'd take little more than hurled words from the balconies—let alone weapons—to give the Talendars and the Soargyl excuse enough for feuding to begin in earnest.

Thamalon did not have to look to know when his wife entered the hall. He could feel the warmth of her regard—and, as always, felt stronger, as if her presence was both cloak and armor raised around him. She must have returned early from the revel she'd expected would last well into morning. Shamur would know the danger here at a glance, and she'd keep their sons and daughter silent.

Of course, one danger always gives way to another. There had never been anyone in Selgaunt, Thamalon included, who could keep Shamur silent.

As if to belie Thamalon's dark thoughts, the hall grew suddenly still, as if everyone in it were holding their breath. With stately solemnity, his footfalls almost inaudible, the butler came into the heart of that heavy, waiting silence bearing the Quaff of the Uskevren on a silver platter.

It stood alone, a large and plain-looking goblet. It looked old, and somehow strong, as unyielding as the old foundation stones of Stormweather Towers. Erevis Cale, evidently well aware of the importance of the occasion, raised the platter high before him and slowed, so that all eyes could look long and well upon the Burning Chalice.

Iristar Velvaunt pointed a peremptory finger at him then at the table, indicating that the butler should set it down in front of him, but Cale stepped smoothly around the mage and brought the platter to his master.

Thamalon gave him a slight smile of approval, and with a gesture of his own indicated that the butler should take the goblet to the man who wore the name of Perivel Uskevren.

The pretender looked at him in surprise. Thamalon gave him a wider smile and gestured at him to take up the goblet.

The pretender stared suspiciously into its depths. It was empty and a little dusty. As if its appearance had suddenly struck the young maid who for some time had been silently gliding around the far reaches of the hall, dusting, she turned and glided forward, a dust rag ready in one slender hand. Thamalon waved her back into the shadows. She inclined her head in a silent nod of acknowledgment, and returned to her work.

Perivel hesitated, and turned his head a trifle, as if looking for some signal from the mage. Presker Talendar stirred, smiling faintly up at the balconies from whence the silent Uskevren stared down—but if the sorcerer Velvaunt gave any sign to the pretender, Thamalon did not see it.

Suddenly the man who claimed to be Perivel Uskevren stretched forth a hand to the platter Cale, as patient and unmoving as any statue, was holding out to him. The pretender stretched out a hand, hesitated, then swooped to snatch up the goblet like a hawk striking at prey.

He caught hold of it, lifted . . . and held on high, up for all to see: a chalice that was not ablaze, but just an old, empty goblet.

"Well?" Perivel Uskevren asked the hall, in triumph. Unburned but not waiting for an answer, he set the chalice back on the table.

The lawmaker, carefully staring across the table at no one, asked formally, "Saer Velvaunt, is this indeed the true Uskevren Chalice?"

The mage inclined his head with a smirk of his own, a bare moment *before* he passed his hand in front of the cup in an intricate flourish. "Indubitably," he replied firmly.

The Lawmaker of Selgaunt lifted his eyes at last to meet Thamalon's gaze. "Well, it seems clear enough," he said, his voice gathering strength with each word. "This is Per—"

The name was chopped off as if by an axe as their host in Stormweather Towers lifted one hand in a signal, and murmured, "Cordrivval?"

The curtains behind him parted, and a gaunt, white-bearded man who moved with the painful shuffle of aging hips appeared through them. "I attend, lord," he announced calmly.

"Mage," Thamalon asked, "before Saer Velvaunt, just a moment ago, has any spell been recently cast on the Burning Chalice?"

"Oh, yes. The Saer cast a spell on it just before he—" Cordrivval pointed at the man claiming to be Perivel Uskevren "—reached forth his hand to touch it. Velvaunt removed that spell just now, when he pretended to identify the chalice. He—"

A sudden spasm shook the old mage, and a shadow passed over his face. "My—lord!" he gasped, voice suddenly thick, "he—"

Cordrivval Imleth had probably not intended to end his days toppling like a felled tree onto an imported Tashlutan carpet woven with a scene of two dragons locked in mortal combat, but it was a splendid carpet. He'd admired it many times, exhibiting superb judgement. So thick and soft was it that his crashing fall made barely a sound.

"Too many lies can kill anyone," Saer Velvaunt remarked smoothly. "His heart must have been weak. Perhaps he was older than he appeared. I hope he didn't owe you over-many coins, Lord Uskevren?"

Thamalon's eyes were as hard and as sharp as two drawn daggers as he met the hired sorcerer's mocking gaze. "So, too, I've heard it said," Thamalon replied, "can the casting of too many ill-considered spells 'kill anyone.' Has that also been your experience, Saer?"

The wizard moved his shoulders in a careless little shrug. "I've seen both faults result in death, before—but hope not to see such things again." He raised his hand as he spoke, and everyone saw that tiny stars of light were winking and circling about it. "I'll just purge the minds of everyone here of all doubt, by casting a magic on the chal—"

Thamalon's left little finger barely moved, but Cale was very attentive. The butler took two steps forward and bent to heave at one leg of the sorcerer's chair in one lightning-swift movement, spilling a startled Velvaunt onto the floor. Motes of spell-light scattered in all directions as various diners half rose, froze, then sat down again. Half a dozen men in full black armor with the gold Uskevren horse head bright upon their breasts appeared through the curtains, drawn swords dripping with sleep-wine ready in their hands. Velvaunt had, after all, been very well paid to deal with just this sort of unpleasantness.

The well-paid sorcerer came snarling furiously to his knees, lifting one hand to point at the butler—but that hand came to a sudden halt as four house guard swords slid eagerly forward to ring it with their glittering points.

"Casting uninvited spells in a private household?" Cale

murmured. "I'm sure you weren't trying to do anything of the sort, Lord. After all, the penalty for that is two years in irons on the docks . . . and the Lord Lawmaker is sitting right there."

He bowed his head and added smoothly, "I do apologize about the chair. I'll have whatever went wrong with its leg fixed immediately, and in the meantime would be pleased to offer you another seat."

Iristar Velvaunt growled wordlessly at him and regained his feet, face dark with rage.

Anger and fear could also be seen in the faces of the other guests. Saclath Soargyl was growling deep in his throat, his knuckles white and quivering on the hilt of his blade. The lawmaker shot him a quelling glance and asked loudly, his voice glacial but firm, "Is the chalice enspelled?"

"It must be," Thamalon said heavily, "and I will not accept here, this night, the results of any magic worked by this hired sor—"

The Flame of Lathander held up one pudgy hand, a spectrum of rings gleaming in the candlelight. "You need not do so, Lord Uskevren. My skills can determine what the Lord Lawmaker seeks to know. If I may?"

He looked with careful formality to Lawmaker Loakrin and to Thamalon, collecting their nods before turning deliberately to meet the eyes of the butler standing with the swordsmen. Cale gave an almost imperceptible nod of his own before wordlessly turning away to pluck up another chair for Saer Velvaunt, lifting it with silent grace.

Thamalon's eyes narrowed at the unfamiliar and intricate prayer that spilled from the fat priest's lips then. It sounded like no supplication after truth or revelation that he'd ever heard, but a binding of some new magic to old.

Before he could stir or say anything, it came to an end, the priest raising the flat palms of his hands in unison to the vaulted ceiling. Everyone looked at him in eager, expectant silence.

"No," said the priest to them all, carefully not looking at Lord Uskevren, "it bears no recent spells, only ancient enchantments—and those astonishingly strong, after so many years."

"I shall have it tested by High Loremaster Yannathar of the Sanctum," Thamalon said flatly, naming Selgaunt's temple of Oghma, "and let him judge." He gave his guests no time for argument as he stretched forth his hand to take up the chalice.

As his fingers closed around the familiar cup, it erupted in leaping flames.

The astonished head of House Uskevren jerked his seared hand back with a gasp of pain, and the man who called himself Perivel Uskevren rose from his seat with a broad smile of triumph.

"Now I think we see who the impostor is," he said almost jovially. "You are not my brother, and you and your brats have no claim here. This house is mine."

The wheezing, whistling thing in the bed looked more like a lizardman than a human. All of its hair was burned away, and burned flesh hung in twisted, wart-studded sheets where there should have been a face. Only the two angry brown eyes told Thamalon that this was his great-uncle Roel.

The rattle in those labored breaths told him one thing more: this might not be Roel for all that much longer.

The eyes caught Thamalon as if they were two sword-points thrusting into his innards and lifting him helplessly, pinioned.

"Promise me," came the horrible, raw snarl that was all Roel could now manage. It broke and wavered on the second word.

"Anything in my power, uncle," Thamalon said quickly,

bending near so the dying man would know he was being heard.

An amiable, roaring bear no longer, Roel had gone back to Stormweather Towers and fought through its flames, seeking anyone alive—had fought in vain and come back like this.

Roel struggled to sit up, clawing at the silent, bone-white lady beside the bed for support. His huge hands were bony, gnarled claws. Their fumbling, shaking grasp must have hurt Teskra terribly as they hauled their owner up, but she made no sound and shook her head when Thamalon reached to help Roel. Silent tears were falling like rain on the linens she was standing over.

"Make the Uskevren great again," Roel snarled. "Rich . . . important . . . respected!" Coughing seized him for a moment, and he shook his head impatiently, the sweat of his shaking effort glistening across the ruin of his face. "Don't waste your . . . time . . . as I did."

"Uncle, I shall rebuild the family to proud prominence once more," Thamalon said fiercely. "This I *swear.*"

"Upon the Burning Chalice?" Roel gasped.

Thamalon nodded vigorously, looked wildly to the servants who stood by the door and said, "Fetch the—"

The clawlike hand that closed on his arm was bruising in its strength. "No . . . time," Roel snarled. "Let me kiss . . . Tessie . . ."

The lady bent swiftly to bring her head down to his, but the light in those blazing eyes went out before she got there.

As Roel's head fell back, Thamalon saw that those ravaged lips wore a last, fierce smile.

"Let me be quite clear about this," the Lawmaker of Selgaunt said carefully, trying not to look at the angry faces of the swordsmen looming over the table. "This chalice tells the watching world who is a true Uskevren and who is not?"

"Indeed!" Perivel boomed triumphantly. "This drinking cup bears magic older than anyone in this hall that cause it to catch fire if the skin of any being not of true Uskevren blood touches it. My ancestor Thoebellon had its enchantments arranged so, as a conceit, after the death of the mage Helemgaularn. Behold!"

All eyes in the room followed the wave of his hand, at the large, plain goblet that stood unmarked on the table, its flames gone.

"No false hand touches it now," Perivel said, with a meaningful look at Thamalon, "so it sits quiescent—waiting. None but those of the blood of House Uskevren can touch the Burning Chalice without awakening it to flame."

"None but those of the true blood of Uskevren can touch the Burning Chalice without it briefly catching fire?" Lawmaker Loakrin echoed slowly, making it a query. He shot a glance at Perivel, received a nod, then turned his head slowly to regard Thamalon.

And the head of House Uskevren nodded his own head, slowly and deliberately.

The lawmaker cleared his throat, and turned his head to regard the chalice.

"Well," he said slowly, "it would then seem . . ."

His voice died away like a drone-horn that someone has left off blowing. His mouth fell open and gaped. Heads turned to follow his astonished gaze, and other jaws dropped here and there around the cavernous chamber.

The maid who'd been quietly dusting and polishing her way around the feast hall had just stepped forward to pluck up the chalice. She was now applying a well-used rag to it with careful concentration, turning it in her bare hands above the table. No hint of flame was coming from the cup.

The men at the table stared at her for a long, tense time as she polished the chalice, apparently oblivious to their scrutiny, before the lawmaker stirred again.

This time, his look was directed at the men seated around him, and it was not friendly. "We sit at the table of one of the mightiest merchants of our city," Loakrin said coldly, "and strive to repay his hospitality by trying to wrest his home—this house I have seen him enter and leave for decades of prosperous trading—from him, declaring he is not who he has been in the eyes of all Selgaunt for years."

The lawmaker let a instant of chilly silence hang in the air before he added swiftly, "I believe, and hereby declare in words I shall repeat before the Lord Sage Probiter and the Hulorn himself, that before such a serious accusation can proceed more proof than flames that may or may not come from this chalice shall be needed. Sembia is a land ruled by law, and ever shall be. I have spoken."

He let fall a heavy hand upon the table. As if in response, the chalice rose into the air to hang head-high above the decanters and spat forth a brief halo of flames.

As murmurs arose from the watching servants, Thamalon allowed himself a smile of relief. At least the few parlor tricks Teskra had taught him to work on the chalice, with the aid of the ring on the smallest finger of his left hand, still worked.

So Uskevren would dwell in Stormweather Towers a while yet. At least until this pretender, or some other scheme, clawed at them again.

Thamalon Uskevren gave his guests a bland smile, dropped his gaze to the cold and motionless figure of Cordrivval Imleth sprawled on the carpet—oh, he'd send for healers, and pay full well for a resurrection, but he knew it was too late, and would avail naught—and made a silent promise to himself. It was not one that would have let any scion of House Talendar, House Soargyl, or anyone pretending to be Perivel Uskevren sleep easily in the nights ahead.

For all Selgaunt knew that Thamalon Uskevren was a man of his word, a man who took care to keep all of his promises.

THE MATRIARCH

Song of Chaos

Richard Lee Byers

As the first scene unfolded, Shamur Uskevren's head began to ache. The overture, with its unexpected discords and irregular, constantly shifting tempos, had been grating in its own right, but now that the vocalists in their chimerical costumes had commenced singing, the opera had become genuinely unpleasant. Neither the lyrics of the arias nor the action unfolding at the front of the open-air amphitheater made logical sense, and yet the willowy, ash-blonde matron with the lustrous gray eyes couldn't shake the vexing feeling that the story had meaning, like a nasty joke whose point she couldn't quite grasp.

Wonderful, Shamur thought sourly. She'd finally managed to drag her hellion of a daughter to an entertainment suitable for a young lady, and it was turning out to be an odious ordeal. She glanced to the left to determine just now blatantly Thazienne was grimacing and fidgeting on the smooth limestone slab of a bench.

A lovely young woman with striking green eyes, raven hair cropped short in the most unflattering coiffure imaginable, and an outlandish red Cormyrean bodice and gown, Tazi was indeed making no secret of her restlessness. She was disgracing herself and her family, and never mind the provocation. Shamur drew breath to whisper a rebuke, then noticed the stout, gray-headed widower seated behind her daughter.

Shamur knew Darvus Baerent, just as she knew all the members of all the best families in Selgaunt. Hitherto, she would have sworn that the aged merchant noble was as stolid and harmless as some old ox long accustomed to the yoke. Now, however, he was breathing heavily and staring fixedly at the nape of Tazi's neck. Despite the evening chill, sweat beaded his brow, and his pudgy fingers played nervously with the jeweled hilt of his dagger. Irked at being ignored, his companion, a buxom girl young enough to be his granddaughter, glowered at him.

Unlikely as it seemed, Shamur could tell something was wrong with Darvus. A fever-induced delirium, perhaps? Taking advantage of a momentary lull in the music, she spoke his name in a cool, dry tone that seldom failed to bring both her social inferiors and her peers up short, even if it had long ago stopped working on Tazi.

Darvus jumped and jerked around to meet her gaze. His eyes widened, and his mouth worked soundlessly, as if she'd surprised him committing some unspeakable crime. He leaped up and ran, trampling and tripping over the feet of the other spectators in his row. To Shamur's surprise, none of them reacted.

Shamur considered going after Darvus, but an instant later a scream shrilled across the amphitheater. Startled, she cast about, looking for the source. Several tiers below her, pretty, auburn-haired Kenna Toemalar sprang up on her seat and tore her clothing open. Eyes rolling wildly, spittle flying from her gnashing mouth, the young noblewoman scrabbled at her newly exposed flesh, which ripped away easily in semi-liquid chunks as if she were melting. Amazingly, none of her neighbors moved to restrain her, nor even recoiled or turned his head to gawk.

Indeed, Shamur now observed, most of the audience sat slack-jawed and staring, stuporous and inert. Some wept, whimpered, or twitched as if suffering the horrors of a nightmare from which they couldn't wake. Meanwhile the singers and musicians played on, seemingly as oblivious to the spectators' incapacity as they were to the pinpoints of violet light that began to flicker in the air around them.

Tazi touched her mother's arm. "Something's wrong," the young woman said. Predictably, she sounded less alarmed than intrigued.

"Obviously," Shamur said. She rose to call out a warning, then, to her ears at least, the music blared. A blaze of violet lightning dazzled her, and a force like a great wind snatched her up and tumbled her away.

Shamur allowed Harric, a grinning, gap-toothed footman clad in blue and gold Uskevren livery, to help her from the carriage. Tazi impatiently scrambled down on her own.

Before them rose a great hall whose essential lines were all but indistinguishable beneath encrustations of parapets, arches, cornices, friezes, entablatures, turrets, minarets, finials, balconies, gables, gargoyles, stained-glass windows, and the gods only knew what else. For a moment, the sight seemed wrong, as if Shamur shouldn't be here, or, shouldn't be here *again*. But the notion made no sense, and when Tazi spoke, it slipped from her head.

"Palace of Beauty, my rosy red arse," the younger woman said.

Privately, Shamur agreed. Andeth Ilchammar's newly constructed theater, concert hall, and art gallery was an architectural atrocity. But she had no intention of saying that and so encouraging her daughter in her disrespect. "You can scoff and jeer out here," she said, "but once we pass through that door, I expect you to be on your best behavior. The Hulorn himself has invited us to partake of a 'unique aesthetic experience'—"

"Oh, bollocks, you don't even know what it is!"

"I know that the invitation said it will be extraordinary, and if you lack the refinement to enjoy it, you will at least pretend to appreciate the honor."

Tazi rolled her eyes. "Oh, very well. Let's get it over with."

Recognizing the Uskevren ladies, the ceremonial guards in their black and silver surcoats stepped aside to allow them to pass. The high, arched doorway gaped before them like a mouth waiting to swallow them up, and as Shamur contemplated it, she felt a pang of weariness.

For a moment, it was as if her daughter's willfulness had infected her, and she didn't want to go inside either. Didn't want to spend another evening listening to dry, stately chamber music and chattering about charity work, culture, and whatever bits of dreary gossip the other merchants' wives had unearthed. She'd spent too many nights that way. She wanted—

Her mouth tightening, she pushed such useless thoughts away. It no longer mattered what she wanted, nor had it for a long time. All that counted now was the obligation to be a staid and proper burgher's wife and to prepare her children to perform their familial duties as well. Lliira knew, the latter wasn't easy.

Oh, Tamlin had turned out fine, whatever his father thought. But Tal, his younger brother, needed both encouragement and guidance. Indeed, she had to oversee every move he made, not that she begrudged him the attention. At least he made an effort from time to time. Tazi didn't. She had the wit to learn manners, music, embroidery, and the other womanly arts which would help her make an advantageous match, or the secrets of accounting and trade which would enable her to take a hand in the Uskevren's commercial ventures. But all she cared about was venery, carousing with riffraff far below her station, playing pranks, and generally getting into trouble.

Well, not tonight, Shamur thought, regarding her grimly. Tonight you'll comport yourself like a demure, refined young maiden, no matter how it galls you. Perhaps intuiting the tenor of her thoughts, Tazi stuck out her tongue.

Beyond the entry was a high-ceilinged foyer, lit by magic and lavishly decorated with a miscellany of paintings, tapestries, and sculptures, including a towering marble equestrian statue in the middle of the terrazzo floor. The piece depicted Rauthauvyr the Raven, founder of Sembia, slaying a gorgon, a feat that, to the best of Shamur's knowledge, the legendary warrior had never accomplished in the flesh. About the pedestal milled a prime selection of the city's aristocracy, the drone of their conversation, the swish of their trailing garments, and the jangling of their abundant jewelry mingling with the harmonies of the glaur, zulkoon, and thelarr players performing in the clerestory.

A lackey thumped the butt of his staff on the floor and announced Shamur and Tazi, whereupon Dolera Milna Foxmantle bustled over to greet them. Still in a glum humor, Shamur had to exert a bit of willpower to stretch her lips into a welcoming smile.

Dolera was a beautiful woman in her forties whose heart-shaped face was, as always, a mask of pigment. She used alabaster powder to whiten her skin, fucus to redden her lips, kohl to emphasize her eyes, and tincture of belladonna to enlarge her pupils. Tonight she wore a low-cut orange mocado gown that reeked of rose water.

"Shamur," she cooed, "how wonderful to see you. And little Thazienne as well. You've extracted her from the taverns and barracks at last, and made her look so pretty, too! Of course, some people don't care for that . . . disheveled look. They say it makes a girl look cheap, or like some clodhopping slattern from a barbarian clime. But *I* find it refreshing."

Shamur didn't even have to glance at Tazi to sense her gathering herself for a furious outburst. She surreptitiously elbowed her daughter in the ribs.

"How kind of you to say so," she replied to Dolera. "How are you, dear? I assume you're still taking instruction in the dance from Maestro Rolando. I'm so looking forward to your first recital."

Dolera's malicious smirk wilted a bit. "Actually, I've taken a sabbatical from dancing to focus on my watercolors. Excuse me, won't you?" She moved away.

"As I understand it, Rolando terminated her lessons in disgust," Shamur murmured to Tazi. "He told her she had the grace of a three-legged sow."

"So you asked about the humiliation to vex her," Tazi said. "But why wouldn't you let me retort with what *I* wanted to say?"

"Because it would likely have been some crude insult, delivered at the top of your lungs, and that isn't how the game is played. If Dolera shakes your composure, she wins."

"It sounds like a stupid game to me," Tazi began. Then the chamber music stumbled to a halt. The glaur player blew a fanfare.

A lanky figure strode onto the landing at the top of a flight of stairs and swept up his arms in a histrionic gesture of welcome. He was veiled from head to foot in a voluminous hood and robe of green velvet and cloth of gold, but from the flamboyance of his entrance, he could only be Andeth

Ilchammar, the Hulorn, a ruler considered eccentric even by his friends and entirely insane by his detractors.

Shamur wondered why he'd chosen to appear in such a bizarre costume. For tendays, the gossips had been whispering that the merchant mayor, who was also a magician of sorts, aspired to transform himself into a titan or some other sort of superhuman creature. Perhaps his garments hid the stigmata of a failed or ongoing metamorphosis. Knowing Andeth, it was just as likely he'd simply succumbed to a childish urge to play dress-up.

"Good evening, my lords and ladies!" the Hulorn cried in his breathless tenor voice. "I hope you're ready to be astonished and exalted, because I have a wonderful surprise for you. As many of you know, I employ agents to seek out the lost artistic treasures of antiquity, and over the years, they've made any number of glorious discoveries." He waved his arm at an example, a carved ebony centaur rearing in an alcove. "But recently, they uncovered the most important find of all. *Visions of Chaos,* a lost opera penned by Guerren Bloodquill!"

Andeth's guests exclaimed and murmured to one another in surprise and genuine interest. Those with a sincere passion for serious music—and over the years, Shamur had affected this passion so doggedly that in the end, it had, to a modest degree, become sincere—were naturally intrigued to learn of a new work by the genius who, three centuries after his disappearance, was still regarded as one of the greatest composers of all time. Those who merely feigned an interest in the arts to be fashionable recalled the sinister side of Guerren's reputation. According to legend, he'd also been a mystic much given to communing with the infernal powers. Some tales even held that he'd bartered his soul in exchange for his musical talent.

The Hulorn paused for a moment, basking in the sensation he'd created, then pressed on. "I have, of course, decided to stage Guerren's work for our delectation. The finest singers and musicians in Selgaunt have been rehearsing in secret for tendays—"

"No!" someone cried. "You mustn't do it!"

Like everyone else, Shamur turned in surprise, to see that a little man with a huge beak of a nose and a shaggy mane of graying hair had somehow slipped into the chamber. Bright scarlet puffing protruded from the slashes in his shabby fustian doublet, and gaudy paste jewelry adorned his chest. Shamur didn't know him, but she knew his type. He appeared to be a member of Selgaunt's sizable artistic community.

Two guards stationed in unobtrusive positions about the foyer sprang forward and grabbed the little man by the arms. "Sorry, Your Grace," one of the pair called to the Hulorn. "I don't know how he got in."

"Please," the small man said, squirming impotently in their grasp. "You have to listen—"

"Master Quyance," Andeth sighed, "we've already had this conversation." He waved to the soldiers. "Remove him." They did, and, when Quyance continued to rave, they silenced him with a blow to the head. Shamur winced in sympathy, and Tazi muttered an obscenity.

"Please excuse the interruption," Andeth said. "The wretch is unbalanced and has been following me about for days. I thought the guards had finally managed to discourage him, but evidently not. Well, enough about him. Come with me. Guerren's masterpiece awaits us."

The merchant mayor descended the stairs and led his guests deeper into the Palace of Beauty. As Shamur moved to follow, she realized she knew what was going to happen next. For the first time that night, her gaze would fall on Gundar, son of Dorin. Her old nemesis, for all that he didn't know it. The wealthy dwarf merchant would be wearing a russet taffeta doublet and a wide, opal-studded belt. He'd have golden chains dangling in his long, white beard.

She finished turning, and her premonition came true.

;undar was there, looking exactly as she'd imagined him. Iow could that be?

"I hate to admit it," said Tazi, "but this might be tolerable fter all."

"What?" Shamur asked distractedly. She struggled to ismiss that disquieting sense of foreknowledge. No doubt : was simply her mind playing tricks on her.

"If a demon-worshiper wrote the opera, perhaps the tory will have slaughter, torture, and monsters raping irgins."

"The important thing," Shamur said coldly, "will be to avor the beauty of the music, not to wallow in any noments of vulgar sensation the 'story' may happen to ffer. There's Dolera. We'll go in and sit with her."

"Why?"

"Because she's my friend, of course."

"How can you say that? The way you snipe at each ther . . ."

"What of it? It's simply the way gentlewomen of our circle behave. Someday you'll understand."

"I hope not."

To Shamur's surprise, Andeth led the company beyond the magnificent theater and into the backstage area with its cramped maze of corridors, rehearsal halls, storerooms, and dressing rooms. Ultimately they passed through a door into the cool night air.

Andeth had ordered that the Palace of Beauty be built into the wall surrounding the Hunting Garden, his private park. Glancing about, Shamur saw that she and her companions had emerged within the enclosure. Before them, ringed by oaks and elms in a natural bowl in the earth, was an ancient amphitheater that predated the city itself. Most people believed that elves had built it, though no one truly knew. Magical lights glowed inside hanging shells of colored paper, and an orchestra sat tuning up in front of the platform at the bottom.

"I wish I could have used Guerren's opus to inaugurat
the new theater," the Hulorn remarked to one of th
cronies walking beside him. "But the master left explici
instructions that the work was to be performed in a settin
like this, and if we wish to appreciate it fully, we had bes
abide by his intent."

"Thanks be to the Frostmaiden that so far, we're havin
a mild winter," Tazi murmured. "You know how Mad And
is when a scheme grabs hold of him. He would hav
dragged us out here to sit through this claptrap even in th
middle of a blizzard."

"Do *not* refer to him as 'Mad Andy,' " Shamur gritted
"particularly when he's walking only a few feet ahead o
us." Then she gasped as another premonition seized her.

This time, it had nothing vague or dubious about it. Sh
was absolutely certain she'd lived through these minute
before and thus knew what would happen next. Sh
started forward, intent on warning the Hulorn, and—

⊙ ⊙ ⊙ ⊙ ⊙

Someone was shaking her by the shoulder. Startled
she pivoted, and saw that it was Tazi. "Mother?" the
younger woman asked, a hint of worry in her voice.

"I'm all right," said Shamur, and that seemed to be
essentially true despite her disorientation. She looked
about and saw that she and Tazi were standing back in the
foyer at the base of the Raven's statue. Dolera and her
equally pretty but younger and more vapid sister Pelenza
were present as well, though all the sentries and servants
had wandered off. Both Foxmantles looked even more
shaken and bewildered than Shamur felt.

"Good," Tazi said. "I was afraid you'd fallen into a
trance, too. Do you remember, a second ago we were in
the amphitheater. Something snatched us up and dumped
us here."

"Yes," Shamur said. She suspected that the force had ctually targeted her because she'd been about to shout, ut since Tazi and the others had been sitting next to her, ey'd gotten caught up in it too. "But . . . were we somewhere, or somewhen, else first? Didn't we relive a bit of the ast hour?"

Tazi eyed her curiously. "*I* didn't."

"What are you babbling about?" Pelenza exploded. What's going on?"

Forget it, Shamur told herself. Evidently her displacement in time had only been a sort of dream, and even if ot, she had more pressing concerns—keeping the Foxnantle ladies from panicking, for a start. "I'm not altogether sure," she replied to Pelenza, "but good fortune has laced us in proximity to an exit, and our best option is to se it and send help back for the others."

Tazi snorted. "*I'm* not going anywhere. This is interesting!"

Shamur glared at her. "For once in your young life, lon't be an idiot. This is not a game. The people in the mphitheater are in peril, and we have a responsibility to uccor them." She had more to say, but at that moment, a leep voice bellowed.

As she pivoted toward the sound, a lackey in the Hulorn's livery plunged through a nearby doorway. A rack of gleaming black antlers had sprouted from raw, oozing sockets in his forehead, and his blue eyes burned with lunatic rage. He clutched a bloody long sword in an awkward, untutored two-handed grip. Shamur—

Shamur crouched among Gundar's coffers, her signature red-striped mask on her face and a silver amulet set with a large, lustrous pearl—the first piece of loot she'd selected to carry away—dangling around her neck. She was smiling in triumph, but the expression felt wrong and unnatural. This time, for the moment at least, she full understood she was reliving the past, and accordingly sh knew what was about to happen.

Sure enough, the door to the treasure vault crashe open. On the other side stood Gundar—clad in a night shirt and nightcap, his beard still black with only a sprinkl ing of white—a pair of his dwarven guards, and a human his household mage.

There was no way out except through that same door way. Shamur sprang to her feet and drew Albruin, he enchanted broadsword, from its scabbard. The weapo shone with an eerie blue light.

Swords in one hand, target shields in the other, the sol diers in their mail shirts spread out to flank her. Gundar who had a reputation as a warrior himself, came straight a her. His battle-axe, whispering and crooning with some magic of its own, shifted deceptively to and fro.

Shamur was so intent on the men-at-arms that she missed seeing the sorcerer—a stunted wisp of a man scarcely taller and nowhere near as solidly built as his employer—point his ivory-tipped wand at her. Suddenly her left shoulder was burning, cooking, as if from the kiss of a white-hot iron, and her loose black silk shirt burst into flame. She dropped and rolled among the scattered coins and gems, knowing she had only seconds to extinguish the fire before the warriors would be on top of her.

Frantically she scrambled back to her feet. Her shoulder still throbbed, and the part of her that had lived these moments before knew she'd carry a peculiar star-shaped scar for the rest of her days. That didn't matter. What did was that as she'd thrashed about putting out the blaze, her mask had come untied.

Gundar stared at her naked face in amazement. No hope that he would fail to recognize Shamur Karn! She and her family had attended a banquet here in his mansion nly a tenday before. That was when she'd determined the ›cation of his hoard.

Taking advantage of his surprise, she bolted past him, !ammed the wizard out of her way, and raced toward the 'indow which had granted her entry. For once she took o delight in the thrill of a narrow escape. How could she? Iow that someone knew that Javis Karn's adolescent aughter and Selgaunt's most notorious robber were one nd the same, she'd have to flee the city forev—

She was back in the foyer, back where a demented ser-ant was about to attack her. She forced herself to think of hat and that alone.

Her body reflexively began to assume a fighting stance, ›ut she stopped herself. Her companions had no idea that he knew how to conduct herself in a melee, and it was mperative that it remain so. Fortunately, she shouldn't ıave to give herself away, not to handle this oaf.

The man with the antlers lifted his sword and charged ıer. She pretended to freeze, then, at the last possible nstant, shifted aside. Trying to make it look as if she were stumbling over her own feet, she dropped, caught herself with her hands, and stretched out her leg. Her assailant ripped headlong over her ankle. The long sword clanged against the floor.

Tazi snatched up a near-priceless porcelain bust of Sune from its pedestal and smashed it over the lunatic's head. He sprawled motionless, scraps of the shattered sculpture caught in his antlers.

The Foxmantle sisters were clutching each other. "Blessed Ilmater, blessed Ilmater, blessed Ilmater," Pelenza whimpered. Given their sheltered existences, it was unreasonable to expect any better of them, but Shamur felt a surge of contempt. Under the circumstances, their case of

the vapors contrasted poorly with Tazi's composure as sh
appropriated the long sword, then brandished it to test i
heft and balance.

Not, of course, that Shamur intended to say anythin
that would encourage her daughter's hoydenish ways c
give her a chance to use her new toy.

"Stop blubbering," Shamur rapped at Dolera an
Pelenza. "None of us was harmed, and now we're leavin
Follow me." The foursome proceeded to the exit, thoug
Tazi trudged along sullenly, casting longing glances bacl
ward at the arena of enticing danger and mystery.

She was so intent on peering behind her that sh
missed seeing the venomous-looking saffron-yello
spider, its bulbous abdomen as big as a walnut, lurking i
a detail of the ornate carving surrounding the door. No
had the quivering, tearful Foxmantles spotted the crea
ture. The arachnid crouched to spring.

Shamur slapped the spider before it could pounce a
any of them and felt its body squish against her palm
Dolera and Pelenza jumped and yelped. Tazi whirle
around. "What is it?" she demanded.

"Nothing," Shamur said. "I lost my balance and had t
catch myself. I apologize for startling everyone." Wonder
ing where the spider could have come from—she'd cer
tainly never seen such a specimen before, and she'd
wandered from Sembia to the southern shores of the
Moonsea in her time—she surreptitiously wiped her hand
on her dark blue skirt.

Tazi pulled open the door, and lesser puzzles such as
the origin of the spider—or a servant who grew antlers
and went insane, for that matter—flew straight out of
Shamur's mind.

The door, of course, should have opened on the
benighted, cobbled, torch-lit turnaround where the carriage
had let them off. Beyond that they should have seen the
lights and towers of Selgaunt, not tangles of underbrush,

ıd towering trees festooned with lianas. Not shafts of sun-
ʒht piercing the canopy to fall through the muggy air.

Speechless for once, Tazi squatted, reached across the ıreshold, picked up the fallen, withered petal of an rchid, and examined it closely. Shamur supposed it was er way of convincing herself that the jungle was actually ıere.

"Everything's all . . . scrambled," the younger woman aid at last. "Changing. People take on new shapes, or go razy. You get whisked from one location to another in the link of an eye. Places that used to be next to one another . . aren't any more."

"Yes," said Shamur. To herself she silently added, it isn't ıst space that's out of joint. Time is a little disordered too, f only in my head. Perhaps, she thought, she was reliving ıoments from the past because she was no longer quite as ırmly anchored in the present as most people.

"How can this be happening?" Dolera wailed.

"I don't know," Shamur replied, "but if we remain alm—"

"Hush, and listen!" Tazi said.

When Shamur did, she heard sobs, bestial roaring, and lemented laughter echoing softly from elsewhere in the uilding. But the most ominous sound of all was the dis-sonant chords and staggering rhythms of Guerren Blood-quill's opera.

"Should we still be able to hear the music?" Tazi asked. "With so many walls between us and the amphitheater?"

"I wouldn't think so," Shamur replied. "That lends cre-dence to the notion that it's the opera itself that is magical and producing the phenomena we're experiencing. That in turn suggests a solution. Since we can't leave the building, at least not through this particular exit, you three will take refuge in a suitable room. One with a door you can lock or barricade. Meanwhile, I'll return to the amphitheater and prevail on Andeth, or the singers and instrumentalists

themselves, to halt the performance. One can only hop
that when that occurs, our surroundings will revert t
normal."

Tazi clicked her tongue in derision. "Have you gon
crazy, too?"

"I trust not," Shamur said.

"I can see why you want to rid yourself of these two,
Tazi continued, indicating the Foxmantle sisters with
casual jab of the long sword. "They're useless." Her ton
was so scornful that, despite her terror, Dolera bridled
"But when it comes to you and me, *I'm* the one who know
how to fight. You need me for protection."

"Nonsense. I can manage for myself, and I'll do so mor
easily knowing you're safe."

"Nobody will be truly safe until the enchantment i
broken," Tazi retorted. "Anyway, I'm not missing out o
the excitement. I'm coming with you, and that's that."

Obviously no argument could dissuade her. Shamu
would simply have to hope that no further dangers woul
present themselves. "Very well," she said, then turned t
the Foxmantles. "My dears, if you'll accompany us, we'l
find you some shelter."

The four noblewomen proceeded down a promising
looking corridor and soon found a small storeroom with a
sturdy door. Blubbering, Pelenza clutched at Shamur
when she tried to leave. The Uskevren matriarch extricated herself as gently as her impatience would allow; then
she and Tazi made their exit.

"And that's what you want me to be like," said Tazi as
she and her mother headed back up the hallway, "those
two weepy, addle-pated geese."

"I concede, they're high-strung," Shamur replied, peering about, checking for potential threats. So far, she saw
none, though strangely, the temperature in the corridor
seemed to fluctuate with every stride, cold one instant and
hot the next. "Even so, they've never brought discredit on

their families by drinking to excess in the lowest, filthiest taverns on the waterfront or lifting their skirts for every likkerish dolt who happens along."

"What happened to turn you into such a dried-up prig?" Tazi retorted. "Is it because you're jealous of Father's dalliances? I can't imagine why. You certainly don't show any sign of wanting him in your own bed." They reentered the foyer, where the madman still lay unconscious on the floor.

"We are *not* going to discuss my relationship with your father," Shamur said icily.

A groaning, grinding sound arose from the center of the chamber.

Shamur pivoted toward the noise. Bands of color—gleaming, metallic blue and black—streamed through the creamy marble form of the gorgon half of Rauthauvyr's statue. In a matter of seconds, it became a living creature, a scaly bull-like horror that stepped off its pedestal almost daintily, its scarlet eyes glowing, its tail twitching, and greenish vapor puffing from its nostri—

Suddenly Shamur was facing a different monstrosity, a huge, vaguely man-shaped thing seemingly made of darkness. Only its fangs and long, jagged claws reflected the light of the lanterns.

It had appeared out of nowhere shortly after the explorers entered the ancient crypt, but even so, everyone reacted quickly. The men-at-arms readied their weapons, and the priests and sorcerers cast spells.

The guardian spirit pounced in among the adventurers and started killing. Neither their blades nor their incantations seemed to hinder it in the slightest. But the magic did have an effect. Around the vault stood immense yet intricate constructions built of bronze rods and faceted crystal spheres. No one in the party, not even canny old

Anax of Oghma, had had any idea of their purpose. Now, however, it became obvious that they were apparatuses of some sort, charged with arcane energies. The adventurers' sorceries had somehow roused them. Dazzling, crackling bolts of power flared from the orbs and arced about the chamber, adding to the general confusion.

A swipe of the demon's inky hand sent Sorn Notchedblade's head flying from his shoulders. Then the horror dropped to all fours, lunged, and caught Kavith the Blue in its teeth. It reared up, lashing its head back and forth, and the magician dropped from its jaws in pieces. Meanwhile the sizzling blazes of power leaped brighter and brighter, faster and faster. The crypt itself began to tremble.

Stalking on silent feet, wishing she hadn't needed to sell Albruin two months ago to extricate her comrades from a predicament almost as dire as this, Shamur circled to take the shadowy colossus from behind. The demon, however, rendered her efforts useless by abruptly plunging away from her and through the ranks of its nearest opponents to charge Eskander, who was piercing it with arrow after arrow. Shamur knew it wasn't cowardice that had prompted the thin, easygoing brigand-turned-treasure-hunter to hang back and use his longbow. He'd done it because his sword wasn't magical, but his silver-headed shafts were.

She also knew, as she abruptly recalled that she'd lived through this ordeal before, what would happen next. Perhaps she screamed even before it did.

Eskander tried to dodge the demon, but he was too slow. The spirit struck with its left hand and impaled the archer's torso on three of its claws. That had likely been enough to kill him instantly, but, perhaps enraged, its head and shoulders bristling with his arrows, the shadowy giant swung him up and down, up and down, battering the only man Shamur had ever truly loved—or ever would—against the heaving sandstone floor.

Shamur charged the guardian, in her anguish scarcely

noticing that the vault was now shaking so hard that it was no longer possible to run in a straight line. The silver amulet she'd stolen from Gundar's hoard bounced against her breasts. Suspecting it to be magical, she'd paid a sage to examine it shortly after her hasty flight years before. He hadn't been able to determine its precise purpose but opined that it might be some manner of protective device, and so she'd elected to hold on to it.

The demon whirled to face her, its agility uncanny in so hulking a creature. Its dark hand lashed out. She dived forward, trying to dodge the blow and get inside the giant's reach. She did avoid the spirit's claws, but its palm smashed into her, flung her off her feet, and tumbled her across the quaking floor.

For a moment she lay stunned, watching stupidly as jagged cracks spread across the rib vault of the ceiling, and the tortured stonework groaned like a god in agony. The demon loomed above her, claws poised to seize her, rend her, and she remembered that she had to keep fighting. When she tried to raise her sword, though, she found it was gone and her limbs were sluggish from shock and pain.

The guardian reached for her, and chunks of stone began to rain down from the ceiling. One of the flares of power from the sorcerous mechanisms struck the pearl in the center of the amulet, and abruptly everything was different.

The demon was gone, and the cave-in was over, though it had buried much of the chamber before it ran its course, demolishing the bronze-and-crystal constructs in the process. Evidently it had also opened some fissures from the crypt to the surface, because a bit of wan gray light was leaking in from somewhere to replace the illumination of the lanterns, none of which were burning anymore.

Dazed and bewildered, Shamur struggled to her feet and cast about for her companions. And she found them, those who weren't buried beneath piles of rubble, anyway.

They were all dead. That in itself grieved but failed to surprise her. The enigma, the grim marvel that made her blink and wonder if she was dreaming, was that they all looked as if they'd been dead for decades. Their remaining flesh was withered and leathery, their eye sockets empty, their garments rotten, their weapons and armor rusty and corroded. Dust covered all.

Numb with shock and sorrow, she couldn't even guess what the condition of the corpses might portend. She walked to the heap of stone that presumably covered Eskander's remains and stood there with her head bowed for a time. Then she made her way out into the daylight.

"Get back!" Tazi said.

Shamur did back slowly away from the gorgon, meanwhile giving her head a shake to clear it. It had been excruciating to relive the slaughter of Eskander and her friends, but she was back in the present now, facing a beast that might well prove as formidable as the guardian of the crypt had been, and this time, her daughter's life was at stake.

The scaly, taurine creature, a third again as tall as a man, turned about, eyeing its surroundings dubiously. Perhaps, Shamur thought, it was feeling so perplexed that it would let a pair of human women withdraw unchallenged. But then, cautiously, stealthily as they were moving, they somehow attracted the gorgon's attention. It glared directly at them, its blank crimson eyes flaring brighter. It bared its mouthful of fangs and stamped its hoof, cracking the terrazzo.

Grinning fiercely, the long sword in one hand and the throwing knife she habitually carried about her person in the other, Tazi interposed herself between the blue bull and her mother. Of course. The girl believed that of the two of them, she was the only trained combatant, and it was unquestionable that she was the only one armed.

Shamur peered about the chamber, seeking a weapon. There was an abundance of art objects that might serve to bludgeon another crazed lackey but nothing that could possibly harm a towering predator with a hide of natural scale armor.

The gorgon bellowed, lowered its head, and charged. Tazi poised herself to meet it. Hard as it was to abandon the girl to fight alone, Shamur forced herself to turn and dash down the corridor that led to the theater.

There had been guards in the Palace of Beauty before the opera commenced. Surely they—and their swords—must be somewhere on the premises still. She prayed Tazi could hold out long enough for her to find one.

Shamur peered into one chamber and alcove after another, to no avail. Until an orc emerged from a doorway immediately ahead of her.

The squat, pig-faced creature in the garish leather rags of orange and purple no more belonged in Selgaunt than had the yellow spider. Perhaps it too was a work of art come alive, or conceivably some other door or window in the Palace of Beauty now opened on one of the wilderness areas such semihuman marauders normally inhabited. In any case, Shamur didn't care where it had come from, only that it had a broadsword in its dirty-nailed, greenish hand.

Not giving it time to come on guard, Shamur sprang in close and kicked it in the crotch. She grabbed it by the front of its filthy tunic and butted it in the face. The impact hurt her own head a little, but the orc's legs buckled beneath it, its bloody snout flattened and skewed to one side, its red eyes crossed. Shamur jerked the broadsword from its grasp, then allowed the orc to drop to the floor.

As she raced back to the foyer, she couldn't help wondering if she was up to the task before her. It had been child's play to trip the befuddled fellow with the antlers, and she'd been lucky enough to catch the orc by surprise.

But only a highly skilled warrior could hope to best an adversary as fearsome as a gorgon, and until this moment, she hadn't touched a sword in twenty-six years.

Yes, damn it, rusty or not, she *would* win! She could tell from the sounds issuing from the archway up ahead—the grunting and snorting, the clatter of hoofs, the clank of steel against the bull's armor—that Tazi was still fighting, still alive, and with the girl's welfare at hazard, failure was unthinkable.

Her skirt flapping around her legs and the slick soles of her gray dress slippers skidding on the polished floor, Shamur plunged back into the chamber. At some point during the struggle, the gorgon had knocked over the remainder of the sculpture that had given it birth—Shamur was fleetingly surprised that she hadn't heard the crash—and now the creature and Tazi were fighting amid the pieces. The girl's bodice was torn, displaying a long, bloody graze across her ribs, while the gorgon bore a pair of shallow cuts, one atop its nose and the other on its flank.

Hearing Shamur's arrival, Tazi glanced around. "No, Mother!" she panted. "Stay out of—"

The gorgon took advantage of the girl's distraction, stepped in, and tossed its head, sweeping its horns in a murderous arc. "Tazi!" Shamur screamed.

Tazi barely jerked back around in time to parry. But the impact of horn on blade sent her staggering, and the gorgon trotted after her, head held low for a thrust at her belly.

Shamur plunged forward, yelling at the top of her lungs to draw the beast's attention. Thanks be to the gods, it spun in her direction, and now all she had to worry about was preserving her own life.

The giant bull loomed over her like a mountain. She dodged its first stroke clumsily, but after that it was all right. Something woke inside her; she could feel the tempo of the gorgon's movements and anticipate what it would do next. Her hand remembered how to cut, thrust, feint, and parry, and her feet fell into the deceptive dance of advance, sidestep, and retreat. She actually managed to nick the behemoth's neck, and when it finally attempted an all-out charge to smash her down and trample her, she spun lightly out of the way and cut it again.

Tazi attacked the gorgon from the other flank. The two women worked as a team, one distracting the bull while the other slipped in an attack or retreated out of danger. Confused, grunting, its sweat and blood suffusing the air with a vile fetor, the gigantic bull pivoted back and forth. Finally it whirled, ran across the room, then turned to face its human foes once more.

"Ha!" Tazi cried. "We scared it!" The gorgon's chest swelled as it drew in a deep breath.

At the last possible instant, Shamur, who had never before encountered a gorgon, remembered the stories she'd heard about them. She dived at her daughter, tackled her, and carried her to the side.

The gorgon blew a cone of green, streaming vapor from its mouth and nostrils. The roiling fumes missed Shamur and Tazi by inches, but the unconscious man on the floor was less fortunate. When the monster's breath washed over him, his flesh turned dull gray, petrifying. In seconds, he became a lifeless figure of stone.

The gorgon bellowed and charged. The Uskevren women scrambled out of its path, leaped to their feet, and resumed fighting.

After another minute, Shamur's heart was pounding, and the breath rasped in her throat. She was tiring, beginning to slow, and no doubt, her youth notwithstanding, the same was true of Tazi. Their immense foe seemed as strong and quick as ever. They needed to dispatch it quickly, before the tide of battle turned against them.

The problem was those cursed scales, which blunted the force of every sword stroke. The creature's only vulnerable spot seemed to be its eyes, but it guarded those so well that despite repeated efforts, neither woman had managed to strike them.

Where else then? Shamur wondered as she sprang backward, narrowly evading a strike that would have plunged a horn completely through her torso. Where else can I hit it and make the blow count? Her memory conjured up the sculpture as it had looked at the beginning of the evening.

The sculptor had depicted the mounted Rauthauvyr laying his long sword across the gorgon's back. If the spot hadn't spontaneously healed over when the beast came to life, there might be a sort of groove up there, free of scales.

"Keep it busy!" she cried. Tazi did just that, assailing it so furiously that she left herself not the slightest margin for error. One slip and the gorgon would surely bury its horns in her vitals.

Shamur clamped her sword between her teeth, ran at the creature's flank, and leaped high, grabbing for the ridge of its spine as, in happier days, she'd grabbed for windowsills or dangling strands of ivy that would help her climb a wall.

She found her handhold and heaved herself up, straddling the gorgon as she would a horse. The bull gave an almost comical grunt of surprise and turned its head to peer at her.

She looked for a notch free of scales and couldn't find it. Unable to reach her with its horns, the gorgon sucked in air. In another second, it was going to breathe on her, but having gotten this far, she had no intention of abandoning her perch. She doubted the brute would permit her to vault up on its back a second time.

She twisted around and found the groove behind her. Gripping the broadsword with both hands, she drove it down.

The bull screamed and tossed its head, the green

vapor fountaining harmlessly up against the ceiling, then collapsed. Shamur frantically dived clear, rolling when she hit the floor.

She wrenched herself around to scrutinize the gorgon. It lay motionless, and after a few seconds, she concluded it was dead.

A smile crept over her face. It was good to know she could still wield a sword. Over the years, she had wondered if her old skills had deserted her for want of practice. Evidently not.

"Mother!" Tazi said. She was so winded, she was wheezing, but even so, there was no mistaking the astonishment in her voice. "How . . . where, when did you learn to fight like that?"

Shamur's satisfaction withered into dismay. Obviously, there had been no help for it—though one could squash a spider and feign clumsiness at the same time, slaying a gorgon was a different matter—but still, here was precisely the question she'd wished to avoid.

"I don't know how to fight, of course. I simply did the best I could in an emergency. I suppose I'm fortunate that my dancing and riding lessons have kept me limber."

"That's the stupidest thing I've ever heard," Tazi said, picking up her throwing knife from the floor. "*Nobody* handles a weapon the way you did without training and experience."

"Well, I've watched your father and brothers fence," Shamur said. She took hold of the broadsword's leather-wrapped hilt and, with considerable effort, dragged it from the gorgon's corpse. "I tried to copy what they do."

"And I still say that's a load of pig manure."

Abruptly Shamur noticed something had changed. Changed for the worse, almost undoubtedly, though at that moment she welcomed anything that might serve to divert Tazi's attention. "The music is louder," she said.

Tazi frowned and cocked her head, listening for herself.

"You're right. I suppose it means the magic's getting stronger."

"Yes. Which makes it even more desirable that we stop the opera without further delay, and certainly before it reaches its conclusion. If my suspicions are right, and it's weaving a kind of spell, then chances are excellent that all the oddities we've encountered thus far are merely preliminaries. The *truly* potent effects will occur at the end."

As they headed for the rear of the building and the amphitheater beyond, they encountered a series of disquieting marvels. The orc Shamur had beaten unconscious was gone but had left a tarry, malodorous stain on the floor, as if it had simply melted away. A tantan floated jingling down a passageway. Small pine trees grew from the molded ceiling of one chamber, and a troop of piebald imps played kickball with a severed head in another. Andeth's theater had become a realm of coral formations and green water in which countless iridescent fish swam to and fro. Tazi gingerly poked her forefinger into the doorway, and the digit came away wet.

The women also encountered more of the Hulorn's retainers, though never in any condition to aid them. Most had fallen victim to the same trance that had overtaken the majority of the people in the amphitheater and proved resistant to any effort to rouse them. Others lay dismembered, slain by some beast now roaming the building. One fellow—or woman, it was hard to tell—looked as if something had reached down his throat and turned him inside out. Several more had changed into inert figures of gnarled wood, red clay, glass, or, in one instance, a patchwork of all three.

Tazi studied the carnage with ghoulish fascination. "This is not a spectacle being staged for your amusement," Shamur told her in disgust. "These were innocent people, senselessly slaughtered."

"If I sniffle and dab at my eyes, will it bring them back

to life?" Tazi replied. "Besides, if it's all so tragic, why are you looking so bright-eyed and chipper?"

"I'm not," Shamur said, yet, now that Tazi had prompted her to consider herself, she couldn't help wondering if the girl was right. Oh, she felt all the emotions that any ordinary woman would if trapped in the same ghastly situation. Pity for the victims of Bloodquill's magic. Anxiety for Tazi's life and her own. But along with the fear came a delicious sharpening of the senses. The addictive *intensity* in pursuit of which a lass from one of the wealthiest families in Selgaunt had embraced the perilous life of a thief.

She was still trying to banish or at least conceal her exhilaration when she and Tazi passed a mirror. The reflections inside the glass lay at right angles to their sources, as if the two women were walking straight up a wal—

No. Shamur wasn't looking at her own recumbent reflection, not anymore. She was standing beside the ornately carved canopy bed of a young woman who looked exactly like her and had even borne her name. Her grandniece, of whom she'd grown fond in the tendays since she'd slipped back into Selgaunt, and who had mysteriously and quite unexpectedly died in the night.

Hook-nosed, curly bearded Lindrian, Shamur's nephew and the dead girl's father, hammered his temple with the palm of his hand. "Why?" he sobbed. "Why, why, why?"

"To destroy us," Fendo growled. He was Shamur's brother, now hideously aged to a bloated, gouty old man and head of the Karn family. Despite his physical decline, his wits remained as keen as ever, and Shamur didn't doubt that his inference was correct. Somehow, his granddaughter had been murdered.

Once Shamur had come to terms with the fact that the interplay of magical forces in the crypt had somehow exiled her in the future, she'd decided to return home and discover what had become of her family. It ought to be safe enough if she was careful. Even after half a century, it was unlikely that the other merchant noble families had forgotten or forgiven her thefts, but they no doubt assumed her dead, or at least withered into a doddering crone.

When she'd revealed herself to Fendo, he'd welcomed her with open arms. Still, all was far from well. The Karns had recently experienced a succession of disastrous business reversals, and now stood on the brink of bankruptcy. Fendo firmly believed some hidden enemy had engineered the family's ruin, but had had no success in discovering the culprit's identity.

Shamur contemplated a new series of robberies, but the Karns' debts were so enormous that even she couldn't steal enough to keep them afloat. The only hope was an alliance by marriage with another merchant noble house willing to provide a massive infusion of cash.

Happily, Thamalon Uskevren then sued for the hand of Lindrian's daughter, the only marriageable child in the family. The Uskevren were rich, but many of their peers still scorned them for once trafficking with pirates. Perhaps Thamalon was willing to pay dearly for a Karn bride because he hoped the union would help his own house regain respectability. Or conceivably, as he professed, he truly loved the girl. Either way, it didn't matter. What did matter was that deliverance was at hand.

Or it had been. Until the Karns' unknown foe had employed poison or black magic to snatch it away. Now . . .

Fendo gripped Shamur's arm with his dry, feeble, liver-spotted hand. Surprised, she turned to face him, and was taken aback by the feverish glitter in his rheumy eyes.

"You look exactly like her," he said, "and no one outside the household knows you've returned."

"Mother?" Tazi said.

"Yes," Shamur said, wrenching her gaze away from the mirror. "I'm all right. Let's keep moving." As they stalked on down the corridor, she wondered grimly why the magic was forcing her to relive all the bad times, the moments when life took a calamitous turn for the worse.

Well, no point brooding about it. Better to stay alert and savor the pleasantly edgy feeling that came from knowing danger was all around. That and the gladsome weight of a broadsword in her hand.

The hallway took a turn that hadn't existed before the start of the opera, then came to a dead end. The obstruction at its terminus resembled a plug of raw, fatty mutton. The Uskevren women backtracked and ultimately found another route that led to the exit they'd used before.

"Let's hope this still goes to the Hunting Garden, and not to the Great Glacier or someplace," Tazi said wryly. She opened the door.

The music swelled, and Shamur's head spun. The dizziness passed in an instant, and she saw that the door did indeed still provide access to the amphitheater, not that the look of the place was especially inviting.

The bowl in the earth seethed with violet sparks, as if millions of fireflies were swarming there. The luminous cloud was so thick that it was difficult to make out the forms inside it, but Shamur could tell that most of the audience still sat entranced. One figure, however, its arms vanished and its legs fused together, was laboriously worming its way up one of the aisles, while on one of the benches farthest from the stage, a man and a woman were feasting on the brains of a corpse with a shattered skull.

A few pinpoints of light scintillated beyond the confines of the open-air theater as well, and here and there, the landscape rippled with miragelike images—a snowy mountaintop, a city of spindly pastel towers floating on clouds, a subterranean flow of glowing lava—as Guerren's magic evidently labored to open gates between the Hunting Garden and elsewhere.

"Come on," Tazi said. The two women strode forward.

"We may have to use force to stop the musicians," Shamur said, "but don't kill them. They don't know what they're doing."

"What kind of bloodthirsty jackass do you think I am?" Tazi replied. Pinwheels of red and yellow light spun in the air before them.

The colors streamed and arranged themselves into shapes, becoming a pair of creatures half human and half leopard, with gorgeous gold rosettes on their crimson pelts. Each held a short, curved, single-edged sword in either hand, and roaring, they attacked.

When Shamur retreated a step, the slick sole of her shoe slipped on the path, nearly costing Shamur her balance. Even so, she succeeded in parrying Shamur adversary's first stroke, then split its skull before it could attempt a second. She pivoted just in time to see Tazi execute the risky but frequently effective maneuver known as the Boar's Thrust, simultaneous squatting to duck the remaining leopard man's cut and driving her point into its belly. The creature made a choking sound and collapsed.

"Nicely done," Shamur said. Tazi stared at her as if her mother's praise was the weirdest prodigy she'd encountered yet.

After an awkward instant of silence, the two women marched on toward the amphitheater, their weapons at the ready. Shamur's blood was up. Conjure up some more servants, she thought savagely. We can kill anything you can throw at us. But, having failed with that tactic once, Bloodquill's magic fell back on its most effective defense.

Once again, the music seemed to blare, and the shining haze in the bowl blazed dazzlingly bright. Something scooped her up—

◉ ◉ ◉ ◉ ◉

Shamur sat beside her grandniece's dressing table suffering a maid to paint her face. Once she might have preferred to apply the cosmetics herself, but she was afraid she'd lost the knack. She hadn't bothered with such fripperies since she'd fled the city.

Ilmater's bleeding wounds, how she wished she could run away again!

Lindrian hovered over her to ensure that the servant made her look precisely as his poor dead daughter would have chosen to look. And to assail her with advice.

"You must always remember," he said, restlessly prowling about her chair, "the girl looked like you, but inside, she was your opposite."

"I know," Shamur sighed. "I was acquainted with her too, if you recall."

"She was refined," the bearded man continued as if he hadn't heard. "Sensitive. Gentle. Timid, even. She would no more have used vulgar language, or spoken an unkind word—"

"Than she would have robbed Vilden Talendar at sword point," Shamur gritted. "I understand."

"I hope so," Lindrian fretted. "If Thamalon ever suspected we foisted an impostor on him! And not just any impostor, but the most infamous outlaw in recent memory! He'd likely have the marriage annulled and demand his gold back. He might even launch a feud against our house. And you, Aunt, he'd hand over to the city guard."

Shamur threw a bottle of hand lotion and hit him in the center of his chest. "I said, I understand! Just get out of here, will you? Get out and let me prepare in peace!"

Lindrian stared at her for a moment, then nodded and withdrew.

Afterwards, as she headed downstairs, she felt faint, and seized the banister to keep herself from falling. Gods above, how could she, who hitherto had always followed her heart, go through with this masquerade? How could she entomb her own nature inside the persona of a woman who'd shared none of her tastes and inclinations? How could she, who had known true love, marry a stranger?

Yet how could she not, when the alternative was to stand idly by and watch her family ruined. Now that Eskander and his comrades were gone, her kin were the only people she cared about or even knew. Moreover, she had a fey sense that it was her destiny to sacrifice herself in this manner. Why else had such a bizarre combination of circumstances landed her in the future? Why else had fate decreed that she and her grandniece would look exactly alike?

The dizziness passed. She arranged her features into a smile that felt like an insipid simper, and, her skirts swishing, her hair scented with lavender, minced on down the steps to greet her betrothed.

⊙ ⊙ ⊙ ⊙ ⊙

Abruptly Shamur and Tazi were back in the foyer. The passage of time had done nothing to sweeten the smell of the gorgon's carcass.

"Damn it!" Tazi spat, kicking viciously as Rauthauvyr's head. The chiseled marble orb rolled clattering across the floor.

"My sentiments precisely," Shamur said. "Our first removal from the Garden could have been happenstance, but this time, there isn't any doubt. Guerren's magic was aware of us somehow, aware we intended to stop it, and it distanced us from the musicians to forestall our efforts."

"That's the way it looks to me, too," Tazi said. She strode to the door and opened it. The jungle was gone, and the turnaround and Selgaunt had returned. "Here's one bit of good luck, anyway. You could still go seek help, if you want to."

"Bugger that," said Shamur. "We can beat this thing by ourselv—" She realized Tazi was staring at her, and caught herself up short. "What I mean is, we might not have enough time left before the opera reaches the finale. Moreover, the way space is twisting and tearing, any rescuers might be unable to find their way into the Palace, and they might fall into a stupor or turn into snails if they did."

"All right, then," Tazi said, closing the door with a thump. "If we can't reach the floor of the amphitheater, what do we do?"

"Remember Quyance, the man who interrupted the Hulorn? He knew dire things would happen if the opera was performed. If we find him, perhaps he can tell us something useful."

Tazi frowned dubiously. "Don't you think the guards dragged him off to jail?"

"It's possible, but he seemed harmless. With Andeth and half the aristocracy to watch over, perhaps they simply locked him up somewhere on the premises for the time being. Let's take a look around."

They started toward a corridor, and Shamur once again felt the minimal traction between the slick soles of her slippers and the surface beneath. She hesitated for a second, then impatiently decided, to hell with it. "Bide a moment," she said. She pulled off the shoes, then used the edge of her broadsword to saw away her cumbersome skirt above the knees and slit the remainder of the garment up the sides.

Tazi watched for a moment, shaking her head, then proceeded to treat her own gown in similar fashion, though she held on to her shoes, which evidently had rougher bottoms. "Not that I'm complaining, but someday you'll have to tell me who you are and what you did with my real mother."

Shamur grinned. "I ate her."

As the two searched, the discordant music swelled louder, and they saw an occasional violet spark glittering here inside the building. Strange odors hung in the passages, and a torrent of water poured from midair, vanishing again before it could strike the floor. Armies of shadows battled on the walls of one of the sculpture galleries, and the conflict bathed the floor in real blood. Most disquietingly of all, Shamur periodically fancied she glimpsed another version of herself and another Tazi prowling along ahead of them, but the pair always slipped around a corner or through a doorway before she could be sure.

Trying not to let the phantasmagoria unsettle her, she kept an eye out for the unobtrusive service passages leading away from the viewing rooms and performance halls. For it was hardly likely that the soldiers had imprisoned an alleged lunatic in a chamber containing valuable works of art, or in any other place the Hulorn's guests were likely to visit.

Eventually the search led her and Tazi downstairs to the cellars. Here, mercifully, the wonders and anomalies seemed less abundant, though the music sounded as loudly as before.

Tazi tested the handle of a stout door reinforced with iron bands, found it locked, and rapped on it. On the other side, someone gave a wordless, gurgling cry.

The two women exchanged a glance, then kicked the door in unison. It banged in the frame, but held firm, and Shamur could tell that they could batter it for hours without effect.

Tazi gave her mother a sidelong, uncharacteristically diffident look. "I . . . may be able to do something here," she said. From the small, beaded pouch on her belt she removed a supple roll of chamois. When she opened it, it proved to contain a shining assortment of steel picks and probes, tucked through a series of loops to hold them in place.

Now it was Shamur's turn to stare at her companion in astonishment. She knew something of her daughter's wild and contrary ways, but still, was it possible? Tazi a thief, just as she herself had been? She supposed she ought to feel outrage, but the emotion wouldn't come, and she surprised both the girl and herself by bursting out laughing instead.

"Yes, get us in," she said. "And may Mask kiss your fingers."

Shamur saw with a wistful twinge of pride that Tazi's touch was as deft as her own had been. The lock, though relatively sophisticated, clicked and yielded in a trice. The older woman gave her daughter time to rise and ready her knife and long sword, then threw open the door.

Inside was a low-ceilinged cell, with shackles intended to secure a brace of prisoners to the far wall. Unfortunately, the power of Guerren Bloodquill's music had altered the nature of the chains. They started out from their mountings as lengths of metal links, but after a few inches turned into thick, lush-smelling green vines, grown and twisted together to become some sort of plant. In the center of the intricate tangle dangled the helplessly writhing form of Quyance, with pairs of serrated, fleshy leaves clamped around his limbs like jaws. Judging from the little man's raw skin and blisters, the leaves secreted a juice that was slowly digesting him alive.

Tazi exclaimed in disgust and hacked at the plant. Three gaping, traplike sets of leaves shot out at her like striking adders. Shamur swung her sword and severed one of them, and the younger woman accounted for the other two.

Killing the plant proved to be far from easy. It had countless mouths with which to strike at its attackers and no obvious vital areas at which the women could aim their blows. Still, Shamur felt confident that she and Tazi would defeat it in time, because she assumed it couldn't pursue them when they found it expedient to retreat. It was, after all, rooted to the back wall, and probably to the floor as well.

Then it made a fool of her by lunging, its roots either stretching or ripping free of their moorings. Shamur pivoted toward the doorway but couldn't reach it in time. A wave of creaking, rattling foliage slammed into her and Tazi, shoving them against the wall.

The mass of the plant pressed all around Shamur, blinding, smothering. Pairs of leaves closed on her, soft but powerful, relentlessly stinging her with their acids and striving to immobilize her. Snarling, she cut at the thing over and over again.

Finally, it stopped moving.

"Mother?" Tazi gasped. "Are you all right?" From the sound of her voice, she was still only a yard of two away, but completely invisible inside the jumble of vines. These were already turning brown, and, from the stink of them, beginning to rot.

"I'm fine," Shamur said. "You?"

"The same, but that was close."

"Close calls are good for you," Shamur said. It was a remark she'd often made to other thieves and adventurers. "They get your blood pumping."

"Sometimes right out of your body," Tazi replied, "but I take your point."

With considerable effort, the women struggled clear of the plant, then turned their attention to Quyance, stripping away the leaves and coils of liana that bound him. To Shamur's relief, the little man wasn't burned as badly as she'd initially feared.

"Thank you," he whispered.

"You're welcome," Shamur said. "I wish we could take you directly to a healer as well, but we haven't time. We have to stop the opera, and we need your help. Exactly who are you, Master Quyance, and what do you know about what's going on?"

"I play the glaur," said Quyance, "and when the Hulorn was assembling his orchestra, he hired me. I was delighted to have the chance to participate in such a historic performance, even though I frankly couldn't understand why a master like Guerren Bloodquill had chosen to spend his talent on such a work. His genius was manifest in every phrase, but the effect was so *unpleasant.*"

"We noticed," Tazi said.

Despite the pain of his injuries, the horn player gave her a wry little smile. "Actually, we didn't have inanimate objects turning into man-eating plants during rehearsal. Still, odd things did happen. Stacks of boxes falling. A rack of costumes catching fire. A rat dancing on its hind legs. A layer of frost in a hallway. And Bors the drummer—strong, young, healthy—keeled over dead. His heart just stopped for no reason at all.

"Given Guerren's sinister reputation," Quyance continued, "I suspected that the music was responsible. I told the Hulorn of my concerns, but if anything, my report made him more eager than ever to have the work performed. I didn't entirely understand him, but he seemed to believe that the opera might contain an arcane message sent down the ages from Bloodquill specifically to himself. A communication that would lead him to some mysterious 'destiny.' "

"Ah, yes, Andeth's destiny," Shamur said. She and Tazi lifted Quyance clear of the dead plant and helped him to a bench in the corner. "He's been seeking it for years, with never a clue as to what it will involve. Though I think we can rule out wise decisions and responsible governance."

"Well, when I persisted in my objections, he discharged me," Quyance said, "and before I left the palace, I purloined a copy of the score. I'm not *merely* a performer, you see." He drew himself up a little straighter. "I'm also an initiate of Milil and a scholar of music in both its exoteric and esoteric aspects. I hoped that if I studied the opera, consulting the texts I've collected over the years, I might find out exactly what was going on with it, and I felt I had a duty to attempt precisely that."

"What did you come up with?" Tazi asked.

"Something more terrible than I could have dreamed. Guerren wove a sort of ritual into the score, which, when it reached its conclusion, would create a permanent region of primal chaos here on the earthly plane."

As a rebellious scapegrace of a girl, Shamur had seldom cared to study, but, gifted with intelligence and a good memory, she'd often assimilated her lessons more or less despite herself. Now she recalled her philosophy tutor explaining that on those levels of reality where chaos, a fundamental force of the cosmos, reigned unchecked by the counterbalancing principle of law, all things were possible, and therefore, nothing was stable or permanent. Under such conditions, human life could not long endure.

"Why in the name of the Abyss would he want do that?" she asked.

Quyance dredged up another weary little smile. "Well, the tales do say that he was mad. But perhaps it was intended as a weapon. You make your enemy a gift of the opera, he has it staged, and it destroys him. In any case, it was only tonight that I finally discerned its purpose. I raced back here, slipped in through a side entrance . . . but you know the rest."

"How big a region of chaos are we talking about?" Tazi asked, restlessly toying with her knife.

"I can't be altogether certain," Quyance said, "but I think it might engulf the entire city."

A chill oozed up Shamur's spine, and the music jangling in the air seemed to laugh at her. She pushed horror to the back of her mind and forced herself to concentrate on practicalities. "There's one thing I still don't understand. During rehearsal, you people must have performed the opera from start to finish. Why didn't the ritual take effect then?"

"It draws power from starlight," the little musician said. "That's why Guerren specified that it be performed outdoors at night. We always rehearsed inside, to avoid the winter cold."

"The important question," Tazi said, "is how do we stop it? The difficulty is that it senses we're trying, and every time we approach the performers, the magic grabs us and flings us back here."

Quyance shook his head. "I'm afraid I have no idea."

"Perhaps I do," Shamur said. "Tazi, we saw the violet sparks filling the amphitheater, and spilling out across the grass, like a ground fog. And when we descended into the cellar, we didn't find as many oddities down here."

"The plant was a fairly impressive oddity," the black-haired girl replied, "but still, you're right."

"Doesn't all that suggest that the magic is most potent at ground level? Conceivably most aware at ground level? Perhaps it we came at it from above, we could sneak up on it."

Tazi frowned. "Maybe, but I can't imagine that buying us more than a second."

"What if we used that second to sap a measure of its power? Then it might not have the ability to displace us." Shamur told the girl the specifics of her plan.

Tazi grinned. "It sounds completely harebrained to me. Let's do it."

They hastily made Quyance as comfortable as possible, then returned to the ground floor, where they discovered that in their absence the chambers and corridors had rearranged themselves into a veritable labyrinth. At last they found their way back to the foyer.

Here they yanked down one of the tapestries—a panorama of life in Selgaunt, with merchants trading, watermen ferrying passengers and cargo about the harbor, beggars begging, and the like—and cut it into manageable, blanket-sized pieces, which they then rolled and secured to their backs with strips of fabric. Shamur wondered fleetingly just how many hundreds or thousands of fivestars the hanging had been worth.

Considerably less than the entire city, one could be certain.

"I intended to find one of the staircases that would take us to the roof," she said, "but given the alterations to the interior of the building, that could take hours even if they still exist. It makes more sense to go up the outside." She smiled at Tazi. "Given your facility with a lockpick, I suspect you know how to climb."

The girl blinked. "Ah . . . yes. But do you?"

"I'll race you to the top."

The two women hastened out the door, then started up the wall beside it. Ridges in the stonework bit into Shamur's bare feet, but the discomfort was a small price to pay for the pleasure of conquering a vertical surface in the dead of night, and she almost wished the ascent could be more of a challenge. Thanks to the Hulorn's abominable taste and the excess of ornamentation it had produced, she found easy hand- and toeholds nearly every inch of the way.

"I've been thinking about what you said," Tazi remarked, climbing along beside her, just the slightest hint of exertion in her voice.

"What?"

"That we shouldn't go for help, because the music might just put any newcomers to sleep, or turn them into snails. How do we know it isn't going to turn us into snails before we're through?"

"We don't," Shamur said. "That's part of the fun." She grasped the black marble balustrade of a balcony. For a moment it felt like solid stone, but when she trusted her weight to it and started to pull herself up, it turned to mush in her fingers, and she fell.

Tazi cried out. Shamur glimpsed the ground four stories below, waiting to smash her plummeting body to pulp. She clutched desperately at the wall and grabbed a fragile bit of cinquefoil molding. It crumbled, and she dropped once more. Certain it was her last chance, she snatched for the narrow protuberance at the top of a cornice.

To her own surprise, she managed to catch and hold on to it. Her momentum dashed her against the wall, and there she clung, heart pounding, her fingers with their torn nails and her wrenched arms and shoulders throbbing.

Tazi peered down at her, then asked, "Was that part of the fun, too?"

Shamur grinned, made a lewd gesture at her, and, once she'd caught her breath, climbed upward again.

The Uskevren women reached the roof without further mishaps. An expanse of fish-scale tile studded with chimney stacks and spires, it rose and fell with a confusion of domes, gables, hips, and pitches.

Shamur rotated her shoulders and swung her arms, trying to work the soreness out. Tiles groaned and rattled. She turned, her hand dropping to the hilt of her broadsword, and a warrior whose immobile face, hauberk, and greatsword were all made of pale stone lumbered stiffly from the darkness. She drew her blade—

⊙ ⊙ ⊙ ⊙ ⊙

The lantern in his upraised hand, Thamalon peered about the benighted forest clearing. Standing behind him, Shamur silently lifted her skirt and removed the broadsword she'd concealed beneath it. It would have been simplicity itself to drive the blade between her husband's broad shoulders, but that had never been her way. Besides, she wanted to watch his face as he breathed his last.

"All right," he said, puzzlement in his voice, "where is this marvel you insisted I must see?"

"In my hand," she replied.

He turned, and his brows—still black, unlike the snowy hair on his head—knit when he beheld the weapon. "Is this a joke?" he asked.

"Far from it," she replied. "I recommend you draw and do your level best to kill me, because I certainly intend to kill you."

"I know you haven't loved me for a long while," he said, "if indeed you ever did. But still, why would you wish me dead?"

"Because I know," she said.

He shook his head. "I don't understand, and I don't believe you truly do either, you're ill and confused. Consider what you're doing. You have no idea how to wield a sword. Even if we did fight—"

She deftly cut him on the cheek. "Draw, old serpent. Draw, or die like a sheep at the butcher's."

For an instant he stared in amazement at her manifest skill with her weapon. Then he stepped back and reached for the hilt of his long sword.

⊙ ⊙ ⊙ ⊙ ⊙

Something slammed into Shamur and knocked her staggering along the edge of the roof. One heel came down on empty air, and the weight of the rolled pieces of tapestry on her back tried its best to drag her over into space, but with a convulsive effort, she managed to throw herself forward onto the tiles.

She realized that, transfixed by her vision, she'd frozen, and Tazi had had to give her a push to keep her away from the stone warrior. She pivoted back toward the confrontation.

Smiling, Tazi advanced and retreated with such surefooted panache that one might almost have imagined she was fencing on the level floor of a training hall, not fighting on an incline where any loss of balance could result in a fatal fall. Her adversary crept after her clumsily. Guerren Bloodquill's music had granted it a sort of life, but here so high above the ground, not to the same degree as the gorgon. It hadn't transmuted the creature's substance into flesh.

Unfortunately, that very fact rendered Tazi's long sword all but useless. It rang and rebounded without leaving a scratch, or at least none large enough to see by moonlight. Meanwhile, other animate rainspouts and statues, some in the form of humans and others bestial, were converging on the scene. Once they surrounded the girl, her superior agility would no longer suffice to keep her safe from harm.

Shamur sprang up and rushed the stone warrior, who turned and swung his sword in a sweeping horizontal cut. She dived beneath the blow and rammed into him, wrestling him backward until he toppled over the edge of the drop.

She nearly went with him but caught herself in time. He shattered on the ground below with a satisfying crash.

"Don't bother to deny that you nodded off on me that last time," said Tazi, a little out of breath.

"Well, perhaps for a moment," said Shamur. "Our friend there advanced on me so slowly, I got bored."

The two women scrambled up the roof. Meanwhile, the stone noose around them tightened, the gaps between the living statues closing one by one until, Shamur observed, none remained.

"All right, then we'll break out," she said. "Help me pull down the fox." The statue in question was an anthropomorphic character from a fable, walking on two legs and clad in a foppish doublet and plumed hat. He carried a yarting in his hand, brandishing the stringed musical instrument like a war club.

The Uskevren women sprang at the fox, and, narrowly dodging both a swing of the yarting and the attacks of the figures on either side, grabbed him, dumped him on his upturned nose, and ran over him. Glancing back, Shamur saw the statues awkwardly turning to pursue. A couple lost their balance, toppled, and rolled rumbling down the roof.

Now that she was no longer in immediate peril, she wondered at her last vision. It certainly hadn't been an episode from her past. Was it possible it had been a glimpse of the future?

No, of course not, because the Thamalon in the glade had spoken the truth. She'd never loved him. Sometimes she'd felt that she despised him. But certainly never enough to kill him, the head of her house and the father of her children. Surely the experience had only been a meaningless phantasm.

Better to forget it, then, and concentrate on the task at hand. The mob of statuary was still hunting her and Tazi, and similar menaces shambled through the darkness ahead. Silently darting and freezing, availing themselves of the cover provided by the complex topography of the roof, mother and daughter managed to make their way toward the Hunting Garden unseen, even when they passed so near their foes that they could have reached out and touched them. Shamur grinned. She'd always enjoyed a good, perilous game of hide-and-seek.

Her pleasure shriveled when the music swelled. Bizarre as the chords and rhythms were, she, who had sat through hundreds of operas, could nonetheless discern that the performance was building toward a climax and she and Tazi were running out of time.

"Come on!" she whispered. "We have to hurry!" She strode forward. Something hissed, and the tiles gave way between her feet, creating a crater three yards across. She toppled helplessly forward until Tazi grabbed her, and, with a grunt, yanked her back to safety on the rim.

The hissing continued. Looking about, Shamur saw that holes were spontaneously opening all across the roof, with no discernable pattern and in such abundance that one could easily believe the whole surface might disintegrate in a matter of minutes.

"I never thought I'd say this," Tazi remarked, "but I may have had enough excitement for one evening. I'm ready for this chore to get easier."

If one of the holes opened directly beneath the women and dropped them down inside the Palace, they'd suffer broken bones at the very least. Before they resumed moving, they needed to discover some sort of warning sign that a given section of tiles was about to collapse. Finally, after several seconds of scrutiny, Shamur observed a subtle shimmering, nearly indistinguishable from the gleam of moonlight, which seemed to presage dissolution.

"Follow me!" she said.

Leaping, zigzagging, and backtracking as necessary, she and Tazi managed to avoid the yawning craters, but it was impossible to do that and keep away from the living statues at the same time. They had to rely on pure speed and agility to see them safely past their enemies. Sometimes these barely sufficed. An alabaster harpy with gilded wings clawed at Shamur, ripping her gown at the shoulder and lightly scoring the flesh beneath.

At last, when so much of the roof had already collapsed that the remainder resembled a spider's web, the Uskevren women reached the eastern edge. Without breaking stride, they leaped into space, grabbed branches of two of the nearest trees, and hauled themselves onto secure perches. A stone axeman clumping along in pursuit stared after them in seeming frustration, then dropped from sight when the tiles eroded beneath him.

Shamur looked down and gasped in dismay. The cloud of violet sparks was brighter than ever, and it was pulsing like a living thing, extruding arms of light and pulling them in again. She suspected that in another minute or so the tendrils would stop withdrawing. The mass would expand and expand until it drowned all Selgaunt in death and madness.

Recklessly, for there was no longer time for even a

modicum of caution, she and Tazi scrambled through the treetops like squirrels, working their way to the limbs that overhung the front of the amphitheater. Once in position, they unslung the rolls of tapestry from their backs, spread them, and dropped them over certain of the singers and instrumentalists below. If the gods were kind, the squares of cloth, by cutting the performers off from the starlight, would so weaken the magic that it could no longer fling the interlopers away.

Tazi jumped down among the orchestra and started wresting the players' instruments from their grips. Shamur leaped onto the stage and moved to club the singers with the flat of her blade.

She silenced a tenor, then a mezzo-soprano, and still Bloodquill's sorcery hadn't displaced her. Tazi was right, she thought, grinning, it's a daft scheme, but by Mask, it's working!

Then a portion of the cloud spiraled high into the air, coalescing into a vaguely manlike form. The giant raised its huge, luminous fist, and she stood motionless, sneering, daring it to attack. Its hand plummeted, and she sprang aside. Despite the spark creature's insubstantial appearance, the blow shook the ground. She kept her feet, and, before the colossus could poise itself to attack again, she clubbed a member of the chorus who was just floundering clear of a section of tapestry.

Shamur repeated the same maneuver several times, until at last, when she and Tazi had silenced the majority of the performers, the giant's form dissolved. Though Shamur didn't feel any wind, the violet sparks whirled like dust caught in a cyclone, then guttered out. The few musicians who were still playing stumbled to a ragged halt. With the glowing cloud and the music gone, the night seemed profoundly dark and quiet.

"Yes!" Shamur crowed, swinging the broadsword over her head. "Yes, yes, yes!"

She saw the people in front of her blinking, shifting, shaking off their collective stupor. She saw Gundar in the front row and realized that her old scar was clearly visible through the tear in her sleeve. In a moment, the dwarf was bound to notice it, and he'd know she was the same woman who'd robbed him so many years ago.

It was imperative that she prevent such a discovery, and yet . . .

She'd denied her true nature for a quarter of a century. Wasn't that enough? If fate had chosen to release her from her dreary masquerade, then fine, let it end!

She stood paralyzed, suspended between duty and desire. Gundar gave his head a shake, rubbed his eyes, and began to turn his head in her direction. Then a layer of cloth settled on her shoulders.

Surprised, she looked about, and saw that Tazi had wrapped her in one of the sections of tapestry. "Somehow I could tell that you didn't want anyone to see your scar," the younger woman murmured.

Shamur drew a deep breath, steadying herself. "Actually, I didn't want people to see all the bare flesh showing through what remains of my clothing," she lied. "But thank you."

In the hours that followed, Shamur discovered that most of the aristocrats and lesser folk in the Palace and Garden had survived their ordeal with bodies and minds intact. Many of the changes wrought by the opera had reversed themselves when the music was interrupted. As she lingered in the foyer, which now served as a makeshift first-aid clinic, making sure that Quyance received proper care and credit for his help, Shamur realized how lucky she was that Tazi had covered her scar. Intoxicated with victory, she hadn't been thinking clearly, but now she knew she had no choice but to continue her imposture. Thamalon could still ruin the Karns. Moreover, if he disowned her, he could likewise have her children declared illegitimate, remarry, and start a new family. Sune knew, the old satyr was still capable of it, even in the winter of his life, and he'd made no secret of the fact that he was sorely disappointed in his heirs.

She was equally fortunate that her fellow aristocrats had sat stupefied while she and Tazi battled Guerren's magic. They recognized in a muddled way that the Uskevren ladies had disrupted the spell but had no idea that they'd needed the abilities of accomplished swordsmen and thieves to do so.

Oh, yes, she'd been lucky all the way around. Why, then, did she feel so empty and cold?

Tazi brought her an inlaid silver goblet of mulled wine. "All right," the black-haired woman said. "Things have settled down, and if we speak softly, no one will overhear us. Tell me."

Shamur arched an eyebrow. "I don't know what you mean."

Tazi gaped at her. "You aren't still going to pretend that no one ever taught you to fight, or climb, or—"

"I assure you, no one did. As I explained before, I simply did the best I could in a crisis."

"Mother, please don't do this. Don't go back to being that starched, frozen creature you were before. I can't believe you truly want to."

"I want to behave as befits my station in life. So should everyone. Indeed, I'd like you to forget all about my undignified behavior. Just as, I imagine, you'd prefer that I not inquire further into your facility with a lockpick. Nor mention it to your father."

Tazi looked as if she couldn't decide whether to laugh or fly into a rage. "That's blackmail."

"If you like."

"Very well," Tazi said, glowering. "I won't talk about tonight anymore. Not even to you, if that's what you want. But I *won't* forget. I *liked* you tonight, Mother. I liked you and I was proud of you."

Shamur felt the ice around her heart thaw a little. "I'm proud of you, too," she said, "even if I don't say so very often." She glanced across the chamber and saw Andeth's chamberlain handing the bandaged Quyance a purse. "Let's find the carriage and go home."

T. NIELSEN

THE HEIR

NIGHT SCHOOL

Clayton Emery

A whistle was their only warning.

Two whistles, one from either side under the dark trees.

Instantly Vox and Escevar planted themselves to bracket Tamlin. Vox, old and huge and dark as the night, hefted a war axe while Escevar, young and fair, drew slim steel.

"Is that some signal?" Tamlin fumbled for his sword hilt in the darkness. The trio could see lights at both ends of the path, for Twelve Oak Park crowned a small hill in the heart of busy Selgaunt by the sea. Yet right here, amid ancient oaks like stone pillars, they might have been stranded in some remote mountain pass.

"Sounds like a shepherd's whistle." Escevar balanced a long sword with the point down and a smatchet, a thick-bladed hacking knife, with the point cocked up. The young men squinted to penetrate the dark night. Tamlin and Escevar were dressed in quilted silks and wool, flashy and fashionable, but the veteran Vox wore workmen's clothes and a black bearskin cape, almost impossible to see. Frost puffing at every breath, Escevar hissed, "We can—Look out!"

The towering Vox grunted and chopped straight down with his long-hafted axe. The blade skinned flesh and chunked in dirt as some animal, fast and low and heavy, slammed into the fightmaster's leg and knocked him reeling. Vox's elbow punched Tamlin so hard the heir almost stabbed Escevar.

In the vanguard, Escevar heard footsteps or hoofbeats pattering toward him. Then he was butted in the gut as if by a charging ram. Vicious teeth snagged folds of his doublet and ripped it clean away. The beast's breath stank like a cesspit. Escevar's exposed stomach felt chilled by the winter night, and the young man gulped, winded and worried: his skin would peel away just as easily. A dog's snarl made Escevar jump and cannon into Tamlin. Escevar jerked a leg more by instinct than training, and heard teeth clash in air. They needed elbow room to fight, thought Escevar, yet he and Vox had to protect Tamlin. A bodyguard's job was never easy.

Angry and scared, the young swordsman flailed steel in a windmill pattern. A leftward swipe of the smatchet struck nothing, but his long sword kissed flesh. Yet Escevar was bewildered: the dog-thing had leaped in, bitten his doublet, then leaped out of sword's reach in an instant. What kind of dogs were that smart?

"Let me fight!" Sandwiched, Tamlin couldn't even raise his sword. Stepping sideways, he picked up his sword tip to deflect an attack, then whipped his cape around his left forearm as a shield, forgetting he carried a smatchet, for they were newly adopted, the latest fashion in fighting.

Tamlin felt Vox's big calloused hand swish for his shoulder. Vox's idea of protection would be to mash Tamlin to the path and straddle him like a baby while swinging his great axe two handed at all comers. Tamlin evaded his bodyguard's reach. He'd outgrown that kind of protection, or so he hoped.

Crouching, unsure what to do, Tamlin waited for an enemy to blunder into his sword tip. Instead, silent and deadly as a crossbow bolt, a stinking dog-monster clamped onto his left arm wrapped in the cape. Tamlin whooped as he skidded on gravel and crashed. Yet even Tamlin, a poor fighter, realized the dog had jumped *down* from a tree branch. Maybe these weren't dogs, but flying—gargoyles? gremlins? what?

Winded by the wallop, Tamlin was dragged across gravel by his arm. Instinctively he flipped the sword toward his attacker, unwittingly saving his life. The dog had let go of the cape to snap at Tamlin's face. Scant inches from the young lord's chin, the dog's teeth clashed on the steel blade. Growls turned to whines as its muzzle was cleft to the bone. Tamlin almost urped from the slaughterhouse breath, and the dog dodged sideways. Tamlin's own blade whacked him like an iron bar on his thick velvet hat. Blood started from a nicked chin.

Disgusted by his ineptitude, Tamlin kicked viciously. His boot thumped muscle, but the dog disappeared in the darkness. Scrambling, with Vox's big paw yanking his shoulder, Tamlin gained his feet. "Nine gates to the night! We're lucky—"

"They're all around us!" Escevar hollered. "Stand back to back!"

Like dominoes falling in a line, growls and chuffs and snarls sputtered around the three nightwalkers. Then some unseen doghandler piped from the gloomy trees, a sharp whistle. With a collective roar, the dog-monsters leaped.

The veteran Vox swept his long axe in a sidewide arc that kissed half a dozen dogs with cold steel. Without reversing the blade, he slung it backward and was rewarded by the meaty smack of the poll spanking a skull and breaking a jaw. A dog skulked low, and its snaggly teeth penetrated Vox's horsehide boot like hammered nails. Vox tugged his leg back to keep the dog hanging on, then kneeled hard on its back. Slapping his free hand on the axe poll, he drove straight down at the belly and felt the blade bite deep. The salt-sweet tang of blood mingled with the beast's open-sewer stench. Another dog snapped at Vox's shoulder, but the big man wore black bearskin in winter, and the dog tore only the cape. Vox shot the axe haft into its gut so it flipped and slammed on its back, kicking and whining feebly.

Escevar and Tamlin, veterans of very few skirmishes, fared less well. A jumping dog snagged Escevar's woolen cape, then hung slack to yank the young man down. Escevar was choked by his metal clasps until the soft pewter snapped. The surprised dog toppled backward, cape tangled in its teeth. Stabbing wildly, the hired man punched a hole through the cape and nicked the dog's breast. Another dog clamped onto his left forearm. Razor teeth sheared Escevar's calfskin glove and ground the bones in his wrist, making him shriek. Frantically he hammered his sword pommel on the dog's head, once, twice, thrice, but it wouldn't let go. Pulled to his knees, Escevar knew it would rip his throat next.

Tamlin wished he'd paid better attention to Vox's lessons in swordsmanship. His cape was gone, ripped off by an unseen beast. Belatedly he remembered his smatchet and jerked it from his belt. Lacking finesse, he slashed the air with sword and smatchet, and hoped he didn't shear his own wrist. When Escevar screamed, Tamlin stabbed at the huge shape hanging from his friend's arm. The blade met flesh tough as rawhide, and for a second Tamlin balked, then shoved hard, leaning into the thrust. The sword grated on ribs, and only then did Tamlin recall a lesson: Never stab the ribs, because the blade might fetch up. Even as Tamlin remembered, the stricken dog dropped, the blade twisted and was trapped in bone, and the pommel ripped from his hand, gone.

"Drat the dark!" burst Tamlin. "Vox will kill me!"

"Lecture you deaf, more likely." Escevar hissed for pain in his shredded wrist. His smatchet dangled by a wrist thong. "Tam, you saved my life!"

"Did I?" Tamlin was astounded. "Oh, it was nothing, old chap, I—*Ulp!*"

For the second time, Tamlin crashed on his rump as Vox's brawny arm knocked him and Escevar sprawling. Tamlin glimpsed two huge shapes soaring down like catapulted boulders, then a silver gleam cut the starry winter sky. Tamlin gasped to see the fightmaster's feat, and thought yet again Vox must have orcish or ogrish blood to see in the dark like a cat. The two dog-creatures that had launched from trees were intercepted by Vox's silver axe blade. Both dogs were blown from the air by the heavy blade. Flesh sheared, blood cartwheeled, the dogs crashed to earth—

—Tamlin and Escevar were lifted bodily and shoved down the path. Vox couldn't speak, but his push spoke. *Run!*

Clinging together, the trio trotted along the slippery gravel path. When the way leveled, they pelted headlong. Ahead the path forked around a shallow pool flanked by upright columns, benches, and flowerbeds: a summer place for parents and nurses to sit while children splashed. In winter the park was deserted, and the wading pool eeriely iced over, gleaming in starlight. Over their panting breath and pounding feet the trio heard more sinister whistles sound behind. They imagined the rapid patter of dog paws drumming the earth. Tamlin was just about to ask which fork to take around the pool when Vox stumbled like a runaway horse.

Knocked headlong, Tamlin and Escevar pitched over the pool's stone rim and slid on their bellies. Escevar hissed as his bare belly slithered across ice. Tamlin slapped down a hand to stop but still held his smatchet. The blade chipped ice, then grabbed so he described a wild, stomach-lurching spin. Flopping like a stranded fish, Escevar rolled until his sword hilt scratched a furrow with a teeth-grating *skreeeeek!* Both young men tried to rise but skidded and sprawled. Grunting, aching, freezing, they chunked weapons into the ice like crampons to drag themselves to the pool's edge.

A one-man army, Vox stood, back against a stone fountain, and killed dog-creatures. His flashing axe walloped a dog's spine, crippling its back legs. It whined like a puppy. A backswing belted a low-flying dog from the air, and the return arc slammed another's skull. Snarling and barking, more dogs surrounded the colossus, yet they were savvy enough not to attack. Tamlin and Escevar grabbed the pool's stone rim as Vox again raised his axe—

Whistles froze the fighter. Different, these tones started high and sank low. Instantly the dogs scampered away. Tamlin and Escevar squinted but saw no mysterious whistlers, only hunched shapes that galloped amidst dark trees.

Cat-eyed Vox saw more. Whipping his left leg forward, swinging his axe far behind, he slung the long weapon at a light-colored figure silhouetted by a dark trunk. Vox's companions heard the *whap!* of steel on flesh and a gargling cry. Vox was already running. Tamlin and Escevar raced after.

Vox hunched over a stricken man whose breath gurgled with blood. The giant fighter snapped his fingers. Escevar pulled a magic candle from a pocket and touched the wick to steel. The paper-wrapped tube flickered aflame, and Vox snagged Escevar's wrist to bring the light close.

"A hillman!" said Escevar.

"We're attacked by barbarians?" puzzled Tamlin. "I expected plain-old city-bred thugs."

Shaggy, cropped hair, a thick beard, and swarthy skin spoke of a lifetime outdoors. The villain wore a long homespun shirt and a laced vest with the hair still on. The hairy hide was a curious dark brown and thickened at his shoulders, giving him a humpbacked look. Vox's cruel axe had ripped the man's belly. Curled in pain, he spilled gallons of blood in a black pool.

Squinting by candlelight, Vox searched at the man's throat but found no wooden or bone whistle, which meant the doghandler whistled through his teeth. The hillman carried only a short club drilled and weighted with lead and a long knife. A squirrel-hide purse dangled from his belt, and Vox used the long knife to cut it loose. Finding nothing else, the veteran spiked the man's windpipe and left him for dead.

"You hardly need loot the man, Vox." Tamlin's voice shook. He didn't often witness death, and his bodyguard's simple savagery always startled him. "Leave the chap some coins so his kinfolk can bury him."

Glaring under dark brows, Vox touched his own forehead, then flicked his fingers away. He pointed to his eyes, then to the dead man, and spread his fingers wide. Used to the mute's sign language, the young men read *Have you lost your mind? There's more to this assassination attempt than meets the eye.*

Moving on, Vox examined a dead dog—or dog-monster. Similar in shape, the creatures proved more squat than dogs, almost humpbacked, with short thick legs. Vox pinched shaggy fur, stroked his breast, and pointed at the dead man. The young men realized the hillman's furred vest was dog-hide. Square skulls of bone bore tiny lop ears and teeth like jagged glass. The rancid smell came from stale sweat, crumbs of dung, and fetid blood on their muzzles.

A second carcass sprang a surprise. Bending, Vox unfolded a leather membrane that stretched from the brute's hocks to its hunch: a lump of muscle to power the stubby wings. Escevar tugged the wing and jerked a dead leg. "It's like a bat's wing! But flying dogs? I never heard of such a thing!"

Vox yanked the wing to test the dog's weight, and found it heavy. He scooped a hand along the ground to say, *More like gliding dogs.* A quick check with the fading candle showed another dog had vestigial wings no bigger than a pigeon's, and a third had no wings at all. Then the candle sputtered out and plunged them into night.

"They're not devil dogs, nor phantom hounds, from what I've heard in pubs," said Escevar. "Wheels of fire! This city's gotten stranger than usual lately. All kinds of oddities crop up!"

"Blame the Soargyls and their necromancers," said Tamlin absently. "Should we alert the Hulorn's Guards?"

"No. They'd ask a thousand questions and we'd have no answers. And I'm freezing." Between battle fatigue, a wounded wrist, shorn clothes, and a lost cape, Escevar shivered uncontrollably. "Let's get somewhere inside."

"What about my sword?"

A nudge from behind was Vox's way of saying, *Leave it.*

Leaving the dead dogs and lone handler, they left the winter-dead park for lighted streets, and safety, and warmth.

"Master Tam," piped the girl. "You're wounded!"

"Eh? Oh, no, Dolly." Tamlin shrugged off torn clothes as the maid assisted. "It's Escevar who got hurt. I'm fine."

"No, you're not." Despite the late hour and hushed

halls, Dolly still wore her uniform and waited up for her master. In the Uskevren household, servants wore a blue shift under a white smock, a gold vest, and a gold turban that set off Dolly's short dark hair. Laying Tamlin's clothing aside, she touched his cheek gently. The master started at a twinge, and Dolly's finger showed red. "This sword cut must be treated right away."

Behind Dolly's back, Escevar and Vox rolled their eyes.

"Sword cut?" Tamlin felt the wound, thrilled at a badge of honor. "My, my. Will it leave a rakish scar?"

"Dolly, if it's not too much trouble?" Escevar hissed as he shucked his calfskin glove. Punctures in the crescent of a toothy jaw leaked red. "Could you summon Cale and his magic box of healing gook? While you dab Deuce's chin, they can lop off my hand and seal the stump with burning pitch."

Thamalon Uskevren the Second, called Tamlin or Deuce, studied his chin scar in a silver mirror. Seven sleepy servants shuffled into the echoing hall bearing hot food, mulled wine, bandages, and fresh clothes. Newly built, Stormweather Towers already felt ancient with jumbled rambling rooms with lofty ceilings that ate any heat and stone walls that echoed every cough and murmur. A fireplace big enough to roast an ox was kicked up, and the three ramblers crowded to the blaze. Gratefully they gulped warm mugs of Usk Fine Old, the sharp and spicy wine that Tamlin's father had originated in his vinyard vats.

Seen in firelight, Tamlin resembled his father, being middling in height and sporting wavy dark hair and deep green eyes. Escevar was rail-thin, red-haired, and profusely freckled, and looked underfed and twittery, which he was not. Vox was a hulk whose single black eyebrow and fierce beard hid a dark face that hinted at orcish or ogre blood. A black braid hung over his left shoulder to mask the white scar that had robbed him of speech. Hired years ago as Tamlin's fightmaster, Vox now served as his bodyguard. The foundling Escevar had been bought off the streets at a bargain, originally to be Tamlin's whipping boy and schoolchum, but now his companion, guard, secretary, and best friend.

As the trio were bandaged and brushed, Escevar asked in a hush, "Is the old owl still up hooting?"

Servants piffed to hear Thamalon Uskevren the First so nicknamed. Dolly, who kept the pulse of the mansion, recited, "The master and mistress have retired. Master Talbot has embarked on a short hunting trip to the hills. He hopes to fetch a hart to the table for the Moon Festival. Mistress Tazi attends a play at Quickley's."

Escevar frowned. "Deuce, maybe we should stay within walls 'til daylight and see what your father advises. Those kill-crazy dog-creatures, whatever they be, were sicced on us by human huntsmen. If we meet Zarrin—"

"We shall meet her." Tamlin pointed his toe as a kitchen boy yanked on his knee-high boot. "Father's entrusted me with a mission, and I'll see it carried out, and damn the riffraff."

Escevar and Vox sighed in mutual suffering. The youth said, "Damning riffraff can lead to early death, friend. Why can't the meeting wait until dawn, though that's hours off since it's winter."

"Father insisted on secret." Tamlin tugged on a quilted doublet of red embroidered with the gold horsehead-and-fouled-anchor badge of the Uskevren clan. Over it he strapped a broad black belt with scabbards for sword and smatchet. An armorer's apprentice roused from bed had fetched a new sword. Servants silently waited for the master to leave so they could return to bed. Dolly brushed Tamlin's dark unruly hair.

The Young Master went on, "Of course, *everything* in Selgaunt is done in secret. What with the Soargyls dropping out of sight, now's the time to snatch up their neglected properties and contracts, Father says. And so we shall, once we strike the stockyards. Uh, where are the stockyards, anyway?"

Escevar rubbed his face and muttered under his breath.

The looming Vox raised a finger for a short lesson, then borrowed Escevar's smatchet. Thick-bladed, with a checkered grip of teak and a thong to circle the wrist, it looked like a gardener's tool for slashing brush. The blade's throat was queerly cut with a deep slot. As an old weapons master, Vox hated the groove for weakening the blade, but new experiments in swordfighting were the rage with Selgaunt's youngsters. This "bladebreaker" slot was designed to replace a cumbersome shield. Carried lefthanded, a fighter slashed down to both fend back an opponent and to hook his blade in the groove. Twisting the smatchet locked or broke the enemy blade, thus exposing him to the right-hand long sword. Escevar and Tamlin had practiced the maneuver, but Vox had proclaimed that "clowning around with toys by day" was no real test of alley fighting in pitch darkness when half drunk.

Vox demonstrated once more how to cock the smatchet up while pointing the long sword down, and how to windmill a "circle of steel" in lieu of a shield. Obeying the fightmaster, Escevar practiced a while, swiping and slashing the length of the hall.

Tamlin fussed with pins and medallions brought on a velvet pillow. As a frequent target of kidnappers and assassins, he had a superstitious awe of good luck charms. One gewgaw featured an imp clutching a gold coin, a charm for business, and that one Tamlin pinned over his heart. From his baldric buckle he hung a tiny chain with a gauntlet symbolizing strength, and to his hat pinned a silver arrow spearing two hearts, in hopes Zarrin succumbed to his own charms. Tamlin donned the round blue hat with a gay pheasant feather and swirled around his shoulders a blue cloak edged with ermine, then struck a pose, hands on his swordbelt. Servants clapped at his smart appearance, and Tamlin smiled and bowed.

"What do you think?"

Vox swiped hands down his front, then mimed circles around his eyes. Escevar interpreted, "I agree. The white fur will make you luminous in the dark."

Escevar tugged on his hat and a borrowed cape. He wore fine clothes but plainer than Tamlin's, while Vox wore a plain brown smock and leather vest under his bearskin cape, and went bareheaded. Both wore small horsehead-and-anchor pins denoting servitude in the Uskevren household. The two waited by the door.

Preening in the mirror, Tamlin scoffed. "Piffle. I haven't any enemies. Only tons of friends. Well, we're off. Wish us well in our venture at the, uh . . ."

"Stockyard," supplied Escevar.

"Yes, jolly good."

A footman opened a big double door that unleashed a blast of frigid air fresh off the sea, then shoved it shut after the trio left. Shivering servants trooped off to bed. Dolly took along Tamlin's torn cloak to mend, knowing he'd probably never wear it again.

"Tamlin! Young Master Uskevren, a word, please!"

"Wheel of the wizard!" groaned Escevar.

The trio toiled against a stiff wind that howled off the Sea of Fallen Stars and sizzled right through their bones. Nightal was the coldest month, and more than once the nightwalkers slipped on patches of ice criss-crossing the rutted streets. Yet the streets were busy as dozens of parties meandered from tavern to tavern. For young folk, the night was still young. Many waved to Tamlin and his bodyguards.

Now a lone man trotted up. Padrig Tuleburrow was called "Padrig the Palmer" because his hand was always out and always empty. Always he had some scheme brewing. Tamlin was a soft touch, the conniver knew, and never could his companions dissuade him.

"Master Tamlin!" Padrig was tall but soft, in a foolish lop-eared fur hat, fur coat, and the layered robes of a prosperous middleman. "You look dashing tonight, a veritable scion of Selgaunt and proper heir to your father's throne!"

"Oh, stop, Padrig." Tamlin smiled at the flattery. "My dear father is hardly a king, just a canny merchant."

"Brilliant merchant!" oozed Padrig, "and it's obvious that canniness carried to his eldest son. Mark my words, Master Tamlin, you'll *rule* this city some day! And I know how to help you gain those celestial heights! There's been talk . . ."

Escevar muttered to Vox, who always stood behind Tamlin, "First you butter the biscuit, then you bite it."

". . . a special deal for only my closest friends and best customers, Master Tamlin. I can't slip any details, it's all very hush-hush, but this plan—"

"Scam!" hissed Escevar.

"—*plan,*" Padrig plowed on, "involves only the best families of Selgaunt. Master Tamlin, if you invest a mere thirty ravens—"

"Thirty ravens?" objected Escevar. "I don't get paid thirty ravens in a year!"

Ignoring the peasant, Padrig went on, "A paltry sum, to be sure, but with great potential for growth. You'd be sorry to miss this opportunity, Master Tamlin. When it comes back five-fold, everyone will know who's the smartest bargainer in town—"

"We know who," grumped Escevar, "and may he sink in the bay to feed the fish and do something useful for once in his life."

"Oh, pay him, Escevar, and stop fretting," said Tamlin.

"Once I've sealed tonight's bargain, we'll be awash in coin."

Grumbling, Escevar counted out thirty silver pieces from a purse but held them until Padrig signed their receipt in Escevar's little red-leather book, marking them "investment." Even as he counted the coins again, Padrig's ears perked. "What mission are you bound to tonight, Master Tamlin? It's clever of your father to entrust you with family business."

"We're bound for the stockyards. We have a secret meeting with—*Ulk!*" Tamlin jerked as Vox's finger jabbed his spine like a dagger. "Uh, that is, we're bound to carouse up one side of Sarn Street and down the other. So much ale, so little time, you know! Ha, ha!"

"Don't I know! Ta, ta!" Laughing, coins in hand, Padrig melted into the shadows like a djinn into smoke.

Rubbing his back, Tamlin groused, "Drat the dark, Vox! I'll pass pink for a tenday from a bruised kidney!"

"If your father hears you blabbed his secret plans," warned Escevar, "you'll be bruised all over from getting hurled down every staircase in Stormweather Towers."

Tamlin had no retort, so they marched on.

Clustered on the Heartland's crumpled coast, Selgaunt was an up-and-down patchwork of jeweled houses, sparkling parks, twisty streets, and proud people. The adventurers waved to friends as they walked the length of Larawkan Lane, for Stormweather Towers crouched hard over the harbor while the stockyards straddled the city's western gate where it opened to farmlands and vinyards.

Gritting his teeth against a stiff wind, Escevar groused, "We'll reek like manure for a tenday! Why would anyone plan a secret meeting in a herd of cows?"

"The contracts concern four-legged beasts as well as two-legged ones, as Father put it."

"What else did he instruct for these negotiations? Or shall Vox and I be as surprised as Zarrin's party?"

"Trust me, Es."

Tamlin's friends only sighed.

The stockyards bustled even after midnight. Many cattlebreeders and sheepherders had driven in animals before the city gates closed so they could adjust to their strange corrals. Calm animals fetched more at auction than skittish ones. Tamlin and his escort circled lowing cattle and gibbering sheep, and watched where they stepped, for the livestock had made their mark on Selgaunt's streets. Translucent globes floated above some cattle like firefly lanterns. Tubes plugged into the cow's hind ends and glow-coals burned the released gas for light, a handy piece of farm magic that always amused newcomers to Selgaunt's marketplace.

Amidst a maze of holding pens sat the Stock Market. The long drafty swaybacked barn held stalls and a judging ring where animals were paraded before bidders. Entering the tall double doors, the Uskevren clan found the building warm as a bakery, steamy as a greenhouse, and fragrant as a spring meadow. Farmers and drovers talked or sang to their beasts to settle them. Some saved pennies by sleeping in the stalls with their beasts, for the clustered animals heated the place better than sheet-iron stoves.

The secret convention was relegated to the second floor, which was partitioned into offices and meeting rooms. As the party's leader, Tamlin made to mount the stairs first, but Escevar blocked him. "We nearly got our heads chewed off in Twelve Oak Park. Let me stick my face in first, please, *milord?*"

The broad stairs stretched over stalls where sheep and cattle contentedly chewed cuds. A farmwife curried a placid brown-and-white beast. Clumping up the stairs, Tamlin whispered, "This is a secret meeting, so look like cattle buyers." Raising his voice, he called, "I say, isn't that a fine looking cow! Yes, indeed, a magnificent cow, madame! And lucky too, with two colors! Just what I need to nurse my calves! I'll bet that one produces buckets of milk!"

The farmwife looked up, puzzled. Vox sniffed, his idea of laughing, and Escevar chuckled. Nodding at the big beast, Vox put two fingers to his brow, stuck one finger before his groin, and made a double pulling motion.

Tamlin shook his head. "Sorry, I don't understand."

"He says your cow is a bull," supplied Escevar. "And good luck milking him."

"Oh." Tamlin followed his friend into the second-floor hall. "They probably teach that in farmer school. It's not something we merchants need to know."

Behind, Vox made a sign of strangling himself. Escevar grinned but drew his smatchet with his good right hand.

Through intermediaries meeting intermediaries, Tamlin Uskevren was to meet Zarrin Foxmantle in the farthest room just after two bells. Tamlin heard the city bells toll, far off but clear in the thick sea air, just as Escevar clicked the latch and threw open the door without stepping forward.

Thunk! A throwing dagger sizzled past and thudded into the door jamb. A female voice shrilled, "You backstabbing bastards! Get in here so we can kill you!"

Warily the three men peeked in the door. At the far left, the corner was lit by three lanterns hung from low rafters. A scarred table was surrounded by rickety benches and stools, the only furnishings. Flyspecked notices and lists were posted on the walls between many pegs for cloaks and coats. Shuttered windows in the end wall would overlook the holding pens. At the table, surrounded by four servants, stood a young and beautiful blonde woman. Her hands were empty of knives, the Uskevren delegation noted, but her snapping brown eyes looked sharp and dangerous.

The Foxmantle quintet had lost a war. The leader's purple embroidered vest lacked gold buttons, she missed her hat and a glove, and her cape hung askew because the chain had broken. Her attendants in purple and blue, two women and two men, were equally roughshod. A woman sported a black eye, and a man carried one arm in a sling. All five bristled with weapons.

Mostly the men marked Zarrin, one of five breathtaking Foxmantle daughters. Pub talk liked to hash over which Foxmantle heir was the fairest, the most hellacious, and the most fun in bed. Zarrin strove hardest to gain power within her family, refusing the role of "a brood bitch who births a bunch of brats for my father and mother to bounce on their knees!" Tamlin and Zarrin were old sandbox chums, for only lately had the two families come into competition. The Foxmantles had always farmed, pressing wine, growing dyestuffs, salting meat, and tanning hides and furs, while the Uskevren had, before the family's Great Fire, farmed the sea. Since Thamalon the First had begun buying and renting farms, dickering with the Foxmantles had become necessary lest they compete in the marketplace and make prices plummet.

Lovely Zarrin fumed but offered no more aggression, so Tamlin plucked the knife from the door jamb and, smiling, offered it to her. "I say, Zar, your welcome lacks the usual Foxmantle cheer. Have you suffered some setback in our city's spangled streets?"

"You're dark-damned right we suffered setbacks!" Zarrin snatched back the throwing knife. Tamlin had unwisely held it by the blade, and now looked at his fingers through slits in his gloves. "What's the idea of siccing gnashers on us?"

"Gnashers? The flying dogs?" Absently Tamlin scratched his chin and made the scab bleed. Escevar stripped his left glove to show seeping bandages. Tamlin said, "We met some too, and their whistling keepers."

"Keepers?" asked Zarrin. "We didn't hear any whistles."

"We did. Vox killed one." Tamlin told about the foreign hillman in the gnasher-fur vest.

Zarrin pouted prettily. Her blonde hair, piled and pinned in back, yet fell about a widow's peak to blonde brows. "We just turned a corner and ran into a howling pack. We thought they were famished wolves that slipped into the city after cattle. They chewed up my retainers and spat us out. One servant's at Selune's temple having his hand amputated."

"Where were you attacked, milady? In what part of the city?" asked Escevar. "And when?"

"Below the Hunting Gardens, not far from the main house." The Foxmantle freehold guarded the northern gate where Galogar's Ride became Rauthauvyr's Road. "Not long after sundown."

Vox held up two fingers, stretched his arms, curled his hands to imitate a tree, showed ten and two fingers, then animals scampering before his eyes. Tamlin interpreted, "Yes, that's near two miles from Twelve Oak Park. How can the keepers move a ferocious pack of monster-dogs through the streets without being seen? Did you notice some had wings?"

The two parties compared notes but learned little. Now and then from below came the bellow of a bull or bawl of a calf.

"Who knows?" Zarrin concluded. "Maybe these hillmen are crazy or cultists. Or maybe they work for someone in Selgaunt. If either of us were kidnapped, the ransom would bring a flock of ravens. We just need to watch our backs, as usual." For emphasis she traced the family crest embroidered on her bosom: three vigilant eyes in purple set on a slant. "Drop it for now and get to business. You and I need to split up the gate tariffs and the drovers' and freighters' trade."

"So Father informs me." Handing his cape to Escevar, Tamlin took a stool and rubbed his hands as his father might. "The Soargyls—May they all be stricken with seven-fold boils!—kept the carters under their thumb by killing the troublemakers and extorting from the rest. But lately none of their thugs have collected the protection money: excuse me, civil supervision taxes. So collections at the gate are haphazardly enforced. Both our houses want to bid on the contracts for the gate tolls. Rather than brawl in the streets, we should reach some agreement."

"I have one: simplicity itself," offered Zarrin. "Consider. My family's house overlooks Rauthauvyr's Road. Your family keeps a tallhouse near the Way of the Manticore. Why not tend our separate gates? We'll negotiate with the Hulorn's seneschal for tolls from the North gate, and you take the Western. You've seen how busy the traffic is in these stockyards. Imagine the revenue you'd collect over a year! We'd sacrifice some duty to maintain the Elzimmer Bridge, but it's worth it to not cross the city just to empty coffers."

They talked. Smiling, smug, and bewitched by Zarrin's beauty, Tamlin failed to see Escevar and Vox signal in the background. Before the companions knew it, Tamlin spit on his palm and shook hands. "I say, Zar, this is smashing! We'll stay out of each others' hair and all prosper! My father will be pleased, and so will yours, I'm sure! We need to celebrate—Escevar, what's all that noise?"

The bellows and bleats of livestock had grown so loud the negotiators had to raise their voices. Every animal within blocks, it seemed, bawled or squawled. Farm dogs barked and farmers shouted. Escevar slid down the hall and trotted back. "Something's spooking the cattle! They're almost breaking down the stalls downstairs! I can't see what's stirring them!"

"Well, go find out!" Tamlin ordered. Escevar trotted off. Zarrin's people shifted weapons. Axe in hand, Vox unlatched the window shutters.

As if shot from a catapult, two winged dogs swooped through the open window and smashed into the sword-trainer.

In that same second, Escevar dashed into the room, grabbed the door, and tried to slam it shut. Three unwinged gnashers bashed the door and knocked the bodyguard sprawling.

Four more gnashers galloped into the room, toenails skittering on the sandy floor. Two more soared through the window.

Everyone fought for their lives.

Tamlin glimpsed brown backs and yellow teeth and smelled the open-sewer stench. Then a gnasher clamped bonebreaking jaws onto his knee-high boot. Another leaped and slammed Tamlin into the back wall. Savage teeth snagged his doublet, and Tamlin was dragged half-over with the dog's weight. A third vaulted its comrade and snapped teeth like a bear trap. Only his wild flailing saved Tamlin's right hand. Tripped by the dog tugging his leg, Tamlin sprawled on hands and one knee, all too aware his throat was vulnerable to attack.

Zarrin snatched up a stool and slammed a dog's head. The stool splintered, but the dog was hammered flat. Snatching out her sword, Zarrin took reckless aim and skewered the gnasher mangling Tamlin's leg. Blood fountained as its throat was pierced. Tamlin kicked the dying dog loose. The other dodged Zarrin's blade, snapping and snarling.

Temporarily free, Tamlin saw they were armpit-deep in rabid killers.

Flat on his back, Vox staved off one beast by the throat while pushing another back with his axe haft. Unable to free his weapon, he kicked a third brute. Escevar danced above him, swiping and slashing at jumping animals with smatchet and sword. A frustrated animal circled Escevar to dive for Vox's face. The swordmaster tried to roll when Escevar was tumbled by a dog ramming his belly.

Escevar flopped over Vox with a pair of snarling dogs atop him. Human and gnasher legs kicked around Vox's head. Escevar's blades swirled like a wind-whipped windmill. The animals gripped by Vox tugged free to escape the circle of steel. The swordsman flipped over on all fours. Escevar was dumped on his side. Dogs pounced on Vox's bearskin back. Swearing like a fury, Escevar stabbed wildly to protect himself and punctured his own thigh with his smatchet. Bleeding, Escevar stabbed, then lunged to gain his feet. Vox bumped his hip, and the two thumped back to back. Where in the name of Seven Sinners was Tamlin?

The Heir of Uskevren lurked behind a table that Zarrin had dumped and dragged against the wall. It formed a solid barricade, but the ends gaped open. A darting dog clamped Zarrin's boot heel. Zarrin shucked the boot but blundered into Tamlin and whacked her nose against the wall. The thought of a bloody swollen nose stoked her fiery temper, and Zarrin screamed as she slashed steel at anything that moved.

Tamlin armed himself with steel in each hand, but wrongly, so the smatchet jutted down and the sword tipped up. He whipped both, but steel clashed uselessly on steel. Still, he struggled to see what went on elsewhere, knowing they had to quit the room.

Shadows swooped and swung as someone banged his head on a lantern. In the crazy light, Zarrin shrieked a battle cry and whacked at milling, growling, jumping gnashers until blood speckled the walls and ceiling. Zarrin's four servants crouched in a corner behind stools and benches, and through cracks and over the tops poked dogs to hold them at bay. Escevar and Vox, bloody and sandy and fighting mad, stood back to back slicing and stabbing. As Tamlin watched, Vox feinted high, then drove his huge axe so hard a dog's head split and the blade chonked deep into pine floorboards. Swiping where he could, Tamlin tried to count, but dogs had overrun the room, a dozen or more. To his left, six monsters breached the makeshift barricade and savaged

Zarrin's servants. Two, no, four more dogs skittered into the room, panting for blood.

Howling, Zarrin jumped the table to protect her servants. Tamlin was left alone as seven dogs scuffled to attack him.

"Can't stay here!" the heir muttered. Flicking his blades wide, gritting his teeth, he vaulted the table and almost landed on a dog. Instantly the monsters champed at his boots and clothes. One winged creature hop-skipped to tear off his head. As Tamlin dodged frantically, the dog sailed by and crashed into its companions. Punching heads with his pommel and snapping his smatchet, Tamlin raced toward Escevar and Vox. His only plan was to die with his comrades like a hero in a folktale, yet to be eaten by ugly dogs seemed a foolish and frivolous death.

"Vox!" Panting, Tamlin kicked a dog headlong. He yelled so the warrior wouldn't whack him with a backswing. "Escevar! We must get out—"

Vox whipped his axe down but missed a dog. The blade bit the wooden floor, and Vox let go the jutting haft. Whirling, Vox's craggy hands grabbed Tamlin and hoisted him bodily off the floor. "Vox! What are you—"

Toted like a baby overhead, Tamlin glimpsed the night lights of the stockyard and a starry sky out the open window. Then he squawled as his boots passed the window frame. "Vox! No—"

Pitched feetfirst out the window, Tamlin wailed as he sailed through the air, but not for long. A howl ended with a grunt as his back slammed a forgiving pile, then a cry as he bit his tongue. Winded and agonized, Tamlin sucked air and a gushing aroma of cows. Vox had chucked him in a towering manure pile heaped beside the big doors.

Groaning, limping, shedding filth, Tamlin tottered to his feet. Head spinning, he sheathed his weapons and looked up at the window. A head flickered and disappeared. Tamlin heard yells and shouts and a vicious unending snarling and barking. He needed to rejoin the fray. He was no great talent as a fighter, but his friends and Zarrin needed every hand to fend off the monsters. Gnashers, Zarrin called them. Curious name.

Groggily Tamlin stumbled to the big barn doors, which stood open a shoulder's width. Faint lights glowed inside, or maybe sparkled in his head, since he felt dizzy. A sound arrested him. A whistle.

The whistle came from outside the barn, so the hillman, the dog trainer, was out here with Tamlin. The heir panted, "Not good news," and made to duck through the door.

An answering whistle piped *inside* the judging hall.

Surrounded, Tamlin froze in the doorway—

—and was almost stampeded by a charging bull.

A big brindled brown-and-white bull bawled and shoved its massive horned head outdoors. Tamlin barely dodged as a horn like a dagger hooked near his breastbone. Bellowing like a war trumpet, the terrified animal banged the doors wide and rumbled past like a war elephant. Cows and sheep gamboled after, bleating and lowing as if fleeing a forest fire.

Unable to get inside, not safe outside, Tamlin spotted an outside staircase and galloped up that. He hoped no animals pursued, but with his luck, he thought glumly, giant apes or mountain goats would climb for high refuge and butt him off the stairs.

A rough door at the top proved locked. Tamlin was debating where to try next when the door was flung open, almost clopping him in the jaw. Escevar and Vox, bloody and disheveled and armed with bare steel, skidded to a halt just before Tamlin was bowled down the stairs.

"Hold hard!"

"Watch it yourself! Are you all right?"

"What's happening in there?"

"Yes! Where's Zarrin?"

"Dunno!"

Tamlin and Escevar gabbled while Vox signaled madly. Below, the livestock still stampeded from the judging hall. Then the full pack of panting gnashers, winged and otherwise, erupted out the door in a brown river. Sharp whistles, three or more, shrilled through the stock market. The pack split and split again and vanished into the shadows.

In the sudden quiet, the men caught their breath. Tamlin asked, "Vox, why'd you pitch me out the window?"

"Oog!" Escevar sniffed. "Deuce, you stink!"

"Thank you, dear friend, for so kindly enumerating my faults regarding personal hygiene. Vox?"

The mute veteran's hands sketched in the air. Tamlin interpreted, "The dog-things, gnashers, were only after me and Zarrin? How do you know that? They broke off the attack once I was gone and Zarrin bolted out the door? Ah. That explains . . . nothing. I don't get it."

"None of us get much," sighed Escevar. He propped one leg on a riser because his punctured thigh throbbed. "The whistling hillmen must have sent the gnashers into the building after you and Zarrin. Remember she was attacked earlier, just as we were? This was a golden opportunity with both you valuable nobles in one cozy room. Why they want to catch or kill either of you . . ."

Tamlin flexed his right hand. Mashed earlier by a table, it swelled so his glove constricted like a tourniquet. "My, my, what a night. We should have gone boozing instead. Oh, well, let's get home and change clothes—again. At least Father will be pleased that I negotiated the gate tariffs before Zarrin disappeared."

⊙ ⊙ ⊙ ⊙ ⊙

". . . mutton-headed, crack-brained, slack-jawed, cross-eyed, granite-skulled acts of depraved *lunacy* and sheer eye-popping *idiocy* it has ever been my misfortune to *witness,* let alone *partake in!*"

Thamalon Uskevren the First was only warming up. Agitated beyond belief, he paced before the fire in his counting room. Tamlin squirmed in a high-backed wooden chair while Vox and Escevar stood equally mute behind.

"Why give away *only* the gate tariffs?" the elder raged. "Why not give away *all* our contracts? Why not rip the key to the family coffers from my aged, palsied *hand,* and *throw* open the gates of our miserable shack of a homestead, and use both hands to *strew* our gold and silver in the *streets* for every beggar to scoop up? What have I ever *done* in this lifetime that the gods *punish* me with a son who carries *cobwebs* in his empty skull? Why did not the fates send me a drooling, gibbering *moron* that I might have, in some tiny way by dint of long hours of excruciating labor, trained to do *useful* work such as fetching wood or slopping hogs? Instead, I suffer the sharpest *torments* by seeing this melon-headed *twit* tear down all my work and hurl my fortunes to the winds from the highest towers of Stormweather, our ancestral homestead *for the moment,* because I have no doubt that come tax time we will be *impoverished* and huddling in the *gutters* because of my son's blatant, ham-handed *blundering—*"

There was much more, but finally the elder ran out of breath. He collapsed in a chair and slugged Usk Fine Old gone cold. Thamalon Uskevren, "The Old Owl," looked like his son. He'd grown gray and seamed but never stooped, and his dark green eyes and still-black brows could summon a scowl to cower a prince, let alone someone who'd squandered his money. The room reflected the man: tidy, aesthetic, intellectual, buttoned-down. A table neatly was laid with a late-night snack, a chess game waited, a stack of books lay open. A hushed ease with luxury and old money and secrets emanated from the walls.

When the echoes of the tirade died, Tamlin cleared his throat softly. "If I don't guess amiss, you seem upset,

Father. Is it possible that, though we shouldn't dwell on an unpleasant subject, you could see fit to say why?"

"Why?" The patriarch glared until Tamlin felt like a chipmunk facing a timber wolf. Thamalon bit off every word. "Because you failed to negotiate a contract to the family's advantage, son. That's why."

"Ah." Tamlin digested the news, but concentrating was an unaccustomed activity. "Uh, might you explain how? I did secure the taxation rights to the, uh, West Gate where the farmers come in. That promises to bring a pretty penny."

Thamalon made a strangling noise and chugged wine as if quaffing poison. Heaving a tremendous sigh, he conceded, "Yes, the gate will bring a penny or two. That's what farmers deal in: pennies. They don't have many to spare, you see, after the Hulorn's tax collectors circulate among the farms and extract the taxes first. All our family can collect at the western gate is a poll tax on livestock: a penny a head. In a good day, we might collect a hundred pennies or more."

"Ah." Tamlin pretended to ponder. "A hundred pennies. That'll buy. . . uh . . ."

"See my son, the Minister of Finance, who doesn't know what anything costs, calculate," snapped the father. "A hundred pennies might buy you a new pair of gloves, Tamlin. Not a lot, considering you've lost twelve pairs so far this winter. Your clothing budget, by the way, is treble what the younger children spend, but we'll scream about that later. For now, let me explain why I wish Zarrin Foxmantle were my son and you, Tamlin Uskevren the Second, were a fish cutter lost in a storm in a leaky boat on the Lake of Dragons!"

The lord rose, as did his voice. "Of course Zarrin would want the North Gate's tariffs! And not because their family manor stands in the neighborhood: What kind of jabberjawed excuse is that? All the traffic from Ordulin and Surd and Tulbegh comes through the North Gate, and unlike the Mulhessens, who use the West Gate and send their tariffs ahead, the northern traffic is completely untaxed, which means the duties are collected *at the gates!* Further, the northern gate overlooks the Elzimmer Bridge, which charges for foot traffic and collects duties on all incoming ships' cargoes! So, while you're standing at the West Gate collecting cow chips and getting dust in your eyes, my lamentably eldest and empty-headed son, the Foxmantles will sprain their backs lugging away all that tax money! I can't believe how badly you botched this mission! How did poor Zarrin Foxmantle keep from bursting a blood vessel holding in her laughter? When word of this gets out, I'll be the laughingstock of Selgaunt!"

In a brittle silence, Tamlin said, "Perhaps, dear father, if you'd explained all this beforehand, I might've—"

Tamlin froze as the Old Owl thrust his face inches from his nose. With eyes smoldering below black brows, the patriarch hissed in an icy frightening whisper. "I—did—explain. You—didn't—listen."

"Oh," Tamlin squeaked. "Quite right. But it was so—complicated. All those variations. 'If this, then that, unless this, in which case that' stuff. I apologize. If there's any way to make it up—"

"There is." Looming upright, looking very tall despite his middling height, the lord pointed a bony finger at the door. "Take your dishonor guards and go. Find Zarrin and undo this miserable deal."

"Uh, now?" Tamlin faked a yawn. "We've been dragged through the mill, Father, what with being attacked twice now by devil dogs and slung across ice and pitched out windows—"

"Go!"

The three listeners rose as if levitated and scurried out the door. Trotting down the wide circular stairs, they heard the liege lord scuffing hard behind in soft slippers.

By the time they reached the door, courteously held open by a sleepy footman, Thamalon had final orders.

"Go," he told his son. "Get out there, find Zarrin, and fix what you've botched. Or I'll cut off your allowance, burn your clothes, sell your goods, cashier your servants, strike your name out of the city registry, and *boil you in red pepper oil!*"

The three deliquents stepped into the cold night, but Tamlin peeked through the crack of the door. "Uh, father, I know I haven't performed to your satisfaction but, just curious, you see, you don't really mean that last bit, do you? About the red pepper oil and such?"

Slowly the door creaked shut. Tamlin watched his father's narrow face grow narrower. Through a slash of a mouth, he growled, "Son, I'm afraid I do."

The door slammed.

Locked outside on high stone steps on a windy wintry black night, Tamlin looked at the door awhile, then at his friends. Grinning, he assured them, "He doesn't really mean it."

Biting their tongues, Vox and Escevar trudged down the stairs.

"Funny, I thought Father would be pleased." The three companions trudged down the middle of Sarn Street, temporarily homeless if one didn't count Tamlin's two tallhouses and three guest apartments scattered throughout the city. The heir rambled, "He should be glad I settled the contract so quickly. When I'm forced to attend his business meetings, they drag for hours. All that talk about money—*ick!*"

"If it weren't for those business meetings," grumped Escevar, huddled against the cold and hating it, "you'd never get any sleep."

"That's true," Tamlin admitted. "Still, Zarrin rolled over

so easily, agreeing to everything I said, I thought she'd been melted by my charm."

Vox walked behind, watching the street to both sides, signing nothing. Escevar stumped beside his charge, muttering, "I don't have any great head for business, Deuce, but even haggling in the marketplace you never pay the first price asked. You agreed to *Zarrin's* proposal in an eye-blink, then moved on to celebrating!"

"True, true. Still, I'm new at this 'work' stuff. So far it's dreadfully dull. What shall we do?"

"Find Zarrin, according to your father." Escevar's voice dripped acid. "It's hard to believe you *are* his son sometimes. Or most of the time."

"Find Zarrin . . . hmm . . ." Tamlin's cape whipped around his shoulders while frozen snow pinged his cheeks. Vox's bearskin had begun to frost over. Escevar cursed the gods of snow, winter, storm, and a few others. "Where do you think she might be?"

Escevar counted to twenty rather than thump his friend's head. The trio had already tried the Foxmantle homestead. The gatekeeper wouldn't admit them, it being enemy territory, but a maid admitted Zarrin had gone to the stockyards earlier and not yet returned.

"If Zarrin's not home," Escevar chided, "she's probably carousing in a pub, feet propped up by the fire and a hot caudle in her hand, toasting her success in selling you down the river!"

"Right." Tamlin nodded, then turned so abruptly he banged into Escevar. "Sorry, old chap. Let's try some pubs. I'm dry anyway. All this negotiating makes one thirstier than sword practice."

Escevar blinked snow off his eyelids as Tamlin drove for a lighted doorway. "Hey, I was joking!"

From behind, Vox voiced a single grunt that said, *The last time you two had sword practice, candles drooped in their sockets from the heat.*

Sarn Street was more commonly called "Souse Street." Sixteen pubs lined the north side of the avenue alone, and over the hours the determined adventurers hit every one. In each tavern, Tamlin greeted friends and strangers, bought rounds of drinks, told droll stories, hooked his arms around laughing women and, at Escevar's prompting, asked if anyone had seen Zarrin. As the night progressed and the pub count climbed, Tamlin made more friends, groped more women, and told longer stories, and even Escevar had forgotten Zarrin. Vox went along dutifully to each pub, drank little, watched everywhere, and tapped his foot in disgust.

Eventually Tamlin and Escevar stumbled into The Black Stag, the last pub on the street, and collapsed onto benches. Unlike most pubs, where the furniture was too heavy to throw and the room stood wide open so barkeepers could see what went on, the Stag had high-walled booths and shadowed nooks and dim lights, which made it a favorite meeting place for flesh-pushers, pawners and fences, poisonous apothecaries, slavers, smugglers, second-story thieves, and other "servants of the underclass." Still, frequenting such a dangerous place made visitors feel dangerous, so noble youngsters in the form of toffs, simps, bawds, and fops congregated. Naturally, many were Tamlin's friends, or at least friendly. Barely had the Uskevren heir plunked down than he called for a round of Stag Stout for his best friends, some of whom he could even name.

"This is a great place to ask for—whatever it is we look for," Tamlin babbled. "The Stag's famous for—trouble and—strangers. Best place for the worst things, what? Barkeep, where's that stout?"

"You might lighten up with the golden touch, Deuce. Even your allowance only stretches so far." Blearily Escevar, who always handled the money, upended a purse. Silver and copper plinked and plunked across the table and floor as booze-soaked Selgauntans cheered. Escevar bent to pick up coins and fell off the bench to more cheers. Some friends helped pick up coins while others pocketed them. Groggy, Escevar counted, getting a new total each time.

"Never mind, Es. I've got credit!" Tamlin called for more stout, though he hadn't yet touched the first one. Drinking, slopping down his doublet, Tamlin tried to focus as Vox made a cutting stroke across his throat. "Cut? Throat? What, there's a cutthroat behind me? Oh, cut! You mean, my father cut off my allowance? Oh, I don't think he means it—Hey, where's everyone going?"

At the deadly words "cut off my allowance," the heir's new-found friends vanished for other reaches. Within seconds, Tamlin, Escevar, and Vox sat alone. No one in the pub, not even dung shovelers and grave robbers and tax collectors, would sit with them.

"Drat the dark." Tamlin slurped stout and belched. " 'Scuse. I wanted to ask those fellows something, but I can't think what. Allowance—Oh, hey, has anyone seen Zarrin Foxmantle? She's blonde, about this high—*Oops!*" Waving an arm almost pitched Tamlin off the bench, and he forgot what he'd asked. Escevar snored, facedown on the opposite bench. Vox listened to a pair of sisterly singers who'd mounted a tiny stage. Growing morose from his friends' rejections, Tamlin guzzled stout and sulked.

I forbid you maidens all,

the two girls sang sweet and high,

Who wear gold in your hair,
For to go to Stillstone Hall,
For young Tam Lin is there.

Tamlin's ears perked. The song was "Tam Lin," a tune old as the hills, and his namesake. Muzzily he followed the words, often heard but never considered. Tam Lin, the handsome knight, fallen from his horse in a hunting accident. Caught by the fairy queen, so enslaved. Forced to serve in her midnight court, which only joined this world under a full moon. Primed for sacrifice to a bloody-handed god. Until a maiden Lyndelle, pluckier than most, entered the sacred hall to meet the ethereal Tam Lin. His only hope of freedom, he told her, was if she caught him falling from a horse. And so they arranged it, Lyndelle lunging into a chaotic raid on a hellish night to catch her newfound lover. And so Tam Lin was freed, the young pair united, and the song ended.

"Still, evil omens. What if she'd missed him? Good luck and good times can't last forever. . . ." Mumbling to himself, Tamlin shivered. Filtered through an alcoholic fog, the sinister song droned in his brain like a dirge. Fairy curses, a young lord snared by ill luck and fate, a ghostly un-life and sentence of sacrifice—and Tamlin himself a young lord banished from home. Was his only hope an innocent maiden's rescue? No one in Selgaunt was innocent—

"Milord Uskevren?"

Jumping at his name, Tamlin pulled his nose from a flagon to see a girl thin and pale as an elf. Under a threadbare cape, really a blanket, she wore only a cambric smock painted down the front, and battered clogs on her feet. Under her arm bulged a sheaf of parchments tied with a faded ribbon. Her big eyes were red from cold or weeping.

Rattled by his own superstition, Tamlin babbled, "Uh, yes, I'm Lord Uskevren, or I shall be some day, if my father ever dies and I don't, perhaps, unless he really carries out his threat, which he might, which I doubt, or I hope . . . Uh, where was I?"

"Milord." The girl licked chapped lips and launched into a speech. "I wonder, sir, if you'd like your portrait painted. My name is Symbaline—"

"Symbaline!" Tamlin burst out. "Like the girl in the song! Another omen! Oh, no, wait. Her name was Lyndelle—"

"S-sir?" The girl hadn't heard the lyrics, so she plowed on, "I'm one of the finest artists in the city. I can show you samples. The smartest nobles agree they're lovely. Every lord and lady should have their portrait painted, and since you're so dashing and handsome—"

"No, no, no. No thank you." Tamlin slugged stout to calm his nerves. "I don't need a portrait. No one wants my face hanging on the wall, though my father'd like my carcass hung from a lamppost. I can't believe he's chucked me out like garbage. . . ."

He stopped babbling because the girl cried. She tried to stifle her grief, but tears spilled down her wan cheeks. Shuddering, sobbing, she couldn't stop. Tamlin gawped, embarrassed. Even Vox, who habitually watched elsewhere, stared.

A barkeep bustled to the table with a billy club dangling from his wrist by a thong. He snagged the girl's pipestem arm. "Here now, you snippet, don't be harryin' the patrons! I'm sorry, milord, I'll pitch the sauce out—"

"No!" Tamlin shook his head in a futile effort to clear it. "Too many people have been tossed out in the cold! We're . . . bargaining. Sit her there. Girl, sit."

Symbaline sat, slowly, as if she'd break. Her stomach rumbled. Tamlin squinted. "What was that?"

Glowering in disgust, Vox flicked Tamlin's flagon off the table so stout splashed on the floor. Snapping his fingers, he mimed to the barkeep for food, enough to cover the table. Soon, a barmaid set down a tray of venison pasties, pickled eggs, ducks' breasts, watermelon rind, black-and-white bread, fresh butter, green and white cheese, figs, raisins, and a cold shoulder of pork. Gruff Vox signaled the bony girl, who tore into the food.

"Oh, she's hungry." Tamlin looked at her thin, worn clothing. "She's poor, too."

Vox's hard hand cuffed Tamlin's head, though the lordling hardly felt it. Gesturing, the swordmaster crooked fingers over his eyebrows and frowned, then swiped his hand down his face, and mimicked someone painting.

"My father. His face. Painted." Tamlin struggled to think. "No, he wouldn't like that. Mother paints her face, but women like—" Dodging another biff cleared Tamlin's head. "Oh, yes, I see! Girl, what's your name? Symbaline? Let me see your samples, if you'd be so kind."

The artist gobbled with one hand and untied the ribbon with the other. Tamlin flipped through sketches of Selgaunt's lords and ladies, then watercolored landscapes. "Lovely, glowing. Full of—colors and things. Yes, I'll hire you to paint a portrait of my father. It's been a while since he had one, and he shan't live forever, if I'm lucky. I'll give it to him as a present for the new year, if he'll let me in the door. And we'll paint one of Mother for the Moon Festival. And Tazi, if we can slap that sneer off her face. And Tal too. We'll hang his picture on the gate to scare away beggars—ha!"

"Thank you, milord, thank you!" Symbaline wiped her mouth with a napkin and wept anew. "I'm sorry I cry, milord, but it's been a hard winter. I had a commission to paint Lord and Lady Soargyl, and I sketched for days to find a pose they'd like, but then Lord Soargyl changed his mind and shoved me out the gate, and I was never paid a penny for all my hard work—"

"Don't fret, dear. We are not the sorry Soargyls. The Uskevren always keep their promises. No matter what. We'll install you in the main house as our court painter. You can sleep there too: we could barrack an army in our guest rooms. And you can eat in the kitchen, if the cook's budget will sustain it, the way you eat."

"Oh, thank you, milord!" gulped the girl. "And I can paint more than just portraits! I'd really love to paint landscapes and seascapes—"

"Ah? That's admirable, I suppose. You can decorate the main hall with a mural. It needs a little color, the gloomy old dump. Or we'll send you up to the north tower to paint a picture of the harbor, then the hills to the west. . . ."

"You're so kind, sir." Symbaline fought to still her tears. "Everyone says you're the most considerate and generous young lord in Selgaunt, and now I see it's true. That's why I approached you. You were my last chance, really. You saved my life. I had no place to spend the night nor any hope for the future—"

"Stop, dear, no need. This way I rescue an innocent maiden, not the other way around, and so banish some omeny beasties lurking about." That confused the girl, so Tamlin covered her cold hand with surprising gentleness. "Anyway, it wasn't I who thought of it, but Vox here. He looks fit to eat babies, but he's really the best companion one could want. With Vox at my side, I'm not afraid to venture anywhere in Selgaunt. He's the finest fighter along the Sea of Fallen Stars!"

Tamlin made to raise his glass, then recalled his bodyguard had cut him off. "Ah. Vox, might I have a tiny drop of something just to toast your health? I'd really appreciate—"

For answer, the swordmaster innocently offered Tamlin a pickled egg and a cold duck's breast.

The lordling's stomach urped as his face drained pale. Tamlin squeaked, "Pardon me a moment," and lurched for the door.

Eventually Tamlin staggered back to the table, wiping his mouth. Symbaline continued to plow through the food like an orc army. "Milord, I hate to beseech, but I need a few coins to buy paints and canvas . . ."

"Easy enough." Frowning at Escevar placidly sleeping on a bench, Tamlin hooked his boot and dumped his friend crashing to the filthy floor. "Escevar, give her some money!"

Roused, Escevar crawled back to the table. "I tol' you, Deuce, we're skint. All this's on credit."

With a sigh of disgust, Vox reached down his shirt, pulled out a squirrel-hide purse, and dumped coins on the table. Tamlin slid silver coins toward Symbaline, counting out seven for good luck.

Escevar's slim hand slapped down on the lot. Tamlin objected, "Es, this is no time to be greedy!"

"No, look!" Shaking off sleep, Escevar became all business. He held up a big silver coin, worn and shiny and stamped with strange sigils. The coin was round but punched at the center with a triangle. "I've never seen triangle-cut coins before. And there are, um, sixteen here. Where'd you get them, Vox?"

Vox mimed a whistle, then cutting a throat. Tamlin translated, "The purse from the dead whistler, the gnasher-handler!"

"Wait, now." Escevar wrinkled his brow. "If the hillmen brought these coins from their country . . . and they spend them in pubs or stores. . . . Wherever we found a batch of these coins, we might find the hillmen's hideout nearby!"

"Why find the hillmen?" asked Tamlin. "They tried to kill us. Shouldn't we avoid them?"

"Don't try to think when you're potted, Deuce," sniped Escevar. "We don't really want the hillmen, but they did try to kidnap or kill you and Zarrin. Maybe they know where Zarrin is. Trained dogs, or gnashers, can sniff people out, you know."

Fuddled, puzzled, Tamlin replied, "You're just making this up to look good for the girl."

"What girl?" demanded Escevar. "Oh, her. No! Would you *think* a moment, for the love of Selune? All you've done tonight is waste money, and get us thrown out of the house—"

Vox mimed bending over and heaving.

"—and puked in the street," added Escevar. "Hardly the hallmarks of a hero."

"Oh, so? I—I—" Indignant but stumped, Tamlin shut up.

Symbaline interjected, "I know how you can find more coins."

"You do?" asked both men. "How?"

"Magic."

"Hoy, Lord Tamlin! A word, if you please!"

"Guts of the gods!" growled Escevar. "Why doesn't someone squash that bloodsucking leech?"

Halting in the wintry windblown street, Tamlin, Escevar, and Vox hunted for the voice. It came from above. The Blue Coot was a three-story tavern of stone and timber. Stepped balconies tilted alarmingly over the street. In summer, whores, male and female, lolled above and called to potential customers. In winter, the balconies were rimed with ice. Padrig the Palmer leaned from a second-floor balcony, pudgy and tall in his fur coat and floppy hat. Before, begging money, he'd worn a syncophant's smile, but now his grin curled like a fox's. Beside Padrig stood an unsavory youth and older man, both fit to cut a cripple's throat for a penny. Third-floor balconies were dark and unoccupied.

"Master Tamlin, your plan proceeds apace!" Padrig bowed theatrically. "Before long you'll sit the tallest chair in Stormweather Towers!"

"What?" Down in the street, Tamlin leaned back and almost toppled, for liquor still gripped him. "Did—Did I miss something, Paddy? What do you gibber about?"

"Your thirty ravens, sir, were invested just in time! All the city knows your allowance is cut off! Ratigan the Green manufactures poison, and now you've engaged a portrait painter to approach your father! You can't enter Stormweather, but she shall! So while you stay the night in Lantern Alley, your minions will do your dirty work!"

Behind Tamlin, Vox tugged his bearskin cape aside to

free his war axe. The fightmaster pointed to the Coot's doors and mimed chopping. Tamlin restrained him, asking both companions, "What's this about? Who's Ratigan? How does he know about the girl? I thought she was innocent! And my tallhouse in Lantern Alley? Wait! If the girl's part of some Soargyl plot—"

"Stop, Deuce! It's claptrap!" Escevar spat in the street. "It's another of his blackmail scams, spinning gossamer out of gossip! He's framing you for some cocked-eyed assassination attempt on your father!"

"Someone plans to assassinate my father?" Tamlin gaped in horror, wishing dearly he weren't drunk. "I mean, it's been tried before, but I'm not involved! But what will Father think?"

"He'll think you masterminded the plot!" Safe on high, Padrig laughed. "I have witnesses and a receipt for thirty ravens! That money will hire enough assassins—I say, what—"

Standing in the street, looking up, Vox suddenly yanked Tamlin back while Escevar bulled him from the front, yelling, *"Move!"*

On the second-story balcony, Padrig gaped upward, bleated, and dived into the tavern, as did the veteran thug. The young tough lingered too long. Tipped from the third-floor balcony, a massive chest of drawers plummeted and smashed to kindling on the second balcony. The young rogue was pulped as the balcony was torn clean off the building. Wood, oak, ice, and a crushed corpse crashed in the street.

Tamlin and friends peeked from the shelter of a doorway opposite. Patrons spilled from the Blue Coot to gawk at the bloody wreckage. Above, Padrig was nowhere to be seen. But on the third balcony . . .

"Tamlin, you owe us!" Grinning from the high rail were Garth the Gimble, called the "Snake of Selgaunt" for his green scaly tunic, and the Flame, always in red. Notorious denizens of Selgaunt's shady underground, they'd shared a drink or two with Tamlin in the past. Garth called, "Pay no attention to Padrig! He seines the wind! Hey, what would you pay for his head, or some other part?"

"Uh . . ." Having said too much tonight, Tamlin curbed his tongue. "Uh, that's not necessary. But thank you, Garth, Flame! I do owe you—something."

With mock salutes, the pair passed into the dark third floor, vanishing like spirits at dawn.

Events rolled by too fast for Tamlin to grasp, but at least his head had cleared. Staring at the shattered balcony in the street, he mused, "I wonder who got squashed."

"A cockroach, if he hangs with Padrig." Wrapped in his cloak, Escevar nodded up the street. "Come on. We've got to gain the Wizards' Guild. They go to bed at dawn, like vampires."

"You have some strange coins and want to find a larger hoard?"

"I guess so," replied Tamlin, still muzzy on details. Then Vox prodded his kidney, and he said, "Yes, that's cxactly it. If you plcasc."

Helara was a striking tall woman with a cascading mane of blonde hair she fluffed up repeatedly, as if posing. Her crimson robe was girded by a triple chain of gold hung with charms of all shapes and sizes. The Wizards Guild was a rambling shamble tucked in the southeast corner of Selgaunt. The upper stories would overlook the city wall and the sea. The gloomy parlor was tricked out with odd-shaped furniture and glittery gewgaws, and reeked of chemicals and ashes and incense. A ten-year-old page waited by the wall and bit down yawns.

"I wish someone would bring us a challenge," Helara rattled. She talked fast yet idly, preoccupied with as many schemes as Padrig the Palmer, except hers usually succeeded. "That's too simple a spell. 'Like attracts like,' whether it's money or love. Prospectors, dwarves, practice it all the time in the mountains: A compass arrow of silver points to silver, with a little coaxing."

"So Symbaline said," Tamlin explained, "though how an artist knows magic I don't get. Can you conjure it tonight? We need to locate these hillmen."

"And?" Helara sensed opportunity. "What will you do when you find them?"

"Eh?" Tamlin blinked. Stuffy smoky air made his head bloat. Too, the guild hall was quiet as a library. Wizards were usually a rowdy lot, but perhaps stayed discreet at home. "I can't really say—"

"When we find the hillmen," interjected Escevar, "and if we can avoid their bloody, gnarly-toothed dogs, we may learn why they tried to snatch Deuce and whether they've seen Zarrin."

"Zarrin Foxmantle?" The mage's blonde eyebrows wig-wagged. "She's missing?"

Vox poked Tamlin to stifle an answer. Escevar hedged, "We haven't seen her lately, but Selgaunt's a big city. These whistling hillmen and their gnasher-dogs are a pest. Can you find them?"

"Can you pay?" returned Helara. "Talk on the street says Tamlin's allowance has been cut off."

"That rumor ran on fast legs," groused Tamlin. "Hasn't anyone better things to gossip about than my pocket money?"

"We can pay later," said Escevar. "Draw up a promissary note and he'll sign it."

Helara pouted rouged lips, but agreed. "Give me the odd coins."

"Summon Magdon," she ordered the child page. "And wake Ophelia. We may need her."

All three men blinked when the summoned pair arrived.

Sisters, though not twins, each had white hair and white skin and pink eyes. Otherwise, they were squat and chunky as farm girls, hearty enough to wrestle an ox. As the men gawped, Magdon spoke, "No, we're not cursed, merely albinos. What do you require?"

Magdon's blue robe was triply wrapped by a black belt, and her bone-white fingers were stained odd colors. Ophelia's yellow gown was unbelted but embroidered with flames at hem and sleeves. She yawned and sat on a bench and scratched her hair. Helara handed Magdon the silver triangle-cut coins and some instructions, and departed the parlor. Magdon told the men to wait and followed. Ophelia yawned and scratched. When Tamlin asked what she did, she replied only, "I have hidden talents."

With nothing to see or do, the guests slumped onto twisty-backed settles and slanted stools. Borrowing the page as a runner, Escevar gave her a coin and a message for Cale, the butler of Stormweather Towers, emphasizing she *not* bother Lord Uskevren. Less than an hour passed before three burly men arrived in Uskevren livery, blue with the gold badge of horsehead and anchor. The housecarls came with boar spears so tall they couldn't stand upright in the parlor.

Magdon returned. From her ivory hand dangled a jangly contraption. The sixteen silver coins were alternately threaded on a silver chain with a black bead, an owl's skull, a scallop shell, three blue feathers, a cork, a lumpy gray stone, and other bits. From the bottom hung a curved strip of gold foil beaten so thin it shivered in no breeze at all. The device looked like a child's windchime.

"What is it?" asked Escevar.

"A compass." Hoisting the charmed chain, Magdon puffed at the gold foil. As it shimmied and bobbed, blue sparkles sizzled up and down the chain. Gradually the gold foil settled and pointed. "It doesn't point north but at a larger hoard of triangle coins."

"Really?" Refreshed by a nap, Tamlin reached to touch, but Magdon steered it away.

"The magic is delicate as a spiderweb. I'll hold it."

"You'll go with us?"

"We all will. Apprentices need guidance." Helara promenaded into the room like a queen. A floor-sweeping robe of red was quilted with a purple lining and hemmed with tiger hide that set off her wild tawny hair. Magdon and Ophelia donned plain cloaks of gray with gathered hoods that almost covered their heads. Escevar nodded to see them. In Sembia, peasant girls bound for "service in the city" were invariably given such cloaks as a going-away present. No doubt the girls' talents had been discovered in some village and they bound over to the Wizards Guild. Yet if Magdon were a "gadget wizard," as Escevar thought, he wondered about Ophelia's "hidden talents" and flaming embroidery.

Passing into a bitter night wind ripe with sea salt, the three men, three women, and three housecarls found Magdon's windchime-compass jingled and jangled, blown every whichway. The three mages had to cluster with their cloaks to shield the flimsy artifact. Settling, it pointed up Rampart Street and onto Rose.

Whipped by winter winds, they pursued tedious rounds of walking, huddling, waiting, and moving on. Slowly, the women assured them, they steered to a trove of triangular coins. The seekers weren't so sure, but Escevar reflected they needn't pay the magicians if they flubbed the magical tracking.

Occasionally they spotted friends scurrying from pub to pub in the cold. By Ironmonger's Lane, a small, lithe woman attached herself to Tamlin. The noble had dallied with Iris a time or two, and smiled as she rubbed against him. Rail thin, Iris wore only a jacket and trousers of rabbitskin, and tilted the neck to show nothing beneath.

"Lovely, dear, if goose-bumpled. We're in a hurry, but I'll stop by later. I hope." Plodding onward, Tamlin mused,

"For some reason, Iris reminds me of Longjaw. Where's she at these days?"

"Haven't seen her since the Sahuagin Wars," said Escevar. "But pirates and smugglers don't live long even in peacetime. What was the name of that artist? She'd make a tasty morsel if you fattened her up."

Rambling, the young men speculated about various women they knew, oblivious to the albino sisters and tawny-haired Helara, who sniffled either in disgust or from the wintry wind.

The keen lessened in the shadow of the Hulorn's Hunting Garden. Not-so-high on a crag was perched the Hulorn's spired palace like a quiver of upright arrows, and at its feet ran a high stone wall enclosing a ten-acre hunting garden of wild weedy woods. Whether any animals lurked within, and whether the Hulorn actually hunted them, no one knew. No one had seen the erstwhile governor for quite a while, and the usual strange stories circulated. Hunting Street ran along the wall, lit in spots by glow-globes to discourage poachers. Opposite the wall, the snobby neighborhood sported houses gaudy even by Selgauntian standards. Mismatched towers, archways, curved staircases, hedged gardens, turrets, tricolor chimneys, false fronts, frescoes, balconies, and other ridiculous trappings decorated the block.

"That's it." Helara pointed to a two-story house of brick and timber behind a jig-jog brick wall with deep arches. A large house shrouded by trees and gardens. As proof, the red-robed mage and the albino sisters shielded the magic compass. Peeking over their shoulders by the light of glow-globes, the men saw the slip of gold foil curled rock-steady toward the house. "It's the only place in the city those triangle-cut coins can be."

"Splendid!" Tamlin stared at the shadowed house. "Uh, now what?"

No answers.

Escevar said, "Perhaps if we tell the Hulorn's Guards that the house owner . . . might know hillmen with flying dogs . . . No, I guess not."

Shivering and sniffling, the statuesque Helara said, "Why not knock on the door and see who answers?"

Lacking a better plan, the nine hunters trooped through a brick archway and bumped into an ornate iron gate, locked. Vox swung his axe's thick poll and the gate popped open. Without speaking, the nine mounted a narrow gallery that ran half around the silent house. Winter shutters rimmed by felt sealed in sound and light, if any. The door was red with a simple iron thumblatch. With no signs of life, the searchers began to feel foolish, like children caught spying. Everyone looked to Helara.

"All right. I'll knock. But if no one—*Yow!*"

One rap set off a shower of yellow sparks that sizzled and skittered across the door's face. Thrown backward, Helara nearly pitched off the gallery before Vox caught her. The door was marred by a smoking scorch mark. Hissing, Helara found her knuckles and fist blistered and her gown's sleeve charred past her wrist.

"You bastards!" she panted. "I'll show you!"

Eight companions reared back as Helara pulled back her sleeves, spat on her palms, and uttered a low spell like a curse. Bracing her feet, the mage slapped both palms against the door. Flashing yellow light blossomed. It lit the gallery, frizzed Helara's hair, and made her clothes smoke. Over the sputtering and spitting of sparks, the mage shouted in a gravelly voice, *"Ras-pal sky-y! Ras-pantle a-too! Ras-pah sen ma-nan-tal!"*

Either her spell worked, or its power merged with the door's charm, or together they doubled and tripled, for Helara got results.

The door and most of the front wall exploded.

Broken bricks and hunks of wood shot in all directions like catapulted missiles. Only Helara's personal shield, her first muttered spell, kept Tamlin and friends from being killed by flying flinders, for the deadly rain blew around the mage in a soaring arc like an invisible bubble. Chunks of wall collapsed, crunching inside the house and on the gallery, though no one saw much because brick dust, smoke, paint chips, and other debris swirled like trash caught in a dust devil. Portions of the second floor collapsed alarmingly, then the house corner slumped with a creak and crunch. People shouted and screamed as the gallery let go, dipping toward the missing door. The companions skidded downslope and blundered into a crumbling brick wall. More dust roiled and boiled, making people sneeze and choke.

Tamlin and the albino sisters were tangled in a gap in the wreckage. Vox gained his feet and yanked them free of the hole. Two Uskevren housecarls tumbled into bushes, and now stayed on the ground to guard. Helara kicked and swore and tore her red robe on iron nails jutting from the door's threshold, which suffered a big, blackened bite.

Above the scuffling and grousing, Escevar called, "Someone's home!"

A foyer and staircase were smothered in laths and plaster and broken tiles. Floorboards jutted over black space. A swarthy black-bearded man in a green robe had slunk down the stairs to peek at the enemy. Stunned by the destruction, he lingered too long.

Handed up by Vox, the tall Helara gained the crumpled littered floor. Batting back her smoking red-and-tigerhide cape, the mage saw the skulker. *"Ratigan?* You fumble-fingered pie-thief! You snake-eyed cross-patch! I warned you *never* to crawl back into my city!"

Screeching an arcane curse, Helara crossed her forearms. Trapped on the stairs, Ratigan reeled as a hailstorm of icicles shattered against his personal shield. Ice stabbed the walls, tore portraits, and chipped the bannister, freezing instantly, making every surface slippery as glass.

Crouching to keep his feet, Ratigan crooked three fingers and conjured a flush of desert heat that steamed the ice into clouds. Yet he barely avoided skidding down the stairs.

Shooting her fingers downward, Helara hurled a second spell. Acid rain gushed from the ceiling. Ratigan writhed as his flesh corroded, and his robe smoked. Gamely he struggled to conjure. Fog blossomed around Helara's feet, then coalesced into snaky heads with teeth. Without a pause in her spellcasting, the red-robed wizard stamped one foot, and the snake heads evaporated.

Over the chanting of mages and creaking and groaning of the house, Tamlin called to Escevar, "I remember now! Padrig mentioned Ratigan the Green! Should we have told Helara?"

Escevar never got to answer, for familiar deadly whistles keened behind the house. Within seconds, fearsome gnashers boiled around the ruined gallery. Lunging low or half-sailing on stubby wings, the beasts barked and snarled frantically, hot to tear into the invaders. After them trotted the foreign hillmen in rough smocks and gnasher-fur vests. They couldn't hang back far as they shouted commands because brick walls hemmed the house.

Mouth open in a mute warcry, Vox slung his axe high and jumped off the gallery to the attack. Escevar, sword and smatchet sizzling, slashed and hacked the first dog that touched down on the tilted porch. Tamlin drew his long sword, but almost stabbed Magdon who, no fighter, whipped behind him for protection, her pale pink eyes round as lanterns. Hollering "Uskevren!" the housecarls stabbed wildly at gnashers and hillmen. Meanwhile, in the crumbling foyer, Helara heaped abuse and spells on the besieged Ratigan.

Amidst this mad melee, the albino Ophelia unleashed her "hidden talents."

With a nerve-grating screech of *"Al-scara-tway!"* her stubby hand sliced a swath in the air. Five stripes of fire pinwheeled into the night, then struck, stuck, and burned—everywhere. Oncoming gnashers suddenly wore burning mustaches and fire-streaked backs. Vox's bear-fur cape charred with a nauseating stink. A housecarl's tunic burned across his shoulders. Paint, brick, splinters, bushes, and leafless trees ignited in stripes that dripped flame like candle wax.

Ophelia flexed her left hand, shouted, and swiped again. Another five-fingered rainbow of fire sizzled on people and gnashers. Primed for more, the fingers of her right hand glowed.

"Doesn't she have any other spells?" Tamlin called over his shoulder.

"We're new to magic!" confessed Magdon. Her sister slung fire to the winds, igniting friend and foe alike.

Squatting, Tamlin surveyed the brawling, spellcasting, shrieking, stabbing, and dogfighting that boiled around and inside the teetering smoking house. He called, "I say, Magdon, everything seems to be under control! I'm going to explore a bit!"

"Don't leave me!" chirped the gadget-mage. Clutching for Tamlin's cape, she missed and skidded backward down the porch.

Sword in hand, cape over his head, Tamlin hopped through the shattered door, dodged the shrieking Helara, skidded on ice, ducked a flaming tapestry curling off a wall, and scampered down a dark hallway.

Not so dark, he discovered. Ophelia's errant spell had rooted in the upper story. Flames licked above Ratigan's head as he clung desperately to the ruined stairs. This old house would burn like candlewood, Tamlin reckoned, unless it collapsed first. The floor wobbled while smoke thickened. The young lord wondered if he should bolt.

A scream came from the second floor. A familiar scream.

Unable to climb the front stairs, Tamlin dashed to the back of the house. While opening doors he found a barracks where the hillmen had obviously bunked, a dining hall, a pantry, a filthy kitchen—and a back stair for servants.

Sheathing his sword, Tamlin clattered to the top. Fire chased across the ceiling and licked at paint and varnish. Above Helara's shrieks and Ratigan's bellows, Tamlin heard the scream again from a front room. The floor was painted with red and yellow squares. Superstitious, Tamlin skip-hopped from yellow to yellow to gain the door.

When Tamlin grabbed the thumblatch, a spark scorched a hole in his kid glove. Cursing, the young lord studied the door. Locked and magically warded, he decided, same as the front door, though not as strong a spell. The ward was probably meant to keep out the hillmen. It shouldn't stop someone really determined, as Tamlin was, perhaps for the first time in his life.

Snagging his cape around his shoulder, the lordling rammed the door. Sparks flared and burned and blinded. His cape smoldered and charred. Hissing, Tamlin gritted his teeth and bulled again, harder. Again. To his surprise, the door burst. The young lord tripped on the threshold and sprawled on a bare dusty floor.

"Tamlin! Thank the gods! Free me, please!"

Scrambling up, Tamlin grinned with delight. Zarrin was disheveled and hollow-eyed but alive. Her wrist manacles encircled a stout post where plaster was gouged from the wall. A sagging settle and bucket were the only furnishings. The floor canted like a ship's deck as the gutted house settled.

"Tamlin!" Tears streaked Zarrin's dirty cheeks. Her purple vest lacked gold buttons, stolen. "Oh, I'm so glad you came! I smelled the smoke and feared to burn—"

"Yes, yes, don't fret. Rescuing's in my blood, after all, like heroism. And we Uskevren always keep our promises." Tamlin fumbled with Zarrin's fetters, feeling immensely smug at finding her. Still, he hurried, for flames licked at the doorway and smoke pooled on the ceiling. "What a story this will make for the pubs! Think how proud Vox will be, and Father—Oh, no! Wait!"

Tamlin let go the chains. "We must settle up first."

Zarrin gaped in horror. "Don't joke, Tamlin! Release me! The fire—"

"No, I'm sorry. Business before pleasure, as Father likes to nag. I have to renegotiate the gate tariffs." Tamlin raised his voice over the crackle of flames, groaning of the house, and clash of spells and arms outside. Smoke made him cough. "Father was not happy with our bargain. You wouldn't believe the nasty names I endured, Zar! Now let's see . . . As I recall, you get to collect duties on the North Gate and we got stuck with the western. Or was it the other way around? No, that's it. So we need—"

"Are you mad? Are you drunk or crazy?" Zarrin rattled her manacles. "Get these chains off immediately! Get me out of here or I'll kill you!"

"No, I'm afraid—*ouch!*" Rubbing his chin, Tamlin gouged a scab from an earlier fight. "Wheels of the wizards, this is my night to suffer!"

"Very well, you can have the gate!" Tears from fright and smoke poured from Zarrin's eyes. "You can have the northern gate and I'll take the western! Just please—"

"No." Tamlin fought to think. It had been a long night. "Escevar said never to accept the first offer. But how about—"

"All right, you can have both double-dark damned gates!" shrieked the woman. "Take them! I, Zarrin Foxmantle, hereby transfer to you, Tamlin Bloody Heartless Monster Uskevren, all taxes and duties collected at both gates! The Foxmantles divest themselves of any gates! Every gate in the city! *Now get me loose or I'll skin you alive!*"

"I guess that'll do." Tamlin coughed as he fiddled with the shackles. The locks were of new brass but the chains antique. Drawing his smatchet, Tamlin whacked the fetters against the wooden post. The new-fangled smatchet, weakened by its fancy blade-catching groove, immediately snapped.

"Drat the dark! No wonder Vox hates these things!" Drawing his long sword, Tamlin used both hands to whack at the chains. Finally he cut them. Zarrin leaped off the settle like a rocket and pelted for the door, chains jingling. Spitting smoke, Tamlin left his sword wedged in the post and followed.

Fire rippled and flared everywhere. No wizards warred on the stairs, for the front of the house had almost crunched flat. Zarrin and Tamlin skidded down the ruined stairs, slithered out the squashed doorway, clawed across the splintered gallery, and finally dashed to the safety of the street.

Panting, breath frosting, Tamlin wrapped his cape around the shivering Zarrin. Huddled, they gaped at the ongoing chaos.

The tilted house burned brightly. Chunks toppled into the gardens. Flaming trees shot sparks that the breeze blew throughout the neighborhood. Citizens scurried in flickering darkness, carrying buckets and lugging firehooks. The Hulorn's Guards worked in teams with spears to kill the last of the gnashers. Other guards fought the fire or shepherded neighbors to safety. Two hillmen lay dead and two more were trussed on their knees. Household goods, books, and clothes were strewn in the street. Proud Helara watched the blaze, a smirk on her face. Magdon and Ophelia stared in awe. Selgauntians milled, clustered, asked questions, and got in the way.

From the madness, Escevar trotted up and clapped Tamlin's shoulder. He was smudgy and bloody but grinning. "Deuce! Thank the fates you're alive! And you found Zarrin! Bravo! We won all around! Ratigan, that green wizard, ran screaming with his clothes half-turned to stone and his hair afire! And you'll never guess who showed up! Padrig the Palmer! He ran up flapping his hands because *his* house was burning! *He* rented it to the wizard! That's how he knew about Ratigan!"

"That answers a few questions." Tamlin spoke over Zarrin's blonde head. "So what did you do?"

"Oh, nothing," Escevar evaded. "What with all those flying sword blades, Padrig got whacked on the head and fell in the cellar, poor chap."

With a rush and gush, the house collapsed into its foundation. Sparks vomited into the sky. Trees sizzled like fireworks. People shouted. Escevar spotted someone and ran off with a laugh.

"I can't believe you took advantage of my misfortune." Zarrin peered from the folds of Tamlin's cape. "That was unfair, Tamlin. It was low and rotten. Holding someone's feet to the fire to drive a better bargain is vile, slimy, underhanded, deceitful and—unkind."

The girl shivered and snuggled into Tamlin's arms. "I'm just cold, so don't get any ideas. I'll admit, though, you were clever. I'd have done the same. Maybe there's hope for you, Tamlin. With all the schemes coming to a boil in this city, my family might find you useful, if you care to stay with business."

"Oh, I don't know." Tamlin looked at the running burning raging chaos that engulfed the early morning street. "I find business so dull."

THE DAUGHTER

The Price

Voronica Whitney-Robinson

"Who are you," asked the lion faced man, above the din of the music.

"I'm not sure myself," giggled his raven-haired dance companion, "and even if I did know, why should I tell you?" With that, she threw back her head and laughed deeply as her partner spun her around the floor. The sound drew a few surprised stares from some of the nearby couples, but most merely smiled indulgently to themselves. Thazienne Uskevren was well known for her exuberance.

Tonight was one of Lliira's celebrations, and the Uskevren had opened the doors of Stormweather to some of the many revelers this evening. The main hall was filled with some of the most renowned members of Selgaunt's elite. The partygoers wore various degrees of costumes for the event. Some sported only masques with their evening finery, while others had gone to incredible extremes to look the roles they assumed for the night. Musicians played nonstop and the aroma of richly flavored delicacies drifted throughout the hall.

"May I cut in," a man asked Thazienne's partner, as he gently pulled the pair aside.

"Now just a moment," the lion began to bluster at the tall, cloaked and hooded figure, "the song isn't yet finished."

The hooded man, however, simply passed his hand in front of the lion's face. All protest faded from his voice. Thazienne's partner immediately faced her and sweetly took his leave. At the lion's departure, the hooded man tilted his head questioningly and held out his hand in offer to Thazienne. She, however, miffed at the turn of events calmly drew out a dagger that was more than just decorative. The hooded man did not move. Something in the manner of the stranger's stance was familiar to her, and Thazienne used the point of her weapon to flick the hood back. Gray eyes, hawklike in their intensity, stared down at her. She moved the dagger under his chin. The cloaked man stood still, staring at her as the nearby dancers, too caught up in the music to notice the scene unfolding nearby, rushed past them.

"I would appreciate it greatly," he finally said "if you would kindly point your little needle somewhere else." He lowered his glance meaningfully at her dagger, which was still under his chin.

"Please forgive me," Thazienne replied in a mock apology. With that, she flipped the dagger around so that it landed point down, on one of her gloved fingers. While balancing the dagger there, she gave a deep bow like a mummer and directed the gentleman to the dance floor. She returned her weapon to its hiding place and accepted his hand.

After a few turns, she sternly admonished the muscular, blond man. "Steorf, I told you never to play those kinds of tricks with me."

"The spell was completely unintentional and unconsciously instinctive," he replied. "I simply did not want to cause a fuss this evening. It appeared the easiest way."

The tenseness melted from her face as she smirked at him. Her deep green eyes lost their harsh glare and she giggled softly.

"To tell the truth," she admitted to him quietly, "I'm a little jealous. Even I can't get rid of men that quickly. Maybe one time you could teach me that trick," she teased.

"You know I don't give away trade secrets, Tazi," he replied, calling her by a nickname only a handful used. "My mother would never forgive me," he added seriously.

Always aware of how somber he could be in public, Tazi picked up the pace of their dance and tried to lighten his mood. "And just what are you supposed to be this evening, all dressed in black," she asked.

"I am simply part of the shadows," was all he would say.

Seeing that she was getting no where, Tazi broke away from his arms and pirouetted in front of him. "What do you think I am, then?"

Steorf escorted Tazi away from the dance floor and then stared at her for a minute. The dress she wore was not a popular style. She had started of late, he had noticed, to wear Cormyrean fashions. The blood-red dress was made from some sumptuous, velvety material and clung to her suggestively. Her flat slippers peeped out from under the loose, full skirt. The tight sleeves accentuated her strong, slim arms and the fitted gold breastpiece accentuated more. Covering her delicate face was an elaborate mask of long, black feathers that blended into her short, equally black locks.

"I would say you are some kind of exotic bird, escaped from the Hulorn's Hunting Garden," he said and then added after a glance, "or you are the bane of your mother's existence." Steorf nodded toward the fuming matriarch of the Uskevren standing some paces distant and watching them closely.

Tazi glanced quickly at her mother and then turned away. "Oh, she's always angry. I can't seem to do anything right in her eyes."

"Is she still furious about your hair," he asked.

"Well," Tazi began, justifying herself, "this length suites me better, and long hair certainly does not go well with Cormyrean dress." She stepped back and curtsied slightly once more.

"Nor does it go well with some of your other activities," Steorf observed slyly.

She was about to shoot back with an angry retort, but fell silent as her mother approached.

"Good even to you, young mage," the matriarch saluted Steorf politely. "Are you enjoying yourself this celebration night?"

Steorf bowed deeply and replied, "I am Madame Shamur. Once again the Uskevren have hosted a most successful fete. I am honored to be counted amongst your guests."

"It seems that your mother, Elaine, is not present," the ash blonde noticed sadly after scanning the hall.

"No, milady. My mother asked me to carry her regrets."

"Well," Shamur offered graciously, "I am sure the premier mage of Selgaunt does not always have the luxury of free time." She turned her steel gray eyes toward her daughter at that last remark. "Speaking of free time, Thazienne, have you seen Talbot this evening?"

"I don't think my big 'little' brother has gotten back from his hunting trip yet. What's wrong, Mother? Has he ruined some secret plan of yours? Did you have a bevy of potential wives to parade past him tonight and now he's missing the show?"

Shamur did not rise to the bait.

"I was a touch concerned," she replied quietly. Before Tazi could add anything else, Shamur continued in a more firm voice, "I wouldn't worry your pretty little head about it." She stepped closer to her daughter and ostensibly straightened some part of Tazi's costume. "I don't suppose you worry about much, though. You don't have to." She stepped back in a crinkle of blue and silver satin. "Enjoy yourselves tonight and see that you share your attentions with some of our other guests, dear Thazienne." She began to walk away from the two.

Angry at her mother's jab, Tazi called out, "Oh, Mother? I love your dress. The silver really brings out the warmth in your eyes." Shamur smiled stiffly at her before continuing to walk away.

"Do you have to do that," Steorf asked as soon as Shamur was out of earshot. "I think she was genuinely worried about your brother."

Tazi dismissed his concern. "I'm sure Talbot stretched out his trip just to avoid this evening, the lucky dog. As for my mother, she just brings the worst out of me. That could be me in a few years, you know," she exclaimed after a brief moment. Steorf took a step closer.

"Never in a thousand years could that be you," he whispered. She smiled up into his face, and he took another step closer.

"Is this a private conversation, or can anyone join in," interrupted a richly, almost foppishly dressed red-haired elf. His amethyst-hued velvet doublet was covered with gold embroidery and the sleeves were slashed to reveal tissue thin undersleeves of lavender silk. His leather boots announced their newness with every squeaky step he took. Unlike many of the other guests, he wore no mask at all.

Steorf stiffened at his approach, but Tazi could only snicker.

"It seems," she replied, "that I have precious little privacy from people tonight. Please, join us," Tazi offered solicitously. The elf immediately stepped past Steorf as though he had been cloaked and stood close to Tazi. He reached for her hand and gallantly touched it to his lips.

"Sweet Ebeian, always the gentleman." She curtsied

deeply, but noticed Steorf's discomfort. She didn't want to see these two start to bicker tonight, so she tried to defuse the situation. "Steorf, would you mind finding me some wine," she asked innocently. "All the dancing we've done has given me a terrible thirst."

"Yes, dear boy," Ebeian dismissed him. "See if you can scare us up some refreshments." Choosing not to notice Steorf's fuming, Ebeian turned all his attention to Tazi. She looked past his shoulder, smiled at Steorf and mouthed the word "please."

"I'd be more than happy to find a full vat for Ebeian and help him into it headfirst," Steorf mumbled to himself. He almost smiled at that image and went off in search of something to drink.

"How radiant you look in that ankle-length red gown." Ebeian used the comment as an excuse to reach over and capture Tazi's hands in his own jeweled ones. "The tight sleeves emphasize your slender arms and, well, that gold breastpiece . . ." His voice trailed off suggestively. "Of everyone in the room, I think only your mother does not appreciate your taste for Cormyrean fashion."

"There's much that my mother does not appreciate," Tazi replied, letting her hands rest in Ebeian's. "But I do not dress to please her."

"It's a good thing you don't. You would be a miserable failure," he said, laughing.

Tazi extricated her gloved hands from his. "What brings you out this evening? When we last spoke, you mentioned other plans."

"Plans change, pretty one," he answered. "You know how that works." He leaned forward and discreetly slipped his hand along the gold breastpiece Tazi wore. Instantly, she grabbed his thin hand and bent it back.

"You forget yourself this evening, Ebeian," Tazi warned him.

"Do I?" He looked at her meaningfully.

"You'll pay for your familiarity one day," Tazi threatened lightly.

"Sooner or later," he countered, "we all pay, Thazienne."

Before Tazi could say anything else, Steorf returned, a servant in tow carrying a tray laden with an assortment of drinks and snacks. He did not miss the grip Tazi had had on Ebeian's wrist, but he said nothing. The three selected glasses of wine, and Tazi and Steorf waited while Ebeian picked through the food until he discovered a satisfactory morsel to nibble on.

"I'm surprised," Ebian began, after dabbing a silken scarf at the corner of his mouth, "to see that you are still here this evening, Thazienne. Normally you do not grace these events for very long."

"Observant of you, Ebeian. I'm actually searching for someone."

"It's not me," Ebeian asked in mock horror, clutching at his heart. "I'm shattered." The ploy worked. Tazi broke up into chuckles and lightly slapped his arm.

"Do you recall the small party my family hosted a few nights back," she asked.

"How could I forget?" Ebeian began to extol the virtues of the beautiful gown Tazi had worn that night. She interrupted him before his commentary became too long. The heavy-handed way he always complimented her was beginning to strain her nerves.

"That's not what I meant. Did you notice the man my mother was throwing at me all evening?"

"Tall, brooding chap, much like our hawk over here." He pointed a delicate finger at Steorf. "Unusual tattoo on his neck, as I recall." For all his pompousness, Ebeian had a keen eye, and very little escaped his notice.

"That's the one. As always, to humor my mother, I flirted with him a bit."

"A bit," grumbled Steorf.

"As the evening wore on," Tazi continued, trying to

ignore Steorf's remark, "I gave him a little something to remember me by. He was dashing, all things considered. Normally, my mother's picks aren't nearly so easy on the eyes. That mark he bore made him seem exotic."

Ebeian reached over and rubbed her gloved hands, though the purpose was more than mere flirtation. "You didn't give away that emerald ring you always wear," he noted astutely. "I can still feel it on your finger. Don't you ever take it off?"

"That always stays with me. It was a gift from a mage a long time ago."

Ebeian gave a high titter of a laugh. "At twenty-one years, there isn't much that was 'a long time ago' for you."

"As I was saying," Tazi continued a bit peevishly, yanking her hands free, "I gave him a token of my affection." She paused and moved a thick lock away from her left ear to reveal a diamond stud. "He has the other one," she explained, "and I plan to liberate it from his dwelling this evening. At some later occasion, I'll demand that he show it to me, to prove how much I mean to him. When he can't produce it, I can denounce him as not being true to me, and then I'm free once more!" Her eyes crinkled in amusement.

"How do you know he won't be home? Or if he is out, that he won't have the earring on him," Steorf asked. "He might be a dedicated suitor, you know."

"Oh ye of little faith, questioning me like that. Have I ever led you wrong? Don't answer that," Tazi quickly added.

"What will you do if you get caught," Steorf asked her.

"You, of all people, should know what I'm capable of. Remind me, Ebeian, to tell you the time I pulled his fat out of the fire." She hooked a thumb in Steorf's direction. "Almost seven years ago to the day, and he still follows me around out of gratitude." She laughed deeply.

"After she does that, Ebeian, allow me to tell you the real story," Steorf returned, as close to bantering as he ever got. The wine had mellowed him.

"He won't be there," she continued confidently. "Everyone who is anyone will be here tonight. And," she added, "I gathered from our conversation the other evening that Ciredor is very eager to see and be seen. He won't be home. Though," she paused to scan the costumed gathering, "I have to admit I haven't yet been able to pick him out in this crowd."

"I hope you're right about him being here," Steorf replied seriously.

"And I hope you don't get caught like when you tried to rob me," Ebeian offered graciously.

With her mask in place, it was next to impossible for either man tell if Tazi blushed at that remark. Underneath it, a frown did cross her face at the memory of a night not too long past. After being introduced to him by her mother, Tazi had attempted to remove some of Ebeian's belongings from his room at the Lady's Thighs Inn. Her timing had been off slightly, and Ebeian had returned before Tazi had made her exit. A struggle had resulted, and Ebeian had discovered quite a bit about Tazi that night.

He sensed her discomfort and winked at her.

She didn't even need to look over to know Steorf was ready to explode after that. She knew how he hated the familiar way Ebeian spoke of their encounters. The last thing she wanted tonight was to cause a scene or alienate Steorf. She valued him too much to allow that to transpire. Just the touch of her hand on his forearm caused his bunched muscles to relax. His black look, however, continued to fester. Ignoring the exchange, Ebeian blithely carried on.

"We must try that again sometime, my dear," the elf chimed, "when you feel you're ready for a rematch."

"You're right," Tazi bantered back. "We can see if you are still up for a battle with me. But there will be time enough for that later."

Ever since Ebeian discovered in such a pleasant way

Tazi's many charms, they often traded exchanges like that in the company of others. He was cautious never to reveal too much; he had his own subterfuges to guard, and Tazi never betrayed those, either. However, they danced awfully close to the truth at times.

"What are you two talking about," Steorf demanded, no longer able to contain his anger.

"You really haven't been around the city all that much, have you," Ebeian said, laughing.

"Enough, you two," Tazi hissed at them as she pushed them apart. "I'd like to be able to slip out quietly, and you two starting a brawl would wreck my plans."

Steorf reined in his termper. "Being one of the few women wearing red this evening, I think you might have a hard time going unnoticed." He nodded in the direction of Shamur.

Tazi thought for a moment before she announced, "Then I will obviously have to be noticed by many. Gentlemen." She curtsied a last time to the men and strode off to select a new partner. Steorf said nothing but left an amused Ebeian standing alone.

Tazi chose a domino-masked man from a pool of nearby suitors and let him lead her to the dance floor. She smiled at his banal conversation and laughed at the appropriate moments. When the tempo changed, she allowed another man to cut in. The rush of changing partners allowed Tazi to put the two men out of her mind. She had other plans for the evening and needed her wits about her.

When the time seemed right, Tazi thanked her most recent partner and discreetly slipped out of the ballroom. From opposite sides of the hall, two pairs of eyes spied her departure.

Tazi couldn't wait to get out of the dress she wore. While the style was chosen specifically to infuriate her mother, Tazi liked it only marginally more than her Sembian attire. All dresses, to her, simply slowed the wearer down and announced her presence to the world. She had yet to discover a discreet one.

As she made her way to her rooms, Tazi noticed Larajin, one of her family's servants, lingering near the end of the hallway. An idea blossomed in her fertile mind.

"Larajin," she called out to the startled maid, "I need your help." She entered her chambers, a bewildered Larajin in her wake.

Tazi walked over to her wardrobe and flung open the doors. She deftly removed a small bundle that was nestled in the furthest recesses of the closet and tossed it onto a nearby settee. Then she turned to face her maid.

"Strip, please," Tazi ordered. "I need you to play a part for me tonight." At her maid's puzzled expression, she burst into giggles.

"I thought you needed some assistance with your gown," Larajin stammered. She slightly emphasized the word "your."

"You couldn't be more right," Tazi confirmed, controlling her laughter as she began to peel the red dress from her body, "I do need help with this thing. And you're just the one to assist me." She brushed Larajin's helping hands aside and pulled her own arms free from the tight-fitted sleeves.

"You might as well start undressing," Tazi said, almost tearing some of her buttons in her haste, "because I don't have all night. I've already wasted enough time here this evening." Larajin began to remove her white-and-gold servant's uniform, still not sure what her mistress had planned but secretly glad to be rid of her own costume.

Tazi slipped off her dancing shoes and stepped out of the pool of red velvet at her feet. Without missing a stride, she padded unselfconsciously over to the settee and began to undo the bundle of leather. When she had her change of clothing laid out, Tazi could see realization dawn across her maid's pretty features. It took only a few practiced motions for Tazi to re-outfit herself. Now she turned her attention to her near-nude servant.

"Come on over here." Tazi pointed to the pile of evening clothes. "Let me help you into this." She could see hesitation in every step Larajin took.

"Oh, don't act so," Tazi gently chided her. "It's not like you never did this before." Larajin looked at her with some surprise.

"What do you mean, mistress?" she asked softly.

"I've seen you in here before, trying on some of my—how shall I put it—less respectable garments. We are, after all, almost exactly the same size." Seeing alarm spread across Larajin's smooth face, Tazi quickly added, "I don't mind. In fact, you can help yourself to any gown you fancy any time. But I need you to do me a favor tonight because you're my size. I need you to be me for the rest of this evening." She nudged Larajin into the center of her discarded evening wear and began to help her dress.

"Mistress Thazienne, this can't work," Larajin implored, holding out her hands beseechingly.

Almost as though she were dressing a child, Tazi caught up her maid's arms and began to slide them into the snug sleeves. "Don't worry about any of this," she soothed. You only have to be me for a few hours."

Tazi walked behind her maid and began to do up the back of the gown. Larajin tried to protest once more, but Tazi cinched up her corset a little roughly, and Larajin's complaints ended in a sharp gasp. Tazi spun her around to face her.

"This will work out just fine," Tazi warned her. Smiling again, Tazi began to tie up Larajin's rust-colored hair into a style that gave the illusion of shorter locks. After a moment, Larajin gathered up her courage to question Tazi again even after that first, painful rebuke.

"Mistress, I only meant that it might be difficult to pass for you because of the difference in our hair and eyes."

Tazi finished Larajin's hair and moved over to where

she had carelessly tossed her feathery mask. She placed it on Larajin and took a step back to admire her handiwork.

"No one should look too closely at your yellow eyes with that on, but you are right about the hair," she said after a moment, tapping one gloved finger against her chin. "Yours looks like it was kissed by the sun and mine is like night." She unconsciously twirled an onyx strand and thought for a moment. "Black," she spoke quietly, "like coal . . . or soot." With a quick laugh, Tazi ran over to the fireplace and plunged her hands into the cold ashes. She then beckoned Larajin closer with a dirty finger.

"I'm sure this will come out fairly easily," Tazi reassured her maid as she powdered the woman's hair with coal dust and soot, "and it does solve the problem of color very nicely." Tazi finished her job and then gave Larajin a pat on the head to have her look up.

"Now," she admonished, "stop biting your lip, stand up straight, and put a smile on your face." Tazi walked around to stand behind her. She placed her hands on Larajin's shoulders and leaned toward her right ear.

"You can do this," she whispered encouragingly. "And you might even have some fun." Stepping around to once again face her, Tazi added a few last instructions. "All you have to do is dance with a half dozen or so of my current suitors. It shouldn't take more than a few hours. Don't look them in the eye too much," she continued her list as she paced around the unmoving Larajin like a drill instructor, "and don't answer any of their questions. I never do. My mother is now too angry to speak to me for the rest of the evening, and Father will be engrossed in business. He won't have time to trade words with you. I mean me," she smiled. "You should be all set."

Some of Larajin's unease had faded at the mention of the word "fun." Tazi could see she was warming up to the challenge of a prank. There might yet be hope for the girl, Tazi thought. Even if things should go awry and Larajin was found out, Tazi wasn't too concerned. She had noticed that since Larajin had been in the service of the Uskevren, she never received many punishments, unlike the other maids. There must be some arrangement between her and my younger brother, Tazi mused to herself. Larajin would be safe enough. "Let's go," Tazi said and pushed the girl toward the door.

Falling into the role of coconspirator, Larajin cautiously peered down the hallway but saw that Tazi and she were quite alone. The two women, now so differently garbed, stepped into the passageway. Without exchanging a word, they headed as one toward the grand staircase. Tazi stopped just short of it, however, and Larajin turned questioningly toward her.

"What's wrong," the maid demanded in a loud whisper.

"Nothing," Tazi reassured her. "I'm simply not going your way. I'm just going to slip out through the window back at the end of the hallway," she gestured.

Surprising Tazi, Larajin said, "Don't worry. No one will recognize you. I hardly do myself."

Smiling, Tazi explained, "Actually, there are one or two guests who would recognize me, and I don't feel like explaining anything else tonight. Off with you now," she ordered in a motherly tone to the girl two years her senior. "Don't have too much fun. I *do* have a reputation to maintain." She only managed to maintain her severe expression for a heartbeat before stifling a laugh. Larajin joined her, and the girls wished each other well.

For a few moments, Tazi observed Larajin as the girl, hesitantly at first, made her way down the grand staircase. At the bottom, Tazi saw with wry amusement that her suitors swarmed around Larajin, each one proffering her an arm and imploring her for a dance. She watched as Larajin carefully selected one and the lucky fellow swept her onto the dance floor. Confident in the subterfuge, Tazi turned to make her way out.

The same two pairs of eyes that watched her leave the ballroom earlier now scrutinized "Tazi's" return. They were not so easily fooled.

Once out in the cool night air, Tazi breathed more easily. It was during this time that she felt the most free. Her days were filled with family obligations and watching eyes, but she had made the nights her own, and she savored the hours. Her first stop would be in the Oxblood Quarter, to gather a bit of information and a drink or two. She moved easily down the streets, so pleased with her escape that she did not notice the dark figure trailing a discreet distance behind her. Soon enough, Tazi had another matter to distract her.

Screams, more terrified than those normally heard in the Oxblood Quarter, caught Tazi's attention. She ducked off of the main street, ears pricked, searching for the source of those uncomfortable wails. It took no more than a moment's hunt down a small back street to locate the cause.

In the rear of the alley, Tazi was able to make out three people. Two burly men had backed a woman against a wall. She must have been responsible for the cries.

The men wore the oily slicks typical of people more accustomed to life on the sea. The boatmen had obviously wandered a bit to be so far from Selgaunt Bay, but Tazi was not surprised in what they had found to distract them this evening. Even in the dim light, Tazi could see the woman was a beauty. She could also see the men appreciated her looks. One of them had unsteadily reached up to touch the woman's face with a hand that did not have all of its fingers. He must not be so adept at handling ropes and nets, Tazi thought mirthfully. Fingers's shorter companion hung back a few paces, content to wait his turn and take another drag from the jug the two had obviously been sharing. The woman was not so content to be their plaything, and she lashed out.

It was either this, Tazi mused, or drinks at the Kit. Without another thought, she charged into the fray.

The woman, her clothes tattered and dirtied, had managed to slash Fingers, more by luck than any real skill. He hissed and pulled back his arm. The sight of his own blood enraged him, and Tazi could see rage burn through his drunken haze. He faced the woman with a hard look. The game was no longer entertaining for him.

"Now you're going to pay," he snarled and balled up his fist.

As he cocked his arm back, Tazi came up from behind and ran her rapier efficiently through the meat of his upper arm. Pain and surprise caused him to fall to his knees. Tazi shot the woman a quick grin, but she didn't respond.

Probably afraid I'm going to be more trouble than these two, Tazi thought to herself. Dressed in black leathers and carrying a sword, she did not give an appearance of respectability.

Tazi placed her foot on Fingers's shoulder blades and levered her sword free. Shorty, slightly less drunk than his friend, stood mouth agape for a moment before throwing the jug aside and coming to his cohort's aid. He had forgotten the woman they had bullied into the dead end, now realizing that everything was turning sour very quickly. Tazi could see the determined look on his face. She had a hunch Shorty didn't like to lose. She now had his complete attention.

Shorty pushed the woman out of his way, and she tumbled to her knees on the cobbled alleyway. Tazi giggled under her breath as the man nearly tripped over his intended victim. The woman made no attempt to get out of the way. Tazi briefly wondered if she was in shock, or perhaps a little slow in the head.

If our places were swapped, Tazi thought, I'd be gone like a flash of lightning.

There was no time for more musings, though, as the second man drew his knife. He lunged toward Tazi's face, but she easily sidestepped his brutish assault. His momentum carried him right into Fingers, who had been unsteadily trying to rise to his feet.

"Come on," Tazi taunted. "I've seen trolls more graceful than you two."

Shorty freed himself from the tangle of Fingers's limbs and staggered to his feet.

"Don't play with me, boy." A rain of spittle carried the shout toward her.

Tazi smirked at Shorty's threat. Once again her leather vest and pants, short hair, skill with a sword, not to mention the poorly lit alley, had done its job. How easy it was, Tazi disdainfully concluded, to deceive people.

"I'm more than man enough to teach you some manners," Shorty threatened.

Tazi planted her rapier point down on the ground, like a walking stick, and leaned jauntily against it with her left hand. "Just what kind of manners could you teach me, you old lech," she demanded snidely. "And what kind of manners were you trying to teach her?" She nodded toward the woman, still kneeling on the street. "I think you and your friend should go back to the Bay," she suggested. "You two are fish out of water here."

The man said nothing but charged her once more. With only a slight shifting of her weight, Tazi brought her sword straight up in front of her face and easily blocked his thrust. They stood facing each other, as close as two dance partners. She looked him square in the eyes and, with an angelic smile pasted on her lips, brought her right hand up and slashed across his thigh with her dagger. Shorty's face twisted in pain, and he sank to the ground, ineffectually clutching his oozing wound. A quick glance at his partner assured Tazi that Fingers was still nursing his arm and no longer posed any threat to her or any other woman this evening. She stepped past the two toward the woman who had finally stopped trembling and had regained her footing.

"Come on," Tazi ordered roughly. "It's time to leave."

In the darkened alley, it appeared to Tazi as though the woman was in a state of shock. She stared blankly at her rescuer. The two boatmen might regain some of their bravado if the women lingered too long. Tazi grabbed the woman's arm and started to pull her out of the alley. And, because she enjoyed being contrary, she paused long enough to yank a black scarf from her throat and toss it at the man with the leg wound.

"Take it," she said disgustedly, "before you bleed to death all over this alley. It's soiled enough already." And with that, Tazi dragged the woman into a busier thoroughfare.

They traveled a short distance before either spoke. Finally, the woman placed her other hand on Tazi's and tugged a little. Tazi stopped her march and turned to look at the woman whom she had just saved. The torches on the street were not very bright, but Tazi could see the woman was not from Selgaunt. The glow of the feeble light reflected blue off her black hair, and illuminated the dusky tones of her skin. Her clothes also marked her a foreigner. The swirl of silks, torn and dirty though they were, hinted of the desert. But travelers from so far afield were not unique in this city of commerce.

"I wanted to thank you," the foreigner began, in a quiet but rich voice. "I believe I am in your debt, lady."

Tazi was shocked that the woman had seen so easily through her disguise. No one had ever found her out so quickly before.

"How did you know," she blurted out. "Didn't the clothes or my hair fool you a little?" Tazi paused to tug at her short, black locks.

For the first time since she had laid eyes on the dark-haired woman, Tazi saw her smile.

"It would be impossible for those things to fool me," she replied in a soft, melodic voice, "as I am quite blind."

Tazi was dumbfounded. She pulled the woman closer to the light and tilted her face upward. By the gentle radiance of the torch, Tazi was able to see the woman's eyes were icy white. There was no recognition in them.

"That explains why you're such a terrible fighter," Tazi said, chuckling. "You really couldn't see them coming."

"While that may be true, I certainly was able to smell them." The woman grinned back.

Tazi's face broke into a genuine smile. She liked this woman. The daughter of Thamalon Uskreven felt herself a good judge of character and acted on her instincts.

"Well, if we are to be traveling together, even such a short distance as this street, it would help to know your name," Tazi remarked.

"I am called Fannah il'Qun," the woman said, with a slight flourish.

"And I," Tazi said with slightly more bravado, "am called Tazi. When I'm out in this quarter, dressed as I am now," she added, "that is the only name I go by."

"Then I will have to 'see' what you are wearing," Fannah told her.

Tazi was perplexed as to what the woman meant by "seeing," considering her condition. She had never before come across someone who was sightless. Curiosity won her over. Tazi rounded the corner, away from prying eyes, and told Fannah to go ahead and "see," whatever that meant.

The foreigner gently raised her hands and reached for Tazi's thick hair. Delicately, she let her sensitive fingers trail through its thickness and moved her hands over her rescuer's features. She could feel Tazi's smooth skin, high cheekbones and delicate mouth. There was the trace of face powder, and a whiff of perfume that hinted at a pampered life. What her fingertips could not reveal was the sea green of Tazi's eyes. She could tell, however, that Tazi was slightly taller than she was. As her hands traveled down Tazi's slender but muscular arms, Fannah could "see" that Tazi was wearing atypical fashion for a lady. In fact, Fannah realized Tazi was not wearing the clothes of a lady at all. Her trained fingers recognized the texture of leather and silk. The cut of Tazi's clothing lent itself more to the style of covert activities, most often carried out by men. Fannah's mouth turned up in a smile.

"I take it that you see now," Tazi asked.

"Yes," Fannah answered in her rich voice. "I think I begin to understand. You're not quite what you seem."

"Well, I am and I'm not. That all remains to be seen," Tazi added, suddenly not wishing this stranger to know so much. "Enough of this! All this playing about has given me a terrible thirst. Would care to join me for a drink?"

Fannah was momentarily at a loss for words. Her confusion was apparent.

"Well, I've obviously ruined your evening plans by bloodying your companions. The least I can do," Tazi offered grandly, "is make my services available in their place."

The raven-haired stranger took only a moment to make up her mind. Life had long ago taught her to accept what was given to her. She graciously offered her arm. Tazi noticed a strange design on it, but she made no mention of it. She gathered Fannah up as a proper escort should, and the two made their way onto Larawkan Lane. Tazi raised her free hand to her mouth in a vain attempt to suppress the giggles spilling out of her. By the time she swung open the battered door to the Shattered Kit Fox, both women were laughing uncontrollably. As the Kit was not the most respectable of places, none of the patrons batted an eye at the scene the "young man" and his lady friend were creating.

Tazi and Fannah seated themselves at a table in a discrete corner of the taproom. A plump serving girl lit the gutted candle sealed to the table by all the melted wax and took their orders. She was new and did not recognize Tazi. That suited the disguised Uskreven just fine. It seemed to Tazi far too many people recognized her tonight. The only one to acknowledge Tazi when she and her companion entered the smoke-filled room was Alall Ulol, one of the inn's owners. Of course he should recognize her, for he was the one she made her monthly payments to. The family's estate, Stormweather Towers, was a grand enough home, but Tazi felt the need to keep quarters that were wholly her own, with no attachment to her more "respectable" life. The Kit suited her completely.

Not certain whom Tazi was with, Alall stiffened behind the bar. His jowls, prominent by their covering of thick, gray sideburns, tightened and Tazi knew he was ready to lend aid if she needed it. She gave a quick nod of assurance, and he relaxed. After three years, he took more than a passing interest in her welfare. She in turn had come to trust Alall and his wife, Kalakalan. Kalli knew more about Tazi than anyone else.

When their drinks arrived, Tazi began to prod Fannah about her predicament. While she herself rarely talked about personal matters, save to Kalli and occasionally to the family butler, Erevis Cale, Tazi made a point of discovering as much as she could about those around her. Cale had taught her that knowledge was a valuable commodity. Plus, a blind woman wandering around unaccompanied in an unfamiliar part of the city must be an interesting tale. Before Fannah could tell her very much, however, Tazi felt a presence behind her. Fannah sensed someone as well and fell silent.

Tazi discreetly leaned forward, as though tipsy, and pulled her dagger from her right boot. The moment the person tapped her on the shoulder, she whirled, dagger drawn. The ragged beggar flinched but held his ground.

"Sorry." Tazi smirked as she recognized the old man. She had a network of informants, and he was one of her most reliable. "Do you have what I want?"

"I wouldn't be here otherwise," he wheezed. He pulled out a small scrap of paper with a few spidery lines on it. "A certain residence you were searching for," he offered.

Tazi sheathed her weapon and snatched up the paper, squinting at it briefly while Fannah calmly sipped her drink. When Tazi was certain she could read the old man's scrawls, she handed him her untouched tankard and discreetly slipped him a coin. Judging from his expression, she wasn't certain which item pleased him more.

Tazi threw her dagger into a timber near the bar to catch Alall's eye. Ignoring his fuming look, she smiled sweetly and motioned for another round.

"I guess I still don't understand." Tazi continued her conversation with Fannah as though there had been no interruption. "What you're saying is that your mother sold you because you were blind?"

Tazi forced herself to stare into Fannah's ice-white eyes. She slowly realized she found them disquieting. She had a difficult time believing Fannah couldn't see her with them. She also had trouble reconciling the life Fannah had lived with the now-composed woman seated before her. Fannah's nonexistent relationship with her mother gave Tazi pause. While she and her own mother, Shamur, bickered bitterly at times, Tazi knew in her heart that her mother could never even think of something so cruel.

Fannah tilted her head, birdlike, and brushed a strand of her blue-black hair from her face. "She wanted to kill me at birth," she replied calmly, "but her religion prevented that. I was fortunate she was so pious, not to mention that she was a beauty. Men paid a great deal of money for the company of Ibina il'Qun. Because of that, a local festhall in the city of Calimport paid well for me. They were sure I would grow to be as beautiful as my mother and perhaps follow in her footsteps."

At this remark, Tazi clicked her tongue as if to say "That's obvious!"

"But what could a young, blind girl offer a festhall?" she asked aloud

"It did not take me long to learn the layout of the Desert's End," Fannah explained. "Once I was comfortable with it I was as competent as any serving girl. There were patrons who would pay extra to keep their identities secret. A blind girl seemed an obvious choice to accommodate them. What most people forget is that it is not just their faces that name them, but their voices and even"—she crinkled her nose in mock disgust—"their smells."

"Did you ever have to take up your mother's profession?" Tazi asked quietly.

"I was fortunate," Fannah answered without hesitation. "That was something I did not have to sell to anyone. When my time was up with the End, someone else bought my contract. He never told me his name, not once during the long journey here. The only demand he made of me was to place a mark on my arm." Fannah stretched out her right forearm for Tazi's inspection.

It was the tattoo Tazi had noticed in the street. She tried to place the familiar design. Tazi knew she had seen one like it recently. In a flash of memory, she recalled the exotic mark Ciredor bore on his neck.

"Once we arrived," Fannah continued, unaware of Tazi's revelation, "he promptly abandoned me without explanation."

"How long ago was that," Tazi interrupted excitedly.

"A few days ago, as best I can tell," the blind woman replied. "He said he would find me when he needed me. It was not long after that I fortuitously ran into you, 'Lord' Tazi."

Tazi's curiosity was raging now. What connection did Ciredor have with this girl? If he had one secret, she reasoned, he probably had more. Anxious to be on her way, she used the pause to take her cue.

"As enlightening as this is, I have some other plans for this evening," she informed Fannah. "I'll be right back."

While Alall finished serving a patron, Tazi freed her small dagger from the timber support near the bar. She leaned against the rail nonchalantly and inspected the point of her blade. Seeing that it had been dulled a little, she pulled a stone from a pocket in her vest and began to sharpen it.

"Dark and empty, I swear you are going to be the death of me, child," Alall scolded her, his apple-round cheeks growing red in indignation. "One of these days, your aim's bound to be off, and I'll be the one left to pay for it!"

Tazi leaned across the bar and lightly planted a kiss on one of those crimson jowls. "Now, now," she soothed, "you know I never miss. And if the impossible ever did happen"—she grinned—"your spirit could rest comfortably knowing that wife of yours would beat me properly. After all, she served in the army of the kingdom of Sembia for more than ten years."

"Why doesn't that make me feel any better," Alall sighed, rolling his eyes at the low ceiling above. But the kiss had already worked its magic. His grim expression softened as it always did around her.

Tazi reached into a concealed pocket and withdrew several coins. She handed him a few and, after some consideration, slid several more in his direction.

"Here's for the drinks. The extra is for you to have another key made for my room."

"Don't tell me you've gone and lost yours, poppet," Alall whispered to her.

"No. You see that black-haired woman at my table?" she said, lowering her voice and motioning discretely at

Fannah. Alall nodded. "She's going to be staying in my room for a bit, and I want her to be able to come and go as she pleases."

Alall managed to hide most of his surprise. Tazi had kept a room at his inn for several years now and he could only think of two others who had ever been in the room after Tazi began renting it. They'd never been allowed to stay long enough to warrant a key.

"It'll be done," he promised. "And I'll let Kalli know about your guest, so she won't think the girl a lovelorn suitor and toss her down the stairs out of reflex."

Tazi grinned at the memory. Not too long ago, she had received a little too much attention from one of the Kit's patrons who had become smitten by the "boy" she seemed to be. Tazi tried to make a discreet retreat to her quarters, but the gentleman had other, friendly ideas. Kalli, however, made sure she was left alone. The man found himself picked up bodily by Alall's six-foot wife and tossed ignominiously down the bowed and rickety stairs. Tazi realized she had found a safe haven and another set of parents at the Kit.

As she turned to leave, Alall gave a few coppers back to her. Tazi smiled briefly at his superstition. There weren't many merchants in Selgaunt who still believed that you gave a little back to the client so that they could barter with you again someday. Alall did.

Returning to the table, she said to Fannah, "I'm afraid I'll have to go elsewhere this evening."

Fannah smiled and nodded, but Tazi could see concern cross her features. Not missing a beat, Tazi continued, "Why don't you take your drink and I'll walk you up to my room. Maybe we can even talk Kalli into fixing you something a bit more substantial to eat?" She went around to Fannah's chair and helped her get her bearings.

With her disturbing eyes fixed on Tazi, Fannah asked with a perplexed tone, "What do you mean by 'your room'?" It appeared that people could still surprise Fannah.

As she steered Fannah toward the stairs along the left side of the bar, Tazi remarked smoothly, "As I said before, I know I ruined your evening's plans. I would like to make up for it."

Fannah stopped before the stairs and resolutely stood her ground. She gripped Tazi's arm with both of her hands and stared hard at her with her sightless eyes.

"You don't know me, nor do you owe me anything. I will find a way to manage on my own," she said with a steel resolve. Now it was Tazi's turn to tilt her head at Fannah.

"I know you can," she reassured her, "but why not take me up on my offer? You don't have a place to go tonight, and I'm not asking anything of you. Why not say yes?"

After a moment of silence, Fannah whispered, "Why are you doing this for me?"

Tazi patted Fannah's clenched hands with her free one. "I like you. It's that simple. I just feel like doing this. Can't you accept that?"

Fannah's only response was to squeeze Tazi's hand and turn her face toward the stairs. Cautiously, the two made their way up to Tazi's room. It was simple enough, with a bed, a wooden table, and some chairs. There were a few locked chests under the bed, but Tazi seemed unconcerned about Fannah's presence in her room of secrets. When she opened, as much as she ever did, the doors into her life, she did so unreservedly.

"Let me light this oil lantern," Tazi began before she foolishly realized the light would not matter to Fannah. This time it was Fannah who smoothed over the awkwardness as she thanked Tazi.

"Leave it. I try to stay in practice and live as much as a sighted person as possible," she explained. "It tends to make people less uncomfortable around me." She flashed a warm smile at Tazi.

"Well, I think you're set for now. I'll see about sending up some food. Don't worry about paying for it."

As Tazi moved to the door, Fannah stopped her once more. Fearing some deluge of gratitude, Tazi raised her hands in protest. But Fannah's next words caught her by surprise.

"Beware tonight. Not everything you see is as it seems."

With those odd words resounding in her head, Tazi returned downstairs. She gave another nod to Alall and stepped out into the night. There, away from the nosy eyes of the Kit's clientele, she pulled out the scrap of parchment the old man had given her and verified the address once more. According to his sources, whatever or whoever they might be, the old man had discovered Ciredor's apartments. They weren't far.

Everything is going exactly the way I want, Tazi said to herself as she confidently made her way down Larawkan Lane. First, I'll relieve Ciredor of the trinket I gave him and, in doing so, relieve myself of his company. Then, I'll find out just what his connection is with Fannah. I don't want him to have any more to do with her. She discovered a protective feeling for her new acquaintance. Serious thoughts, however, never clung to Tazi for long, and soon she found herself envisioning Shamur's search for a new suitor for her. The picture of her exasperated mother caused a wave of giggles to well up in Tazi. As usual, they passed quickly.

Without warning, a group of gaudily costumed party-goers burst from around a corner. Tazi automatically reached for her dagger, but when she saw they offered no threat, she composed herself and gave a quick nod to the merrymakers. The encounter further reinforced her belief that everyone of note would be out tonight at one celebration or another.

Tazi walked more and more quietly as she left the

concealing seediness of the Oxblood Quarter. To the few people still milling about on the cobblestone roadway, she looked for all the world like a young man out on a lark. Tazi was well practiced at effacing herself and becoming part of the backdrop around her. But she was not the only one this night with such skills, and the shadow that had followed her from Stormweather Towers was still near.

It was not too long a walk, but it was long enough, and Tazi used the time to prepare herself. The tang of salt in the air meant Selgaunt Bay was close again. Though she would be loath to admit it, her mouth always dried out at the beginning of her excursions. Her heart beat just a little faster, too. It was the end of her "wildings," though, that were sweetest. Words could not describe the surprise and pleasure she felt when they were over and she was triumphant once again. She had to admit to herself that she was secretly pleased she had discovered someone to share a few of these outings with, someone who enjoyed them as much as she did. But even though Steorf made a wonderful companion on nights like this, Tazi ultimately found the wildings on her own to be the best of all.

The accomplished thief made her way down Larawkan Lane, lost in her own thoughts. A few shops were still open. This was Selgaunt after all, and business was business, no matter the hour. The few lingering patrons were lost in their own trades and paid little attention to the darkly clad youth traveling quickly down the road. Soon Habrith's Bakery came into view.

Tazi nodded to herself at the sight of the landmark and turned right at the bakery, a business closed now but one that would be bustling with the coming of dawn. Down a few paces on Sarn Street nestled a small garden. There was a scattering of such islands of greenery in Selgaunt, the largest being the Hunting Gardens. The one before Tazi was much, much smaller, but Ciredor's temporary lodgings were said to be adjacent to the corner of the wooded lot. Tazi made her way through the grove to her intended target.

She moved silently through the sparse brush adjacent to Ciredor's walled-off garden, glad she had oiled her leathers earlier in the evening, for there wasn't the slightest creak from them. She was not as fortunate as her absent companion Steorf, who had learned to cast wards to ensure his own silence, regardless of what he wore or carried. Tazi had to admit when they were together his skill impressed her. He was becoming as formidable as his mother. He would make a worthy successor to Elaine one day, Tazi thought, assuming he could give up this kind of mischief for a respectable life.

She discreetly approached the garden wall, which had a limited view of the back of Ciredor's rented tallhouse. Most of the buildings nearby were tallhouses, stone edifices hard to distinguish from one another. Tazi hoped her information was correct, that she had got what she paid for. If not, she would probably help herself to a few sundry items from whoever's residence this was. Later she could throttle the old man back at the Kit.

The garden wall, still in fairly good repair, was about twice her height. The garden beyond was dense with trees and little else. Through their leaves, Tazi observed a little of the household. Two of the upper rooms had small balconies jutting out over the greenery. Several others appeared to be dimly lit, probably by some kind of continuous light spell. Tazi watched those rooms for several long moments. When she saw no shadows cross them, she deduced the house was empty of its master. At this time of night, the few servants she knew Ciredor had retained would most likely be in the kitchen or pantry, drinking ale. Tazi knew from experience that her own family's butler, Erevis Cale, kept a small supply of brandy in his own pantry, a brandy she had warmed herself with in his company more times than she could remember.

Tazi wasted no more time lost in memories. Deftly and soundlessly she scrambled up the side of the wall. She had picked a spot covered by tree branches and, when she arrived at the top, crouched there motionless for a time. With her dark hair and clothing, she was another thin shadow. The garden appeared to be empty, but it paid to be cautious. Some of these houseowners kept great, lumbering hounds and Tazi had learned quickly that dogs were not creatures she wanted to tangle with. Her right wrist still bore the scars of her first encounter with just such a beast. This garden, though, contained only trees. Across the lane, the dark figure watched Tazi and waited.

Unaware of being observed, Tazi swung herself down and slipped through the garden. She caught some movement in one of the rooms on the first floor, toward the west end of the house. The servants, no doubt, in the pantry, she thought. Tazi made her way stealthily to a set of double doors to the east, doors that opened onto what was probably a sitting room. She reached into the sleeve of her shirt to the slim wire tools tied to her forearm. Tazi had carried such lock picks with her since she was fifteen. A quick twist of the wrist and she heard the gratifying click of the lock disengaging. She smiled to herself and added another number to her mental tally of successes.

As the tallhouse was in such good condition, the door inched opened smoothly without a hint of sound. Now the sands were running. Tazi started her search of the house.

She moved easily from the first floor with its receiving rooms, actively avoiding the kitchen and pantries, and slipped up the stairs to the next floor. They were austerely furnished, and it looked as though Ciredor had not traveled with many of his own possessions. That added to the puzzle. The merchants Tazi knew never traveled so lightly. There were few wall decorations, save for the rich drapes that hung at the windows, and no ornamentation or personal trinkets anywhere else.

Tazi slid skillfully from one room to another, looking for a strongbox or jewel casket. She'd burgled the tallhouse of rich merchants before, and knew all the tricks: the secret alcoves, false stones that moved aside, hollow doors, and the obligatory traps. But each of the spots in which she expected to find such things was empty. Frustrated, she kept searching.

While searching in the bedroom Tazi was startled by something. The room was littered with many small, obscene carvings and pagan statues. "Interesting," she thought, with not a little distaste. A cursory glance revealed nothing of any monetary value, but Tazi began to wonder about the kind of man Ciredor was.

Her sharp eyes caught the glint of silver on his bed-table. Tazi slipped the shiny object out from under one of the shameful carvings. It was a badge with silver swans against a backdrop of green. Tazi knew this coat of arms all too well.

"The Soargyls," she whispered harshly. "What does Ciredor have to do with them?"

Knowing that the longer she dallied, the greater her chance of discovery, Tazi left the bedroom, frustrated by her lack of progress. Her mind raced. He must have a study somewhere, since there was no office attached to the tallhouse. Perhaps there she could discover what kind of connection existed between Ciredor and her family's most hated enemies—enemies whose motto was "Always even in the end." Ciredor would regret any association between himself and that loathsome brood, of that Tazi would make certain. No one threatened her family and walked away.

The only place she hadn't searched was the cellar. Tazi hated cellars; they were dead ends and, therefore, traps. Reaching the cellar would also mean sneaking through the occupied pantry, but she would be damned if she was going to leave empty handed.

She wound her way more quickly now back down the stairs and moved close to the kitchen. The room was dark. She could see pots and skillets hanging near the windows. Obviously the servants had cleaned up and were enjoying the emptiness of the household. As she passed the window, Tazi gave a quick squint to see if she could anything or anyone outside. As far as she could tell, Tazi thought she only had to worry about the men in the other room. In the blackness, she did not make out the figure crouched on the garden wall. But he saw her.

As she neared the pantry, Tazi plastered herself against the wall. She could hear the low voices of a few men coming from the room. At the edge of the doorway, Tazi glanced inside. A single, ancient oil lantern cast a dim light in the room. Evidently Ciredor's manservants didn't rate the same light spells as the rest of the house. There were three of them huddled around a table in the far corner of the room, lost in whispered conversation. There was something furtive, almost secretive in the manner in which they were speaking. Perhaps, Tazi thought cheerily, they were planning to rob their temporary master. Wouldn't that be terribly ironic, she wondered delightedly?

The lighting and the location of the table made her next move much easier than she'd anticipated. Most of the pantry was in shadows, and Tazi slid slowly along the wall. She had done this before, but the nearness of the men and the possibility of discovery made her heart pound harder. She felt as if it might burst through her fitted vest at any moment.

Four steps and she was at the stairs. Part of her still felt uneasy at searching the cellar, but now she was committed. She had her family to protect. Carefully avoiding the well-worn center of each step, Tazi made her way down with almost no sound. Pleased with her skill, she took a few steps and was suddenly hard pressed not to gag. The room was filled with a powerful stench of mold and decay.

She could almost taste the dampness. The room reeked of it. The odor was so overpowering, she almost changed her mind. The challenge was irresistible to her, though. Resolutely she pressed on, one hand clamped over her nose and mouth.

Tazi noticed many footprints in the grime on the flagstones of the floor. Too many, she thought, for just the normal traffic of servants fetching liquor. Ciredor hadn't been in town that long, and hadn't hosted any large gatherings, as far as Tazi knew, to warrant such a substantial supply of spirits. Something else must have drawn him here. She began a careful search of the room.

Along a back wall, Tazi found what she had been looking for: a secret door near some ale casks. She knew from experience not to blunder through. To the right of the door, were stacked several crates. She climbed on top of them, her head practically pressed into the low ceiling. From this angle she was better able to check for traps or wards along the door. Strangely enough, there weren't any.

"Is he that arrogant," Tazi whispered incredulously, "to think no one would get this far? My, my, he's got a lot to learn about life."

The lock was a simple matter, and the door soon swung open to reveal a clean, dry room. Spells tripped by the door's movement banished the darkness but revealed something so foul it made the bile rise again in Tazi's throat. She had seen a lot in her years in the Oxblood Quarter and even darker locales, but she had never seen a thing like this atrocity.

The room was an antechamber, with two other doors at either side, near the entrance. At the back, against a wall, was an overstuffed divan with a mountainous pile of pillows. Right beside that was a desk covered with scrolls and a strongbox resting on the corner. The floor was comprised of two different colors of flagstones, one darker and one lighter. The dark flagstones formed a huge circle, its diameter slightly larger than the height of an average person. But it was what rested in it that caused Tazi's world to reel.

In the circle's center was what must have been a teenage boy. The tattered remains of his clothes marked him as a boat person, one of the many souls living in communities of ships lashed together in Selgaunt Bay. One of the faceless hordes whom only a handful might notice missing and none would dare report gone. Just like a newly arrived foreigner, she thought. The boy lay with limbs outstretched, with no sign of restraint. Bonds were pointless.

He was split from stem to stern. The skin of his torso had been carefully spread open like the pages of a book. Each of his larger internal organs was placed neatly near his body. Through horrified eyes, Tazi could see that blood vessels and connective tissue still bound those organs to his body. Muscles were pulled out and stretched taut from his bones. Almost against her will, she was drawn closer to him. The coppery smell of blood was everywhere.

As she neared, Tazi could see that huge lengths of his intestines had been yanked out and arranged in strange patterns. They appeared to form sigils, spelling messages that meant nothing to the sickened thief except for one sign that she had seen earlier this evening: the tattoo on Fannah's arm. A mark that both the foreigner and Ciredor bore. Was this what he had planned for Fannah, she wondered. But what Tazi had to force her mind to accept at that moment was the fact that the lad was still breathing! Some wicked magic kept his lungs working and his heart pumping. His lips were quietly moving, and the eyeless sockets in his head seeped with bloody tears. She knew with a heart-wrenching despair that he was beyond help and must be put out of his misery. There was no way she could bring him to a healer in time. He was beyond that.

How? her mind demanded. How could she kill him? Tazi slowly moved toward his prostrate form.

A cold hand gripped her shoulder, and a scream tore from her throat. Tazi whirled around, instinctively drawing her blade. Standing there, a slow smile spreading across his face, was Ciredor. He was still arrayed in his costume from the fete; he looked like a malevolent salamander. His mask hung about his shoulders. More than a head taller than Tazi, his slim build made him look even taller. He had a thick head of dark hair, which he kept closely shorn. And his mustache and goatee emphasized his hollow cheeks. But after what she had seen tonight, Tazi no longer thought him to be so dashing.

"What a lovely surprise to find you here, Thazienne Uskevren. I was disappointed by your shoddy replacement at the party and thought I wouldn't get the chance to see you this evening," he said knowingly, slowly walking around her. "I would have brought you here soon enough, but it looks as though you couldn't wait."

With horror, she saw her diamond stud winking in the dimming light from his left ear.

The door slammed shut behind her. Tazi jumped and raised her sword higher. Ciredor paid no heed to her weapon. He moved past her to the far wall where his desk was situated. Casually, he began to sort through some of the many scrolls that lay there, all but oblivious to her presence. Tazi's heart was hammering in her chest, and there was no moisture left in her mouth.

"What are you," she managed to croak out, "that you could do this?" She pointed at the boy with a trembling hand.

Ciredor barely glanced up from his papers. "Oh, come now, Thazienne. You're a bright girl. Why ask such foolish questions?" He put down a scroll and advanced on her. "I'm a mage, of course, and some magic demands a high cost. This"—he nodded at the boy—"is nothing, really. I have many such as him who carry my sign, scattered throughout the lands. As one fades, there is always another to fill the void." With an easy wave of Ciredor's hand, Tazi's sword flew from her grip and spun across the room. It landed with a hollow clang on the flagstones. He put out one index finger and tipped her ashen face up to meet his gaze. "Everything demands a price, pretty Thazienne."

She slapped his hand away and stumbled back a bit. "What business do you have with the Soargyls?" she asked, buying time, giving her mind a chance to find an escape. She knew, with a kind of quiet dread, that death or worse was close at hand. There had to be a way out.

Ciredor answered, "I have been retained by, how shall I put it, those 'acquaintances' of your family to accomplish certain tasks. They do not ask for all that much, really, considering what they pay." He moved closer to her. "They ask for you, among other things," he whispered silkily, walking around her unyielding form. "But you might be able to outbid them. They have, after all, only procured my temporary loyalty."

The wooden entrance to the room fairly blew off its hinges. Both Tazi and Ciredor lost their footing as the foundation shook and debris flew everywhere. Steorf stormed in, eyes blazing, like some avenging spirit, no longer a mere shadow. Blinking dust from her eyes, Tazi was certain she had never seen him like this. Without a moment's hesitation, Steorf grabbed the lighter Ciredor by his shoulders and slammed him into the nearest wall, treating the mage to the same kind of punishment his three servants had received upstairs. Steorf should have finished the fight then, but he paused to glance at Tazi as she staggered to her feet, concern etched on his face. That hesitation was his undoing.

Ciredor brought up his arms between Steorf's grip. At the barest touch of his hands, fine, green sparks engulfed Steorf and blasted him the length of the room. Steorf's thickly muscled back absorbed the worst of the blow and barely saved him. The force of the explosion, however, stunned him and he slumped to the floor.

Tazi, in the meantime, had used the distraction in an attempt to retrieve her sword. She did not get far. Ciredor whispered a few words, and Tazi found herself slammed to the ground, her sword only a tantalizing few inches from her reach. Pain exploded inside her. She curled into a ball. Her mouth was thick with the taste of blood and fear.

"Dear, dear Thazienne, it doesn't look like you are ever going to grow up," Ciredor chuckled. "You've spent far too much time playing in your short life." As he spoke, he began to circle her crumpled body. "Just look at you," he continued, savoring the moment, "still playing dress up like some silly child. Don't you think it is high time you grew up?" He made another gesture. Tazi noticed the lights in the room dimmed, before a white, hot pain blurred her vision.

Somehow she managed to roll to her knees, her forehead against the cool flagstones. She was certain her brains were burning. A thousand daggers sliced into her scalp. Blood oozed from the pores atop her head as her hair began to grow at an unbelievable rate. She balled her hands into tight fists against the agony. Even through the suffering, she could feel her emerald ring bite into her finger. The words spoken to her years ago by a mage she had met as a child echoed dimly in her fevered mind.

"That's better," Ciredor cooed. "Now you look more like the slightly outdated portrait the Soargyls sent to me. That short style never suited your looks. I might even keep you for a while longer."

Tazi blindly reached for her sword. Ciredor deftly kicked the blade away.

"I can't believe that you have managed to survive this long, little girl," Ciredor hissed. "You are so obviously ill equipped for life."

"You might be surprised by what I'm capable of," Tazi

spat back, forcing herself to stare at him through blood and her once again waist-length hair. Steorf had also risen unsteadily and moved up to stand behind her.

Suppressing a snicker, Ciredor nodded toward Steorf and remarked, "Even your hired help won't be able to pull you from this fire."

"He's not my 'hired help,' " Tazi, still in pain, moaned.

"Oh, excuse me," Ciredor replied with a mocking bow. "I meant to say *your father's* hired help."

Those words sliced through the agony her body was feeling. Forgetting her immediate danger, Tazi demanded, "Just what do you mean by that?"

Ciredor smiled and crossed his arms over his chest. A cat could not take more pleasure in playing with a mouse. Tazi could sense that to him the game was sweet and the pain emanating from the room was exquisite and addicting.

"Do you mean to tell me, Thazienne Uskevren, that you are completely ignorant of your father's machinations? Have you truly been unaware of the fact that for these past seven years yonder fledging mage," he paused to gesture at Steorf, "has been in the service of your father? He only stays by your side because he's been paid to do so!"

Tazi, oblivious to the deadly mage in front of her, staggered to her feet and slowly turned to Steorf. Her emotions rolled down her face like the wax of a tavern candle. A dark rage fixed itself there. For the first time in her life, Tazi was a fearsome sight to behold. Steorf took a step back from her.

"What is he talking about?" she hissed.

"It isn't what it seems," Steorf was quick to offer.

"Then this serpent is simply dripping venom to poison me against you. Is that what you're telling me?" she growled. There was no forgiveness in her voice.

"I'm your friend," Steorf said. "I always have been."

Tazi didn't give him a finger's length. "Do you accept money from my father?"

Steorf lowered his head, uable to meet Tazi's burning glare.

"I'm afraid," she continued through gritted teeth, "that I'm having trouble hearing you."

Ciredor leaned against the far wall grinning at the scene unfolding before him. Evidently he intended to let it play out for a few more moments.

"Yes, I do," whispered Steorf.

Tazi's world crumbled. She squeezed her eyes against the tears that threatened to spill forth. Her rage welled up within her, and she let her right hand curl into a fist. She cocked back her arm to swing at him.

Ciredor could no longer contain himself. He clapped delightedly at the pathetic tableau they presented. Before Tazi could strike her would-be rescuer, the mage whispered a word, and a green light shot from his outstretched hands. The light split into four glowing balls, and each found its way to Steorf's ankles and wrists. He was lifted and bound to the wall as efficiently as if iron manacles had been used. He struggled, but there was nothing in his mystical arsenal that could counter Ciredor's own arcane strength. In the growing gloom, Ciredor turned to face Tazi once more.

Blood ran down her face and throat. Her newly grown hair was matted in several places. Her leathers hung in tatters. She could barely maintain her footing. But a small, grim smile was planted on her lips.

"Enough, child. Time for us to leave," Ciredor stated. He clasped his hands together, and a sharp, green light burst from them.

"This ring is not something to be taken lightly." The warnings of Durlan, a moon elf, resounded through Tazi's mind. "There is a price to this magic," he had warned her a lifetime ago. "You will feel a great pain, more severe than anything you can imagine, and it will leave you spent, but the ring will keep you safe from any evil magic."

As the deadly bolt flew toward her, Tazi stretched out her left hand in a gesture of defiance and spoke an ancient word. The pain from Ciredor's earlier torture was nothing compared to the hot knives that stabbed her body. A pale, gray shield formed in front of her and deflected Ciredor's attack.

The mage stood amazed. His magic had never failed him before.

Tazi seized his hesitation. Nearly blinded by the pain, she still managed to slide her right hand into her boot and grab her small dagger. No playful, practice throws at the Kit any longer; her life depended on her skill now. She flung her arm out.

The dagger caught Ciredor below his heart. His face a mixture of surprise and shock, he doubled over and sank to his knees. Tazi didn't waste the opportunity. She had noticed the lights flickering and dimming during their battle and suspected the fight was draining Ciredor, though he still had a reserve. The only possibility was the boy. Somehow, his waning life was feeding Ciredor.

As the mage struggled to pull out her dagger, Tazi ran across the room to the divan. She grabbed a large pillow and stumbled over to where the boy lay. There was only one thing to do. Tazi dropped to her knees, no longer feeling any pain, and leaned over the eyeless boy.

"I'm so sorry," she whispered, the tears barely in check. "You never had a chance." With that, she lowered the pillow over his face and leaned against it with all her weight.

The child did not last long. It only took a brief moment for Tazi to take her first life.

The room grew very dim. The shackles binding Steorf began to flicker. Ciredor, who had managed to remove the dagger, tried desperately to staunch the flow of blood with part of his costume. Things were not going as he planned. Wounded and with little energy left, he gave way.

"I'm not nearly through with you, Thazienne Uskevren," he warned darkly. "We are bound, you and I, and the end has not yet been written." With that, he tossed her dagger aside, and summoned the last bit of his remaining magic. A bright glow filled the dark room. When it finally faded and the dancing stars had left Tazi's eyes, Ciredor was no where to be seen. Tazi was alone with Steorf and a crumbled pile of dust that had been the boy's body.

For a time, there was no sound in the room. Tazi simply knelt over the dead boy's ashes and gently rocked back and forth, hands on her knees. She felt a hand on her shoulder.

She knocked it away and leaped to her feet. "Don't you touch me," she warned Steorf through gritted teeth. He looked shocked and weary at the same time. "You don't have the right to, and I'm sure"—she added a bitter laugh—"my father isn't paying for that."

"Tazi—" he began feebly, but she didn't give him the chance.

"Just how much is he paying you?" she demanded. "How much to ensure your loyalty?"

Steorf looked torn. Despite herself, Tazi could see that what he said next cut him to the bone.

"Please don't make it sound so horrible, Tazi. Everyone has a price. You should know that. This is a city for buying and selling. Don't act so shocked. Even you have one." After a moment, he added, "I have always been loyal."

"And how many 'suns' would it take for you to be loyal to someone else?" Tazi turned sharply from him. She would not let him see her like this. It would be the bitterest of defeats, and she refused to lose anything else tonight. Looking down at what was left of the boy, she abruptly changed the subject. "This must be taken care of."

Seizing the chance to help, Steorf hastily said, "Don't worry, I'll see to it that the remains are put to rest." He moved a step closer to Tazi, but she would have none of it.

"Well, that's what you're paid for, isn't it? To take care of things, and clean up after me?" Not waiting for a response, she absently collected her dagger and stuffed most of the scrolls that seemed so important to Ciredor into her vest. Dimly, she knew she would need whatever information she could gather about him in the days to come. She strode to the door.

"Wait," Steorf shouted after her. "Let me accompany you home."

"Don't bother," she snarled, without turning around. "The only thing you'd need to protect me from now is my rage against you." With that, she left.

Once out in the street, Tazi leaned against a wall, raising her hand to her mouth. The tears were so close, as were a collage of memories: times she and Steorf had spent together, near captures, jaunts, and larks. All of it seemed far away now, as if they were someone else's memories. Everything she had held true was thrown back in her face. She was more alone than ever now.

Somehow she managed to stumble the short way down Sarn Street to Stormweather Towers without being seen by anyone. It would have been hard, if not impossible, to cxplain her appearance now, looking both like a noblewoman and thief. She moved automatically. When she entered her family home, the party finished long hours past, she dropped into the first chair she found in the darkened parlor on the main floor. It was while she was in this near comatose state that Cale, still cleaning up after the departed guests, discovered her. The sight she presented shocked him mightily.

"Thazienne," he blurted out, "what has happened to you?" The sight she presented—torn and bloody, her hair restored to its former length—shocked him into calling her by her first name.

Tazi turned glazed eyes up to his pale visage. "Oh,

Erevis," she choked out. His pale, gaunt face had never seemed so dear as it did now. But a seed of doubt had taken root, as well. She caught herself before she said anything, and after a moment, she asked, "Do you have a price, Cale? Aside from what my father pays you for your loyalty and your service, do you have a price?"

Cale was silent. Something had changed the normally laughing girl into something else tonight. He was unsure of how to proceed.

"Never mind, Cale," Thazienne continued wearily. "I know you are loyal to us. But I suppose, I must be careful. You could also be loyal to someone else one day."

She turned from the stunned Cale to carefully climb the grand staircase to her rooms above. Her whole body and soul ached tonight. She wouldn't have cared if anyone had discovered her as she was this evening, but no one did. It was too late in the evening for the rest of the family and servants. She arrived at her rooms unrevealed.

Once inside, she walked to her dressing table and sank onto the cushioned chair beside it. Some part of her mind knew she would have to clean herself up, rid herself of the blood and soil, cut the long tresses that hung in her way. But she was exhausted. She found herself staring at her face in the mirror and not recognizing the woman who stared back at her. The change was more than just the blood and hair; it ran deeper than that. She found herself remembering the boy and how she had ended his life.

Moving slowly, as if underwater, she reached out with her bloody hand to touch the face in the mirror. At what cost, she asked herself quietly, is this life of mine?

The woman in the mirror remained silent.

T. NIELSEN

THE SECOND SON

THIRTY DAYS

Dave Gross

Through the dark boughs of the Arch Wood, Talbot Uskevren fled for his life.

Black branches slashed at his face as brambles clutched at his cloak. A hideous force snagged it from behind, snapping his head back painfully. The clasp cut into his throat before tearing away with the cloak. Tal twisted and nearly fell, but his boots dug into the slippery ground, and again he ran. He dared not look back.

The creature was almost upon him. Tal heard its labored breath, felt its massive heat radiating through the darkness. He imagined the vice of its jaws on his neck, then thrust the thought from his mind and poured all his strength into his pumping legs.

He ran toward the only beacon he could see, a

bright patch of moonlit clouds at the edge of the wood. If he remembered correctly, the moonlight marked the edge of a clearing. He hoped some of the others had escaped and waited there with spears.

Just as his hopes rose, Tal smashed into a solid branch. The blow slammed him flat onto the ground, blasting the breath from his lungs. His pursuer flew overhead, narrowly missing Tal as it briefly eclipsed the moonlit clouds. The branch that clobbered Tal snapped crisply under the creature's bulk, and the thing crashed to the ground, blocking Tal's path.

Tal couldn't discern the thing's shape, but he felt its coiled energy as it tensed for the attack. Fear gripped his body, but Tal rolled away just as the creature pounced. Too slow, he cried out as claws raked his back.

Tal tried throwing himself to the right, but snarling jaws clamped his arm and shook. Tal flopped as helplessly as a rag doll in the teeth of a vicious dog. He hurtled through the darkness to smash painfully back on the cold winter ground.

As he scrabbled to his knees, another blow buffeted his head. Sparks burst in his skull, and he felt a cool wetness on his scalp. The image of his exposed brain flashed bricfly through his mind, and his mouth opened widc to scream, but then he was running again, saving the breath for flight.

Tal could no longer feel his legs, and his left arm hung uselessly at his side. He ran by force of will, by force of terror. He knew the thing was inches behind him, but it was death to glance backward. Not while he was still in the grip of the deadly Arch Wood, where the owlbears were clearly not hibernating after all.

Tymora, the goddess known as Lady Luck, must have heard one of his half-formed prayers, for Tal struck no more trees before exploding out of the choking forest.

He leaped into the clearing in a rapture of hope, only to

realize that Beshaba, the Maid of Misfortune, must also have heard one of those prayers, for it wasn't a clearing that lay beyond the darkness.

It was a cliff.

Tal's body turned as he plummeted, and the brief instant of his fall stretched into one long moment of perfect clarity. He saw the huge figure of his pursuer silhouetted and silvered against the moonlit clouds. It perched at the very edge of the precipice over which Tal had run, seeming to debate whether to leap down after him.

"Rusk!" called a harsh voice from behind the beast. Before Tal could see whether the thing would turn away or leap down after him, the dark ground rose up to smash him senseless.

A pixie kept beating his skull with a tiny club, so Tal reluctantly opened one gummy eye. He tried to swat the pest but managed only to poke himself in the eye. His arm was feeble, and his fingers felt thick and limp as cold sausages.

That thought made the pixie's accomplices jump with laughter from their lair in his stomach. Tal rolled to one side and vomited onto the floor.

Blinking, he peered into the thin yellow mess, expecting to see the soggy little nuisances wringing out their caps and cursing. Maybe he could squish one.

There were no pixies in his vomit, and Tal began to realize that the rhythmic pounding came from outside.

He swallowed painfully. The vile taste in his mouth was familiar. What nasty medicine had he been fed? How long had he been sleeping? With an effort, he rolled onto his back and blinked at his surroundings.

He was in an unfamiliar cottage. Of course, any mere

cottage should be unfamiliar to a scion of the Uskevren family, whose Stormweather Towers was among the finest mansions of Selgaunt. Instead of the warm scent of incense, Tal smelled the earthy odor of wood smoke. Rather than rich tapestries, he saw bunches of drying herbs and clusters of garlic, onions, and a confusing variety of other roots hung from the rafters. Amid it all was a squat stone fireplace, its flames dancing upon a trio of withering logs.

Cold fresh air and thin rays of morning light swept in from under the crude wooden door and through the simple shutters. Tal took a deep, cleansing breath. Even through the sickness, it felt grand to be alive, and better still that someone other than his father had rescued him from the disastrous hunting expedition. Recovering in a woodsman's home would give him time to put a better face on the fiasco.

Tal stopped kidding himself. This was far more serious than spending a night in jail for a tavern brawl. For all he knew, he was the only one of the hunting party to survive.

Tal tried sitting up, but his head spun. Only then did he begin to feel the stiff pains of his wounds. He cautiously lifted the woolen blanket and surveyed the damage.

His left arm was neatly bandaged and bound against his chest, which was swathed in more bandages. His scalp itched, and he felt more dressings on his head. Tal gently probed his skull but thankfully found no boneless wound. Whoever had found him must have been a skilled healer, perhaps even a priest. Tal wasn't particularly observant of the gods, but he made a mental note to donate next month's ale money to the shrine of Tymora back in Selgaunt. She had certainly showered him with enough good fortune to make up for the regrettable mistake of the cliff.

Tal tried rising once more. He managed to put his good elbow under him and swing his feet over the side of the bed. His back prickled and ached from lying too long on the straw mattress. He realized that the chopping sound had stopped, replaced by muted voices.

Tal rose from the bed but couldn't unfold his body completely. He shuffled hunchbacked to the window and peeked through the shutters. Snow glare made him blink at first, but then he saw a neat row of firewood and the flat-hewn stump that served as a chopping block. Upon the stump sat a figure so heavily bundled in shawls and coats that Tal knew it was a woman only by her voice, rough but strong as old hide. She was speaking to someone Tal couldn't see.

". . . gone already. Fetch some from Abell. Hurry, and you'll be back before night."

"What if it doesn't work?" replied another, younger woman's voice. Tal fumbled to unlatch the shutter for a better look, but the younger woman added, "We'll have to kill him, won't we?"

Tal left the shutters closed. He crouched down, just in case one of the women should glance his way.

"If we can keep him sleeping another tenday," said the old woman, "and if Dhauna Myritar approves, and if he submits himself to Her will . . ."

"And if the search party doesn't return," said the younger woman. "Even with the fresh snow, I don't think they believed . . ."

"Feena," interrupted the old woman. "None of these ifs matter unless you run your errand soon."

"Yes, mother," replied Feena contritely. Tal heard her reluctant footsteps crunching in the snow as she walked away.

"Don't dawdle," called Feena's mother. The sound of chopping resumed. "He's a big lad and getting his strength back."

A thrill of fear surged through Tal's veins. He had no idea why these women might kill him, but it had to have something to do with the attack on his hunting party. Did they command the owlbears that charged through the camp? If so, why hadn't they killed him already?

The obvious answer was ransom.

Thamalon Uskevren, Tal's father, had objected to his hunting trip for many reasons. Among them was the constant threat of kidnapping the child of one of Selgaunt's most wealthy and influential men. In the city, Tal was almost always in the public eye, and he always suspected that his father sent bodyguards to shadow him and his siblings. Tal tried not to care, as long as he never saw them and they never interfered with him.

Kidnapping didn't seem like the right answer, though. True, the hunting party consisted almost entirely of young scions of wealthy Selgauntan families, but the sounds Tal heard the night of his attack were not those of young men and women being captured. It was of their being torn to pieces.

Tal shivered. The fire was burning low. Soon, he knew, Feena's mother would return with more wood.

He considered climbing back into bed and pretending to sleep, waiting for a chance to escape, but he realized that this might be his only chance. He considered the position of the door in relation to the old woman. Yes, she would see him if he tried to slip outside.

His mind racing, Tal looked for his clothes. There was no sign of his shirt, but he found his boots stuffed under the bed. He tried putting them on with the use of just one hand and nearly overbalanced himself. Frantically, he searched for a blade among a jumble of cabinets, finally turning up a short paring knife.

He cut his arm free of his chest, then gingerly extended it, wincing at the anticipated pain. Surprisingly, the arm felt good, if a little numb from long restraint. He cut away the bandages. Underneath, the scars were pink and faint. Even if someone had used magical healing on him, Tal had expected scabs, at least.

How long had he been sleeping?

Tal used the knife to make a slit in the middle of two woolen blankets. He cut himself a twine belt to secure his makeshift tabard. Finally, he used both hands to put on his boots. Not only did his wounded arm not hurt, but he felt a surge of exhilarating power. He knew it was the thrill of fear, but it cleared his head and gave strength to his limbs.

He crept to the door and turned his head to listen. He heard no sound of chopping, just a muted grunt and a creak as the door was grasped from the other side. Tal felt a sudden bout of indecision. He wasn't sure whether he could bring himself to hit an old woman. On the other hand, he was quite sure he couldn't let her kill him. Without thinking, he snatched a burlap sack from the wall, wrapped it around his hand, cocked a fist, and waited for a target.

The door opened, and Tal saw a short lump of clothes clutching a huge bundle of wood. Tal's punch landed squarely in the center of the bundle. Logs scattered in all directions, and the old woman fell to the floor, stunned.

"Sorry!" blurted Tal. He felt a sharp pang of guilt as he saw the old woman's surprised face, round, matronly, and even kind, but he remembered that she might be the spell-caster who had healed him. One word from someone like that would be enough to defeat him.

"Sorry," he said again, and knocked her head against the floor. This time her eyes rolled straight up, then closed. Grimacing, Tal put his ear to her mouth. He heard a breath, much to his relief.

He lifted the woman in his arms and carried her to the bed. She was much lighter than he'd expected, or else he was stronger than he felt. He made her as comfortable as he could, then bound her securely to the bed with the remaining twine.

"Feena will be back before dark," he said to the old woman. He felt foolish consoling the unconscious form of his would-be murderer. Still, he touched her bruised cheek gently before he turned to go, wishing he knew exactly why she'd planned to keep him hidden.

Outside, Tal squinted at the white landscape. In the distance was what he took to be the edge of the Arch Wood. Judging from that and the position of the sun, he figured the direction of Selgaunt. It would be a long journey on foot, but at the end lay home and safety, and maybe some answers.

The first day was the worst. Tal was much hungrier than he realized upon escaping the cottage, and he didn't know the first thing about hunting without a spear and a dozen servants to flush out the quarry. He whooped with joy when he came across the Daerloon-Ordulin caravan trail just as his strength was beginning to flag.

The wind turned cruel after dark, and Tal squatted in the shelter of a snow bank to escape the night's howling. He couldn't sleep—he'd slept too long already. Instead, he listened for the knifing wind to subside, then he continued the trek eastward throughout the night.

A few hours after dawn, Tal's perseverance was rewarded by thc appcarancc of a tinker's cart. In other circumstances, Tal would gladly have traded an Uskevren promise for services rendered. Considering recent events, however, he omitted his family name when asking for a ride. Fortunately, the tinker was lonely enough to welcome an unarmed passenger. Four days later, he left a leaner, hungrier Tal just outside the nearest city, Ordulin, while he continued west on the road toward the port of Yhaunn.

Tymora continued to smile on Tal, perhaps enjoying the irony of a noble's son reduced to makeshift clothes and begging for food and rides. Just as he began to rue the decision to turn south, away from the scowling guards at the gate of Ordulin, he begged a ride from a southbound cart drover. The kindly fellow not only offered him a ride in his hay wagon but also gave him a warm meal each day. Tal resolved to repay the man a hundredfold.

Nine days after Tal's escape, the farmer's cart passed through the streets of the town of Overwater, the staging grounds for caravans arriving or leaving Selgaunt. In summer the place would be teeming with travelers and traders. Even in the dead of winter, it was spotted with tents, wagons, and pack animals snorting plumes in the cold air. Most of these were from nearby Ordulin, small merchant caravans keeping trade with the port city brisk. Their activity churned the dung and mud into a pungent morass that threatened to engulf them all on warmer days. To Tal's nose, the stink was welcome. He was coming home.

They emerged from Overwater to pass over the High Bridge. Aptly named, the seven-story structure was lined with shops, market stalls, taverns, and enough guard-houses to keep them all in line. At its far end, Tal saw the Klaroun Gate. Magnificent water horses were carved into its face, seeming to leap from the river to form the bridge of the central arch.

After long absence, Tal felt keenly aware of the city's pulse. He heard it in the chatter on the bridge, in the irregular clop of hooves on cobblestone. He smelled the human musk of the place, diminished but not hidden by Mulhorandi perfumes and Thayvian spices.

He peered everywhere for some sign of a friend, some-one he could surprise with his miraculous return. The urbane citizens of Selgaunt were giddy for fashion, and a thousand colors and styles of clothing were paraded through the steets each day. The farmer had driven nearly the entire length of the bridge before Tal spied a familiar face.

Tumbling out of a little alehouse, a sandy-haired man nearly collided with a squad of Scepters, the city guardsmen.

With drunken grace, the man wove neatly among the five Scepters, barely disturbing their dark green weather-cloaks. The guards looked formidable in their silver-chased black leather armor. One of them made a show of fanning the air before his face and wincing at the invisible cloud surrounding the drunk.

"Get yourself home, Chaney," warned the Scepter wearily. He'd obviously had this conversation with the man before. "Get off the streets, before you're run over by a night-carter."

Tal put a hand on the cart driver's arm. "Wait a moment," he said.

Duly chastened, Chaney swirled his own red cloak around one arm and made an elaborate, unsteady bow. His tousled hair fell over his eyes as he slurred, "I thank you, and I shall. Soon as I purchase a jug in which to drown . . ." Chaney's eyes lit upon Tal, and he stared in astonishment.

The Scepters glanced back at Tal, then turned back to Chaney, frowning their disapproval. One took Chaney by the arm. "Let's find you a nice pallet down—"

"Wait," called Tal, climbing down from the cart. The Scepters looked at him dubiously, while Chaney continued to stare in disbelief. "I'll make sure he gets home safely."

The Scepter holding Chaney's arm looked Tal up and down in obvious disapproval of his makeshift attire. One of his companions nudged the Scepter impatiently, and he relented.

Chaney continued to stare at Tal even after the scepters walked away. Tal grinned back at him. "Is it Tal?" Chaney asked, peering dubiously up at Tal's new beard. It had grown in thick, black, and curly.

"More or less."

"They didn't get you!" slurred Chaney. He reached carefully to touch Tal's rude imitation of a tabard, then clutched it to keep his balance. "They just stole your clothes."

Chaney seemed tiny beside his big friend. Where Tal

was broad, Chaney was slight and narrow. His intelligent eyes sparkled even through the fog of ale, and his fine nose and pointed chin gave him a look of perpetual mischief. Softening his impish appearance were his smooth cheeks, preserving an illusion of youth that made him seem the younger of the two, though he was in fact a year older at twenty.

"How much money do you have with you?" asked Tal.

Chaney fumbled for his purse before Tal took it from him. Peering inside, he frowned at the contents before tossing the entire thing to the farmer.

"If you stay at the Outlook tonight," he said, "I'll have something more sent over to you."

"That's all my money!" complained Chaney, reaching after it long after the farmer had caught it. The farmer's bushy eyebrows rose in surprise at the heft of the purse.

"This is more than enough for what I done," said the farmer.

"All the same," said Tal. He had it in mind to reward the kind farmer with more money than the man had seen in a decade, and even that wouldn't put a dent in Tal's monthly stipend.

"I won't say no," conceded the farmer with a friendly nod. He snapped the reins and continued across the bridge.

Tal got an arm under Chaney's shoulders and turned him back toward the Klaroun Gate. "Let's get you wrung out."

Chaney needed sleep before he could sober up, so Tal delivered him into the care of a frowning housekeeper in Chaney's flat. Soon after, Tal stood before his tallhouse.

It was a narrow building of equal parts gray stone and brown vines, which in spring would smother the building in vibrant green. It stood amid five similar buildings, each divided from its neighbors by a narrow alley.

Tal ascended the short flight of steps and pounded cheerfully on the door. He couldn't wait to see the expression on Eckart's face when the fastidious valet saw Tal wearing a pair of old blankets and a twine belt.

After a few moments, Tal banged on the door again, to no avail. Of course, realized Tal, Eckart must be back at Stormweather Towers. He slipped around to the side alley, where stairs descended to the side entrance. Tal had hidden a key behind a loose stone there, despite Eckart's protests about burglars. He was pleased to see that it was still there.

As he turned to open the side door, Tal heard a sudden hiss. He looked up to see the neighbor's fat orange tabby perched on the ledge above. It was one of a dozen cats who haunted this street, and Tal often saw it near the steps, where Eckart often placed leftovers or a saucer of milk in the morning.

"Well again, kitty," said Tal. He reached up to let the little beast smell him, but the cat spat furiously and vanished.

Tal sniffed at himself and frowned at the sour odor. "Can't blame you," he muttered. "I do need a bath."

Inside, Tal was surprised to find the wine cellar illuminated by two bright lamps. More alarming was the sight of the empty wine racks and a stack of crates. One was still open and overflowing with packing straw.

"Don't tell me they've sold the house," muttered Tal wearily. He knew he'd been missing for a long time, but surely his family wouldn't have given up hope already. He reached into the open box and removed a bottle of Thamalon's Own, the precious pear wine his father gave him for his birthday earlier in the year.

"I must warn you," called a prim and tremulous voice from the stairs, "that I am armed and have no compunctions about shooting a burglar."

Tal put away his smile before turning around and adopting his father's own voice. "Put that toy away, and tell me where in the nine hells you've taken the rest of my wine!"

"Master Talbot!" squeaked Eckart, lowering his hand crossbow so quickly that he shot a bolt into the stairs. Glancing down, he paled at the bolt quivering neatly between his feet. Looking back at Tal, he whitened even more. "Bu-Bu-but we thought you were—"

"Still waiting for an answer about my wine!" roared Tal. He struggled to keep a straight face. He rarely used his father's voice to fluster Eckart, but it worked every time. Chaney insisted it was because Eckart received exactly such rebukes each time he reported on Thamalon Uskevren's wastrel son.

"It's at Stormweather, sir, along with the rest of your belongings." Eckart gulped as he saw Tal's brow's furrow in another perfect imitation of the elder Uskevren. "Lord Uskevren thought it best to remove everything to your rooms at home."

Eckart's earlier words finally sank in, and Tal said quietly in his own voice, "Because he thought I was dead."

"Oh, no, sir," replied Eckart in a tone of genuine distress. "Your father—all of us—never gave up hope. Your father merely felt that, upon your return, you'd prefer the safety of—"

"You mean the *confinement,*" interrupted Tal, now genuinely angry. His sudden flare of temper surprised him, for as much as he resented his parents' continued coddling, he also appreciated their concern—especially after his recent ordeal.

Tal noticed Eckart's pale lips working soundlessly, looking for all the world like the gasping of a fish out of water. "It's all right, Eckart," said Tal more gently. "I realize I've been missing for an awfully long time."

Eckart swallowed his distress as best he could, but Tal realized he had to make sure the servant wouldn't have time to report his return before he himself could go to Stormweather.

"Just see that everything's back in order here by tomorrow morning," said Tal with an impish gleam in his eye.

"Tomorrow!" sputtered Eckart. "But—"

"But first, draw me a hot bath. Is the tub still here?"

"Yes, but—"

"And summon a barber." He scratched under his chin. "I don't like this beard."

"Yes, but—"

"And fetch me some clean clothes—not from Stormweather, mind you. Buy new ones."

"Yes, but—"

"And have you any funds on hand?"

"Yes, but—"

"Good. Once you've drawn the bath, summoned the barber, and fetched me some clothes, take one hundred fivestars to the Outlook Inn, and give them to a farmer named Mott."

"A farmer! But sir—"

"Thank you, Eckart. That will be all."

With a look of genuine pain, Eckart nodded his assent. Tal felt briefly guilty for harrying him so.

"Oh, and Eckart?"

"Yes, Master Talbot?"

"It's good to see you again."

Before approaching Stormweather Towers, Tal stopped to observe his reflection in the frozen waters of a public fountain.

His gray eyes glittered beneath his black hair, now trimmed neatly above his short collar. Eckart had found him some warm woolen hose whose dove gray hue matched the shirtsleeves that showed through the slashes in his blue doublet. The ensemble was completed by Tal's favorite longboots, into which he'd tucked a fine but simple dagger at the right hip. It was his concession to going armed out of doors. As much as he enjoyed sword practice, he loathed the inevitable confrontations his size attracted from the city's bravos. Sometimes, it was more trouble being a big man than a small one.

Straightening his warm weathercloak, Tal left the fountain and came to Stormweather Towers.

The mansion was one of the newest in Selgaunt, but at first glance it looked like the accumulated accidents of a dozen different architects. The house itself was a great stone collection of towers and turrets, each with its own character. It took a thorough observation to realize that the seemingly random collection of structures formed a unified if complex whole.

Stables and a guardhouse formed the shorter branch of the L-shaped border around the open courtyard. The quadrangle was completed by a cunning array of intimate gardens bordered with fruit trees.

The only people standing outside in the cold afternoon wind were a quartet of family guards. Their leader tipped Tal a wink that told him his arrival was expected. With a sigh, Tal smiled his thanks for the warning and went to the door. It opened at his approach, and there stood Erevis Cale, the family butler.

"How good to have you returned home, Master Talbot," said the gaunt man. His head and face were immaculately shaved, but his clothes hung loosely on his angular frame. Somehow Cale always seemed taller than Tal, though he was a few inches shorter.

"You're not surprised to see me, are you, Cale?" Tal smiled to take the edge off his disappointment. He liked the butler, who had an uncanny knack of knowing what was about to happen before it did. Tal had never decided whether the talent was supernatural or merely criminal.

Cale smiled faintly, a rare expression on those thin lips, and one that might seem chilling to someone who didn't know him better. Sometimes Tal's elder sister teasingly called the man "Mister Pale," though Tal would never dare do so. He had no doubt that Cale would hear of it, and Tal shrunk at the thought of the man's disapproval.

"I don't know how you do it," said Tal, shaking his head. "Still no chance of your replacing Eckart?"

Cale's smile nearly turned warm. "I suspect Lord Thamalon might forbid it, young sir."

"Yes," agreed Tal. "I suspect he might, too."

"Your father awaits you in the library, Master Talbot."

"Thanks, Cale," said Tal, stepping into the foyer. "Does everyone . . . ?"

Tal's question was smothered as a veritable comet of older sister crashed into him. All he saw before the powerful arms clamped around his neck was a flash of scarlet fabric and ink-black hair.

"Tazi!" he gasped before the last of his breath was cut off.

"You great buffoon! You should have come here as soon as you returned to the city. Don't you know how worried we were?"

Tal hugged her back, just hard enough to make her ease up on his collapsing lungs. She was tiny compared to him, but she was fierce and strong. "You'd feel differently if you'd had a whiff of me when I arrived."

Thazienne, more often called Tazi, pushed herself back and held Tal at arm's length. For a moment, Tal thought he saw the hint of tears glimmering in her eyes, but she wouldn't let them come. "They looked everywhere, and there was no sign of you."

"I know," said Tal. "I came back as soon as I could." He made a point of looking over his shoulder as if to examine his back.

"What are you doing?" asked Tazi.

"Just making sure you haven't pinned a tail to me."

They laughed as Cale looked on with his inscrutable neutrality. As well as he knew the Uskevren children, he wasn't present for the many childhood pranks Tazi had played on Tal. Once she had talked him into drinking a potion that turned him green for most of a tenday. Loyal to the end, Tal took the blame—and the punishment—when their mother had to endure the embarrassment of Tal's appearance at the appropriately timed Greengrass Festival.

That was the least of Tazi's pranks. The one that most threatened their youthful alliance came when Tazi embroidered bunnies and lambs on all of Tal's underclothes just before he went on a swimming trip with the young sons of a half-dozen other families. On the bright side, Tal learned a lot about fistfighting, and he came back the most formidable brawler of his cohorts that summer. Moreover, he made fast friends with Chaney Foxmantle, who until then had borne the brunt of the other boys' torments.

"It's just like you to keep us all waiting," called another familiar voice from the inner hall. Tal looked up to see his elder brother standing in the doorway.

Thamalon Uskevren the Second was better known as Tamlin. Even at six year's Tal's senior, he was much smaller than his younger brother, but he carried himself as if he were much greater in every way. He leaned casually against the doorjamb, idly glancing at his fingernails as if to observe his reflection there. His fine clothing made Tal's new attire seem as mangy as his recent makeshift clothes. "I'm glad you're not dead, little brother."

Tazi scowled at Tamlin, perhaps expecting him to be more gracious at their younger sibling's miraculous return. If he had been the least bit friendly, however, Tal would have suspected an imposter. "I'm glad you're not dead, too," he said.

"Ah, we have something in common at last," observed Tamlin. He smiled winningly, and once again Tal understood what Tamlin's friends saw in him. He could be a charming fellow, as long as he wasn't your brother.

Before Tal could frame a suitable reply, a hulking form

emerged from behind Tamlin. It was Vox, Tamlin's mute bodyguard. He loomed above Tamlin like a mountain shadow, black hair spilling all over his square head until it collected in a single barbaric braid over his left shoulder. The man's size and blunt features suggested ogre blood, and Tal secretly despised him.

When the Uskevren children were much younger, Tamlin and Vox threw the admittedly annoying Tazi from a window. Torn between running to his sister's aid and beating his brother senseless, Tal had gone to Tazi rather than risk facing the monstrous Vox. His anger burned brighter when he discovered they had broken Tazi's arm. Tamlin insisted that the children agree to a lie to avoid their parents' punishment. Tazi was quick to forgive, but ever since that day, Tal had found it impossible to trust Tamlin, and he had forever after hated the brute who had kept him from dealing a deserved punishment to his arrogant older brother.

"I should visit Mother before going up to face Thamalon," said Tal.

"She's in her parlor," said Tazi. "We just returned from the opera when we heard you were back." She squeezed Tal's arm and grimaced for him. She knew how little Tal enjoyed confronting Thamalon after a disaster. He smiled his thanks back at her.

"We'll catch up later," he promised. He walked toward the west hall, pointedly avoiding Tamlin and Vox. The gesture wasn't lost on Tamlin, on whose face Tal glimpsed a smile just before he left.

Shamur Uskevren was in her parlor. The room reflected her personality, for it was feminine without seeming dainty, expensive but not garish. Its deep purple draperies were complemented by a half dozen paintings, from a serene landscape to a glorious montage of the events of the Time of Troubles, when gods walked Faerûn, made war with each other, and died.

Tal worried that his mother would turn this latest proof

of his irresponsibility into another lecture on the many wrong streets his life was taking. Why consort with those theater scoundrels, she might ask, when the opera was a respectable venue? Why not explore sculpting or painting or composing? At least she wouldn't insist that he follow in his father's footsteps and look after the family business. That fate was reserved for Tamlin or, more likely, for Tazi once Tamlin proved himself inept.

When he arrived in her parlor, however, Tal found his mother less than argumentative.

Shamur remained seated on an elegant fainting couch as Tal entered the room, greeting him with the poised smiled reserved for honored guests. It pierced him to the heart, for there was no greater sign of her displeasure.

"Mother," he began. "I'm sorry for all the worr—"

"Come here, Talbot," she said.

Tal knelt beside her couch. She looked into his face for a long moment, then pulled his head onto her shoulder and held it there.

"Mother," he began.

"Hush," she said, and he obeyed. She held him there for a quarter of an hour, without saying another word. At last she stroked his hair a few times, lifted his head up to look into his face, and said, "Now go to your father."

As Tal walked slowly down the hall to his father's study, he heard the whisper of slippers and a gentle tinkling of silver bells. A servant had withdrawn to a side passage ahead of him, no doubt to avoid the conflict between Thamalon and his wayward son.

As he reached the narrow hallway, however, Tal saw that the servant stood waiting for him, hands folded demurely beneath her breasts. Her gaze was locked deferentially on the carpet.

She wore the knee-length white dress of the Uskevren domestic staff, the family colors shown in the slashes of her sleeves and a tight gold vest. From a turban of the same gold dangled the bells he had heard, a device to warn family members of a servant's intrusion.

"Master Talbot," she said, looking up at him. Her pale hazel eyes looked yellow in the steady golden light of the corridor's enchanted sconces.

Tal summoned his best look of exaggerated disappointment, then looked pointedly up and down the empty hallway. "Where is the audience that makes me 'Master Talbot'?" he asked. "Have you forgotten our promise?"

Four years his senior, Larajin had been with the Uskevren for as long as Tal could remember. As children, they were frequent playmates. One summer night, after escaping the flustered adult servants at an Uskevren family picnic, they tramped about the nearby fields until the fireflies rose from the ground. Exhausted, they lay upon the heather and gazed at the stars. After a long silence, Larajin told Tal this was their last night together. Upon returning to Stormweather Towers, she must assume the respectful demeanor of the other servants. She was no longer a child.

"But we're friends," protested the six-year-old Tal. "That isn't fair."

"I'll always be your friend, in here," replied Larajin, placing the tip of a finger over her heart. "But now I must call you 'Master Talbot' and answer only when you speak to me."

"That's stupid," said Tal crossly. He furrowed his brow and considered the options.

"If I don't, I'll be punished," she said reasonably.

"Not if nobody else hears you," argued Tal. "When we're alone, you can call me Tal, and we can be friends, and nobody will know."

Larajin looked ready to protest, but then she agreed. "We'll be secret friends, then."

Tal reached for her hand in the secret pirate handgrip. It was secret because pirates was the one game that would win him a thrashing if he were discovered. Father hated pirates.

"Promise," said Tal. "We'll be friends forever, even if it has to be a secret."

"Promise," agreed Larajin, returning the secret sign, her hand gripping Tal's wrist, then making a fist inside his own hand, already almost as big as her own. "Forever."

Thirteen years later, Tal remembered that promise.

"I haven't forgotten," she replied, "but we aren't children anymore." A beat later she added, "Tal."

"No," agreed Tal, "but a promise is a promise." He gently covered her shoulders with his massive hands, intending to embrace her as he did his sister. Before he could, however, he felt a most unbrotherly stirring and dared not draw her close.

Larajin must have seen something on his face, for she took his hands from her shoulders. "Lord Thamalon the elder awaits you," she reminded him. Her tone was formal, but she took the sting away with a last, warm squeeze of Tal's hands.

Tal smiled in agreement, took a deep breath, and turned to enter the library.

The Uskevren family library was not by any means the most comprehensive in Selgaunt, but what it lacked in volume it made up in comfort and beauty.

Besides the inevitable shelves of scrolls and books, the library contained a fantastic collection of artwork. What separated it from the many other collections in the city was that each piece was distinctly elven.

Most citizens of Selgaunt would rather rub shoulders with Red Wizards or Tuigan barbarians than consort with the elves of the great forest north of Sembia. Centuries of rivalry and conflict had burned deep resentment into the hearts of Sembians, so much so that their scorn was not limited to the elves of the kingdom of Cormanthor. Very few elves of any sort lived in Sembia, and any association with their kind was considered disgraceful.

While Thamalon Uskevren did not share the bigotry of his countrymen, he was wise enough to confine his love for things elven to the privacy of his library. Tal was not surprised to find him there, surrounded by the fabulous masks of the green elves, the wondrous dreamcatchers of the gold elves, and the excruciatingly beautiful crystal of the moon elves.

Amid all these beauties, Thamalon Uskevren sat beside a chess table. Upon it were arrayed exquisite figures of ivory and mahogany, no doubt carved by an elven artisan.

Tal could tell by his father's expression that there would be no small talk.

"Start from the beginning," said Thamalon Uskevren. The white-haired patriarch had already made his standard opening, pawn to queen's four. He frowned intently at the ivory pieces before him, his black brows forming a dark chevron above his deep green eyes.

Tal took the seat behind the mahogany pieces and opened with his knight, a move that invariably irked the elder Uskevren, who considered it reckless. "After some debate, we decided that the owlbears would be hibernating."

Thamalon moved to protect his pawn without hesitation. Tal knew at once that this would be a match of lightning chess, which he preferred. He soon became bored during a longer, more considered match. He advanced his other knight, a dragon rampant. "We decided to hunt boar. There's little for them to eat in winter, so they root for yams."

Thamalon advanced a pawn, threatening Tal's knight. Still, he didn't speak.

"Right after a kill, you gut the boar and make sausages. They're filled with sweet yams, you see, and you roast them on an open flame." Tal advanced his knight again, looking at his father's face for a reaction. "You slice them while they're still steaming hot."

At last the elder Uskevren's patience cracked. "Unless you've been missing for nigh on a month because of food poisoning, I fail to see the point." He pressed the attack against Tal's first knight with another pawn.

"We killed a boar on the first day," said Tal. He retreated the knight. "It was when I left the camp to relieve myself of some of the your Usk Fine Old that we were attacked."

"So, you were drunk," said Thamalon. He followed the retreat relentlessly, intent on showing Tal the folly of his twin knights' attack, as he had done so often.

"I wasn't drunk," said Tal with a hint of indignation. His knight safe at last, he advanced his own pawn. "Being away from camp probably saved my life. I heard shouting, not all of it from the other hunters. By then it was dark, and men were screaming. I ran back to the campfire. Before I could reach it, something began chasing me."

"An owlbear?" Thamalon freed his king's bishop by advancing another pawn.

"I think so." Tal opened the outer line of his own king's bishop.

"Did you see an owlbear?" persisted Thamalon.

"No, I didn't see it. Maybe it was something else. Whatever it was, I didn't have a spear, so I ran." Tal described his terrified flight through the Arch Wood in unadorned terms, pausing only briefly to respond to the ever-changing board. "Eventually, I escaped."

"And how was that?" asked Thamalon Uskevren.

"By cleverly throwing myself over a cliff," said Tal dryly.

At last the old man's eyes met Tal's, suspecting a jest.

"Honestly," said Tal. "I couldn't see where I was going, but it probably saved my life."

Thamalon pressed an attack on Tal's king's flank, threatening his second knight with pawns while advancing his own king's knight, an ivory unicorn. "Tell me the rest."

The rest of the story unfolded much like the game of chess, quickly and in short bursts. Tal told the story, and Thamalon interjected a question here and there. The elder Uskevren explained that Chaney and the other survivors had already given their accounts to the city guard, and Thamalon had interviewed them afterward, learning little more.

"I called upon High Loremaster Yannathar," explained Thamalon. "His acolytes cast divinations at once. Nothing."

"I knew that old woman was a wizard," said Tal, "or maybe a priest. She must have hidden me from magic."

"We'll find her," asserted Thamalon. "Then we'll have the truth of it."

"She mentioned a name—Dhauna Myritar."

"Hmm." Thamalon tapped his chin with a forefinger as he considered the name, momentarily distracted from the game. "That has a certain familiar echo." Snapping out of his reverie, he resumed his attack on Tal's chess pieces. "Continue."

Tal resumed his tale, eventually coming to the point when he ordered Eckart to return his belongings to the tallhouse.

"By no means!" snapped Thamalon. "You're to stay in Stormweather until this business is sorted out."

"Check," said Talbot.

"What?" Thamalon observed the board. He had captured one of his son's knights and two of his pawns at the cost of only three of his own pawns. What he hadn't realized was how badly he had exposed his king's flank in the process. Fortunately for him, it was not a fatal check, and he moved quickly to block it with a protected bishop.

"I'll be staying in the tallhouse," said Tal. "I didn't come home rescued by your men—but thanks for sending them."

Thamalon's jaw tightened, but he controlled his voice as he replied, "Son, it's foolishness to leave yourself exposed after such an obvious attempt."

"Who knows that it was aimed at me? There were ten other sons of equally wealthy families—"

"Not quite as wealthy," interjected Thamalon. "And not my sons."

"Father," said Tal evenly. "I'm not moving back into Stormweather."

"I can stop paying your rent," warned Thamalon.

"Yes, and you can cut off my stipend, too. I'll move in with Chaney and start taking my shares at the theater."

"You'll do no such thing!" roared Thamalon. Tal had to suppress a smile at the thought that he'd been acting his father's part just a few hours earlier. Had he looked so furious to Eckart? "That wastrel is the worst possible influence—"

"Check," said Tal, meeting his father's angry gaze. He wasn't even sure it was true until Thamalon looked down at the board and scowled.

"Speaking of Chaney," said Tal, trying not to sound curt and failing, "he's probably looking for me right now. It's good to see you again. Thanks for looking for me. I'll visit soon." He stood before he could lose his courage, but he faltered as he reached for the door and heard his father's voice.

"Tal," said Thamalon. He almost never contracted Tal's name. "I want only the best for you, my boy. I just wish you could be—"

"More like you," said Tal with a rueful smile, finishing the unspoken refrain of their relationship. He opened the door and stepped through.

"You don't have to be exactly like me," said Thamalon

as the door closed. "Just be *something*. Just *do* something. Make something of *yourself*."

"I will, one day," promised Tal from the other side of the door. "You'll see."

Chaney was sleeping so soundly at his own flat that Tal left him alone. He knew Eckart would still be busily supervising the return of the household furnishings rather than risk Tal's wrath. While the servant was no Erevis Cale, Tal noted with amusement and a little guilt that he'd put the fear of Thamalon the Elder into the man. If he could imitate the bearing as well as the voice, perhaps he could persuade Mistress Quickly to cast him as something other than a soldier in her next production.

Thoughts of the theater reminded Tal that the troupe probably had not yet heard of his return. Today's last show had begun over an hour earlier, but there was still time to visit before the play's end.

Outside, Tal looked up and down the street for his father's guards. He smiled as he spotted the corner of a blue cloak whipping back into a nearby alley. Sometimes he'd play a game with his father's paid men, darting into an alley or using the back door of a tavern to slip away from them. Considering his recent ordeal, he didn't mind a few guards tonight.

Tal cupped a hand beside his mouth and cried, "I'm going to the theater!" One of the family guards poked his head back around the corner. He touched the brim of his helm with an expression composed of equal parts guilt and gratitude. Tal returned the courtesy by not looking back over his shoulder at each corner.

The Wide Realms was a simple open-sky theater in the round, with a few permanent enchantments in place to keep out the rain and cold. Mistress Quickly had invested a fortune in constructing the building with such conveniences, so none of the troupe complained of her generous shares in each production. She had even paid to lift an expensive enchantment she'd commissioned to mute the audience. Rather than improve the actors' concentration, it had made them constantly nervous that they weren't evoking sufficient laughter, sobs, or—most importantly—applause.

Tal knew by the hour that tonight's show was nearly over, so he went directly to the stage entrance. He had to repeat the company rap three times before the door opened, seemingly by itself. Beyond, Tal saw the familiar chaos of rigging and storage.

"Tal!" cried a high, whispery voice at his feet. A tiny green creature with bright feline eyes clambered up the front of his clothes and clutched affectionately at his hair.

"Lommy!" exclaimed Tal. When the little tasloi wasn't capering about on stage as a clown, he was usually up in the rafters, operating the mechanicals with his brother, Otter. Tal gave the minuscule creature a gentle hug before trying to peel him off. Lommy refused to budge, pressing his long, flat forehead against Tal's cheek. Tal had never seen the intimate gesture extended to anyone but Otter or Mistress Quickly, the tasloi's adoptive mother.

If Tal had stretched Lommy straight out, the tasloi would measure little more than two feet tall. He looked even smaller when loping across the floor or swinging through the rigging, his fine black hair forming a wake behind him. More often than not, both Lommy and Otter were invisible to the casual observer, lurking in the upper shadows.

"Lommy is *very* happy," whispered the tasloi. "Lommy was afraid Tal died, but Otter said Tal would come back."

"Tal is happy Otter was right," grinned Tal. The tasloi indifference to pronouns was infections among the actors, and the creatures often bore the curses of actors who flubbed their lines after chatting with one of them. Tal was half certain the idiosyncrasy was not a cultural trait but one cultivated by Mistress Quickly for exotic effect.

"Shh!" warned an actor standing near one of the stage entrances. Then the young woman recognized Tal and threw him a friendly wave. With Lommy perched happily on his shoulder, Tal joined her at the curtain, where they watched the final scenes of the play.

Mallion Dray had taken the part Tal would have had if he hadn't disappeared. As the hotheaded son of an unlawful king, he was about to meet his doom at the hands of the rightful prince, played by Sivana Alasper, a woman of such androgynous beauty that she often took the role of young men. Such gender trading was a hallmark of Mistress Quickly's troupe, and she often composed comedies based on the old trick.

As the hero, Sivana stood before the company's prized prop, an enspelled long sword with the conveniently theatrical powers of producing light, flame, or a variety of thrilling sounds upon command. As Tal watched, Sivana grasped the weapon and spoke a line in which the command syllables were carefully hidden. The weapon blazed with blue light, proving the young hero's claim to the throne.

Tal had choreographed the fight scene months ago, eagerly anticipating the chance to play the dark prince. He tried not to feel jealous as Mallion leaped to the attack with the aid of a springboard hidden behind a small pile of artificial stones. The slender actor flew gracefully over the shoulder of his opponent, landing behind her to strike the first blow.

The fight varied from Tal's original design here and there, usually to take advantage of Mallion's lighter build. Tal noticed with some chagrin that the death scene had changed to include one of the stage's four hidden trapdoors. He felt that Quickly overused the device, but he had to admit that it pleased the crowd to see the vanquished pretender pulled down into the ninth hell as the triumphant prince dealt him the killing blow.

As the applause died and the actors left the stage, Tal found himself the center of attention. The resources of House Uskevren might have detected his arrival as soon as he set foot in the city, but everyone at the Wide Realms was astonished to see him in the flesh. Soon he was dizzy from the hugs, kisses, and occasional friendly gropes.

"Don't think this means you get the part back," warned Mallion.

"How could I top that performance?" said Tal. "But next time it's my turn to use the sword."

"You'll have to take it from me, first," declared Sivana, sketching a flourish with the blade before leaping up to grab the bars of a big steel cage hanging behind the stage. The troupe still hadn't found a use for the gigantic prop, which Mistress Quickly had bought for a production of "The Royal Prisoner" the previous spring.

Tal grinned at the challenge and started toward her, but before he'd taken a second step, powerful arms closed around his waist and lifted him off the floor.

"My boy!" cried a husky voice. Mistress Quickly set him down just long enough to kiss him full on the mouth. As usual, her breath smelled of garlic and pipeweed.

Quickly was a big woman, almost six feet tall and wound tight with muscle. She was the only one in the troupe who could have lifted Tal off the floor, and when she held him at arm's length to look him over, he doubted he could escape her powerful grip.

"You look little worse for the wear," she said appraisingly. "Tasty as always," she added with a leer, revealing a prominent gap between her front teeth. Her features were broad and almost comical, even without the garish makeup she wore on and off the stage. No one dared guess at her age, though to account the thousands of stories she told of her five late husbands, she might have been a hundred.

"Let's hear the whole story," boomed Quickly, "and not

in any tavern full of tilting ears. Who'll be a dear and fetch us a keg?"

The long journey and the many reunions since his return finally caught up with Tal shortly after dark. With some difficulty, he extricated himself from his friends with a promise to return soon.

His tallhouse wasn't far from the theater, so he walked. He made it all the way home before realizing that he'd forgotten to call out to his father's guards. Mindful of the irony, he hoped he hadn't lost them by accident.

He'd forgotten to ask Eckart for another key to the front door, so Tal went to the cellar entrance again. As he descended the stairs, his boot struck something, causing a ceramic clatter. He bent down to pick it up. A bowl from the kitchen.

With a startling scream, a furious animal threw itself from a ledge at Tal's face. Razor claws tore his skin before the creature pushed away and dropped to the ground. Tal turned to see the orange tabby retreating across the street, hissing and yowling as it was chased out of its territory.

"Damn it!" hissed Tal. He touched his cheek and felt the wetness there. His affection for the local cats was diminishing by the day.

"Take that, you scoundrel!" cried Tal. His sword was a blur against a weakening barrier of retreating parries. Between each sharp rap of the blades, he could hear his opponent's labored breathing. Tal hadn't yet broken a sweat, despite a night full of troubling dreams. "Had enough?" he called.

"Nev—!" puffed Tal's adversary. "Never!" He withdrew

with haste, crossing back quickly without lowering his guard.

"Have at you, then!" cried Tal. Grasping his blade in two hands, he unleashed a punishing series of head and neck attacks. They lacked finesse, but his superior strength beat his opponent's weapon down. When he saw that he'd forced the man into too short a guard, Tal feinted a slash to the left. As expected, his opponent overextended his parry.

Instead of striking the unguarded right, Tal whirled low and threw a sweeping reverse kick at the man's legs. His quick-thinking opponent turned his parry into a straight thrust at Tal's hip. A quicker swordsman might have succeeded. This one fell to the wooden floor with a resounding thud. Before he could move, Tal's blade was at his throat.

"I yield!" cried the fallen man. He dropped his sword to clatter loudly on the floor.

"You should have jumped," offered Tal. He removed his practice helmet single-handed and set it on the floor. "That would have looked great."

"Gods know I've suffered enough humiliation at your hands. You are truly a master swordsman."

Tal offered Chaney his free hand and lifted him from the floor. "I'm a sober swordsman, at least," replied Tal, pulling the other man to his feet. "You'll beat me after you've had a few more days to dry out."

"May the gods forbid," said Chaney. Even among the notoriously hedonistic Foxmantle family, he was known for his excesses. Even on the rare occasions when he was momentarily sober, Chaney couldn't best Tal at sword play. In fact, Chaney was without rival the worst of Master Ferrick's thirty-two students.

Tal used these matches with his friend to devise maneuvers for the fighting scenes at the theater. More often than not, that meant a sharp rap or two from Chaney's wooden practice sword as Tal tried flashy but unsound attacks.

"I'll need a bottle or two just to dull the pain from this hangover," added Chaney, struggling to remove his padded helmet. "I hope—"

The sound of loud, slow clapping interrupted their conversation. Chaney and Tal looked up to see that two other men had entered Master Ferrick's practice hall.

One of them strode forward as he continued his mock applause. He was narrow-hipped and broad-shouldered, with long blond hair held up in ivory combs that matched the piping on his burgundy doublet. He wore an elegantly curled mustache above a thin red slash of a mouth. Alale Soargyl fancied himself the most accomplished swordsman of Master Ferrick's school.

"Bravo," said Alale. "I shall endeavor to recall that inspired maneuver. It will undoubtedly prove useful when next I am faced with a blindly drunken sailor."

"I doubt he's ever *facing* the drunken sailors he meets," observed Chaney in a stage whisper. Tal couldn't quite hide his smile.

"If your sycophant wishes a lesson in manners or sword play, Master Uskevren," sniffed Alale, "it may address me directly."

Tal felt the hairs on his neck prickle. It wasn't the first time Chaney had been insulted in this fashion, but it still rankled. Ever since they were childhood friends, Chaney was perceived by his peers as little more than Tal's henchman. Chaney derived from a particularly disreputable and very nearly destitute branch of the Foxmantle tree. There was no stopping gossip that he courted Tal's friendship to improve his own standing.

Never one to ignore a barb, Chaney opened his mouth to retort, but Tal interrupted. "I could stand a lesson."

Alale's mustache twitched. Tal couldn't tell whether the man was pleased or irritated. Tal was a much better fighter than Chaney, and he was big enough not to fear the rumors that Alale paid longshoremen to thrash those who bested him at practice.

"Very well," replied Alale after a long pause. "One must assume responsibility for one's pets."

"To three?" asked Tal.

"To three, then." With a last sneer at Chaney, Alale plucked off his gloves before returning to fetch his gear. He would need a few moments to warm up.

Tal smiled inwardly. He considered Alale a poor swordsman and expected to win. He was more concerned about Chaney. Tal hoped he hadn't hurt his feelings by interceding. He turned to see his friend's expression, but Chaney was still glaring at Alale as the man unlaced his doublet.

Tal glanced at the other man who had entered with Alale. It was Radu Malveen, second son of one of the lesser merchant families in Selgaunt. Radu was nearly Tal's height, and his hair was just as black. There the resemblance ended, for while Tal was massive, Radu was whipcord thin. His black eyes were cool as a snake's, and Tal knew from experience that the man was serpent quick. Tal was certain that Radu was the finest swordsman of the school.

Radu returned Tal's gaze but said nothing. He had finished lacing his padded tunic and hooked the back of his ankle over the stretching bar. He bent as gracefully as a swan, touching his high forehead to his shin.

"Be careful," said Chaney. "If you beat him too badly, you'll have to watch your back for a month."

"That's your job," replied Tal. "Which means showing some mercy to the local vineyards for a while."

"Curses!" spat Chaney. He shot Tal a genuinely grateful smile. "But it's the least I can do for my faithful bodyguard."

"The very least," agreed Tal.

Alale announced his readiness with an imperious sniff. He stood upon the middle circle of the central practice ring. Half the diameter of the red outer boundary and twice that of the green inner circle, the black line represented balance and equal opposition.

Tal took his place opposite Alale and met his opponent's eyes, as Master Ferrick always insisted. They donned their wicker helmets. Without another word, the two swordsmen saluted, Alale affecting a delicate little Tethyrian flourish at the end. The maneuver seemed clumsy and ridiculous with a wooden sword.

"Be careful, Tal," called Chaney. "He means to tickle you into submission."

Alale kept his eyes on Tal, but he scowled at the taunt. Tal grinned. He loved sword practice, and he had a mind to do a little tickling of his own.

"Stand the middle . . . " said Chaney, ". . . attack!"

Tal stood his ground at first, watching as Alale crossed over left, then forward, then back. Instead of obliging his opponent's invitation to dance, Tal exploded forward in a loud, stamping rush that startled Alale into a premature parry. Tal's attack, a beat later than anticipated, rapped Alale smartly across the knuckles. Alale didn't drop his weapon, but as it fell out of guard, Tal lunged and smacked the top of Alale's helmet.

"One," said Tal, returning to his position in the middle ring. He could almost see the red glow of Alale's cheeks beneath the nose and cheek guards of his practice helmet.

"One," agreed Alale crisply. He sounded as if he wanted to complain about the ignoble attack, but he knew it was perfectly fair. He should have been more careful.

"Stand . . ." called Chaney, ". . . attack!"

This time, Alale came on in a direct but cautious attack. First he explored Tal's outer guard, always careful of a riposte. Tal restrained himself from a counterattack at first, looking for a chance to strike a particularly humiliating blow instead of settling for an ordinary cut.

Alale's feints were good, and soon he added a low cut with a thrusting riposte. The first one nearly came through, and Tal realized that remaining on the defensive would be more difficult than he had expected.

Before he could change tactics, however, Tal misjudged a low cut by half a beat and felt a smart blow to the thigh.

"One and one," said Alale triumphantly. Tal shrugged an apology at Chaney and took his place again.

In the next pass, Tal tried to take the offensive once more. He beat Alale's blade to the outside with all of his strength. Rather than lunge forward for the point, however, Tal whirled around, taking the blade from his right hand to his left, throwing an ambitious backhanded sweeping cut at Alale's padded shoulder.

It would have been spectacular, had it landed.

Instead, Tal nearly threw his arm out of joint as Alale thrust the tip of his wooden blade into his shoulder.

"I suppose that sort of thing appeals to the groundlings," observed Alale scornfully. Normally immune to such barbs, Tal felt his cheeks warm. It was a silly attack, but it might turn into something good for the next show. If it had landed, how Alale would have simmered!

Tal evened the score in the next pass by pressing with his superior strength, then luring Alale into a hasty counterattack. Tal deftly deflected the cut to his head and thrust under Alale's blade to poke him with a two-handed thrust in the biceps. Annoyed, Alale slapped the wooden blade away before Tal could withdraw it.

As he took his position for the final pass, Tal noticed that Radu Malveen stood outside the fighting circle, opposite Chaney. Even when he turned his eyes back to Alale, Tal could feel Radu's leaden gaze upon his back.

" . . . attack!" Tal realized that he had lost his concentration almost too late to parry Alale's running thrust. Had Alale moved before the command? Tal twisted to evade

Alale's body, then quickly raised his blade to block a quick but weak slash as Alale recovered from his lunge. Unfortunately, the maneuver left Tal on one knee. Before Tal could recover, Alale kicked the side of his forward knee, spinning him to the right and opening his entire left flank to attack.

Ignoring the pain in his knee, Tal threw himself to the right, rolling to evade the attack. Alale followed him, the sharp rap of his sword against the floor striking three times just behind Tal's helmet before he came to his feet in a low guard position. Tal feared he might have rolled out of bounds, but he heard no call from Radu or Chaney.

Without looking down, Tal knew he stood on the red outer line. If he took one step backward, the touch would go to Alale, who even now unleashed a furious attack designed to make Tal retreat. Tal was determined not to move.

As he pushed aside his burning embarrassment at putting himself in such a weak position, Tal felt a gentle calm envelope him.

Tal's blade moved faster as his heart grew quiet. Soon he could no longer feel the weapon in his hands, then his arms were more a memory than a tangible presence. His blade was no longer his conscious defense. It had become the mirror of Alale's own weapon, moving where it did not by will but simply because it must.

Frustration built on Alale's face, and Tal didn't sense so much as he later remembered when the man's fury broke into a desperate lunge. Instead of another sword strike, Alale threw his entire weight toward Tal's chest.

Tal shrugged as smoothly as if donning a robe, rolling beside and behind Alale as his opponent threw himself out of the red circle.

Alale landed with a painful crunch and a muffled curse.

"Yes!" shouted Chaney gleefully.

Tal blinked as if coming out of a trance. Then he grinned

and turned toward Chaney. "I thought he had me," said Tal, shucking off his helmet.

Chaney didn't have time to voice a shout, but the expression on his face was warning enough. Tal dropped and spun to the right, just in time to see Alale's practice blade slash down where his unprotected head had been an instant earlier.

Before Alale could recover, Tal had the man's wrist in his hand, squeezing hard. "That's enough," said Tal.

Alale's face was white with hatred. Tal saw his eyes go wide and watery as Tal squeezed his wrist harder, feeling the bones grind together before Alale gasped. The wooden practice sword clattered on the floor.

Alale choked back furious tears as Tal released him. "You'll regret that, Uskevren."

Tal growled, low and throaty. The inhuman sound transfixed Alale. For long seconds he stood looking up into the eyes of the bigger man with naked terror in his eyes.

The moment passed, and Alale twisted his thin lips an ugly, flickering sneer. Still, he kept his tongue still as he scurried away to stand near Radu Malveen.

Radu looked at the frightened man with the expression of one noticing that he was standing next to a pile of steaming dung. With the barest widening of his nostrils, Radu stepped gracefully away, turning his back on Alale.

Abandoned Alale scurried off to collect his things and left, still cradling his bruised wrist.

"That went well," suggested Chaney. "Don't you think?"

Outside the fighting school, Tal and Chaney blinked into the strong sea breeze that wound through the warehouses. They paused for a passing ale wagon before entering the street. As they did, Radu Malveen appeared beside them. Tal noticed that the wind did not disturb the man's hair or clothing and wondered what sort of enchantment he carried for the effect.

Tal barely knew the man, but Radu's younger brother, Pietro, had been on the ill-fated hunting party. Fortunately for the Malveens, Pietro was one of the few who reached their horses in the early moments of the attack. Like Chaney, he had escaped unharmed.

"My apologies for disturbing your practice, Master Malveen," offered Tal.

Radu inclined his chin.

"Perhaps I can make amends for chasing off your opponent. Shall we practice tomorrow?"

"No," said Radu.

"Perhaps another time . . ."

"No."

"Why not?" asked Chaney, cocking his head as if detecting a sound he didn't like. "You came here with that fool Alale."

"It's all right, Chaney," said Tal. "Let's see who's at the Green Gauntlet."

"No, it isn't all right," insisted Chaney. "What's wrong with Tal, Malveen? He's twice as good as Alale, and you were going to face him. Weren't you?"

"Chaney!" protested Tal.

Instead of flattening Chaney, as was the usual custom among their peers, Radu merely nodded again, as if acknowledging Chaney's point. "That is true. Master Uskevren is mechanically proficient with the sword."

Chaney's head bobbed as if he'd just scored a touch, ignoring the caveat of "mechanically." "So what's the problem?"

Tal wished Chaney would shut up.

"I will face you in the circle," said Radu, turning his unreflecting eyes on Tal, "once you begin treating it with respect."

Chaney opened his mouth to retort, but Tal shushed him with a raised hand.

"This is not theater rehearsal," said Radu. Few of Tal's peers thought much of the theater, but Radu sounded particularly scornful.

"I was just having fun with Alale," said Tal. "I intended no disrespect."

"You don't understand," said Radu coolly. "You should never have permitted Soargyl to touch you. Your antics are an offense to the circle, to your sword, and to yourself." With that, Radu Malveen made the most perfunctory of bows and turned away.

Chaney gave a little snort, but Tal noticed he didn't cast a snide remark after Radu.

"He doesn't know what he's talking about," said Chaney. "You're one of the best swordsmen in Selgaunt."

"No," said Tal slowly, "I'm not." Radu's words had disturbed him more than he thought possible. "But maybe I ought to be."

⊙ ⊙ ⊙ ⊙ ⊙

That evening, Tal returned alone to his tallhouse. The sun had just set, and his shadow stretched across the cobblestones in the deceptively warm-looking glow of the street lamps.

He'd had more than a few flagons of ale throughout the afternoon, but he was sharp enough to keep his eyes on the shadows. The figure trailing him for the past few streets was probably one his father's men. At least he made an effort to stay out of sight.

Throughout the day, Tal and Chaney had traded gossip and sung songs with longshoremen and market girls at the Green Gauntlet. When the wealthier patrons began arriving, they moved along to the less savory Black Stag, where they shared rude jokes and flirted with the tough women of that den of smugglers.

Chaney slipped out with a fetching young servant of the

Hulorn's palace. Like Tal, he preferred common women to merchant nobility. Chaney considered them exciting and dangerous, the more disreputable the better. Unlike his friend, Tal simply found such women more approachable, free of the inevitable pretensions of the rich.

Unfortunately, even common women who learned Tal's heritage often became more ambitious than interesting. At the first sign of an ulterior motive, Tal's interest evaporated. Thus his experiences were considerably less epic than Chaney's.

The idea made him angry at no one in particular. He hated thinking his most valuable attribute was the accident of his birth.

These sour thoughts distracted him so much that he walked completely past his tallhouse. Turning back, he glimpsed a hooded figure gazing at him from the corner of his house. A woman's face framed in auburn hair, bright eyes—maybe blue or green—that was all he saw before she slipped into the dark alley.

She'd been watching for him. He was sure of it.

Tal ran to where she'd been. In the dark alley, only the glittering rails of shallow balconies and stairwells shone in the streetlight. Tal wished the moon had risen to shine straight down into the darkness. The woman could be hiding almost anywhere in that gloom.

Opening his eyes wide against the darkness, Tal stepped carefully forward. He debated whether to call out to the woman. But what would he say?

Before he found any trace of his mystery woman, a light appeared from the tallhouse beside his. A big-bellied woman stood on the second-floor balcony holding a lamp. She wore a gaudy, embroidered robe over her nightgown.

"Precious?" she called. "Is that you?"

"It's me, Mistress Dunnett," said Tal. He stepped out of the shadows and into the dim circle of her lamplight.

"Oh," she said, disappointed. "It's good to see you've

come back home, Master Talbot. Have you seen my precious Pumpkin?"

"I'm afraid not." Briefly, Tal wondered whether his mystery woman had done away with the cat, but he couldn't think of a reason why she would. After the scratch the little bastard had given him yesterday, Tal found himself unmoved by the thought of Pumpkin's untimely demise.

Tal said goodnight to Mistress Dunnett and went inside to bed.

In his dreams, Tal relived the terror of the Arch Wood, only this time the beast had him cornered. It harried him time after time, tormenting him yet witholding the killing stroke.

Gray light filtered through the draperies of Tal's bedroom window, but it was the noise that had awakened him from the vexing nightmares. This time, Tal awoke clear-headed enough to realize that someone was banging on the door to his bedroom. In fact, someone else was banging on his closet door—from the inside.

"Master Talbot!" called Eckart from the hallway.

"Help me!" cried an unfamiliar voice from the closet. "They're still out there!"

Tal began to rise but paused, sensing something strange about the room. The curtains flapped at the open window, raising goose bumps on his naked flesh. That was odd, for he wasn't one to sleep in the nude.

Tal threw his feet over the side of the bed. Standing, he slid in some nasty slickness on the floor, crashing down beside it.

His head hit the floor beside the torn and bloody face of Alale Soargyl. Tal had slipped in the man's scattered guts.

Tal screamed, the voice from the closet screamed, and

Eckart screamed from the hallway. Tal was the first to stop, scrambling through the horrid mess toward the hallway door. He found the portal blocked by a heavy chest pulled from the foot of Tal's bed. Crammed into the corner behind it was another dead body, or most of one, its remaining features unrecognizable.

Tal screamed again. So did the man in the closet. Eckart had never stopped.

Swallowing the bile that rose in his throat, Tal shoved the chest away from the door to let Eckart in. His manservant took one look at Tal and began to scream again, but Tal quickly clamped a big hand over his mouth. His arms were bathed in blood, and he felt the stickiness all over his naked body. It was on his legs, his chest, his arms, even his face.

"Let me think," said Tal, but a horrible realization had already taken shape in his mind. At last he knew the nature of his mysterious attacker back in the Arch wood. He understood now why he had been followed to the city.

"Fetch Chaney," said Tal, taking his hand from Eckart's mouth. "No one else, and I mean it. You don't want to be the one to describe this to my father, do you?"

Eckart demonstrated a certain amount of iron as he calmed himself. He plucked a handkerchief from his vest and dabbed hastily at the bloody handprint over his mouth. "No, sir," he said emphatically. "I should not desire that."

⊛ ⊛ ⊛ ⊛ ⊛

"I know some men from the Stag who'll take care of the bodies for a few coins," offered Chaney.

"Yes," said Tal, "but how much for their silence? And for how long?"

"True," agreed Chaney. "Once they realized who you were, there'd be no satisfying them."

"Cale would know what to do."

"What Cale knows, your father knows."

"Sometimes I'm not so sure of that," said Tal. "But eventually my father must know. I can't afford a cure with my own money. Even if I could, there isn't a priest in Selgaunt who wouldn't tell father later."

"I thought a cure worked only before you actually . . . you know. Changed."

"That I don't know," sighed Tal. "I don't know *anything* about being a werewolf." He'd washed himself soon after Eckart had left to find Chaney, but he still felt unclean. "Maybe I should just turn myself in."

"Don't be a fool!" said Chaney. "If nothing else, think of the harm it would cause your family."

"I've just killed two men!" countered Tal. "The third one's still locked in my closet. How much more harm can I cause?"

The lone survivor of the night's massacre had been eager to tell his story, though it was hard to make out the details through his terrified babbling. He was a lockpick who prided himself on working for only the wealthiest employers.

Alale Soargyl offered him and his hulking companion two hundred fivestars each to beat Tal into submission, then hold him as Alale threw a few punches of his own.

They'd broken into the tallhouse and found their way to Tal's bedroom, where they had planned to lie in wait. Instead, they'd found a monster.

"What if it's not your fault?"

"How can that be?"

"What if someone did this to you on purpose?" said Chaney.

Tal considered that suggestion. "That's too fantastic," he said at last. "Even if the attack on our party was planned, how could they know who would survive?"

"Maybe they didn't care which of us it was," suggested Chaney. "Or maybe we were all supposed to die."

"The old woman knew I'd been attacked by a werewolf," said Tal. "But was she part of the plot? Or was she just trying to help?"

"She had to be in on it," said Chaney. "It's too big a coincidence that she'd find you out there in the woods."

Tal nodded. It was all too convenient.

"The important thing is that we put you someplace safe tonight. Too bad the closet's already occupied."

"That wouldn't be enough, anyway," said Tal. "I need a strong cell. And in case I get out . . ."

"It takes an enchanted sword to slay a werewolf," said Chaney. "You'd be safe as long as you didn't run into a wizard or someone with a magical weapon."

"There's that big, solid cage at the theater," said Tal.

"And you can trust Quickly to keep things quiet." Chaney was brightening, even if Tal was full of despair.

"There's the sword, in case I get out."

"You won't get out," said Chaney. "I mean, it won't get out. You said yourself you don't remember anything from last night. That proves it's not you. It's . . . you know. The thing. The wolf. *It.*"

"But if *it* does get out," said Tal, "I need someone I can trust to take care of it. I need you there with the sword."

"Listen," said Chaney, "Eckart and I can take care of things here. You go talk to Quickly."

"I'm serious, Chaney. I need you there tonight, and I need your promise that you'll kill it if it gets out of the cage."

Chaney sighed. "I'll be there."

"Promise."

"I promise."

"You're a what?"

"A were—"

"No, no, I heard you the first time," said Quickly. She bit

the tip of her thumb and turned away to pace beside the big steel cage. "Do you suppose we could work it into a play? Of course, we'd be limited to a few shows each month, and—"

"Quickly!" exclaimed Tal. "This is a serious problem, not an opportunity to . . ." He saw from the sly look on Quickly's face that she'd been putting him on. "Can I count on you to keep this quiet?"

"You know you can, lad. I'll cancel today's shows and put out word that half the cast is down with river fever. That should keep the other half from snooping about tonight." She gave Tal a comrade's hug. "We'll see this thing through, just you and me."

"And Lommy!" cried a voice from the dark rafters. Tal looked up to see two pairs of yellow eyes peering down. "And Otter!"

"Eavesdroppers!" scolded Quickly.

Tal hesitated a moment. "Chaney, too," added Tal. "He'll be here before nightfall. We'll need him in case the cage doesn't hold."

"What do you expect he can do about it?"

"We need the sword, Quickly."

Even the false cheer at last drained from her cheeks. "You can't mean it, Tal. There must be another way."

He shook his head. "I'd rather die than kill again. Even Alale didn't deserve what he got. Imagine if I woke up at Stormweather tomorrow morning."

"The cage will hold," affirmed Quickly, grabbing one of its bars and pulling. It didn't budge.

"Let's hope so."

Chaney arrived an hour before moonrise with assurances that he'd taken care of the problems back at the tallhouse. He'd also done something he assured Tal would keep Eckart quiet for a while, but he wouldn't reveal what it was.

"In you go," said Quickly. Lommy and Otter had lowered the cage to the ground, and Tal stepped inside. Quickly locked the door and set the key on a prop table, well away from the bars.

"You want us to turn our heads or anything?" asked Chaney.

"Would you if I said 'yes'?" asked Tal.

"Well, no," admitted Chaney. Quickly laughed, but Tal could see the tension on both their faces. He thought of the tasloi peering down from above.

"No matter what happens," he called up to the darkness, "you two stay up there."

Lommy and Otter squeaked their assent.

"Well," said Chaney, "I don't plan to stand the whole time." He found a couple of chairs for himself and Quickly, then eased himself comfortably into the better one.

"The sword!" said Tal suddenly. "Don't forget the sword."

"Right, right," said Chaney in a tone that convinced Tal that he hadn't forgotten it.

"You'll never find it on your own," said Quickly. "I'll show you were it is." She led him down the narrow stairs to the small prop room under the stage.

Tal found himself wishing one of them had stayed. He looked up toward the ceiling, but there was no sign of Lommy or Otter. He stopped himself from calling out to them. They were probably more frightened than he was and had run off to avoid witnessing his horrid transformation.

A muffled thump came from the prop room.

"Chaney?" called Tal. "You haven't been drinking already, have you?" He tried to keep his tone light, but a new fear crept into his heart. "Chaney? Quickly?"

Neither of them answered.

He tried again. When no one replied, he fell silent, gripping the bars of his cage. Time oozed at a gelid pace.

Tal heard two pairs of footsteps rising from the prop room stairs. "Come on, now," he said weakly. "Stop kidding around, you two." The echo of his voice made him fall silent, and he watched as two people emerged from the stairs. They weren't Chaney and Quickly.

The intruders each wore long, gray cloaks, the hoods pushed back to reveal their faces. Tal immediately noted the family resemblance. Feena had her mother's determined jaw and slightly upturned nose.

"What have you done with my friends?" demanded Tal. He'd meant to sound intimidating, but he failed to conjure his father's voice.

"They are well," assured the old woman in the voice Tal remembered from his confined convalescence. She turned to her daughter and gestured toward Tal in his cage. "Does this reassure you?"

"Yes, Mother. Perhaps I was hasty."

"There is hope for you, young Uskevren," said the old woman, "but only if your faith is strong."

"What are you talking about?" demanded Tal. "Who are you?"

"My name is Maleva. I am a servant of Selune."

"The goddess of the moon," said Tal.

Maleva nodded, then gestured to the young woman beside her. "This is Feena, my daughter and acolyte. We pulled you from the brambles of the Arch Wood and tried to cure you of your affliction. Now we offer you one last chance to escape the curse of the beast."

"But there's a price," said Tal suspiciously.

"There is indeed a price," agreed Maleva. She produced a crystal flask from beneath her cloak. A thick, pearlescent liquid glowed within the container. As Tal watched, the stuff seemed to move, undulating like a jellyfish. "This is moonfire. I have traveled far for the privilege of offering it to you."

"It can give you control over the beast," said Feena, "but

only if you have not hunted and devoured your fellow men."

Tal felt a heavy sigh escape his chest. "Well, that's where we have a problem. You see—"

"I have seen," interrupted Feena. "While mother traveled to the city of Ordulin to beg a fraction of moonfire from Dhauna Myritar, I followed you here, to Selgaunt. In the past two nights, you have slain no one."

"You must have nodded off," said Tal. "This morning there were two dead bodies in my room." He realized suddenly how easy it would have been to lie, but something about the strange women made him blurt the truth.

Maleva's faint smile told him that he had passed a little test. "We were not the only ones to follow you," said Maleva. "Rusk slew the men who watched over you, then tracked you to your home."

"Rusk . . ." said Tal slowly. "That's the name I heard the night I was attacked."

"Rusk is a servant of the Beastlord" said Maleva, "a priest of the god Malar. We children of Selune are charged with checking the atrocities of his kind. It is he who led the attack on your hunting party. Now he claims you as his disciple."

"He's the werewolf who mauled me?" ventured Tal. The women nodded.

"He rarely ventures from the wood," said Maleva, "but something brought him . . ."

A beam creaked noisily from the rafters above. At the sound, Maleva and Feena stepped back as one, clutching the talismans they wore about their necks, their voices chanting two different spells.

Harsh laughter boomed from the rafters. It wasn't a sound Lommy could have mimicked.

Feena raised her talisman like a shield. A pair of eyes surrounded by stars blazed on the amulet. Before Feena could finish the words to her spell, a great dark figure crushed her to the ground.

It was a huge man, bigger even than Tal. His leather jerkin was open to expose thick gray hair on his muscular chest and arms. A beaded headband kept his unruly locks at bay and held the bronze image of a ragged claw upon his forehead. His mustache grew down either side of his broad mouth, while grizzled stubble covered his cheeks and throat.

He crouched growling over Feena, who moaned and shook her head dazedly. Rusk turned his blazing blue eyes on Tal and made a savage smile.

With a flash, a blue-white blade of light appeared in Maleva's hands. Without a word, she raised the weapon high. Rusk whipped around to face her and spat a single word: "Stop!"

Tal saw Maleva's arms tremble, but her conjured blade was fixed fast above her head. Rusk stood, towering over the old woman.

"Your powers are weak," he declared, balling a fist scant inches from her grimacing face. "Strength lies only within the heart of the beast."

Rusk punched Maleva in the stomach hard enough to lift her feet from the floor. Her paralysis broken, she fell back hard. Tal heard the crack of her skull on the wooden floor.

"Stop it!" he shouted from the confines of the cage. Real anger empowered his voice, making a weapon of it.

Rusk turned back again. "Don't worry, brother wolf. I am saving them for your first true hunt."

"Let them go," said Tal. He felt powerless within the cage, but he couldn't silently watch Rusk murder the women. He hoped he could buy enough time that Chaney could recover from whatever Maleva and Feena had done to him. He hoped Rusk's melodramatic manner ran true.

"Oh, that I will," agreed Rusk ominously. He turned to Feena, who was crawling across the floor toward Maleva. Again he spoke a prayer to Malar, the Beastlord, god of hunters. To Feena he said, "Take your mother and flee."

Feena obeyed so quickly that Tal knew Rusk's words carried the power of the Beastlord. She dragged Maleva toward the back stage door.

"You, my cub," said Rusk, turning again to Tal, "have disappointed me. You ran like a hart last moon, but you must learn to be the hunter as well as the hunted."

"Then teach me," said Tal, hoping to buy a few more minutes. Too much, however, and the moon would be upon him, too. He hoped he was a better actor than he thought, and he prayed that Rusk was not the most discerning audience.

Rusk's grin told Tal that the man did not yet trust him. "This is your last chance, little brother."

Tal winced at the phrase. He wanted no relation to this monster.

"You must do better than one miserable cat before you can join the great hunt," snarled Rusk. "This is the last time I will show you."

"What about the moonfire?" ventured Tal. "Shouldn't we take it? The old woman said it would give us control of—"

"A lie!" spat Rusk. "It is a trick to place you in thrall of their mewling, feeble goddess. It saps the power of the beast and bends your will to theirs. Tonight they shall be our prey."

"I should have known." Tal made fists of his hands, a stone of his face. He paused as long as he dared for dramatic effect. "I never trusted them."

Rusk glanced sidelong at Tal.

Tal clenched his teeth and thought of all the attempts to control his life: his mother, his father, even Maleva and Feena. He summoned his father's voice. "I'll take the old bitch first," he thundered. "She tried to tame me with her potions, but now she'll feel my teeth on her throat."

Rusk leered and watched Tal closely.

"Let's stand beneath the naked sky," rumbled Tal. "Let the moon come. We'll wash it in blood."

Tal nodded toward the table, and Rusk found the key. He put it in the cage lock but then paused. "I'll tear out your heart if you run from me," he warned.

"No more running," said Tal. "It's time to hunt."

Satisfied, Rusk opened the cage. Tal walked past him, out onto the stage. Rusk followed closely, watching for any sign of weakness. The floor lamps cast unsettling shadows on the faces of both men.

Tal paced the length of the stage, his real anxiety making it easy to appear restless and eager. As he walked across one of the trapdoors, a plan began to form in his mind.

"The moon is coming," rumbled Rusk. "Can you feel it?"

Tal noticed the pressure on his ears and eyes. "Yes," he said. "It's like a storm."

"That's it!" encouraged Rusk. "Open your heart to it. The beast sends you strength and courage."

Tal stood squarely on the trapdoor. He couldn't open it himself. Glancing at the open galleries, he peered for some sign of Lommy or Otter. "Open, heart!" cried Tal. "Open your depths to the beast!" *He hoped the tasloi understood.*

Rusk raised his arms toward the sky. "Malar, Beastlord, Master of the Hunt, hear my prayer and bestow your blessing on my acolyte. Give us your—"

The trapdoor opened, and Tal vanished into the small prop room.

"No!" screamed Rusk. He pounced toward the closing door. His fingers slipped into the crack and prevented the door from closing. "Fool! Weakling! I'll kill you!"

Tal heard wood popping as Rusk pushed against the trapdoor. He found what he wanted, then ran to another trapdoor across the dark prop room. He pulled the lever and rose back onto the stage.

"Here I am," Tal called from behind Rusk. He raised the

enchanted sword and spoke the words. Hot flames whooshed along the long sword's blade.

Rusk began chanting another spell. Tal rushed to strike him before it could be completed, but he saw the effects before he reached his foe. The man's fingers grew long and thick. The nails extended into sharp, bony knives.

Tal's sword glanced off Rusk's terrible new claws. The scraping vibration made his teeth ache. In his rush to strike the first blow, he opened his guard far too wide.

Rusk swept a backhanded slash across Tal's belly, ripping through fabric and flesh. Tal gasped at the pain and tried to restore his guard.

The beast man pressed the attack, slashing furiously with both gigantic hands. Tal felt a horrible looseness in his guts as he struggled to sustain a defense, parrying left and right as he backed across the stage.

Even through the pain, Tal felt another keen sensation. The hairs all over his body pricked up, and his joints ached. The transformation was starting.

Rusk felt it also, and he stopped to howl at the sky. Tal felt a wild scream rising in his own breast, but he fought to keep it down. Rusk lowered his eyes to meet Tal's. He approached slowly, savoring the fear he saw in his prey.

Tal retreated until he ran out of stage. The pain in his belly sprang to agonizing life. He wondered briefly if he'd live long enough to die as a wolf. Part of him hoped he would die first.

Then he noticed the springboard.

A mad grin stretched across Tal's face. Win or lose, he would finish this fight on his own terms. Clutching the flaming sword in both hands, he ran toward his enemy.

Rusk braced for a headlong attack, his god-granted talons spread before him in a shield of blades. Tal hit the springboard with both feet and flew high above Rusk's bony shields, flipping forward as he guided the sword in a great overhead arc.

Rusk moved just in time to save his skull. The sword swept past the werewolf's cheek to cleave through the meat and bone of his shoulder.

Tal collapsed heavily before his enemy, defeated. He felt his guts spilling through his belly but didn't even have the strength to clutch at them. He raised his head to face his death.

He looked up just in time to see Rusk's severed arm fall away from his body. The arterial spray was black in the yellow light.

Rusk's agonized howl was deafening as Tal fell backward onto the stage. Their blood mingled in a widening pool.

Tal's second convalescence was much more painful than the first. Maleva and Feena returned in time to save his life, but they had yet to use Selune's power to heal him properly. When they returned to his tallhouse the next day, they found Chaney and Eckert at his side.

After they'd mended his wounds, Maleva produced the moonfire. Tal had already told Chaney and Eckart his story. The servant was especially quiet this morning, still angry at having spent the night trussed and locked in the closet beside the captured lockpick. His cold glare followed the unrepentant Chaney wherever he went.

"At last," said Chaney, admiring the vial of moonfire. "Here's the solution to all your trouble."

"No," said Tal. "I don't want it."

Feena's eyebrows jumped, but Maleva seemed nonplussed.

"But sir," said Eckart, breaking his silence at last, "how else can you put an end to this curse?"

"That stuff won't work for me unless I pledge myself to Selune. Right?"

"That is true," replied Maleva evenly.

"I can't see you as a priest," said Chaney with a little whimsy.

"Neither can I," agreed Tal.

"There are many ways to serve Selune," said Maleva. "All that is required is devotion."

"You mean obedience."

Maleva inclined her head with a little smile.

"The difference between you and Rusk is only the purpose you intend for me. You both demand my obedience."

"Rusk sought to turn you into a beast, like him," said Feena.

"I've been wondering about that," interjected Chaney. "There were more than a dozen of us in that hunting party. None of this 'Hunt' came after me or the others who escaped. Why are they so interested in Tal?"

"It *is* strange that he followed you to the city," allowed Maleva. She looked Tal in the face as if considering him for the first time. "He has a special interest in you, Talbot Uskevren."

"He isn't done, either," said Feena. They had found a trail of blood leading to the theater entrance, but Rusk had escaped. "You would be wise to trust in Selune. She offers the power to oppose his kind."

"I appreciate what you've done," said Tal. "Eckart will see that you're well paid for healing me. But I'll need more time to consider this business of the moonfire and Selune."

"If you let the beast rule your heart," warned Feena, "you must be destroyed." The heat in her voice was startling.

"I'll find a way," promised Tal. "But I'll find my own way."

"Sometimes that is the best course," said Maleva. "We will remain in Selgaunt until you have found that way."

Feena gave Tal a long look to emphasize her mother's point, a threat mingled with some other emotion in her steady gaze. "We'll be watching you," she said.

"I understand," said Tal. He knew Maleva and Feena would deal harshly with him if he surrendered to the monster Rusk had placed inside him. "I have thirty days."

THE BUTLER

RESURRECTION

Paul Kemp

Cale sprinted down the alley, flattened himself against the wall, and shot a nervous glance behind. No one—just darkness and empty cobblestones. Winded from the run, his lungs heaved like a bellows. He sucked in the stink of the alley, a sour reek of urine and vomit, and blew it out in a cloud of frozen mist.

Take it easy, he ordered himself. But that was easier thought than done. Someone was following him; someone had been since he had left Stormweather Towers. But who? And why?

He slid along the wall until he reached a shallow, garbage-strewn recess hewn from the bricks. Blanketing himself in shadow, he concentrated on slowing his heart and steadying his breathing. He knew a cloud of exhaled breath would betray his location as surely as a shout. With an effort of will, he calmed himself.

The roughness of the bricks at his back tempted him to try climbing, but he quickly dismissed the idea as too risky. If his pursuer caught up to him while he hung helpless on the wall. . . .

Blowing out a soft, tense sigh, he quietly eased his dagger from its belt sheath and peered through the darkness behind him. Still no one. Perhaps he had lost—

A silhouette suddenly appeared at the mouth of the alley, a short, wiry body framed by the light of a street torch. Cale froze and held his breath. The figure wavered uncertainly for a moment, as though sniffing for a trap, then stalked down the alley. The soft *sshhk* of a blade being drawn rang loud in Cale's ears. He gripped his own dagger in a sweating fist and tried to sink deeper into the shadows.

The figure prowled down the narrow alley with short sword drawn. Its wary gaze swept the shadowy recess where Cale hid but passed over without a pause. Still holding his breath, Cale studied the man. Darkness hid his features, but Cale nevertheless recognized the ready blade and deft movements of a professional killer. An old adage he had learned back in the pirate city of Westgate popped into his head—only an assassin knows an assassin.

The man stopped mere feet from Cale's recess and peered ahead into the darkness. Apparently satisfied, he muttered something under his breath and started to stalk farther down the alley—

Cale leaped out and smashed a fist into his jaw. The impact dislodged teeth and knocked the man across the alley.

Cale easily sidestepped the dazed assassin's retaliatory stab and landed another vicious punch, this one to the nose. Bone shattered like eggshell, and blood exploded from the assassin's face in a spray of crimson. Stunned, he dropped the short sword and crumbled to the street with a moan. As soon as the assassin hit the ground, Cale had a knee on his chest and a dagger at his throat.

"Move and you're a dead man," Cale hissed.

Unable to breathe through his ruined nose, the assassin wheezed through a mouth rapidly filling with snot and blood. "All right. All right. I ain't movin'."

Even up close Cale didn't recognize him, though he knew most of Selgaunt's professionals.

"Speak," Cale ordered. "All of it. And if I think you're lying . . ." He pricked the assassin's throat with his dagger and let the threat dangle.

Fear cleared the man's watery eyes. "Sure. Sure. What's it to me, right?" He tried to force a laugh but choked on his own blood.

Cale waited for the coughing fit to pass, then asked, "Who hired you?"

The assassin hesitated only an instant. "House . . . Malveen. Pietro Malveen."

Cale nodded. That sounded about right. Turning an assassin loose on the Uskevren would be just like Pietro Malveen. Foolish, ham-handed dolt. He pressed his knee further into the assassin's chest.

"Who was your target?"

"No one," the assassin managed between gasps, then hurriedly added, "I mean, anyone . . . any Uskevren. I thought you were one of the sons." He turned his head to the side and spat blood. "Who in the Nine Hells are you?"

Cale replied with cold silence and a hard stare. Stupid question, he thought. If you knew the answer, you'd already be dead. He kept his dagger to the man's throat while he tried to decide what to do. He could hardly turn the assassin over to the Scepters, Selgaunt's city guard. Too many questions there. But he had to get to the Stag soon. Riven would be waiting. Perhaps . . .

"You're the butler," the assassin blurted, certainty in his

voice. "Dark, but you don't move like any butler I've ever seen."

Cale grimaced. Foolish, foolish man.

"What?" The assassin's voice rose an octave. He sensed he'd made a mistake. "What'd I say? You are the butler, aren't you?"

Cale stared down at the now frightened man with cold eyes. Though he knew now what he had to do, he nevertheless found it distasteful. Apparently realizing his danger, the assassin began to struggle. Cale held him in a grip like a vise.

"Hey, wait, wait, *mmph—*"

Cale covered the assassin's mouth with a powerful hand and leaned in close. "You're right," he whispered into the man's ear. "I am the butler."

He flashed the dagger and opened the assassin's throat. The dying man screamed into Cale's palm while his blood poured steaming onto the frozen cobblestones. Cale watched him, emotionless. It was over within seconds.

Cale wiped his blade clean on the man's cloak and stood. He took no pleasure in what he had done, but he had to do it. If he had allowed the assassin to carry word of his skills back to the Malveens, someone would have grown suspicious—Radu Malveen if not that idiot Pietro. Cale could not allow that.

Some secrets have to be kept, he thought, irrespective of the cost.

Without a backward glance, Cale left the cooling corpse behind him and headed for the Black Stag.

The hearth stood unused, the coals cold. Only the wan orange glow of a single oil lamp provided light in the Black Stag. Hanging crookedly from a hook behind the bar, the lantern's flickering wick emitted wisps of oily black smoke that twisted upward to mix with the clouds of pipeweed smoke hovering around the ceiling beams. The dim, dancing flame created a confusing patchwork of shadows and smoke shapes that played eerily across the dead eyes and hard faces of the Stag's hushed clientele. They looked like the lost souls some said wandered about the uppermost of the Nine Hells in search of peace.

Cale stood in the Stag's windswept doorway and grimaced. Lost souls indeed.

He had just left a man lying dead only three blocks away.

Perhaps twenty other patrons sat huddled in pairs and trios at the Stag's greasy wooden tables. Their hissing whispers remained indecipherable even to Cale's sharp ears, but he could imagine the content of their conversations well enough. He had been party to many such conversations himself once—black market deals, bribes, assassinations. . . .

Drasek Riven, he saw, had not yet arrived. Irritated, Cale walked across the common room to the bar and exchanged four coppers for a tankard of ale. He took a table far from the Stag's only public entrance, in a corner that commanded a view of the rest of the room. The stink of sweat, spilled ale, and the lantern's fish oil created a distinctively vile stench unique to the Stag, and disturbingly familiar to Cale. The smell recalled to him the man he had once been, a man who did black deeds in the cover of night. He thought again of the corpse back in the alley and knew that the ghost of that man yet haunted his soul. He still did black deeds.

Trying to banish the image of the assassin's panicked gaze, Cale threw back a gulp of sour ale and slammed the tankard down on the table. A few wolfish faces jerked his way at the sound, but his cool stare quickly turned them back to their own business. He mopped his bald pate with a suddenly sweating hand, a hand that had slit a throat only minutes before.

"You are not that man anymore," he chanted, as though invoking a spell. "You are not that man anymore."

The corpse he had left in the alley made a mockery of his claim and he knew it. No matter that he had played the loyal servant to Thamalon Uskevren for the past nine years. He remained a killer. Anything else, no matter how well played, was a sham. If Thazienne ever learned of his fraud . . .

Shaking his head angrily, he dismissed Thazienne from his mind. Now was not the time for distractions. He could not afford to show weakness when facing Riven. That black-hearted bastard smelled weakness like an Inner Sea gray shark smelled blood in the water. Cale needed to be focused.

Endless minutes passed and still no Riven. Cale grew increasingly edgy. His long fingers beat an impatient drumbeat on the arm of his chair. Why had Riven contacted him? Their scheduled meet was still a tenday away. Where in the Nine Hells was he?

The door to the Stag flew open, and Drasek Riven strode into the common room as if he owned the place. Without a glance to either side he stalked directly up to the bar, his scarlet cloak billowing behind him like a pool of blood. Wordlessly accepting a tankard of ale from the skinny, greasy-haired barkeep, he turned to survey the common room with a contemptuous sneer. His right hand rested comfortably on the hilt of one of his two sabers.

Gazes that had nervously followed the assassin's trek to the bar hurriedly turned back to their own business and dared not look up. Drasek Riven fairly stank of murder. He had a reputation among the Night Knives as a man who loved to kill. No one in the Stag risked eye contact. Except Cale.

Cale met Riven's hard gaze with a cool stare. The

assassin's one good eye flashed recognition, and he strutted over to the table. Licking his lips, Cale tasted the salt of sweat. Riven reminded him of a hunting cat—compact, powerful, and predatory.

Calm down, man, he ordered himself. Though he towered over Riven physically, Cale knew his own bladework was no match for the temperamental assassin's slim sabers. He made his face an emotionless mask as Riven slid into the chair across from him.

"You're late," Cale announced matter-of-factly.

Riven regarded him over the rim of his tankard while swigging a gulp of ale. He set the tankard down softly and sneered. "So?" Clearly, the assassin was itching for a confrontation.

Cale gave no ground, though it meant risking naked steel. He pointed a single finger at the assassin's pockmarked face and hissed, "So the next time you make me wait, I walk away. You understand? We'll let the Righteous Man decide who's in the wrong."

That struck home. Cale was Riven's only rival for the guildmaster's ear. Where Cale urged caution and patience to the Righteous Man, Riven urged violence, and violence now. Most times, events had proven Cale's counsel the better. Riven would not want to make the Righteous Man choose between them. Not yet.

Cale watched with satisfaction as Riven's smug sneer twisted into a scowl. Tight lipped, the assassin fixed him with a menacing glare. "You push me too hard, Cale, and I'll gut you like a bluefish. The Righteous Man be damned."

Still unwilling to back down, Cale leaned forward and stared unflinchingly into Riven's scarred face. The assassin had lost an eye on a job years ago but disdained an eye patch. The scarred, empty hole in his face provided a window into a soul equally scarred and empty. "You know where to find me," Cale calmly stated.

To his credit, Riven gave no ground either. "That's right," the assassin replied softly. "I do." He flashed stained teeth through a neatly tended goatee. "The Righteous Man won't be able to protect you forever, Cale. When he's gone, I'll still be here. Then we'll have this conversation again." Riven's hard gaze promised blood.

Cale leaned back in his chair and tried to look unconcerned. "It's starting to stink in here. Be about your business, errand boy."

Riven jumped to his feet and whipped a saber from its scabbard before Cale could even get a dagger drawn. Suddenly staring down the point of Riven's blade, Cale slowly removed his hand from the dagger's hilt. His heart raced. Riven stared at him a long moment, waving the saber blade under Cale's chin. Cale said nothing, only stared. At last the assassin sheathed his blade and slowly sat back down. His signature sneer returned tenfold.

"You're slow, Cale," he mocked. "Very slow. You're like a little dog . . . lots of yap—" he leaned forward and champed his teeth, his one eye burning a hot hole of hate into Cale's consciousness— "but no bite." He sat back and smugly crossed his arms over his chest.

We'll see, bastard, Cale thought. You show me your back, and I'll show you your grave. Though he itched to say those words aloud, Cale kept his calm and said, "The information, Riven."

The assassin made a deliberate show of slowly quaffing from his tankard before speaking. "The information is this, Cale: Naglatha has hired us—"

"Naglatha! Since when do we work for an agent of the kingdom of Thay?"

"Since she started paying in platinum suns," Riven snapped. "Now shut up and listen." The assassin leaned forward and spoke in a whisper. His breath made Cale want to gag. "An issue is soon to be before the Hulorn, and Naglatha wishes to see it decided in Thay's favor. The

Righteous Man assured her that he could see to it."

"What issue?"

"Not my business," replied Riven easily. "Not yours either. We're just providing the leverage."

Cale saw immediately where the conversation was going. He shook his head and spoke hurriedly, trying to head it off. "I've already told the Righteous Man that I've got nothing on Thamalon Uskevren. I'm working on it, but the man is clean."

"So you say," replied Riven. "But you've been 'working on it' for years. The Righteous Man is growing impatient, and so am I. No one is that clean, Cale. Your inability to come up with some dirt makes a man wonder."

Cale leaned forward in his chair with narrowed eyes. That comment hit too close to the mark. "Wonder about what?" Under the table, his left hand fingered a dagger hilt.

Riven returned his cold stare, unflinching. "About where your loyalties lie."

Cale sniffed derisively and leaned back in his chair as though unconcerned. "It's no wonder you're a lackey. You don't see the value of having a Night Knives agent in the Uskevren household? I've proved my worth to the Righteous Man ten times over, but I can't find something that doesn't exist. We'll have to use someone else."

Riven laughed, a sound like a hacking cough, and said, "It's already been decided. We're using Uskevren. He's got the most influential voice among the Old Chauncel. Since you've been unable to come up with anything, I've convinced the Righteous Man to address matters more directly."

At the words "more directly," a pit formed in Cale's stomach. The Old Chauncel was a common name for the small set of wealthy families that comprised the money—and power—elite of the city of Selgaunt. Few were nearly as "clean" as the Uskevren, but fewer still deserved the attention of the Night Knives. The Uskevren had Thamalon at its head, and Thamalon commanded respect. Cale knew what was coming next.

Riven went on with a grin, "It's like this: You're going to arrange the kidnapping of his youngest son. What's his name . . . Talbot? While we're holding the little bastard, his father will do exactly what we say. If not, I'll split little Talbot from gut to gullet and move on to the next son."

With difficulty, Cale contained the storm that exploded in his soul and managed to maintain a calm facade. Talbot to be kidnapped! The boy had only recently returned to Selgaunt after being involved in a hunting accident in the forests outside the city. He wasn't even living at Stormweather Towers, the family's city estate. Since the accident, he had been residing in one of the tallhouses the Uskevren had scattered around the city. Where he's an easy target, Cale thought. Riven obviously knew none of that or Talbot would have been taken already, without Cale's involvement.

Cale took a deep breath and tried to craft an excuse on the fly. "Kidnapping the boy is unwise," he said. "Thamalon will retaliate afterward. All the Scepters in the city will come down on the guild." Selgaunt's Scepters could make business difficult if a noble like Thamalon forced them into action. Cale shook his head. "No, it's definitely unwise. Tell the Righteous Man it can't be done."

"I'm not telling him anything," Riven spat and slammed his fist down on the table. "You'll do exactly what you're told. The Righteous Man understands the risks. You figure out a time when the boy is vulnerable and leave word for me here, with Jelkins." He jerked a thumb over his shoulder to indicate the skinny barkeep. "I'll assemble the team. You've got two days."

Somehow, despite his numbness, Cale managed a nod. He pushed back his chair and stood on legs gone weak. Two days! A mere two days! He must betray Thamalon, disobey the Righteous Man, or confess his past and lose everything that mattered. Either way, nothing would stay the same. If he betrayed his lord, he could not live with himself. If he disobeyed the Righteous Man, he would be dead within a tenday. If he confessed his past, Thamalon would dismiss him and Thazienne would hate him. He could not bear that.

In a flash of desperate inspiration, he saw a way out—plunge his blade into Riven's throat right now. No one in the Stag would bat an eye, and he could concoct an explanation for the Righteous Man afterward. Hells, he had been doing exactly that, concocting stories for the Righteous Man, for the past nine years. Everything could go on as it had.

His hand drifted to his dagger hilt. Riven hunched over the table, finishing his ale, unsuspecting. Cale stared at the back of the assassin's neck, the exposed flesh visible, beckoning. One thrust through the throat, a gurgle, then it would be over, just as with the man back in the alley.

"Unwise," Riven said without looking up. *"That,* Cale, would be unwise."

Cale heard the smile, and the challenge, in the assassin's words. Without a word, he spun on his heel and stalked out of the Stag. He needed to think.

When he reached the street, he nearly collapsed. The hopelessness of his situation weighed on him like a hundredweight. He bitterly recalled a concept from dwarven philosophy and mouthed it like a curse. *"Korvikoum,"* he hissed. Linguists often translated the term as "fate" or "destiny," but Cale knew its meaning to be subtly different—something more like "the necessary consequence of previous choices."

In that instant, he hated dwarven philosophy. "Fate" put responsibility on a cosmic force with designs of its own. *Korvikoum* put responsibility squarely on his own shoulders.

"I will not betray the Uskevren," he vowed to the night. "I will not. I'll die before I see Talbot hurt." He found the explicitness of the resolution unexpectedly liberating. "I will die first," he vowed to himself again, this time with a grim smile.

He took a great breath of cool winter air, tasted the salt tang of the wind blowing off Selgaunt Bay, and began to walk. And think. He had to find another way out.

The well-tended streets he trod fairly reeked of wealth. Shop after shop lined the broad avenues, and even the most common sported at least a colorful awning and fresh paint on the shutters. Many had custom stonework on the rainspouts or carved windowsills made from exotic wood. Sculptures of the oddest creatures—centaurs, chimeras, and even satyrs—stood in nearly every public square, the artisans no doubt commissioned by the city's ridiculous ruler, the Hulorn. Cale found Selgaunt laughable. The city tried hard to look the center of sophistication and gentility but only managed to look like a street whore in full makeup. The veneer of wealth obscured a city full of decadent, back-stabbing nobles little better than well-educated guttersnipes. Except for his own lord, of course.

Since taking his position at Stormweather Towers, Cale had come to respect Thamalon Uskevren as fair, honest, and self-made—a rare man indeed among the jaded nobility that made up Selgaunt's Old Chauncel. Cale admired the Old Owl's mettle. Over the years he and Thamalon had become friends of sorts, colleagues even, and if Cale wanted to maintain that relationship he had to thwart Talbot's kidnapping without revealing that he was a spy for the Night Knives—Selgaunt's guild of assassins and thieves. Only one option seemed open to him, and it was desperate. And dangerous.

He had nothing else.

He thought through the rudiments of a plan as he walked, then turned east and headed for the gambling dens along the wharf. If his plan were to succeed, he would need help. He could trust only one, very short person.

He sought Jak in three gaming houses before he finally spotted the halfling seated at a card table in the Scarlet Knave. A disreputable establishment with a mediocre bar and eatery attached, the Knave had of late become popular among Selgaunt's lesser nobles. The place drew bored second sons eager to gamble away their families' fivestars like a sugar-ice street vendor drew children. Nobles, however, made up only a fraction of the thick crowd. Everyone from itinerant adventurers and legitimate merchants to rogues and pimps thronged the gaming tables and pleasure rooms. In places like the Knave, Cale observed, Selgaunt's true nature bobbed to the surface—the otherwise clear lines of social hierarchy gave way to the universal brotherhood of vice.

Before approaching Jak's table, Cale wove through the crowd and flashed enough fivestars at the barkeep to secure one of the many private meeting rooms upstairs. Typically, the rooms were used for exclusive games, secret business deals, or illicit liaisons. Cale wanted one for a more mundane purpose—what he had to tell Jak was for their ears alone.

After watching the door for a time to be sure Riven had not followed him, he casually worked his way across the carpeted floor until he stood opposite Jak's table, perhaps seven paces away. Through the shifting crowd, he glimpsed a sea of coins glittering on the table before the trim, three-and-a-half foot-tall halfling. The little man's mop of red hair bobbed up and down as he chattered good-naturedly with the six disgruntled nobles who shared his table but not his good fortune. They were playing Blades and Scales, a card game that required skill and luck in equal parts. Cale knew Jak Fleet to have plenty of both, despite the fact that he looked as much like an adolescent human boy as a professional gambler. The fops hadn't a chance.

With his suede cap, embroidered blue doublet, and Sembian high boots, Jak looked every bit a miniature fop himself. Only his long, pointed sideburns and shrewd green eyes indicated his maturity. In truth, the little man was both a priest of Brandobaris, the halfling god of thieves, and a rogue of no small skill. He was also Cale's only friend in Selgaunt.

After a few minutes, Cale caught Jak's eye. The little man's expression of happy surprise vanished in an instant when Cale surreptitiously shook his head to indicate caution. Instantly, Jak returned his attention to the game and only occasionally cast a guarded glance toward Cale.

Though Jak operated as an independent in Selgaunt's gang-dominated underworld—a situation Cale thought of as akin to swimming the shark-infested Inner Sea with only a table knife for protection—the little man still knew guild hand-cant. So while Jak seemingly paid full attention to the card game, Cale used a series of subtle hand gestures to communicate a message: "Upstairs. Number seven. Urgent."

Jak gave a slight nod while laughing at a noble's joke, and Cale made his way upstairs. The halfling would come as soon as he could.

Cale did not have to wait long. Within a quarter-hour, the meeting room door opened and Jak strolled in, teeth shining and purse chinking.

"This must be important for you to interrupt *that* run of Tymora's favor," he observed, invoking the name of the goddess of fortune. What's going on, Cale? Have I stepped on the Righteous Man's toes again?" Jak often inadvertently interfered with the Night Knives' operations. The fact that he was still alive showed he did indeed have the favor of Tymora.

"No, no, it's nothing like that." Cale blew out a sigh and ran a hand over his head. "I have a problem, Jak. I need help."

Jak's face grew serious. He slid into the chair across from Cale and rested his small hands on the table. "Go on."

"The Knives want me to arrange the kidnapping of Talbot Uskevren." He did not need to explain the dilemma further. Jak knew all about Cale's position with the Knives and that for the past several years he had been secretly shielding the Uskevren from the Righteous Man, rather than exposing the family's vulnerabilities.

The little man eased back in his chair and blew out a soft whistle. "That does bring the boil to a head now doesn't it? Dark, Cale! I told you to get out of the Night Knives years ago."

Cale smiled tiredly. "Easier said than done, my friend. The Righteous Man isn't going to let me walk away. I'm too valuable to him. If I tried, he'd either kill me or tip my past to Thamalon, and . . ." He shook his head, unwilling to voice the thought aloud.

"And that would be that," Jak finished. His green eyes flashed angrily. "The *Righteous* Man indeed! He's a murderous priest of Mask, by the Trickster's hairy toes." He drummed his hairy-knuckled fingers on the tabletop and stared earnestly at Cale. "What are you going to do?"

Cale steepled his fingers before his face and looked Jak in the eye. He had already decided not to mince words. "I'm going to ambush the hit team and kill every one of them. Afterward, I'll tell the Righteous Man that a rival gang ambushed us and only I escaped."

Cale had expected Jak to tell him he was mad, but to the

halfling's credit, he merely nodded. "That could work, assuming no one escapes. Who's leading the team?"

"Drasek Riven."

"Riven," Jak softly hissed. "That figures." He sat back in his chair and stroked his chin, considering. Cale waited silently, unwilling to press. He was asking a lot of the little man.

To his surprise, Jak took only a few moments before flashing a grim smile. "We've been friends a long time, Erevis," the halfling said. "If you need me, I'm in."

Cale stared solemnly at his friend. Though grateful for Jak's offer, he could not yet accept it. Not before he told the little man everything. Cale could not ask Jak to risk his life without knowing the kind of man he had agreed to help.

"Jak, I need . . ." He stopped, cleared his throat, and started over. "You don't know much about me, about my past I mean, before I came to Selgaunt."

Jak held up a small palm and shook his head. "That's true enough, but that's your business, Cale. You don't owe me any explanations."

"I know that, but under the circumstances . . . I think you should know who you're helping."

Jak studied him carefully, trying to read his face. At last, the halfling blew out a sigh and sank into his chair. After crossing his arms over his chest, he looked like a man bracing for a storm. "All right. If you insist."

Cale hesitated, suddenly unsure of where to begin. He longed to get the secret off his soul, but feared Jak's response. If the little man balked, he had no one else to whom he could turn. He forced himself to begin. "You know that I came to Selgaunt from Westgate?"

Jak nodded. Westgate straddled the trade route between the Inner Sea and the Sword Coast; a large, rich city brimming with merchants and thieves, pirates and assassins.

"I came here because I was running."

Jak leaned forward at that, his green eyes curiously intense. "From what?"

Cale looked at his hands while he spoke, embarrassed by his past. "When I was just a boy, I was recruited by the Night Masks."

Jak gave a low whistle at the mention of Westgate's infamous, but now defunct, thieves' guild. "Dark," he softly cursed.

Cale ignored him and continued: "I received all the standard training . . ." He hesitated at Jak's raised eyebrows. The halfling obviously had some idea of what Night Mask "standard training" entailed. Cale hurried on. ". . . but got moved to letters work pretty quick."

Jak gave a start. "You? A letters man? Translations and such?" He chuckled softly at Cale's nod. "I always knew you were too damned smart for your own good, Cale. How many languages do you speak?"

"Nine."

"Nine!"

Cale sighed in exasperation. "If you'll stop interrupting," he snapped, "maybe I can tell you the rest before dawn."

Jak started to say something, thought better of it, and closed his mouth with *pop*. He sank into his chair, sulking.

Cale suppressed a smile. The little man looked like a petulant child ordered into a corner. Cale spoke his next words in a soft, tense voice. "For a lot of years, I did what Mask guildsmen did—steal, kill, intimidate. I got tired of it, even doing letters work, so I started skimming coin. When it got too hot, I ran—here." He gestured expansively and gave Jak a slight smile. "You know the rest."

Jak sat silently for a moment, staring at Cale as though wondering whether or not it was all right to speak. When Cale gave a nod, Jak sat up in his chair and adopted an overly serious mien. "Indeed, I do know the rest of your sorry tale, my bald friend. It goes something like this: Despite the advice of your intrepid and fearless halfling friend, Jak Fleet, you foolishly fell in with the Righteous Man and his gang of thugs. The guild being otherwise filled with incompetents, you rose quickly through its ranks. Ultimately, you developed this harebrained scheme to place guild operatives in the noble houses." He looked up with a straight face, his green eyes all innocence. "So far, so good?"

Cale smiled despite himself. Jak grinned and went on.

"Unfortunately for you, you came to actually like Thamalon Uskevren and to care for his daughter even more. You protected them over the years by feeding the Righteous Man harmless information. Oh, you occasionally dropped some juicy bit that hurt this or that noble family but never anything that seriously compromised the Uskevren. Now that very scheme has turned around and bitten you in the tail."

Korvikoum, Cale thought.

"And now your pigeons have come home to roost."

Cale nodded.

"And now—"

"I get the point," Cale snapped.

"Good." Jak sat silently for a moment. He shook his head and his face grew serious. "That's a tangled web, my friend, and a lot for one man to carry around. I don't know how you've done it."

Cale held his tongue. He suddenly felt very tired.

"Erevis Cale isn't even your real name, is it?" The halfling spoke softly. "Can you tell me?"

Cale shook his head. "You don't want to know."

Jak accepted that with a slow nod. "I guess what I call you doesn't really matter anyway. I already know what makes up the man." Thoughtful, the halfling reached into his belt pouch and pulled out his ivory-bowled pipe. Cale watched silently while his friend tamped the pipeweed and lit. His entire life turned on Jak's next words. After a time, Jak spoke.

"This doesn't change anything, Cale. I'm still your friend and I'm still in." He blew out a cloud of aromatic smoke.

Cale merely nodded, overcome, too grateful for words. He had a chance.

"Plan?" Jak asked from around his pipe.

Cale smiled. "Ever drive a nobleman's carriage?"

Near midnight, Cale returned to the brooding turrets of Stormweather Towers and found the household dark. He quietly entered via the servant's entrance and padded up the spiral staircase to the spartan suite that served as his quarters. Needing to speak to Thamalon right away, he changed into his butler's attire—ill-fitting black pants, white shirt, purple-and-black laced doublet—and silently made the rounds of the great house for what might be the last time.

After tomorrow night, he thought sadly, I may never set foot here again.

The plan to ambush the Night Knives hit team presented tremendous risk. He and Jak would need Tymora's own luck to get out alive.

I've got no choice, he reminded himself. Telling Thamalon the truth would cost him everything. The Owl would not trust him again, and Thazienne would never forgive the betrayal. He could run away, of course, as he had from Westgate.

Back in Westgate, though, he had had no friends, no home, no loyalties, nothing to keep him from turning tail. Now, he had a family, he had a friend, people he loved.

I'm through running, he resolved. Fortified, he strode downstairs to look for Lord Uskevren.

He found him seated amidst the book-lined walls of the first floor library, his lord's typical nighttime haunt. Thamalon sat in his favorite chair—a plain high back fashioned from Archendale walnut—and considered an unfinished chess match that sat on the low table before him. A pair of silver goblets and an open bottle of Storm Ruby rested on the floor beside his chair, the wine nearly half gone. The glow of the blazing hearth fire highlighted the tense lines of Thamalon's face.

Cale stood silently in the doorway, suddenly unwilling to disturb his lord. Taking in the wine and incomplete chess match, he knew that another game between Talbot and Thamalon had ended in shouting. Perhaps now was not the best time—

"Erevis!" Thamalon caught sight of him and gave a tired smile. "It's good to see you back. How went the business with your cousin?"

Cale winced inwardly. Years ago, when it had become clear to him that information about the goings-on in Selgaunt's underworld would be useful to Thamalon, he had concocted a fictional cousin, a disreputable man who moved in the darker circles and with whom Cale remained in reluctant contact. While the information Cale provided under the guise of this cousin had repeatedly proven useful to Thamalon in sniffing out this or that plot by a rival house, mention of it only served to remind Cale that his life was a lie.

"The business went well, my lord. It took an unexpected turn, but all is well. Or will be. The affair is yet incomplete, and I must ask a favor."

"Of course." Thamalon gestured at the cushioned chair on the other side of the chessboard. "Come in and sit down, old friend."

Cale strode slowly across the hardwood floor and sat rigidly in the chair.

"Wine?" Thamalon asked as he refilled his own goblet.

"No thank you, my lord."

"Care to finish?" Thamalon gestured at the chessboard, the beginnings of a smile playing at the corners of his mouth.

Cale returned the smile halfheartedly and studied Talbot's jade pieces. Thamalon always played ivory. After a few moments he shook his head. "My lord seeks to entrap me. Ivory checkmates in four moves."

Laughing aloud in his deep voice, Thamalon raised his goblet in a mock toast. It pleased Cale to see his lord's spirits lightened. "Excellent, Erevis, excellent. How is it that we've never played?"

Cale smiled softly. "Because I have no desire to challenge my lord's skills. A wise man knows better."

Thamalon dismissed the flattery with a tired wave. "If that were true, old friend, then one would be forced to conclude that Selgaunt is filled with fools, for I find challenges at every turn. Without your aid . . ." He trailed off and bowed his head in fatigue. When he looked up, he again wore a tired smile. "I forget myself. You spoke of a favor?"

At that instant, Cale came within a bladewidth of confessing everything. Seeing his lord refuse to bow under the weight of disappointing sons, an aloof wife, and constant plots by rival houses, he found himself overcome with admiration. How could he keep secrets from this man who confided everything to him?

His past rushed up his throat, the story eager to be told. It would be so easy . . .

No! he thought. Not even Thamalon could forgive such a lie.

With a conscious effort of will, he swallowed the temptation and instead said, "Yes, Lord. Forgive my presumption, but my cousin remains in some minor difficulty. I wonder if I might have leave to use one of the old carriages and the tallhouse on Lurvin Street for the next two days."

At that, Thamalon sat forward, eyes intent, his bushy brows narrowed in thought. "This must be a serious matter for you to put yourself out so, Erevis. Perhaps I can be of some help."

"No, Lord," Cale quickly replied, even while loving Thamalon for the offer. "I must do this alone. I cannot risk the Uskevren reputation by having the doings of my cousin associated with the family. This is a matter to be kept between him and me."

"Hmm." Cale saw discernment in Thamalon's gaze and knew the Owl suspected the story to be false. Yet his lord respected his privacy and probed no further. Cale loved him all the more for that.

"Very well then, Erevis. The carriage is yours, as is the tallhouse."

"Thank you, Lord." Cale unfolded his tall frame from the chair and rose. "Lord Uskevren, I do not know how this business will play out, but—"

"Erevis," Thamalon cut him off, eyes aglow with worry, "will you not let me help? I see that you are distressed. You of all people need keep no secrets from me. I have trusted you utterly for years. Will you not trust me with this?"

Cale choked on the bitter taste of his own lies. He lowered his head to hide his suddenly welling eyes. *I have trusted you utterly.* He did not even trust himself enough to reply.

After an uncomfortably long silence, Thamalon sighed and nodded. "I understand. We all have our secrets. Take care of yourself then, Erevis."

"Yes, Lord," Cale managed to mutter, and hurried from the library.

Overcome with guilt, he stumbled to his quarters. After lighting a candle on the night table he collapsed into his reading chair and held his head in his hands. He sat that way a long while, inhaling the smell of his deceptions. It had been his idea to plant a guild spy within House Uskevren. It was he who had arranged for the previous butler to die in a street robbery. His doing, all of it.

That was before I knew them, he rationalized, before I changed—

He had left his door open, and a soft knock on the doorjamb snapped his head up.

Framed in the soft glow of the candlelight, Thazienne's beauty stole his breath. Tight-fitting leather breeches and a laced jerkin highlighted the sleek curves of her figure. She wore her raven hair cut short, Cormyrean fashion, accenting a smooth complexion and shining green eyes. She somehow managed to look both naive and self-possessed all at the same time. That beauty—that fearless innocence—drew Cale to her like a lodestone to iron.

"I heard you come in," she said with a playful smile, "and saw that your door was open—" When she saw his face, her smile vanished into a look of worried concern. "Erevis, what's wrong?" She rushed across the room and sat on the arm of his chair. Her light touch on his forearm sent his heart spinning. Her smell, of lavender and rose oil, intoxicated him.

She is beyond you, fool, he reprimanded himself. Ten years your younger and the daughter of your lord. What would she have to do with a fraud and liar like you?

His internal protestations melted in the warmth that came off her body.

"Erevis, what is it? Has something happened?"

He got a firm grip on himself before looking into her eyes. "Are you going out?" He made a gesture that took in her thieving leathers.

She shot him a look that would have done her mother proud. "Do not change the subject, Erevis Cale. I asked you if something has happened." Despite her stern tone, her soft eyes glowed with concern. Cale wilted.

"Yes, Thazienne. Something has happened. Something . . .

terrible. I have to go away for a while. I hope . . . I hope to come back soon."

She sat bolt upright. *"Hope?* What do you mean? Where are you going?"

He shook his head. "I can't tell you, Thazienne—"

"Is this some task my father set you on? If he is putting you in danger . . ." She jumped to her feet and looked as though she might storm off to find Thamalon on the instant.

"No, no, it's nothing like that." He brushed his fingers across her arm to turn her around. Her skin was so smooth. "It's nothing like that," he said again, the feel of her flesh still tingling on his fingertips. "It's personal business."

"Personal? Then tell me what it is. Maybe I can help." She pulled back her jerkin to reveal a dagger at her belt and Cale caught a tantalizing flash of skin. "You know I'm no amateur to our kind of work."

Our kind of work. Thazienne knew that he could handle himself in the shadows but nothing more about his past. He had played down his skills and explained them as the result of a wild youth.

"No," he conceded, "I know you're no amateur." He studied her eyes, seeking her soul. She stared back for only a moment before turning shyly away. Despite her "wilding," he was confident that her hands remained free of real bloodshed. He wanted them to stay that way. "This is a different kind of work."

"You think I can't handle it?" Her stance and the hard set of her jaw told him only one answer was acceptable.

"No, it's not that. I have to do it alone."

"Why?"

"Damn it, Tazi, I can't tell you why!"

She gave a start at that. He never called her Tazi, only Mistress Uskevren in the presence of others, or Thazienne when they were alone. She shook her surprise off quickly and said, "You mean you *won't* tell me why."

He hung his head, frustrated but unwilling to give in to anger. Not when this might be the last time he ever saw her. "I just can't, Thazienne. Please? I can't."

She huffed and considered him coolly for a long moment. "Very well then, Erevis Cale. Have it your way." She spun on her heel and stomped for the hall. Her steps slowed as she crossed the room, as though with each step she took her anger dissipated fractionally. When she reached the doorway she stopped, quivering, her back to him. "You be careful, Erevis," she said without turning. "Whatever this is, be careful. You take care of this the same way you take care of everything, all right? Then . . . come back."

Cale could hear the tears in her voice, but before he could say a word, she pulled the door shut and hurried down the hall.

"Goodbye, Tazi," he whispered through welling eyes.

A fitful sleep came with difficulty and he rose before dawn.

The red wax dripped like blood onto the parchment, sealing the letter, likely sealing his fate. Cale had written it earlier in the morning, his light script an ironic counterpoint to the weight in his soul. *Tonight,* the letter read. *Tenth hour. Drover's Square. Minimal Guard.* A simple letter with a message that would be meaningful only to Riven—but its delivery would change Cale's life. Or end it. This letter would set everything into motion, and make his choice irrevocable.

All choices are irrevocable, he chided himself. That's why you're in this fix in the first place.

He had made most of the necessary preparations before dawn, while the Uskevren still slept. He thought it best to act quickly so that Riven would have minimal time to assemble the hit team. Without explanation, he had informed the staff of his upcoming absence and set the household affairs in order. He had personally readied the carriage and loaded it with a locked wooden trunk taken from his quarters.

Like a coffin holding a long dead corpse, that trunk entombed the trappings of his past life: enchanted leather armor taken from the bloody body of a rival, Selbrin Del, on a wharf in Westgate; the still keen-edged blades, both long and short, with which he did his work; and the deadly, magical necklace and the potion of healing given him by Amaunt Corelin, a grateful mage. He had hoped to leave that trunk locked forever, the contents never to be exhumed, but circumstances had made that impossible. The old Cale had to be resurrected.

Smiling mirthlessly, he rose from the walnut desk and strode across the parlor to the orange uniformed messenger boy standing in the doorway.

"Take this to the Black Stag," he said, handing over the letter. The boy abruptly cut his bored yawn short, and his eyes grew to the size of coins. Cale suppressed a smile. "You know it?"

"Yes, sir," the boy said, not quite able to hide a nervous quaver.

"Good. Hand deliver this to the barkeep there. His name is Jelkins. Tell him this is for Riven. Do you understand?"

"Jelkins, the barkeep at the Black Stag. For Riven. Yes, sir."

Cale pulled a shining fivestar from his vest pocket and pressed the gold coin into the nervous messenger's hand. The boy gasped; messengers usually received only a silver raven.

"Thank you, sir!"

"You're welcome. That will be all."

"Good day then, sir." Grinning, the boy buttoned his

coat against the chill, pulled on a pair of wool mittens, and hurried out. Cale figured the grin would last only until the boy forgot the shining coin and remembered his dark destination. He needn't have been afraid, though. The Stag wasn't dangerous by day. The animals only came out at night.

Cale glided through the darkness like a ghost. Stalking through the shadowy streets of the warehouse district with long sword and dagger at his belt, he felt surprisingly—and horribly—*right*. Though he normally suppressed his dark side, tonight he consciously gave it the reins. If he were to succeed, he would need the old Cale: Cale the assassin and thief, not the reborn butler. He just hoped he could separate the two again when the night was done.

He approached Drover's Square from the south, stopped a block short, and ducked into the shadows of a wheelwright's workshop. Before him loomed the tall brick warehouses typical of the district. The wide streets that he would use as his approach sat empty but for the occasional whirlwind of snow whipped up by the bitter wind. He frowned thoughtfully at that. While the cold month of Nightal was hardly the height of caravan season, it was still unusual for the streets to be so empty. Trade never stopped entirely in Selgaunt, even in the height of winter, even at this hour. The strangely forlorn streets made him uneasy.

Calm down, he ordered himself. There's no one here because those guards who weren't driven off by the cold were paid off by Riven. Standard Knives practice on a hit.

Still, Cale had not survived years in the underworlds of Westgate and Selgaunt by acting incautiously. He silently watched the approach to the square for another few minutes, wary. Still no one. His keen hearing picked up no sounds. Even the ubiquitous rumble of carts along Rauncel's Ride was swallowed by the howl of the wind. Satisfied at last, he prowled through the shadows toward the three-story warehouse that was his first target.

He had only a bit more than a quarter of an hour to do his work—a narrow margin. When the bells of the Temple of Song sounded the tenth hour, a disguised Jak would drive the carriage in from the west, then all the Nine Hells would break loose.

Cale knew what to expect from the Night Knives hit team. Since his letter to Riven had specified only a light guard, he anticipated no more than twelve men. The Righteous Man could spare no more; after all, the guild numbered only thirty or forty men in total. Six or seven of Riven's team would be stationed on the ground of the square, armed with nets and mancatchers. Another four or six slingers will be stationed on the rooftops, he thought grimly, as he flattened himself against the rear of the warehouse and gazed up its towering brick face. To provide cover if something goes wrong.

They would be the first to die.

Pleased with how easily his skills and killer's mindset had returned to him, he gave a hard smile. He had moved soundlessly from shadow to shadow. He wore his leather armor more easily than he did his butler's doublet. His longsword and daggers hung comfortably from his belt. The Night Knives were about to die.

This is who you are, a voice whispered in his mind, an uncomfortable thought to which he hurriedly added, at least for tonight.

He ran his hands over the wall. The bricks were uneven, weathered, craggy. An easy climb, even in his leather gloves. He began to ascend.

Within minutes he had scaled the forty feet to the roof. Still he heard nothing, and still he saw no one on the street below. Slowly, he peeked over the edge, careful to keep his mouth below the lip of the roof so the cloud of his breath would not give him away.

He spotted them fifty feet away on the opposite side of the rooftop, two Knives assasins holding slings stood silhouetted by Selûne's pale light. They were leaning over the far edge of the building to look down on the square, their backs to Cale, their cloaks whipping in the wind. Without a sound, he slipped over the low safety wall and crouched in the darkness. No response from the Night Knives. Slowly, he withdrew his long sword from its oiled scabbard, his eyes on the assassins all the while. Still no movement. He allowed himself a cool, satisfied smile.

His approach would have to be flawless. Except for a large wooden rain vat and some unused crates, the rooftop provided no cover. Undeterred, he stalked forward, hugging the shadows near the roof's edge, staying out of the moonlight. When he was within five paces, he closed his eyes for a moment, steeled himself, and rushed forward.

Before he had taken three strides, he slipped in a pool of fluid. His feet flew skyward and his back slammed down on the roof—hard.

"Ooomph." The impact blew the breath from his lungs. Gasping, he struggled to rise and bring his blade to bear, knowing two Night Knives were rushing him, knowing he had only seconds to live.

Nothing happened.

Still gasping, he sat up and reoriented himself. Inexplicably, the assassins had not moved. The fluid he had slipped in, the sticky, still-warm fluid that now soaked his cloak—

Blood. The ground near the assassins was covered in it. He stared dumbly at his blood-covered fingers while a nervous shudder raced up his spine. He jumped to his feet and pulled both Knives back from the edge. Slit throat and a stab through the chest. Both had been bled out and put back at their posts. Professional work.

"Dark," he softly cursed.

He looked down on the square and saw nothing. What in the Hells?

The bells of the House of Song began to sound the tenth hour. Jak would be coming.

A terrible thought took shape in his mind. He raced to the eastern edge of the rooftop and looked across the alley to the adjacent warehouse. He could see nothing in the darkness. Without hesitation, he leaped across the eight-foot void and hit the adjacent roof in a roll. He leaped to his feet, caution thrown to the bitter wind, and sped to the edge overlooking the square. Two more corpses lay in a bloody pool, their unused slings at their feet.

The bells ceased tolling and the sudden silence felt ominous. Still nothing in the square. "Dark and Empty," Cale muttered. "Jak is driving into an ambush."

Jak whipped the snorting horses into a steady canter. At that pace the carriage bounced through the wide streets like a skipping stone over water, but he thought it best to have some speed as he approached Drover's Square. Don't want to be too easy a target, he thought wryly.

He would have taken this job for no one but Cale. While he regularly took incredible risks in the name of his god, Jak generally preferred calculated gambles to blind leaps. The Master of Stealth himself might enter the endless inferno of Baator on a mere whim, but Jak would do so only after due deliberation and for a good cause. A good cause like a friend in trouble. It might not have been how Brandobaris did things, but . . .

"But you're a god," Jak murmured to the sky, reaching

under the oversized cloak and twice tapping the holy symbol that hung from his belt. "And I'm a man. Your margin for error is bigger." Grinning sheepishly, he hurriedly added, "No offense, of course."

Tonight was hardly the night to irritate the Lord of Stealth with his oft-criticized impertinence. Jak and Cale would need all the Trickster's wiles to come through this little affair unbloodied.

Nearing Drover's Square, he hurriedly rechecked his "disguise." He stood balanced precariously atop the coachman's seat, wearing a large gray overcoat that draped past his real feet to reach a pair of human-sized boots nailed into the floorboards. Cale had insisted on the disguise. Everything must look normal, he had said, or the Night Knives would sniff out the ambush. A halfling driving a nobleman's coach in Selgaunt was decidedly abnormal.

So I get to play dress-up, he thought, while Cale does the real work.

Satisfied that he looked at least passably human, he turned to the west and headed toward the square. The steady drumbeat of hooves on cobblestones echoed off the bricks. The snow-dusted streets stood empty. He steered the horses under the arch that spanned the western entrance to Drover's Square, slowed the team a bit, and guided the carriage into the killing field.

If Cale had meant to choose an ideal ambush point in order to minimize suspicion, he had chosen well. Drover's Square offered an unparalleled field of fire. There was a wide-open expanse of cobblestones bordered by tall buildings—perfect perches for snipers. The area was littered with unhitched wagons and piles of discarded crates—perfect for hiding ground forces. Moonlight trickling between the looming warehouses cast a crazy quilt of shadows. Jak felt utterly exposed. The Knives could be anywhere.

They won't take chances with bows, he assured himself. They want the boy alive, and they won't want a stray arrow to eliminate their prize.

Still, his heart raced. Mouthing a prayer to Brandobaris, he guided the carriage across the square.

A sudden sound jerked his head skyward. Cale's voice—shouting in Lurienal, the halflings' tongue—from a nearby rooftop. *"Get out of there, Jak! This isn't a Night Knives oper—"*

Shouts from all around drowned out Cale's warning as armed men burst from the surrounding buildings and swarmed toward the carriage, blades and crossbows bare.

"Trickster's hairy toes," Jak grumbled, then thought, There must be thirty or more!

They ran toward the carriage from all sides, screaming for him to halt. The horses bucked and snorted, skittish as the men began to close.

Thinking fast, Jak stripped off the oversized cloak and hurriedly murmured a prayer to the Lord of Stealth. On the instant, he vanished from sight. Invisible now, he leaped from the carriage and swatted the already nervous lead horse in the rump. "Hyah!"

The team bolted and took the bouncing carriage with it. Two of the ambushers tried to halt the speeding carriage, and the panicked horses ran them down, crushing bones under a flurry of merciless hooves. The rest of the men sped after the bouncing coach, still shouting for a nonexistent driver to halt. Crossbows twanged, and bolts thudded into wood. Somehow, another of Cale's monumental shouts managed to rise above the din, again in Lurienal.

"Take cover, Jak!"

"Dark!" Jak breathed, and raced for the nearest warehouse.

Hurriedly, Cale affixed his grapnel to a carved rain-spout and fed the rope down the side of the warehouse. "Dark," he murmured as he worked. "Dark and empty." This had turned bad fast. Jak would need help. He hoped the little man had heard his warning.

There must be thirty men down there, he thought. Who in the Nine Hells are they?

Shouting men scrambled around the square and tried to corral the panicked horses. Several of the ambushers had already been run down. Their crushed bodies littered the cobblestones, broken limbs cocked at grotesque angles. It would only be a matter of time before the rest either calmed the horses or shot the team down. Cale had to move now.

He selected the most tightly packed group of men within range, plucked a large crystal globe from his necklace, and hurled it through the air across the square. When the globe struck the cobblestones in the midst of the crowd, Drover's Square exploded in fire. The force of the blast blew bodies apart and threw the pieces into the air like dry leaves in a gale. Screams and the stink of burning flesh filled the air. Many of the men scattered, unsure of where their attacker lurked, while others still pursued the carriage. Cale spared the carnage only a glance before climbing over the edge and shinnying down the rope.

Halfway down he peered over his shoulder, chose another cluster of men, and hurled a second globe from the necklace. Again orange fire blossomed, and again men burned and died. The fireballs would attract the city watch, he knew, but he intended to be gone before they arrived. He would retrieve Jak and get the Hells out of here.

He descended into a chaotic furnace of thick smoke, screaming men, burning wagons, and rearing horses. No one had yet sighted him. He dropped the last ten feet to the ground, whirled, and whipped out his longsword.

He stood face to face with Drasek Riven.

"Riven? What in the Hells—"

The assassin lunged forward, both blades low. Cale leaped back like a cat but felt the points of Riven's sabers slice the cloth of his cloak. He clumsily parried one of the assassin's follow-up slashes but took a shallow cut across the forearm from Riven's other saber. A minor wound. Sneering, Riven backed off.

"What are you doing, Riven? You—" In that instant, everything crystallized. Riven had been the betrayer of the Knives, the betrayer of the Righteous Man. But why? Cale asked himself. Who's he working for?

"I've been waiting a long time for this, Cale," Riven hissed. "So I'm going to bleed you slow. One nick at a time." He waved his sabers threateningly. His one eye glared with an evil glow.

Breathing hard, Cale backed up against the warehouse wall. He briefly considered trying to climb back up the rope, but quickly dismissed the idea. The assassin was too fast. Riven would cut him down the moment he turned his back. Cale knew he had to get out of there. Though skilled with a blade, he was no equal of Drasek Riven.

Where in the Hells is the Watch? he thought. They must have heard the explosions.

"What? Nothing to say?" The assassin sneered.

Behind Riven, Cale saw through the flames and smoke that the men near the carriage had finally grown impatient enough to shoot down the horses. They would have the carriage door open in moments. The rest, still unsure of the source of the fireballs, began to cautiously regroup. Riven continued to gloat.

"Cale the Clever with nothing to say? Scared silent, eh?" the assassin scoffed. "I always knew you were a coward." He stalked forward, but the shouts from the men checking the carriage turned him around and stopped him cold.

"It's empty!" they yelled from across the square. "The carriage is empty!"

Riven whirled on Cale, his triumphant smile replaced with a hate-filled glare. "W-where's the boy, Cale?" he sputtered. *"Where!"*

Cale shot him a smug smile. "I always knew you were an idiot, Riven."

Roaring in rage, the assassin charged.

Riven's sabers cut a whistling swath through the smoke-filled air, his promise to kill Cale slowly apparently forgotten. Cale sidestepped a stab at his vitals and lashed out with an overhand slash. Riven deflected the blow wide with one saber, spun, and slashed backhand at Cale's throat. Cale dropped into a roll to avoid the killing stroke, instead taking a painful gash across his scalp, then leaped to his feet. When he stood, Riven shot him a hateful smile and stabbed him through the shoulder.

Desperately, Cale pulled free of the saber, swept Riven's other blade wide with his longsword, and landed a vicious kick square in the smaller assassin's chest. The impact blew the breath from Riven's lungs and drove him back three paces. With blood and sweat pouring into his eyes, Cale used the reprieve to gulp his healing potion. Skin knit painfully and abruptly back together. The wounds in his scalp and shoulder stopped bleeding instantly.

"You're . . . a . . . dead . . . man," Riven managed between gasps.

Behind the assassin, Cale could see the other men moving across the square toward the combat. Wiping the remaining blood out of his face, he resolved not to go easily. He fingered a globe on his magical necklace and thought, We'll all go together, you sons of whores.

"Come on," he said to Riven, and beckoned him forward with his long sword.

Riven's signature sneer returned with his breath.

"Cale, yo—*ahhh!*" The assassin's words turned into a howl of pain as the tip of Jak's shortsword burst from his gut in a shower of blood. The now visible halfling, standing behind the assassin, jerked his blade free. Riven fell to his knees, gurgling blood, then collapsed into a groaning heap.

As Jak walked past the bleeding assassin, he spitefully said, "You talk too damned much, Drasek Riven." The halfling bounced up to the surprised Cale and shot him a smile. "Bet you're glad to see me, huh? Come on, let's—"

"I'm finishing this," Cale pronounced, and walked past Jak toward the writhing Riven. Jak's small hand closed on his wrist and pulled him to a halt.

"Forget him, Cale. *Erevis!* Forget him. We've got to get out of here."

Cale's gaze followed Jak's pointed finger to see the rest of the hit team speeding toward them. The flaming, smoke-filled square swarmed with shouting men. A crossbow bolt buzzed past his ear to slam harmlessly into the side of the warehouse. Another followed, then another. Jak was right.

"Let's go," Cale said.

"Which way?" he asked. The nervous excitement in Jak's voice was plain. "They're everywhere."

"Up." Cale reached around the halfling and grabbed the end of the rope. "You first. I'll coil it behind me as we climb." He looked back to the square. Their pursuers were only a long spearcast away and closing fast. "Go! Go!"

Without a word, Jak leaped up and began climbing. Cale quickly wrapped the end of the rope around his waist and followed. Halfway up, he spared a glance down and saw a crowd of eight or nine crossbowmen taking aim.

"Crossbows, Jak," he shouted up to the little man. Trying to make himself as small a target as possible, Cale held the rope with only his hands and pulled his legs into his chest.

Bowstrings twanged, and a shower of bolts peppered the walls around him. Two of the barbed missiles struck him square in the back but ricocheted off his enchanted leather armor. Still, the impact was enough to nearly knock him off the rope. He looked up to see Jak still unwounded. *Brandobaris takes care of his own,* he assumed.

"Go, Jak! Now, while they reload!" The halfling sped up the line like a red-headed spider, but before they had climbed another ten feet, Cale's keen ears picked up the telltale intonations of spellcasting below.

Dark! he cursed inwardly. *Who in the Nine Hells are these men?*

"Hang on!" Cale shouted. "Spell!"

At that instant, a searing bolt of lightning shot upward from the ground and exploded into the building. The force of the blast shattered bricks, showering Cale's exposed skin with a hundred stinging chips of stone. The rope swung across the face of the building like a pendulum. He gritted his teeth and held on. Jak held on too, he saw, but barely. Clinging to the rope with only his hands, the halfling's feet dangled loosely over empty air. He looked stunned.

We can't take another one of those, Cale thought. He looked down through the smoky air and saw the crowd of crossbowmen preparing another volley. In the midst of them stood a gray-robed mage, fingers even now weaving another blast. Without a second thought, Cale plucked another of his precious missile globes—one of only three left—and hurled it downward.

"Eat this!" he shouted.

Too late the mage and crossbowmen scrambled for cover. With a deafening roar, the globe exploded into a blazing inferno that left the men mere piles of charred meat and exposed bone. Though thirty feet up, the blast of superheated air still curled Cale's eyebrows and warmed his boots. That globe had been his most powerful.

Free from the threat of crossbows, he and Jak quickly scaled the rest of the wall. When they reached the top, Cale raced over to the trapdoor that provided access to the roof from the warehouse below and stuck his dagger in the latch.

"There are still more of those bastards," he explained to Jak. "They'll try to reach the roof to cut off our escape. We've got a minute or two at best."

Swaying on his feet, Jak nodded absently.

Cale hurried over and gently gripped the little man by the shoulders. "Are you all right? Did the lightning bolt catch you?"

Jak returned Cale's concerned gaze with green eyes only now beginning to unglaze. "Yes . . . partially. I'll be all right though."

Stubborn as always, the halfling squirmed out of Cale's grip and shook his head as though to clear it. Afterward, he withdrew his holy symbol—a platinum snuff box he had stolen from some mage—and mouthed the words of a healing spell. Immediately he looked better. Recovered, the little man blinked and looked around the roof as though seeing it for the first time.

"Trickster's toes, Cale," the halfling cursed. "Mages *and* Drasek Riven? What's going on here?"

Before Cale could answer, the latch on the trapdoor began to rattle. Without a word, he and Jak raced to the eastern edge of the roof. Eight feet of empty space stood between them and the safety of the adjacent rooftop.

"Can you make it?" Cale asked the halfling.

Jak shot a glance back at the trapdoor just as a body slammed into it with a loud thump. The dagger held, but it would not do so for long. "I'll make it," he promised.

They backed up to get running room, then sprinted forward and leaped into open space. Cale made it easily, Jak barely.

Hitting the rooftop in a run, Cale pulled his last dagger

and headed for the trapdoor in this roof. Before he reached it, it flew open and a blond head poked through, facing away from him. Without hesitation, Cale rushed forward, grabbed the man by the hair, and lifted him through the opening. The surprised man squawked in protest and awkwardly swung his long sword.

"Dark! Hey . . . wha—"

The man's protests ended in a groan when Cale buried the dagger in his back, all the way to the hilt. Holding him aloft like some macabre marionette, Cale let him bleed and spasm away the last seconds of his life. From the warehouse below, he heard the shouts of still more men. He disdainfully flung the corpse to the side and reached for the trapdoor. As he did, he caught sight of Jak.

The little man stared at him, ashen faced, eyes aghast. Cale's gaze went to the corpse, then back to Jak. He pointed at the body with his bloody dagger. "It's either this or we don't get out of here alive."

Jak nodded, but his eyes remained haunted.

He's never seen this side of me, Cale realized. Little man, I hope we live long enough for you to decide later if we're still friends.

Shouts and the heavy tread of boots on stairs pulled him back to himself. He grabbed the trapdoor, threw a missile globe down into the warehouse, and slammed the door shut. The explosion shook the building. Smoke poured from the cracks around the trapdoor. He could hear the screams of burning men even through the wood and brick.

Without looking at Jak, he bent down and rifled the corpse. He quickly found what he sought. "Dark," he softly cursed.

From the inner lining of the corpse's cloak he removed a small token. Shaped as a black triangle with a yellow circle inset and a "Z" superimposed over the whole, the badge told him all he needed to know.

"Zhentarim," he breathed. No wonder there had been so many men. An immense organization comprised of warriors, mages, and the fell priests of the mad god Cyric, the Zhentarim sought to dominate trade and politics throughout the lands of Faerûn. Their methods ranged from legal trade agreements to assassinations.

Jak's intake of breath was as sharp as a razor. "Zhents! Gods Cale, what's going on here?"

Cale stared down at the badge in his palm while his mind worked to make the connections—Thayvians, Zhents, Riven, the Night Knives. But it was too much, and now was not the time.

"I don't know," Cale replied at last. "We'll have to figure it out later. We need to get out of here fast." What he did know was that the Zhentarim rarely left survivors. They were thorough. Very thorough. Already, more armed men had probably secured the block. Getting out would be difficult.

"We'll get no help from the Watch," he said to Jak. "The Zhents will have bought them off. So we stick to the roofs until we clear this block. When we hit Rauncel's Ride we go street level and make a run for uptown. You capable of that?"

Jak, holding a dagger in one fist and his holy symbol snuffbox in the other, nodded. "I'm capable, but . . ."

"But what?"

Jak shook his head. "Nothing."

They started to head off, but Jak abruptly stopped. "Wait, Cale. I . . . I've got a better way." The halfling sounded strangely reticent. "There's an abandoned cordwainer's shop off Stevedore's Way. The alley beside it has a secret passage that leads into the sewer system. We're at low tide, so the sewers should be passable. We can get out that way."

Cale paused, thinking, weighing the options. Both were long shots, but Stevedore's Way was closer. "Are you

certain it's secure? If the Zhents catch us in the sewers . . ."
He left the result unspoken.

Jak hesitated only an instant. "I'm sure," he said at last. "The Zhents don't know about it."

"All right," Cale acceded with a nod. "Let's go then."

They raced headlong across the rooftops, heedless now of anything but escape. Moving from building to building, they leaped an endless succession of alleys, the voids beneath their feet promising death for any misstep, all the while harried by the shouts of men below and behind. At last, winded and sweating even in the cold, they descended the face of a warehouse and stood in the shadows of Stevedore's Way.

"There," Jak whispered. The halfling's stubby finger indicated a narrow alley ten paces ahead.

Two black-cloaked men stood near the mouth of the alley with blades drawn. Their wary stance and alert gaze proclaimed them Zhentarim. Cale silently slipped his long sword from its scabbard. Darkness would provide cover enough to mask his approach. The Zhents would be dead before they ever saw him. "Stay here," he hissed to Jak. "I'll take care of them."

Jak gripped him gently by the forearm. "Wait, Cale. Wait." The halfling's voice sounded strained. "No more . . . no more blood tonight, all right? I'll use a spell to immobilize them."

The halfling's pleading gaze dredged up enough of the reborn Erevis to dilute the now predominate old Cale. The butler gave a reluctant nod. Jak blew out a soft sigh and patted him on the arm.

Hurriedly, as though he was afraid Cale might change his mind, Jak closed his eyes and uttered a soft prayer, invoking the power of Brandobaris. He pointed a finger at the Zhents, and both emitted startled gasps. After that, they did not move. The power of the spell held them rigid.

"Nice," Cale acknowledged.

Jak nodded and they jogged forward. The moment they broke from the shadows, shouts erupted from the street behind them. Cale shot a glance back to see four armed men running toward them. They were two blocks away but closing fast.

"Let's go, Jak. We've got more company."

"Follow me," the halfling said, and sped down the alley.

On his way past, Cale plowed through the rigid Zhents and knocked them flat—just for good measure, he told himself—then sped after Jak. Stacks of crates, bricks, and broken wood littered the ground and made passage difficult. Jak navigated the refuse with the skill of a man well accustomed to the placement of every barrier. Forty paces down the alley the little man halted before a wooden pallet that stood upright against the wall. He reached between the slats and felt for something, muttering. After a few moments, Cale heard a click.

"Got it," Jak said, satisfied. He swung the pallet open like a door.

Ingenious, Cale thought. A small, brick-walled room lay beyond, with a well dug in its center.

"Mind the hole," Jak said. The two piled in and pulled the secret door closed behind them. In the darkness, Cale heard Jak click the locking mechanism back into place. They stood in silence while the footsteps of their Zhent pursuers thumped by and faded into the distance. Afterward, Jak pulled forth a small metal rod that emitted a soft blue glow from its tip. His excited smile shone brighter than the magical rod.

"Close one, eh?"

Cale returned the smile despite himself. "Close," he agreed, and the two shared a tension-relieving chuckle.

"The well descends eighty feet before reaching the sewers," Jak said. "There's a ladder affixed to the side. I'll go first."

The halfling slipped over the side and began descending

the iron rungs. Cale followed and soon they stood in Selgaunt's sewers, three inches deep in stinking muck. Cale had to stoop to avoid hitting his head on the low ceiling. The narrow passage led off in three directions.

"Which way?" he asked.

"This way." Jak hurried off down the left-hand passage.

Surprisingly, the sewer did not reek as badly as Cale had expected. Still he tried to keep his mind off the composition of the muck that sucked at his boots. To occupy himself, he tried to put together the events of the night.

Riven, clearly a Zhentarim double agent, must have tipped his true masters to the Night Knives ambush. He and his Zhent allies had murdered the Knives hit team and waited for Cale to bring them Talbot. Why? Because if the Knives had succeeded and turned Talbot over to the Thayvians, Naglatha could force Thamalon to advocate Thay's interests before the Hulorn. The Zhents, bitter rivals of the realm of Thay, would want to prevent that. Winnowing out a few Knives and hurting the Righteous Man in the process would have been an added bonus. After the failed Knives ambush, Drasek Riven, the lone Knives "survivor," could have concocted any cover story he wanted. With Cale dead, that one-eyed bastard would have become the Righteous Man's chief aide. The Zhents would have had effective control of the Night Knives *and* Talbot to use as a bargaining chip with Thamalon.

Cale's own secrets had thrown the whole affair into disarray.

He shook his head in disbelief, chuckling, amazed that a violent clod like Riven could have been so subtle. If Jak hadn't known of the secret door in the alley and how to trigger its lock. . . .

If Jak hadn't known. . . .

A chill ran up Cale's spine. "Jak?"

The halfling stopped and turned, his face eerily lit by the blue light of the wand. "What?"

"How did you know how to trigger that lock?" Cale's hand closed over his sword hilt.

The halfling hesitated for an instant too long. "You're asking me about the lock *now?* Come on, Cale. It's only a little farther." He turned and started to walk again.

Cale grabbed him by the shoulder and whirled him around. *"What's* only a little farther?"

The little man's eyes went wide. "Hey! Take it easy, Erevis."

"The lock back in the alley. How'd you open it? You didn't pick it, and you sure as Hells didn't install it your—"

"Do not move," said a voice from the darkness ahead.

Cale pushed Jak away and fell into a fighting crouch, blade ready. "Who are you working for, Fleet?" he snarled.

Jak took a step back and held his hands palms up. "Easy, Cale," he softly said. "We're safe now. Take it easy."

"What?" Cale still did not see the source of the voice. "Safe? What are you talking about?"

Jak gestured at the darkness ahead. "They're Harpers, Erevis. Harpers." He paused a moment before adding, "So am I."

Cale's dagger fell limply to his side. He stood dumbfounded as three men splashed out of the darkness ahead, each armed with broadsword and crossbow.

Jak was a Harper.

The Harpers worked covertly throughout Faerûn to stem evil and promote good. They were everywhere but nowhere. Cale had always thought them irrelevant—too timid to seize power and too decentralized to stop anyone else from seizing it. Given tonight, he would have to rethink that view.

That Jak belonged to the Harpers called their entire friendship into question. The halfling could have been using him as a source for information about the Night Knives.

The tallest of the Harpers, blond and bearded, gave Cale

an appraising stare before turning to Jak. "You shouldn't have brought him here, Fleet."

The little man stomped up to the blond giant and bristled like an angry badger. "Shut the Hells up, Brelgin! It was come here or die. The ambush turned out to be a Zhent operation."

"Zhents? Hmm. . . ." Brelgin made a show of considering. "Still, you've been warned not to bring someone outside the organi—"

"Well I've already done it. Now go clear out the safe house. He's only seen us four, and he can be trusted not to tell anyone." Jak turned to give Cale an apologetic shrug. "We know his secrets just as he knows ours. We can trust him to keep quiet."

Brelgin remained hesitant. Cale, still too taken aback to speak, merely stood silent.

"That's the way it's going to be," Jak said firmly. "He can't go back."

Brelgin looked down at Jak, then looked up and shot Cale a meaningful glare. "He better stay quiet." Brelgin and the Harpers turned and plodded back through the darkness. Jak faced Cale.

"Couldn't be helped, Erevis. I'm sorry." Jak patted him on the arm. "We'll give them a few minutes to clear the safe house of personnel, then we'll go up. You all right?"

"I'm all right." He stared at the little man as though looking at him for the first time. "But you're a stranger to me, Jak."

The halfling took a step back, a wounded look on his face. "Nonsense, Cale. You already knew everything important about me before tonight. Just as I already knew everything important about you before you told me about Westgate. We're friends. Why do you think I came with you tonight? This . . ." he waved a small hand in the air to indicate the safe house, or the Harpers, ". . . is just what I do. Not what I am. You understand?"

Cale considered that and nodded slowly. This is what I do, not what I am. He hoped it was true, for Jak and for him. "I understand."

"Good." Jak smiled and waved him forward. "We've waited long enough. Come on, let's get out of these sewers and go home."

Cale nodded in agreement, though he knew that Stormweather Towers was not his destination. At least not yet. He had unfinished business with Riven. If the assassin yet lived, Cale knew where he would find him.

⊙ ⊙ ⊙ ⊙ ⊙

Other than Cale and Jelkins the barkeep, only a few snoring drunks still lingered in the stinking, late night dimness of the Stag. Cale sat with his back to the wall, facing the door. An untouched ale sat on the table before him. He inhaled deeply to steady himself.

He'll come, Cale thought. If he's alive, he has to come.

"I'm closin' in fifteen minutes," announced Jelkins from behind the bar. Cale nodded in acknowledgement and continued to wait. The drunks snored on, oblivious.

When the door to the Stag did finally open, Cale had to remind himself to breathe. Drasek Riven staggered in, leaning on the door for support, and surveyed the common room. Seeing Cale, the assassin's mouth formed into a twisted, hate-filled rictus. Cale gazed back impassively, unflinching. They stared across the room at one another like that for interminable seconds, predators evaluating prey.

Finally, Riven eased the door closed and walked unsteadily toward the table. Watching the assassin's pained strides, Cale had to suppress a triumphant smile. Riven had been able to buy healing enough to keep him alive but not enough to totally assuage the pain of Jak's backstab.

"Cale," Riven said with a nod, as he eased painfully into the chair across from him.

"Riven," Cale replied. The assassin still stank of blood and sweat. Cale could see the tension in his face, the barely controlled rage. Riven was a kettle ready to boil over at the slightest flame. Cale decided to stoke the fire. He smiled smugly and asked, "Well, what now?"

"What now?" Riven's voice sounded like the growl of a wounded animal. "I'll tell you what now, you whelp."

He lunged across the table, snarling, but stopped halfway, hissing in pain and reaching for his wounded back. Cale took the opportunity to grab him by the cloak and jerk him fully across the table so they came face to face. The assassin's mouth twisted in agony.

"You won't show me anything, you traitorous bastard," Cale hissed. He allowed his own flaring anger to fuel his strength. He shook Riven like a rag doll. The assassin hissed through teeth clenched in pain. "You're a godsdamned Zhent! I should drag your wounded arse to the Righteous Man. Or maybe split you open here and now." He drew his dagger and held it to Riven's exposed throat.

"Go ahead," Riven snapped, spraying spittle into Cale's face. "You think I haven't told someone about your little betrayal tonight? If I don't walk out of here safe and sound, the Righteous Man hears all about *your* treachery. Anything you say about me then will sound like the excuses of a desperate man. You'll die ugly, Cale."

Cale stared into Riven's face and tried to discern whether the assassin was bluffing. I can't take the chance, he decided. He let Riven go, and the assassin slid back into the chair with a pained, yet satisfied sigh.

"It was a good play, Cale," Riven said. "You and your boy did quite a job. I lost seventeen men." He chuckled, a gurgling sound that made Cale want to vomit. "A good play and that's certain. What I can't figure out is why?

You got a fondness for this Uskevren boy?"

"Not your concern," Cale replied tightly.

Riven smiled knowingly, grunted, and reached across the table to take a gulp of Cale's ale.

"My question remains," Cale said, this time less smugly. "What now?"

"Now nothing," Riven replied easily. "We go on as before. I betrayed the Righteous Man, and so did you. We keep that little tidbit between us and explain the failed ambush by telling him the Uskevren boy had more guards than anticipated. He'll believe it if both of us tell him. Knowing how much we . . . dislike each other, he'll never suspect collusion." He smiled evilly through his goatee. "Good enough?"

Cale sat back in his chair and considered the offer. It meant that he would stay in the guild—an undesirable outcome—but it also meant he could go back to being the Uskevren butler, feeding useless information to the Righteous Man and protecting his adopted family. Given the convoluted events that had unfolded tonight, he could hardly expect anything better. Besides, what was one more secret for a man who lived a lie?

"Good enough," he agreed at last. "But no more attempts on the Uskevren. We both steer the guild clear of them. Agreed?"

Riven frowned but nodded. "Agreed."

Cale pushed back his chair and rose. "Before I go, Riven, tell me why the Zhents did it. What's their real interest in this?"

"Not your concern, Cale," Riven replied. He took another gulp of ale.

Cale nodded. He had expected as much. "Watch your back, Riven," he said. As he walked past, he slapped the assassin between the shoulder blades. Riven spat ale and gave a satisfying hiss of pain.

"You're a bastard, Cale."

Cale smiled, walked out of the Stag into the cold night air, and headed for home.

I might be a bastard, he thought wryly, *but still I have a family.*

THE MAID

SKIN DEEP

Lisa Smedman

Larajin yanked the gold turban from her head and tossed it angrily aside. The tiny silver bells sewn onto it tinkled as it rolled to a stop in the corner of the workroom.

"I've had it," she said, shaking out her long, rust-colored hair. "I can't seem to do anything right."

Kremlar looked up from his oil press. "What's wrong?" the dwarf asked in a soft voice. "Did you have another run-in with Erevis Cale?"

Larajin gave an exasperated sigh. "It wasn't my fault that the wine goblet spilled on the table," she said, hooking a finger into one of the royal blue slashes on the sleeve of her dress. "How could anyone be expected to serve a luncheon in a uniform like this? The sleeves catch on everything."

"That explains the stain then," Kremlar said, nodding at her skirt. He pulled the handle of the press, and oil trickled out into a bowl.

Larajin looked down. The white fabric of her dress had a blotchy red line across the front. She stared at the dwarf as he sat at his worktable, which was scaled to Kremlar's stocky but short body. The dwarf was surrounded by the ingredients of his trade: stone mortars filled with powdered spices; pots of bright red and blue and purple dyes; trays heaped with fragrant flower petals; and bowls of sticky, pungent tree sap. A lot of messy ingredients were involved in the manufacture of perfumes, yet somehow Kremlar was always immaculate. His gray hair and beard were neatly braided, and his doublet and richly embroidered sleeves were spotless. Even his hands—with a gold ring on every finger and a locket ring on one thumb—were clean and pink, without a grain of powder or smudge of sap anywhere on them.

"How do you do it?" Larajin asked as she unfastened the lacings on the front of her tight gold vest.

"Eh?" Kremlar looked up again. "Do what?"

"Stay so clean," Larajin answered. "Mister Cale is always lecturing me about my uniform and not keeping up the standards of the Uskevren household. He expects me to carry coal without getting dusty, and to scrub pots without wetting my sleeves. He's always whispering to Mistress Shamur, and I'm sure it's about me. The mistress gave me a look colder than winter when I stoked the fire in her room this morning, and she's always watching me. I'm sure Mister Cale told her that I was the one who left the dust mop out in the hall that her guest tripped over, and that I scorched Tazi's masquerade dress with the pressing iron. If it weren't for my parents, she'd have turned me out by now—which just isn't fair, because I do try. It's just that—"

Kremlar finished her thought for her. "You're a square

peg in a round hole," he said. "Try as you may, you're unable to smooth off your corners."

Larajin frowned. "Are you saying I'm not trying hard enough?"

Kremlar shook his head. "No. Someday, you'll find a square hole, just as I did." He held up blunt but neatly manicured fingers. "Could you imagine these hands working a pick or shovel? I felt the same way when my father tried to make a miner of me. I loved the sparkling gemstones, but the dust and sweat—ugh!"

"At least they let me out to do the shopping," Larajin said. "Mister Cale never complains about how long I take. I think he's glad to be rid of me."

Larajin began to tug her dress up over her head. Kremlar politely declined to look up again until she'd changed into the more serviceable clothes that she kept hidden in the back of his store: a brown trouser-skirt and a gray shirt with sleeves that buttoned tight from wrist to elbow. Kicking off her black velvet slippers, Larajin pulled on fur-lined, oiled leather boots. Like the rest of her outfit, they were serviceable: they kept her feet dry, even when she was standing in a foot of sewer water.

It felt good to be out of the foolishly fancy maid's uniform. Larajin stood and ran fingers through her hair, raking it back out of her eyes. She reached for her cloak.

"You're going to the garden?" Kremlar asked. It was more of a statement than a question; Larajin always snuck into the Hunting Garden when she needed to clear her head.

Larajin nodded.

"Will you fetch me something?" Kremlar asked. "I'll make it worth your while: thirty ravens if you can find it."

"Find what?" Larajin asked. She could guess. This wasn't the first time she'd turned an illicit venture into the Hulorn's private estate to her profit.

The dwarf rose from his worktable. He stood only as

tall as Larajin's waist, and so he had to balance on tiptoe to lift a thick book from its place on the shelf. He flipped through pages, then tapped a finger against the hand-tinted illustration of a brilliant red flower whose twin petals resembled a woman's lips.

"It's called Sune's Kisses," he said. "There's also an elvish name for it, which I won't even try to pronounce. The flowers bloom only in the depths of winter, and the leaves are flecked with gold. The name's poetic: the plant is said to have sprouted after the goddess kissed the barren ground in the depths of an especially cold winter. The flowers have an exquisite fragrance. The plant is extremely rare, but the Hulorn is said to have a specimen or two in his garden. That is, if he hasn't trampled them under his horse's hooves while out hunting or let weeds strangle them."

"Better that someone who appreciates the plant should have it," Larajin agreed, "and that they should turn it into a beautiful perfume, worthy of Sune herself."

"Indeed," Kremlar said reverently. He looked up at her. "Our usual arrangement, then?"

Larajin handed the dwarf her shopping list and the knotted kerchief of silver ravens that Mister Cale had given her. "Done," she said. "If Sune's Kisses are in the Hunting Garden, you'll have them by eventime."

Larajin rubbed grease into the hinges of the grate, waited a moment, then carefully pushed it up. The metal was cold enough to stick to her bare fingers, and a light snow had started to fall. Snow meant footprints: she'd have to stay in the deepest parts of the garden, lest someone see her tracks.

She climbed out of the sewer grate into the fountain that was the garden's centerpiece. It had been drained for the winter. The hideous collection of leering sirens at its center, carved from pink marble, were no longer squirting water from their breasts.

Larajin stepped out of the fountain and made her way into the Hunting Garden. When it had first been laid out, more than a century ago, the garden had contained beds of flowers and only a scattering of trees, but now it had a more natural, forested appearance. Trees arched overhead, and the ground was covered with soft, springy moss. Not so long ago, when the Hulorn's father ruled Selgaunt, the garden had been carefully tended. But Andeth Ilchammar had neglected it for more than a decade, preferring to spend his fivestars on lavish clothes and parties. Meanwhile the gravel paths sprouted grass, and the flowers and shrubs outgrew their weed-choked beds.

Larajin found the Hunting Garden beautiful even in winter, with the flowers gone to seed and the leaves blown away. Frost sparkled on bare tree branches, and winter berries added spots of ice-bright blue to the underbrush. The garden called to her as no other place in the city did—not even the temple of Sune. Its silences and dappled shadows spoke to a part of her that yearned for the beauty of the wilderness. Already she could feel the knot of tension between her shoulders beginning to unravel.

Larajin kept her eye on the ground as she walked, diligently searching for specks of red. The dusting of snow would make Sune's Kisses easier to spot. She stopped to straighten a shrub whose branch had been broken by someone's careless footstep and heard a small animal rustling through the bushes. A squirrel? She clucked her tongue, but there was no response.

Her eye fell on a neat line of footprints in the snow. She recognized them by the size of the oval pads and the lack of claw scuffs as having been made by a house cat, probably one of the Hulorn's many pets.

The tracks were as fresh as her own. They had a curious

drag mark beside them. Had the cat become tangled in something?

Larajin rubbed her fingers together. "Here, kitt-cat," she said. "Come, kitt."

The bushes to her left rustled, and Larajin saw a flash of color. Her breath caught in her throat.

It was no ordinary cat that slunk cautiously out of the undergrowth, but a tressym: a cat with large, feathery wings. The creature had sleek blue-gray fur and wing feathers as colorful as a peacock's, with spots of brilliant turquoise, rich red, and vibrant yellow, all edged in tabby-stripe black.

One of the wings was folded neatly against the creature's back. The other dragged in the snow, its feathers wet and bedraggled. Larajin could not only see that the wing was broken, but she could also see the cause. Someone—probably the Hulorn's spoiled children—had tried to force an infant-sized shirt over it. The shirt hung in tatters from the broken wing, and the cat mewled in pain and stopped abruptly as it snagged against a branch.

Larajin clenched her fists in anger. Tressym were magical creatures, sacred to Sune. How dare the Hulorn give one to his children as a plaything!

Slowly, murmuring her reassurance, she let the winged cat sniff her fingers. "There, little blessed one," she said. "Let me help you."

The tressym growled softly and lashed its tail as Larajin's fingertips touched its wing. It tried to move away, but the shirt was caught fast on the branch. Hissing, the cat swiped at it with its claws. Larajin heard a soft crack, as something inside the wing splintered further. The tressym's hiss rose to a howl.

Worse yet, Larajin could hear someone approaching through the woods. It wouldn't be one of the few remaining groundskeepers. They did little enough in summer and ignored the garden completely in winter. It had to be a member of the Hulorn's family, or one of his invited guests. Whoever it was, if Larajin were discovered in the garden, she'd be in big trouble. However, she couldn't leave the tressym to suffer.

As the footsteps approached through the wood, Larajin prayed to Sune. As she whispered, the cat fell silent. It looked up at Larajin with luminous yellow eyes, as if suddenly understanding what she meant to do. This time, when she reached down to gently tug the shirt away from its wing, its only protest was a soft growl. It remained utterly still until the instant Larajin pulled the scrap of cloth free, then bounded away into the woods, its broken wing trailing behind it.

Larajin suddenly smelled a sweet fragrance. Looking down, she saw that she was kneeling beside a plant with tiny red flowers and leaves flecked with gold: Sune's Kisses! She was certain the plant hadn't been there a moment ago, but perhaps her knee had brushed away the snow that had covered it. Wherever it had come from, there was no time to dig it up now. Larajin scrambled behind the trunk of a wide tree, just as the source of the footsteps strode into view.

She was just in time. The walker in the woods was none other than the Hulorn himself. Larajin recognized him at once by the insignia on the breast of his black velvet doublet and his carefully coifed, raven-black hair. He wore hose and a codpiece of royal purple and had an ermine-skin cape wrapped around his broad shoulders. Snow had settled upon it like downy white feathers. He muttered to himself as he walked, his fingers twisting a heavy gold ring on the forefinger of his left hand.

As the Hulorn passed, Larajin saw that his left hand ended not in fingers, but in clawed, birdlike talons. His face was even more horrible. The side of it turned toward Larajin was covered with glossy black scales, and the bulging eye that stared out of it was slitted like a reptile's.

For the second time that afternoon, Larajin gasped. So the rumors were true! The Hulorn had altered his body with foul magics.

The Hulorn slowed his stride. Larajin froze in terror, convinced he had heard her or seen her footprints in the snow. His mismatched eyes searched the forest as if he were looking for something. After a moment he turned and strode away. As he left he stepped on Sune's Kisses, crushing its tiny red flowers underfoot.

When the sound of footsteps faded, Larajin emerged from hiding and carefully dug the crushed plant from the ground. She looked around for the tressym. She wanted to take it to the Temple of Sune, to ask the priests there to heal its wing, but the tressym's footprints ended at a tree, which it seemed to have climbed. Larajin scanned the branches overhead but couldn't see any sign of the creature.

It was nearly dusk. She'd never find the tressym now. She'd have to come back tomorrow and look for it then.

It was dark by the time Larajin changed her clothes at Kremlar's and picked up the basket of purchases he'd made on her behalf. The dwarf hadn't been happy with the condition of the plant she'd handed him, but after hearing how she'd nearly been caught—by the Hurlorn, no less—he'd given her ten ravens, just the same. He didn't seem particularly surprised when he heard of the Hurlorn's strange appearance, but he did have a word of advice.

"You'd best keep that to yourself, Larajin. The rich and powerful don't like it when the common folk know their secrets."

Larajin hurried back through the streets, past the street lanterns, which tindermen were lighting with long, candle-tipped poles. The snow was to the top of her sodden slippers now, and her feet were numb with cold.

Engrossed in her thoughts, it took her several moments to realize that someone was following her, dogging her shadow. The figure darted from one shade to the next, silent as falling snow. Was he a cutpurse—or worse? Only when he passed briefly through the pool of light cast by a street light did she catch a better look.

He was a slight man with a narrow face, clad in an unfashionable forest-green cloak whose hood was pulled up over his head. His hair hung to one side in a long braid tied with a feather, and his feet were clad in high soft boots. Noticing that Larajin had spotted him, he stepped quickly into the shadow—but not before she had seen his almond-shaped eyes. Below them, his face was patterned with strange marks.

Now Larajin was scared. The fellow was an elf. Not only that, but one of the wild elves of the lands north of Sembia. Master Thamalon the Elder might see the wild elves as noble savages, but to Larajin—to most Sembians—they were one step removed from animals, reportedly incapable of compassion or pity. What was one doing in the city?

For a heartbeat or two, Larajin froze, uncertain what to do. If she took her usual route back to Stormweather Towers, her pursuer would catch her within a block. No members of the city guard were in sight. She was on her own.

She darted suddenly into a narrow alley that was a shortcut and broke into a run. Her sudden doubling back caught her pursuer by surprise, but the fellow was as fast as a tiger. He ran up behind her and caught her wrist in his hand. As she tried to jerk away, his cloak fell open. Larajin saw the bone-handled dagger at his hip, hanging beside a pouch.

Larajin dropped the basket, which fell to the snow beside her. She opened her mouth to scream, but the elf clasped his free hand over her mouth. His fingers were long and slender, as brown and hard as tree roots. They smelled of leather and earth.

He whispered fiercely at her in a foreign language as sibilant as the whispering of tree leaves. Then he drew her close. She tried to pull away, but his narrow arms were as strong as tree roots. He lifted the hand that had been holding her mouth a finger's breadth away from her lips.

Larajin's heart pounded in her ears. Should she scream? The snow fell thickly, muffling all sound. Her lips began to move in a whispered prayer for mercy.

"Please," she begged. "Please don't. . . ."

Larajin suddenly smelled flowers. The elf's nostrils quivered. He sniffed—then his eyes widened.

The elf's hand clamped back over her mouth. His other hand fell to his waist, to the spot where his knife was sheathed. Suddenly realizing that he could draw it and slit her throat in an instant, Larajin threw herself backwards as hard as she could and wrenched her head to the side.

"Leave me alone!" she screamed. Then, "Help! Guard!"

Strangely, the fragrance of Sune's Kisses was even stronger now, as if Larajin were standing on a crushed field of flowers, instead of on snow. Stranger still, the elf released his hold on her wrist. His body stiffened, and his brow furrowed as if he were fighting against some inner demon. Then he turned on his heel and walked briskly away, his soft leather boots padding on the snow.

Larajin sagged back against a wall, trembling with relief as she saw a member of the Selgaunt Guard round the corner at a run. By the time he reached her, the elf was gone, swallowed by the shadowy streets. The only assistance the guard could offer was to help her scoop her soggy loaf of bread out of the snow, then escort her home to Stormweather Towers.

"Are you sure it was the Hulorn?"

Tal's voice echoed out of the darkness behind Larajin. He splashed through the sewer behind her, just at the edge of the pool of yellow light cast by the lantern in her hand. As soon as he'd spoken, he clamped the perfumed handkerchief that Kremlar had given him back over his mouth and nose. The tunnels reeked, even at low water when the retreating tide had carried most of the effluent away.

"Don't you believe me?" Larajin asked.

"I believe you," Tal said.

He probably meant it. At nineteen, Tal was four years younger than Larajin. He'd always listened respectfully to whatever she had to say, even though she was just a servant and he the second son of the noble Uskevren House that Larajin served.

Last night, when Larajin had told him about the Hulorn and how she used the sewers to sneak into the Hunting Garden, Tal had insisted on accompanying her when she went back. He tried to talk her into waiting a day or two, saying that he needed time to memorize his role in Mistress Quickley's new play, but Larajin insisted on rescuing the injured tressym as soon as possible. Tal at last gave in after being assured they'd be back well before dark.

"The person you saw in the Hunting Garden may have been someone who just looked like the Hulorn," Tal continued. "Or if it was the Hulorn, perhaps he was wearing part of a costume. I heard that the Hulorn's face and hand were injured when a lantern spilled flaming oil on him. Maybe he's wearing a mask and glove to cover his burns. Theatrical devices can be quite realistic—"

"The scales and talons were part of his body," Larajin asserted. "It was magic—I'm sure of it. Now hush, or we'll be discovered."

They were approaching one of the street gratings. Pale morning sunlight poured in from up above, together with the sounds of street vendors hawking their wares. The skies had cleared since yesterday, and a trickle of meltwater dripped off the long icicles that hung from the grate. The clouds were breaking up. Larajin could see the full moon in one of the patches of blue sky.

They passed under the grate and turned down a side tunnel, then down another. Tal's splashes were uneven now, and Larajin paused to wait for him. When he caught up to her again, his face looked gaunt. Then she saw it was only a growth of beard, giving his normally clean-shaven face a shadowed appearance. Odd, that it had grown so quickly. He was sweating, despite the fact that the air in the tunnel was cold enough for Larajin to see her breath.

"Are you all right, Tal?" she asked.

"How close are we?" he asked.

Larajin studied the tunnel. They'd reached a point where it was reinforced; the high stone walls surrounding the Hunting Garden must have been directly above. "Almost there," she answered.

Tal nodded and waved Larajin on.

She continued up the tunnel for a few paces more but paused when she saw a pair of small bright eyes glinting at her out of the darkness ahead. After a moment, their owner scurried into view along one of the raised ledges: a large brown rat.

Larajin stepped to the opposite side of the tunnel to let it pass. She froze in mid-step as it crawled into the light. That was no ordinary rat. It fumbled along the ledge, crawling with one front leg that was a feathered wing and another covered in thick white fur. Its rear legs clicked against the brickwork like tiny hooves. Its face . . .

Larajin raised the lantern. "By all that's unholy, Tal, you won't believe this," she said in a trembling whisper. "This rat has a human face."

In that same moment, Tal—who once more was well

back of the lantern light—turned and fled. His feet splashed rapid echoes around the corner the tunnel.

"Tal!" Larajin shouted. "Where are you going?"

She turned to follow Tal—and the movement of her swinging lantern illuminated dozens of pairs of eyes, up on the ledge. The tunnel filled with the whispering, clicking, dragging sound of dozens of malformed legs scurrying. With soft splashes, the rats began dropping from the ledge. They swam toward Larajin, their malformed bodies leaving rippling wakes through the murky water.

One of the rats clawed its way up Larajin's leg. She felt a sharp, stinging pain in her thigh and the hot trickle of blood. She slapped at the writhing creature, knocking it from her, then felt another rat land on her shoulder. It had the beak of a bird and pecked her ear. Screaming, she whirled around, only to lose her grip on the lantern. It plunged into the sewage, and the light snuffed out with a loud, hot hiss.

Larajin could feel rats everywhere on her now. Their teeth tore into her skin; their feet plucked like human hands at the fabric of her shirt. She slapped at them furiously, knocking more than one off her body, but others replaced them. One twined itself into her hair.

Larajin turned and ran. Though the tunnel was in near-total darkness, she knew every step of this sewer. Her eyes were keener than most, especially in dim light—she could just make out the dim reddish-brown blurs of the rats that covered her body. She turned right, then left, back the way they'd come, shedding rats with each step. Several still clung to her, rending her flesh with their teeth.

Praying she wouldn't slip and plunge face-first into the sewage and be eaten alive by rats as she floundered helplessly in the stink, Larajin ran on. She nearly cried when at last she saw the patch of light looming ahead. When she was under it she jumped—and her flailing hands snapped off one of the icicles. She caught it on the way down, landed miraculously on her feet, and used the pick-sharp icicle to stab at the half dozen rats that still clung to her body. She punctured her own skin by accident once, and after killing just two of the rats, the icicle broke. She leaped again—missed and splashed down into the sewage—then leaped a third time and managed to snap off another icicle. Holding it with cold-numbed fingers, she continued stabbing furiously. One by one the rats dropped from her and either floated or swam away.

Larajin stood panting in the barred patch of sunlight. A dead rat with the lolling, forked tongue of a snake floated in the water at her feet. Above the grate, carts rumbled past, their drivers oblivious to the battle that had just taken place in the sewer below.

Now that it was over, Larajin's shoulders began to shake. She found herself crying: not so much at her near brush with death but at the fact that Tal had abandoned her when she needed him most.

At first, Larajin didn't realize that anyone was in the library. The crackling of flames in the fireplace muffled the slight creak of leather, and the high back and wings of the armchair hid the person sitting there. She dusted the shelves, too distracted by her thoughts to replace the elder master's books in exactly the same order, even though she knew she'd catch a tongue-lashing from Mister Cale later for her carelessness. The books were all the same to her: musty, leather-bound tomes filled with stories about folks long dead. Elven folk. After being accosted by the wild elf yesterday, elves were the last thing Larajin wanted to think about.

It was only when she moved closer to the fire to dust the chessboard and collect the empty wine goblets from the table beside it that she smelled a faint hint of sewage that wasn't quite masked by the smell of soap. She peered around the edge of the wing chair and saw the very person she'd been looking for all afternoon: Tal.

He was staring into the fire with troubled eyes. His broad hands were knotted together in front of his face, his chin resting upon them. His face was clean shaven, and he'd changed into fresh clothes.

Larajin rapped the duster down against the table. A pawn toppled over and rolled across the chessboard, then clattered onto the stone floor.

Tal looked up, noticing Larajin for the first time. A series of emotions crossed his face: surprise, relief, guilt. He sprang to his feet and reached out to pull her into one of his bear hugs, but Larajin jerked back. Her leg struck the table, knocking the rest of the chess pieces over. She didn't even stop to worry about the fact that she'd just demolished a game in progress—another contest of wits between the Mister Cale and the elder master. Mister Cale's wrath seemed inconsequential, now.

"Larajin, I—" Tal lowered his arms. "Thank the gods you're all right. Those rats—"

"Why did you run away?" Larajin asked. She wanted to rage at him, to smack her hands against his broad chest and tell him how terrified she'd been and say that she'd nearly been killed. She'd suffered nearly a dozen bites, and though they were only superficial wounds, they stung.

"I had to leave," Tal said. A desperate look crept into his eyes. "I couldn't take the chance that . . . I might have . . ."

Larajin sat down on the table beside the jumbled chess pieces. Now that she was face to face with Tal, the hurt inside her was as chill and sharp as the point of the icicle she'd used to kill the rats. Wordlessly, she pulled up the hem of her skirt to show him the bites on her leg. The skin around the bandages was puffed and red.

"Did you get them treated?" Tal asked, concern in his eyes. "Rats are diseased creatures. Their bites—"

"You know how to use a knife," Larajin said. "You're one of Master Ferrick's top pupils. If you'd stayed to protect me, I wouldn't have any bites. I just want to know why you ran, Tal. Why?"

Tal sagged into the armchair with a heavy sigh. He stared at the bandage on Larajin's wrist. This time, when he reached out for her, Larajin let him take her hand. For a long moment, they sat in silence, listening to the crackle of the fire as something warred with itself in Tal's troubled eyes.

"Larajin," he said, leaning closer. "There's something I must tell you about myself. I'm—"

The door to the library opened at just that moment. Master Thamalon the Elder strode into the room, then stopped as he saw Larajin and Tal seated by the fire. Dark eyebrows drew together as his penetrating eyes took in Larajin's hand in Tal's. Startled, Larajin jerked her hand away and hurriedly pushed the skirt of her servant's uniform back over her knee. The elder master's eyes narrowed. When Larajin realized what he must be thinking, her face flushed.

As Tal stood to face his father, Larajin bowed her head and began nervously setting the chess pieces back on the board. They kept falling over, and soon black and white were jumbled together.

Tal read his father's stern look instantly. "Father, I can explain. Larajin was . . . We—"

"Tal, I want a word with you," the elder master said. He used his quiet voice, the one he'd always employed when Larajin and Tal were just children, romping through the halls together and running headlong into dignitaries and guests.

Out of the corner of her eye, Larajin saw Tal's shoulders slump. Once again, the second son had proved a disappointment to his father. This time, he wasn't at fault, but he couldn't explain why—not if he wanted to keep Larajin's foray into the sewers a secret.

Larajin knew exactly how Tal felt. Mustering up her courage, she straightened and met the elder master's eye, but the look in it silenced her.

"Leave us, Larajin," he said. "It's time that my son and I had a little chat about self-control."

Tal's expression was a mixture of frustration and fear. With one last look at him, Larajin hurried from the room.

⊙ ⊙ ⊙ ⊙ ⊙

"Tal and I didn't do anything wrong!" Larajin said sullenly. "The master is lying if he says we did."

As her father raised his hand, Larajin suddenly realized she'd gone too far. Defending herself was one thing, but calling the word of the elder master into question was quite another. She winced, but stood her ground, waiting for the sting of a slap against her cheek.

Her father stood with his open hand trembling, visibly fighting to restrain his anger. Thalit Wellrun was a gentle man who had never taken so much as a whip to the horses under his care during all of his four decades of service to the Uskevren household. Even though he and his wife quarreled frequently, Larajin had never seen her father strike her mother. Now, as he looked at Larajin, his eyes were blazing.

Thalit stared at his hand as if it had betrayed him, then ran a callused palm across his close-shaven scalp. He paced in frustration between the lines of linen, limping slightly on the leg that had been damaged years ago. The old injury only troubled him when the weather was changing for the worse. Outside the closed window, the evening air was still and cold, but Larajin could sense a storm of emotion coming.

They stood in the drying room among the crackling braziers and clotheslines pinned with tablecloths, where Larajin had been folding the clean linen. Thalit had come straight from the stables and was still dressed in his leather apron. His white cotton shirt with its gold and blue ribbons was smudged with dust and smelled of horses and hay. Unlike the household servants, his work ended early in the eventime, after the horses were fed. However, he often worked late into the night. Larajin did the same—except that her extra duties were a punishment from Mister Cale, performed under silent protest, and not by choice.

"You have to understand the consequences," her father said in a strained voice. Not once did his eyes meet Larajin's. "Affections between master and servant always turn out for the ill. Young master Talbot would be honor-bound to provide for the upkeep of any child resulting from such a union, but an illegitimate child would be an embarrassment to the Uskevren household. You could be unable to continue in your duties while you were bearing and nursing the infant and—"

"Is that what matters most to you?" Larajin interjected. "The master's embarrassment? And my duty? What about the truth?"

Her father turned to her with a pained expression. "Duty is sometimes more important than truth," he said gruffly. "Duty keeps households together—and families. If it wasn't for my duty to your mother, you—" He bit off the rest, as if he had said too much.

"You care more about your horses than you do about mother," Larajin muttered. "Or me."

She hadn't meant for her father to hear the remark. She'd half turned to unpin a sheet from the line, but now her father wrenched it aside.

"I care for you," he said, in a voice trembling with emotion. "Even though you often disappoint me. Even though you are not my daughter."

Larajin blinked in surprise. She opened her mouth to ask her father if she had heard correctly—if he had truly uttered those words. All that came out was a whisper: "What?"

"Ask your mother," her father said. He let the sheet drop like a curtain between them.

Larajin stood, stunned, as her father limped out of the room. By the time she thought to run after him, he was gone.

She walked slowly down the hall, her thoughts whirling. Suddenly, her father's long-simmering anger toward her mother made sense. If Larajin was another man's child, it was only logical that Thalit's jealousy had turned to bitterness over the years. Larajin could see that her father still loved her mother, but until now she'd never understood why he held back his affections—or why he sometimes stared at Larajin as if wondering who she was.

Larajin already knew that she didn't look a bit like her father, nor did she share any of his mannerisms. While her father went about his duties as quietly as a horse bred to the bit, Larajin chafed at the very touch of her servant's uniform. They were as different as shadow and light.

Larajin found herself in the doorway to one of the smaller kitchens. Her mother was the only servant in it. Shonri Wellrun leaned over a heavy wooden table, kneading dough. Behind her a fire blazed brightly in the oven, and the warm air smelled of yeast and cream. Her hands white with flour, Shonri rolled the dough into long, thin lines, then deftly braided it. She squeezed juice from a tart-smelling fruit onto the dough, then dusted it with a sprinkle of brown spice.

Larajin stared at her mother, trying to see her through her father's eyes. Shonri had just turned sixty. Her red hair had faded to the color of pale ash, and her hands were creased with wrinkles. Even though she had been a servant all of her life, Larajin's mother had a hint of pride in her bearing and a gentle beauty that years of toil hadn't quite erased. She was one of the elder master's favored servants and was often summoned to the big table to be praised for her delicate pastries, made with rare spices from the four corners of Faerûn.

Had Shonri been summoned by one of the master's guests for attention of a different sort? Was Larajin the illegitimate child of a union like the one her father thought he was preventing?

As if sensing Larajin's intent gaze, Shonri looked up. She smiled at her daughter and gestured at a mortar that held greenish nuts. "Larajin, if you've finished with the linen, would you crush those for me?"

"Mother, I need to know . . ." The question died on Larajin's lips. But her expression conveyed it silently.

Her mother covered the braided dough it with a damp cloth. "Something's troubling you," she said, gesturing Larajin closer. "Come tell me what it is."

Larajin found herself unable to move from the doorway. She gripped the door frame tightly and spoke in a rush. "Father says I'm not his daughter. I believe him. I want to know who my real father is."

A flash of anger crossed Shonri's face. An instant later it was replaced with an expression of resolve. She patted a stool beside her. "Sit down. It's time you knew the truth."

Like a sleeper walking in a dream, Larajin slowly crossed the room. She sat beside her mother and waited while her mother carefully cleaned her hands on a rag. Then Shonri herself sat down.

"You are a daughter to your father," she said in a careful voice, "as much as you are a daughter to me. Always remember that."

Larajin nodded. She already knew that her mother and father loved her. She considered the relationship between herself and her mother a close one, even though it was to her Aunt Habrith that Larajin turned when she wanted to confide her secrets.

Shonri stared at the oven, not really seeing it.

"Twenty-three years ago, I lost a child," she said slowly.

Larajin was confused. This wasn't what she'd expected to hear. "I don't understand."

"You will," Shonri said. She continued. "I was accompanying Master Thamalon the Elder on a trip north to the Dales, a trading expedition. He'd asked me to come with him to evaluate the quality of the wild forest nuts and fruits he intended to purchase. It was a very important journey, a keystone in the household's economic well-being, and the meeting had been set up a full year in advance. It was a singular honor for me. So I agreed to accompany the master, even though I was pregnant and near to giving birth."

Shonri's eyes grew sad. "Your father didn't want me to go. We'd been trying for a child for so long. . . ."

She sighed. "I lost my child on that journey. When the birth came, we were deep in the woods, far from a cleric. The child died."

Larajin touched her mother's hand. "How—"

"The trading expedition was not a success," Shonri said. "More than half of the nuts had been damaged in the harvest, and the fruits hadn't ripened properly. We stayed only a short time—long enough for the master to conclude that the yields would never be large enough to turn a profit.

"While we were there, the folk in the place we were staying at learned that I had just lost a child and approached the master to ask a favor. One of their women had died in childbirth, and no other woman had milk to suckle it with. They asked the master if his servant would care for it. I took one look into your beautiful hazel eyes and immediately agreed."

Larajin had listened carefully to every word her mother said, yet she still found them difficult to believe. "I . . . I am not your daughter, either?" she asked. "Who am I, then?"

Shonri gave a slight shrug. "An orphan. The mother was unwed, and no one knew who the father was."

Larajin wanted to know more. "Was my mother a Daleswoman?" she asked. "From what town?"

"I don't know," Shonri answered. "We were deep in the Tangled Trees, far from any town. The meeting was held in a place where the nuts and fruits grew wild. The master never inquired as to the woman's name."

Even though she was firmly seated upon a stool, Larajin felt as if she were floating. Her mind groped for something—some as-yet unspoken detail—then seized upon it.

"You never told Father that you lost your own child, did you?" she said. "He was just guessing when he said that I wasn't his daughter. He didn't know how right he was."

Shonri rose from her stool and picked up a metal tray. Lifting the cloth away from the bread, she carefully eased it onto the tray, then opened the oven and slid it inside.

"Have you finished folding the linen?" she asked in a businesslike voice.

Larajin suddenly realized that her mother wasn't going to tell her any more. The familiar distance between mother and daughter was back. The time for confidences was over.

"Not yet," Larajin answered.

"Well get back to it, then, before Mister Cale finds out."

Larajin stood quietly, listening to the lap of the water against her ankles. The Temple of Sune was quiet this early in the morning. Its priests tended to serve the Lady of Love with nightly revels, then sleep late the next day. Only on mornings when there was an especially beautiful sunrise did they rise to greet it.

It was snowing again outside, and a chill wind was blowing, but the waters of the great fountain that filled the temple's courtyard were as warm as a stream on a summer day. Powerful clerical magic kept the temperature balmy at ground level. The snowflakes that were falling into the open central courtyard, with its beautiful natural rock formations and magically animated fountains, gently melted away before they hit the ground. Driftglobes floated just above the surface of the main pond, filling the temple with soft-hued light.

The only other occupant of the temple at this hour was a young girl about eleven years old, wearing the crimson robes of the temple. She was an auburn-haired child, one whose high cheekbones and long eyelashes suggested that she would grow into a great beauty one day. Like Larajin, she was of uncertain parentage. The priests had found the girl on their doorstep one day and taken her in.

Larajin had been worshiping at the temple long enough to know the serving girl's name: Jeina. She knew little else about her. Was Jeina as tormented by questions as Larajin was? Or had knowing ever since her birth that she was a foundling allowed the girl to come to terms with her unknown ancestry?

Larajin watched Jeina tip a bowl of pale yellow rose petals into the water. For a moment, their eyes met. Jeina smiled, then shyly turned away.

Larajin waded through the ankle-deep water to one of the pools near the center of the fountain. Formed over decades by pebbles that had gradually worn a boulder into a natural bowl as the water swirled them round, the pool was one of those used by lay worshipers who wanted to ask questions of the goddess. Its stone was veined with gold and tufted with velvety mosses that were blooming in the unseasonable warmth.

Larajin stared into the clear water that filled the pool, watching the pebble trace a lazy circle around its bottom and the ripples flowing across the pool's surface. They distorted her reflection, softening the rust-colored hair that straggled out from under her turban and blurring a face that was too long and angular to ever be considered pretty. Usually a petitioner would ask the pool to reveal the face of a future beloved. Larajin had other questions on her mind.

"Who am I?" she asked. She dipped a finger in the water, then touched it to her heart, leaving a damp spot on the gold fabric of the vest of her serving uniform.

Larajin felt a tickle on the back of her neck, like a lover's breath, and smelled the unmistakable fragrance of Sune's Kisses. A moment later, a tiny red flower petal slid down the trickle of water that was falling into the pool, then another. Even though water was still falling into the pool, its surface became still.

Larajin looked down upon a reflection that she only half-recognized. The face was her own, but the turban was gone. Her hair was tucked back behind her ears. Her ears were . . .

"A golden morning to you, Larajin."

Larajin started, and her hand fell into the pool. Ripples covered its surface once more, distorting her reflection. She whirled around and saw the one person in Selgaunt she'd least expected to see. Diurgo Karn, a young noble about her own age, was a priest of Sune. He wore holy vestments: tight-fitting crimson hose capped by a thickly padded codpiece, and a shirt slashed to reveal his muscular arms and chest. His features were every bit as handsome as Larajin remembered, with fair hair containing just a touch of red swept back from his high forehead and forest-green eyes. Not so long ago, Larajin had thought herself in love with him and had dreamed that the goddess would smile upon this "impossible" match between servant and noble.

"A golden morning to you, Diurgo," she said in a choked voice. "When . . . when did you get back?"

"Ten days ago."

Ten days ago, and he hadn't once thought to inquire as to Larajin's well being or even to let her know of his return.

Larajin intended to say no more to him, but curiosity burned inside her. "Was Lake Sember as beautiful as they say? Did you see its crystal towers?"

Diurgo made a dismissive gesture with his hand. "I was forced to turn back before I could reach the lake. The elves would have killed me had I tried to continue."

"You knew that before you set out."

"Knowing and seeing are two different things."

"Yes they are," Larajin said, seeing him even more clearly than before. Several months ago, in the flush of spring, she'd been caught up in his quest: a pilgrimage to famed Lake Sember, a body of water sacred to both Sune and the elf goddess Hanali, Sune's rival for worshipers of beauty. Larajin had stolen away from Stormweather Towers to follow Diurgo but had traveled only a short distance before agents sent by Master Thamalon the Elder had forced her to return to Stormweather Towers. She'd pleaded with Diurgo to persuade them to let her accompany him, but he'd refused to speak on her behalf, sharply reminding her that she was only a serving girl, and a hindrance to his quest. Now it seemed he'd given up his "holy pilgrimage" as soon as the path became too steep for him.

Larajin stared at Diurgo, not bothering to hide the hurt she felt. "What do you want?" she asked.

"I saw a faint pinkish aura around you just now as you were gazing into the pool," Diurgo said. "I'm certain it was a manifestation of the goddess. I thought I could help you to channel it into—"

"A manifestation," Larajin spat back at him. "Like my rust-colored hair? Your lies worked on me once, Diurgo, but I'm not listening to them any more. You can find another naive young woman to conduct your 'holy revels' with."

The young priest had the good grace, at least, to look uncomfortable. Even so, he persisted. "I'm not lying, Larajin. I saw the aura clearly."

"Just as I see you clearly, Diurgo." Larajin folded her arms across her chest. "And I no longer like what I see."

Haughty annoyance flashed across the young priest's face. He waved a finger at her. "You shouldn't talk that way to the son of a noble house, girl." Without another word, he splashed angrily away.

Furious with herself, Larajin waded back to the edge of the main pool. Ignoring the towel Jeina offered, she jerked her slippers onto her feet, then picked up her cloak and strode out through the temple's main door.

She'd gone nearly two blocks before she noticed that her arms and legs were no longer stinging. Stopping, she untied the bandage on her wrist, and found to her amazement that the bite there had completely healed.

As she walked toward Kremlar's perfume shop, Larajin clutched her cloak tightly around herself. The sun was just rising over Selgaunt's eastern wall, and snow drifted down out of a leaden gray sky. Larajin pushed the thoughts of Diurgo out of her mind. Unlike him, she would complete her quest. Today, no matter what foul creatures lay in wait for her in the sewers, she would sneak into the Hunting Garden and rescue the injured tressym.

She was nearly at the shop when someone hissed at her from an alley. Instantly on the alert, Larajin poised herself to run. When she saw the person who beckoned to her from the shadows, she faltered to a stop.

It was as if Larajin were looking into a mirror. The woman was in her early twenties, and wore the turban, vest, and serving dress of the Uskevren household. She had the same height and slender build as Larajin, and the same angular features. She even stood with the same awkward posture, aping Larajin's surprise. Then she winked and pulled off the turban to reveal short, dark hair.

"It's me: Tazi," the double said. "Pretty good disguise, don't you think?"

"Mistress Thazienne," Larajin gulped. "Why are you dressed in a servant's uniform?"

"Call me Tazi," the mistress said: a reprimand that had become automatic between them. She chuckled. "I was just having a little fun. Remember the day when I caught you in my room, dressed up in leather armor and posing in front of the mirror? You looked so much like me—aside from the clumsy way you held my sword—that it gave me an idea. I wanted to see if I could pass as you."

Larajin blushed, embarrassed to be reminded of her transgression. She'd always admired Mistress Thazienne for her boldness, and when Larajin had set out after Diurgo she'd pictured herself an adventurer like the young mistress. In the wake of her one adventure's disastrous ending, Larajin was even more aware of the vast gulf that separated the two of them. Thazienne, she was certain, wouldn't have even blinked at the malformed rats in the sewer.

Which reminded Larajin of the injured tressym.

"I have to go," she said, glancing up the street in the direction of Kremlar's perfume shop.

Thazienne's playful expression instantly sobered. She caught Larajin's arm. "Not that way," she said. "There's three elven gentlemen just up the street that I don't think you want to meet—much as they'd like to make your acquaintance."

Larajin's eyes widened. "Is one of them a wild elf?"

Thazienne's eyebrows raised in surprise. "You've run into them before?" she asked. "They look like pretty tough customers. They nearly succeeded in grabbing me—and I'm a pretty slippery eel. What do they want with you?"

"I don't know," Larajin said with a shiver. "Maybe they're members of a rival house who want to kidnap an Uskevren servant."

Thazienne shook her head slowly, her green eyes sparkling. "I don't think so," she said. "I understand a bit of the elven tongue—enough to have overheard one of them say, 'Is it her?' and the other answer, 'She's the one. I could smell it.' It's you they're after, Larajin."

Larajin glanced around fearfully. "Where are they now?"

"I pretended to run away, but then I followed them. They're lying in wait outside your friend's perfume shop."

Larajin didn't know which surprised her more: the fact that the young mistress knew about Kremlar, or that the wild elves knew her movements.

"You shouldn't go back to Stormweather Towers either," Thazienne advised. "Is there some other place else you could lie low?"

Larajin thought for a moment, then nodded. "I could go to Habrith's," she said. "Or do you think they'll be waiting for me there, too?"

A strange look crossed Thazienne's face; it was almost as though she knew something Larajin didn't. "Habrith's bakery should be safe enough," she said. "Go there now. I'll distract the elves and lead them back to Stormweather Towers, so they'll think you're there."

Larajin felt a rush of relief. "That's very kind of you, Mistress Thazienne."

"Think nothing of it—I haven't had this much fun in ten-days," Thazienne said. She winked. "And for gods' sake, call me Tazi, would you?"

Larajin peeked out the window of Habrith's shop at the busy intersection. Wagons rumbled past, shoppers hunched along through the snow, and nobles in all their finery rolled past in glass-enclosed carriages, high above the dung-splattered slush in the street. She saw Kremlar stride past under a multicolored snow parasol, followed by a servant of the Soargyl family who was laden with boxes of Kremlar's perfume samples. But there were no other figures she recognized—and she was especially relieved to note there were no green-cloaked elves in sight.

"I don't understand any of it, Habrith," Larajin said, letting the curtain fall. "I'm not my parents' daughter, and now there are elves trying to kidnap me. Wild elves."

Habrith must have heard the faint note of disgust in Larajin's voice. "Elves have their place in the world, just as humans and dwarves do," she gently chided. She waved away a customer who had come to buy bread and hung a "Closed" sign on the shop door.

Larajin wasn't listening. "What are they doing in Selgaunt, anyway? Wild elves are too simple and shy to cope with city life. That's why they hide in the forest. They have no use for money, the elder master says. Nothing to spend it on. Why would they want to ransom me?"

"It's not ransom money they're interested in."

The certainty of Habrith's tone caught Larajin's attention. She stared at Habrith. The baker was in her late sixties—older than Larajin's mother—but though her face was wrinkled, her hair was still a rich nut brown. She wore it in a simple braid down her back. Her clothes were fashionable, but a little on the plain side. In a city where even peasants decorated their bodies with enough adornments to attract a flock of greedy crows, Habrith's only adornment was a silver crescent moon pendant, worn on a leather thong around her neck.

Habrith's philosophy—"simplest is best, and all ingredients in balance"—was reflected in her shop. She was known throughout the city for her bread. While other street bakers and household cooks, including Larajin's mother, cut and shaped their bread in intricate patterns, Habrith's product was simple, square loaves, shaped like the pans they'd baked in. But the tastes . . . that was where

Habrith excelled. She made loaves using ingredients even Larajin's mother hadn't heard of.

Shonri and Habrith had been rivals, back before Larajin was born, and for a time there had been a war of loaves in the Uskevren household. Over the intervening years they'd developed a close bond, based on their shared love of their craft. Habrith, who seemed to embrace Larajin's own thoughts on the foolishness of fashion, had become like an aunt to the girl.

Now Larajin wondered how much Habrith really knew about her. The baker hadn't seemed one bit surprised when Larajin had told her that Shonri and Thallit weren't her parents.

Habrith seemed to have heard Larajin's thoughts. "I know who your mother is," she said.

"You do?" Larajin asked, startled.

Habrith nodded. "I've been waiting for the right moment to tell you. Now it seems that moment has been forced upon us. I just hope you're prepared to listen."

"I am," Larajin said, jumping down off the counter she'd perched upon. "Tell me!"

Habrith thoughtfully fingered the pendant at her throat. "You asked about wild elves. That's a subject I know a thing or two about. I was the one who set up the trading mission that your mother spoke of. Thamalon Uskevren hoped the fruits and nuts that grew wild in the Tangled Trees could turn a profit, and that this would encourage the preservation of that forest."

"What have the Tangled Trees got to do with me?" Larajin asked. "Aside from the fact that a Daleswoman gave birth to me there."

"Your mother wasn't a Daleswoman," Habrith said. "She was a wild elf."

For a moment, Larajin sat in stunned silence. Larajin refused to believe it. Her mother couldn't have been one of those tattooed, wild creatures. She shook her head.

"My mother can't have been an elf," she said. "I'm human."

"Half-human," Habrith said.

"But my ears aren't—" Larajin's eyes widened as she remembered her reflection in the pool in Sune's Temple. She'd seen her own face—but with an elf's delicately pointed ears.

"So that was what the goddess was trying to tell me," Larajin said in a whisper. She stared at her fine-boned, slender fingers as if seeing them clearly for the first time, then ran them over her narrow face and pointed chin.

Habrith looked intently into Larajin's eyes. "The goddess?" she prompted.

It was all the encouragement Larajin needed. She told Habrith about what had happened in the Temple of Sune: about her wounds magically healing and the reflection she'd seen in the pool. She told Habrith about the rat bites, and the sewer, and her encounter with the tressym. She also told Habrith about the Hulorn's strange appearance and the magical appearance of Sune's Kisses, whose fragrance the wild elves seemed particularly interested in. When she finished, Habrith was quivering with excitement.

"Do you know the elvish word for that plant?" Habrith asked.

Larajin shook her head mutely.

Habrith spoke two words in a fluid language, then translated. "The name for it in the Common tongue is Hanali's Heart. It's also sacred to the elven goddess of beauty: Hanali Celanil. The gold flecks on the leaves are her symbol. The fragrance is said to emanate from priests of Hanali when they are working their magic."

"I'm no priest," Larajin protested, "and I worship in Sune's Temple."

"Sune and Hanali are rivals for mortals' love and affection, but they share one thing: the sacred pool of Evergold. While the goddesses might quarrel over whether humans or elves are more beautiful and often try to steal each other's worshipers—especially if they are half elven—they are on friendly terms with one another. It is possible for a mortal to worship them both—and to be blessed by both."

Larajin's head was spinning. "You're saying . . . that I'm blessed? By an elven goddess?"

Habrith nodded. "And by a human goddess. That brings us back to another point: your human father."

"Who . . . was he?"

"Who is he, you mean," Habrith corrected. "None other than your master: Thamalon Uskevren the Elder."

Larajin sagged, and caught herself against the counter. "My master?" she whispered. Habrith's words made sense. No wonder Thamalon the Elder had been so incensed at the thought of any romance between Tal and Larajin. Tal was her brother—or half-brother, at any rate, as was the younger Thamalon. Mistress Thazienne was Larajin's half sister. No wonder they resembled one another!

Larajin understood, now, why she had never been turned out of her servant's position, despite Mister Cale's unfavorable reports. Why the master had sent agents after her to fetch her back after she followed Dirugo.

Even so, Larajin was hard pressed to believe that the elder master was her father. Thamalon Uskevren was a solemn, respected man of noble birth and impeccable character who loved and respected his wife. What would have possessed him to sleep with a barbarian elf maiden?

"Your mother was a beautiful woman," Habrith said. "As beautiful as you have yet to become, once you find your way. She was well respected by her people, even though she accepted a human's seed inside her."

"Is that why I was given up by the elves?" Larajin asked. "Because I was half human?"

Habrith shook her head. "You weren't given up," she said. "Thamalon took you. Now the wild elves want you back."

"Back?" Larajin croaked. "Back where? And why?"

"In the Tangled Trees," Habrith answered. " 'Why' is the question I'm trying to find an answer for."

Larajin looked at Habrith with fresh eyes. The grandmotherly woman was more than she seemed. She knew things a mere baker should not.

Habrith nodded, and tapped the crescent moon that hung against her throat. "I have friends. I ask questions and hear things. The answer shouldn't be long in coming."

Larajin realized she was supposed to understand what Habrith was hinting at—the crescent moon represented something. But she had no idea what.

Habrith's hand dropped away from her throat. She rummaged behind the counter, pulling out a change of clothes, which she thrust at Larajin.

"Take your uniform off," she said, "and put these on. That should keep them guessing. Wait here, and open the door for no one. I'll have a word with these fellows who have been bothering you, then I'll come right back."

Larajin held the clothes in her hands. "But—"

Habrith pressed a finger to Larajin's lips. Then she smiled. "We'll speak more when I get back," she said. "Be sure to lock the door behind me."

After changing into the clothes Habrith had given her and waiting a few moments to ensure the baker wouldn't see her leave the store, Larajin made her way through the sewers to the Hunting Garden. She didn't see any malformed rats, this time. The only thing that slowed her down was an overactive imagination. Every splash behind her sounded like the footsteps of the green-cloaked elf. She whirled around more than once, a knife from Habrith's bakery in her fist, to confront what had proved to be only a shadow.

Inside the garden, she hurried to the spot where she'd last seen the tressym. It mewed in response to her call—but so faintly that Larajin barely heard its cry.

The winged cat lay at the base of the tree, barely looking up when Larajin stroked its fur. It looked even more bedraggled than it had two days ago, its fur wet and matted and its wing feathers shredded. A large lump over the broken portion of its wing was oozing pus.

"Oh, kitt," Larajin said, tears welling in her eyes. "I should have come back sooner. I'm so sorry."

She touched a hand to the lump on the tressym's wing. It was hot under her fingertips, despite the fact that the creature was shivering. The tressym growled softly but made no other protest.

Larajin wanted to pick the wounded creature up and carry it back to the temple, but she was afraid that if she moved the tressym, it would die.

She did the only thing she could: she prayed. First to Sune, then to Hanali. She begged whichever of the goddesses was listening to save the tressym, to prevent this beautiful creature from dying.

Larajin caught a whiff of something sweet: Sune's Kisses. Or, as she knew it now, Hanali's Heart. The flower was nowhere to be seen. The Hunting Garden was shrouded with snow. Yet the scent grew steadily, as if dozens of the tiny mouth-shaped flowers were suddenly blooming.

The tressym began to purr. Larajin looked down in alarm, mindful of the old wives' tales that spoke of cats purring just before they died. She was surprised to see that the tressym's fur looked a little less matted, that the lump on its wing was a little smaller.

Most surprising of all, her hand that lay over the lump had a rosy red glow. It pulsed out from her fingers and into the tressym, beating with the steady rhythm of Larajin's own heart.

She swallowed down her wonder. If this was magic—if she really were channeling the power of the goddesses—she didn't want to lose it. She concentrated on the wounded tressym, putting every ounce of her will into her desire for it to be whole and well.

She heard voices headed in her direction. One, she recognized—the Hulorn. Every instinct told her to flee, but she continued to focus upon the tressym, doing her best to ignore the approaching danger. The only sign of her rising panic was a slight tremble in her hands.

Finally she heard something that broke her concentration.

". . . this blasted ring," the Hurlorn said. "It seems to bear a curse. It regenerates flesh but twists it to its own dark design."

The other voice, also male, was unfamiliar. Now Larajin could hear feet crunching on the snow.

"Its magics seem to be linked to that of the wand," the second man said with a wheeze. "I cannot dispel the magic of one without affecting the other. You will have to make a choice: both, or neither."

The tressym stirred under Larajin's hand. The lump was almost gone.

"By the gods! Who is that?"

Larajin looked up. Not more than a pace or two away stood the Hulorn, his half-serpentine face twisted with alarm and rage. Behind him was a tall, dark-skinned man who leaned on a knotted staff. Clad in smoke-gray robes that made him little more than a shadow in the snowy forest, he stared at Larajin with an expression that was equally surprised.

"Who is she?" he asked, his voice wheezing.

"What does it matter?" the Hulorn said. "She's seen us together. She's seen this." He held up his bird-taloned hand.

The dark-skinned man nodded. He moved his staff slightly. "Shall I?" he whispered.

Fear coursed through Larajin in a violent shiver. She had no idea who the dark-skinned man was, but she understood the look in his eye. The Hulorn had just condemned her to death, and the dark-skinned man was to be her executioner.

Larajin crouched, too frightened to move, as the mage pointed the knobby tip of his staff at her. In that same moment, she felt the tressym stir under her hand. Finally healed, it rose to its feet and stretched brilliantly colored wings wide, fluttering them and testing their strength.

The Hulorn laid a hand on the staff. For a moment, Larajin thought she had been reprieved.

"Wait a moment," the Hulorn said. "The tressym cost two hundred suns. I don't want it damaged."

With a loud howl, the tressym launched itself into the air, fleeing into the treetops. Larajin stood, holding up her hands and begging for her life. "Please. I didn't mean to trespass. I found the injured tressym and just wanted to—"

The end of the dark-skinned man's staff crackled with magical force. Black sparks spat from its tip. Larajin started to turn but knew she'd never escape. Out of the corner of her eye she saw a bolt of crackling black force leap from the staff . . .

In that same instant a figure hurled itself from behind a tree. Still turning, Larajin caught only a glimpse of him: green cloak, feather-tipped braid, narrow tattooed face. Then the bolt from the staff took the leaping figure full in the chest. The wild elf screamed in agony, body suddenly going rigid. Sparks leaped from the tips of his fingers and booted toes, then his clothes and hair burst in tatters from his body. His charred husk fell to the ground, smoking against the snow.

Larajin gaped in horror at the blackened corpse. Now a sound registered in the silence left by the explosion. An urgent whisper, in a language she didn't understand. Again, in the common tongue: "Run! Run!"

She needed no urging. Somehow her feet found their footing in the slippery snow. She caught a glimpse of another cloaked figure leaping down from a tree branch onto the Hulorn, who had drawn his sword, and yet a third cloaked figure rushing out from behind a bush at the dark-skinned mage. As she ran through the woods, her heart pounding, she heard two more explosive crackles behind her.

With frantic haste, Larajin scrambled over the lip of the fountain and wrenched the grating free. She'd barely wriggled through when she heard thudding footsteps approaching the fountain above. Sobbing, she realized that they had followed her footsteps in the snow. They wouldn't be able to trail her through the sewers. However there were too many twists and turns in the darkened tunnels—and sewer water didn't hold any tracks.

She leaped down into the tunnel, and fled with splashing footsteps through the darkness.

Larajin slipped in through one of the servants' entrances of Stormweather Towers, still panting from her run across the city and stinking of sewer water. She'd seen no signs of pursuit—neither the Hulorn's guard, nor the dark wizard, nor even wild elves. She was reasonably certain the Hulorn wouldn't be able to identify her if he saw her again, since nobles tended to see only the uniform and not the servant underneath. That didn't mean she was safe, though.

As she slipped off her muck-covered boots and toweled her hair, Larajin could hear murmured voices coming from the stairs that led to the main part of the household. That would be the master, in the throes of yet another business discussion with the Talendars, a very important meeting that Larajin was supposed to be working.

A meeting presided over by Master Thamalon Uskevren. Her father.

The thought was still too incredible to believe.

Larajin heard a slight scratching at the door behind her. She opened it, and saw the tressym perched on the boot scraper outside. The winged cat walked into Stormweather Towers as though it had always lived there and rubbed against Larajin's leg.

"What is that creature doing here? That's an expensive pet—send it back to wherever it came from."

The winged cat scuttled back out the door as Mister Cale marched down the hall. The head servant's deep-set eyes were blazing. He drew himself to a halt and pressed thin lips together, giving Larajin the full benefit of his scowl as he took in the fact that she was out of uniform. His nostrils sniffed.

"Just where," he said, with heavy emphasis on each word, "have you been?"

Larajin saw the tressym fly away, a splash of vibrant color amid the falling snowflakes, and shut the door behind her.

"To worship Sune, Sir," she said meekly. "The winged cat followed me back from the temple, and I was all this time trying to get rid of it."

"Hmph." Mister Cale seemed to accept this explanation. "Get into uniform. At once. Tend to the master. There's an important meeting going on upstairs."

Larajin bowed her head. Despite her posture, she was anything but contrite. She stared at her folded hands—at the fingers that had wrought the healing magic of Sune—or Hanali—or both.

I'm somebody, she thought to herself. Somebody who three elves just died to protect. Not just a servant—a square peg in a round hole—but something . . . else.

Everything was the same in the Uskevren household, but for Larajin, everything had changed. Master Thamalon the Elder, engrossed in his business meetings and haunted by memories of his past, was no longer just her employer. He was her father, and the people who had died when the original Stormweather Towers burned were Larajin's own kin. Mistress Shamur now was someone to be doubly cautious around. Larajin didn't even want to imagine the icy treatment she'd get, if the mistress knew that Larajin was the result of her husband cheating on her.

Mistress Thazienne—Tazi—was still the same roguish troublemaker she had always been, but now Larajin saw her with a different eye. The same blood flowed in their veins. Perhaps Larajin might be just as adventurous, one day.

Master Thamalon the Younger was still as much of a playboy and spendthrift as ever. Knowing that he was her half-brother gave Larajin a new empathy for the struggles he faced. Though she had heard the details only secondhand, while waiting at the Uskevren table, she now could appreciate the dangers Thamalon had faced while patching up the Foxmantle trade agreement.

Larajin even saw Tal in a new light, not just a friend who deliberately stepped over the line that devided master and servant but as a brother. She prayed that Tal would react in his usual, relaxed way to the news that they were kin.

Only one person in the Uskevren household had not changed, in Larajin's eyes. Mister Cale was still the same mysterious, slightly ominous figure he had always been.

Larajin edged past Mister Cale and marched briskly to the servant's change room to put on a uniform. Out of the corner of her eye, she saw him staring at her. Hard.

He sees the change in me, she thought. I wonder if he can guess why.

Larajin, for the life of her, had no idea what lay ahead. But she knew the answer was waiting for her somewhere. Not here in Stormweather Towers, nor even in the Hunting Garden whose artificial solitudes had called to her all these years, but elsewhere: among the wild elves of the Tangled Trees.

The Sembia Seven

Ed Greenwood is the creator of the FORGOTTEN REALMS® fantasy world, which became the setting for his home D&D® game in 1975. Play still continues in this long-running campaign, and Ed also keeps busy producing Realms lore for various Wizards publications. Ed works as a library clerk and has edited over a dozen small press magazines. When not appearing at conventions, he lives in an old farmhouse in the countryside of Ontario, Canada.

Richard Lee Byers holds a Master's degree in Psychology. He worked in an emergency psychiatric facility for over a decade, then left the mental health field to become a writer. He is the author of more than fifteen books, and his short fiction can be found in many anthologies. A resident of the Tampa Bay area, he spends much of his leisure time fencing foil, epee, and sabre, frequently competing in local tournaments.

Clayton Emery is an umpteen-generations Yankee, Navy brat, and aging hippie who grew up playing Robin Hood and War in the forests of New England. He's been a blacksmith, dishwasher, school teacher in Australia, carpenter, zookeeper, farmhand, land surveyor, volunteer firefighter, award-winning technical writer, and other things. Read more of his stories at www.claytonemery.com.

Dave Gross discovered Ray Bradbury in fourth grade and was hooked on fantasy forever. Books soon overcame underwear as his most common birthday gift, and he grew up with idols like Roger Zelazny, H.G. Wells, Boris Karloff, Isaac Asimov, and Mary Stewart. Instead of becoming a shuttle pilot as he'd always dreamed (damned corrective lenses), he taught English for six years before joining the disreputable ranks of magazine editors. Dave lives in

Seattle, where he doesn't mind the rain so much as the SUVs.

Paul Kemp is a graduate of the University of Michigan-Dearborn and the University of Michigan Law School. He lives in Garden City, Michigan with his wife and four cats. If all is going well, he has a six-pack of Guiness extra-stout and a Dunhill Altamira in the house.

Lisa Smedman has been designing for TSR/Wizards of the Coast since 1987, and has contributed numerous adventures and sourcebooks to the ADVANCED DUNGEONS & DRAGONS® line. She has also done freelance design work for a number of other roleplaying game companies. Her fiction has appeared in *Dragon* Magazine, as well as in various science fiction and fantasy anthologies. She is the author of four SHADOWRUN novels to date. She lives in Vancouver, B.C., with her partner (who thankfully, is also a gamer) and their ever-expanding litter of felines (none of whom, thankfully, have wings).

Voronica Whitney-Robinson's first book with Wizards of the Coast, *Spectre of the Black Rose*, was co-authored with James Lowder. Voronica is probably the only one of the Sembia Seven who has been mistaken for a reincarnated witch doctor, an unsettling experience that pales when compared to some of her other experiences as a world traveler and a Peace Corps Volunteer in Africa. She has also done a stint as a veterinary assistant in the wilds of New Zealand and is currently a marine biologist in the wilds of Seattle.

Sembia

Shadow's Witness
Paul Kemp
November 2000

Erevis Cale must battle ghosts from his own dark past if he is to save the family he dearly loves. The first full-length novel in this exciting new series—your gateway to the Forgotten Realms!

The Shattered Mask
Richard Lee Byers
May 2001

Shamur Uskevren is convinced that she must kill her husband Thamalon. When the truth is revealed the great lady realizes that her husband was not to blame . . . but will the truth come too late for her to avoid a terrible mistake?

Black Wolf
Dave Gross
November 2001

The young Talbot Usevren was the only one to survive a horrible "hunting accident." Now, infected with lycanthropy he must learn to control his urges and come to terms with what he has become.